About the author

Arthur Curtis was born during WWII. He was a railway signalman for a number of years, until Dr Beeching's cuts. He went on to several accountancy roles in the private industry and in the Civil Service. Arthur served the last ten years in Government statistics as an Archivist before he retired in 2000.

SEEING OLD FRIENDS

Arthur Curtis

SEEING OLD FRIENDS

Vanguard Press

A CIP catalogue record for this title is
available from the British Library.

ISBN 978 1 784656 79 9

*Vanguard Press is an imprint of
Pegasus Elliot MacKenzie Publishers Ltd.*
www.pegasuspublishers.com

First Published in 2019

**Vanguard Press
Sheraton House Castle Park
Cambridge England**

Printed & Bound in Great Britain

Dedication

To Mum and Dad for making this book possible.

Acknowledgements

My thanks to Buddy Holly and Peter Tinniswood.

Chapter One
Rogerstown

It had been Arthur's plan to revisit Rogerstown ever since he had received the wedding invitation from his niece Nicola, two weeks earlier. Now, into his second day back in South Wales, the rustle of taffeta and the seemingly unending chatter regarding various popular brands of make-up, and the pluses and minuses of sling backs and court shoes for the coming ceremony, was starting to get to him.

Feeling hemmed in on all sides by the constant movement of females wandering about the house with mobile phones pressed to their ears, the old man could not wait to get out of the house and put into action his plan to visit the old haunts of his youth.

Arthur stood in the hallway, dressed as though he was about to go on a first date, looking critically at the grey-haired image that stared back at him from the mirror, the eyebrows were too bushy and the sideboards were straight out of the nineteen sixties and far too long for a man of his age, but he dismissed these as minor points, his immediate concern, was the errant strand of hair that would not lie down. "Balls!" he hissed, exasperatedly, combing at the grey mane for the umpteenth time, while, in between passes of the comb, attempting to smooth it down with the aid of some spit.

Finally, he gave up trying and shrugged dismissively at his reflection, *What the hell, no one's going to notice anyway.* Inwardly, however, he felt that his appearance had to be acceptable, otherwise he wouldn't feel right, hence the effort with the hair, for, ahead of him lay the prospect of his seeing Rogerstown again for the first time in more years than he cared to remember, and now that he was back, and just a couple of miles from where he had spent some of the more important years of his youth, he was not about to waste the opportunity that his visit to his niece's house in Newport presented.

As Arthur straightened his tie and brushed at the shoulders of his jacket for non-existent dandruff traces, the image of his niece, Nicola, joined his in the mirror, her handsome face set for confrontation.

"Why you want to go traipsing off along that canal path to Rogerstown is beyond me," she said, her hands on her hips, in a posture that dared him to argue. "It must be all of four miles, and the climb up that Black-Ash path, is not for the faint-hearted, I can tell you. Why you can't catch a bus like any normal person is beyond me?" Arthur opened his mouth to defend himself, but her diatribe kept his protests at bay. "We do have buses in Wales; believe it or not," she exclaimed. "This is not the Wild West. And, it's not as though they're few and far between, either, they're every twenty minutes from town and the bus stop is only just down the road by the paper shop." She pointed towards the front door. "So there's no excuse not to catch one, is there?"

Nicola was now well into her stride, and his getting-a-word-in-edgeways, was proving to be futile. Soon she would be firing on all cylinders, and there would no chance of her letting up.

"And, what's so special about Rogerstown?" she asked pointedly. "There is nothing there, apart from a supermarket and a golf club." She sniffed with disdain, "Overpriced little boxes, I wouldn't live there if they paid me. It's just one big housing estate; you wouldn't know it any more."

Seeing that her argument was falling on deaf ears, his niece tried a new tack. "Besides, it must be over forty years since you and Avril lived there. So why go there now? Looking for ghosts?" She shook her head and her glossy, nut-brown hair bounced on her shoulders. "I would have thought you'd want to forget all about that little episode, anyway, Arthur Tanner." She gave a try-and-get-out-of-that-one stare that only women seemed to have the mastery of.

His niece caught sight of her own image framed in the hall mirror and she noticed a stray strand of hair, which she quickly guided back behind her ear.

Arthur took full advantage of the opportunity that this momentary pause presented. "Avril has nothing to do with it, For Christ's sake! I just want to have a look at the old place, see how it's changed, and that. I had a lot of mates up there, at one time, you never know, some may still be around, I might just bump into one or two, who knows?" He plunged on, regardless, "And don't forget, I worked there long before Avril came on the bloody scene, remember?"

Taking the battle to Nicola was having a certain amount of success, for she was now shaking her head in resignation.

Arthur then went and lost the initiative, by adding lamely, "Besides it'll get me out of the house and out from under the feet of all you females, and away from all the talk of weddings and the like."

The wedding ploy of his didn't work.

"No, I don't remember," his niece replied, again trying to regain the high ground, irritation showing from the fact that he had had the temerity to retaliate. "I was too young to remember any of the goings on, at the time." She tossed her head again. "Anyway, that's neither here nor there, that still doesn't explain what a man of your age thinks he's doing, going all that way?"

The old man opened his mouth to speak, but words failed him, he was back on the retreat.

"You'll have a heart attack or something similar," she continued, "which is all we need, what with our Petra's wedding tomorrow, and all." She smoothed away imaginary creases from her non-crease skirt and moved a vase of flowers, which sat on the polished surface of a gate-legged table beneath the hall mirror. With all of the precision of a watchmaker, she repositioned it a quarter of inch away from its original position.

Arthur sighed, "I'm not going to have a heart attack, for Christ's sake! Nicola, I'm not totally senile yet, I know exactly what I'm doing." He placed a hand reassuringly on her shoulder, and delving into his trouser pocket, he produced a mobile phone with a flourish. "If there's a problem of any sort, I'll ring you on this gadget, OK?" He brandished his bright-red new toy, for her to see.

"I didn't know you had a mobile. How long have you had that, then?" Nicola said, now completely wrong-footed by his apparent, newfound grasp of modern technology. His niece was now definitely on the back foot and beginning to lose the battle.

"I bought it in St Ives about two months ago," he replied, pressing a button with a thumb, and a tinny version of the Dam-Busters March filled the air. "It took me a while to get used to it, but I've sorted it now. I sent a text to old Lanney at the Hotel Porthcurno yesterday, no problem." He gave her an innocent smile, turned off the 'phone and returned it to his pocket.

His astonished niece gave a huge theatrical sigh, shook her head, and, with a half-smile on her handsome face, she kissed him on the cheek. "What are we going to do with you, you stubborn old man?" She pushed more hair back behind her ear, and shrugged her shoulders resignedly. "Oh, all right, have it your way, you apparently seem to know best, so go and see your precious Rogerstown, but the moment you start feeling tired, you ring me, promise?"

The old man nodded his agreement, and she opened the front door for him and he stepped out into the bright sunshine. "Don't worry love, I'll be fine." He gave her another smile and strode off down the road. "See you at teatime," he called over his shoulder.

"Take care Arth," she called after him, concern showing in her voice.

Arthur continued on his way without replying, on hearing the noise of the front door closing behind him.

Once out of sight of the house, he quickened his pace, reaching the canal in record time and he strode along its towpath, his adrenaline working overtime, as he anticipated the prospect of seeing some of the old haunts, and maybe some old pals from his youth.

While it was not in his nature to admit such things, he had to admit that he was feeling quite excited at the thought of seeing Rogerstown again, and he was relishing the prospect at what this long overdue return promised; so much so, that he was undaunted at the thought of the three-mile walk that lay ahead.

In fact, the minutes and the three miles sped rapidly by, and he arrived at the canal basin terminus in a little over an hour, feeling surprisingly fresh. *That was a bloody doddle, I don't know why our Nicola was getting her knickers in such a twist, Jeez, I could walk here and back a dozen times, no problem.*

Continuing along the towpath for a further hundred yards or so, he came to a rusting anti-sheep gate that guarded the entrance to a short lane dotted with dock leaves and dandelions.

He remembered the lane and he entered through the gate, which complained as he swung it ajar. The lane was hedged with hawthorn, brambles, ivy and the young shoots of dog roses. "Hips and haws," he murmured. *In a month's time this will be a picture.* In his mind's eye he pictured the array of the pale, pink petals of the dog roses as they competed for space with the scarlet berries of the hawthorn and the young pale green fruit of the newly formed blackberries. The thought lifted his spirits and he carried it with him to the end of the lane, where he stopped to get his bearings.

Arthur found himself standing in a hushed suburban road where grass-verged pavements fronted a line of 1950 bow-windowed bungalows, where ubiquitous saloon cars and four-by-four SUVs occupied many of the driveways.

It was the sort of road that one would view with disinterest through a railway carriage window, as the train clattered through suburbia.

Not a soul was to be seen, nothing stirred, the road had the atmosphere of an inside of a cathedral, hushed yet ominous in its silence, even the whine of a nearby lawn mower and the continuous, muffled roar of distant traffic seemed to make little impact on the sullen stillness of the road.

Looking right and left, he studied his surroundings with a frown, for, having arrived at what he supposed was his destination, disappointment now wrapped itself around him like a cloak. It was not at all what he had expected.

Thirty odd years is a long time, he told himself. *They've probably built dozens of little cul-de-sacs, similar to this one in and around about this area, this could be any one of them.* Dismissing the thought, he argued, *this is the only road leading from Fifteen Locks lane, so it must be the right one.* He looked back at the lane, sure in his mind that it was the same lane that he'd known those many years ago. *Now, that, I do remember,* he told himself. *I bet that old lane hasn't changed in the last hundred odd years.*

Now satisfied that he was where he was supposed to be, he turned his attention back to the line of bungalows, which unlike the lane, were not as instantly recognizable as he had hoped. Shrugging his shoulders, he shoved his hands into his trouser pockets and shook his head, nonplussed. *What did you expect? You daft old sod,* he said to himself. *Time doesn't stand still, for God's sake, over a period of years, changes would be almost certain to happen.*

Concluding the debate, he shrugged, and, accepting the inevitable, he looked in the opposite direction. Fifty yards along, on the opposite side of the road, was the entrance to a smaller cul-de-sac, which he definitely did not remember. He headed for it.

The tang of freshly mown grass reached his nostrils, perking him up considerably, and as he reached the cul-de-sac, the sound of the traffic grew louder, drowning out the lawn mower.

He stopped at its entrance and studied its cast-iron nameplate. It bore the legend: Whernside Glade.

Giving a snort of derision he entered the short road and studied the dwellings, all of which appeared to be clones of the bungalows from the previous road, half a dozen of them facing each other, their driveways and their carports mirror images.

Evenly spaced rowan trees stood on sentry duty along both sides of the short road, their feathery leaves cast speckled shadows across the grass verges, as he made his way towards the vehicular turning point at the end of the road, where he stopped and leaned on the wooden boundary fence and took in the panorama that was now spread out before him. An empty briar pipe was now clamped between his teeth, as he surveyed the other side of the fence, where a grassy bank sloped steeply down and away towards a six-lane motorway that resonated with a low-pitched hum from the constant stream of vehicles moving along its surface, nose to tail, like inquisitive dogs.

Scratching at his chin, he studied the rest of the landscape, particularly the background of surrounding hills, which he recognized at once. The foreground, however, was entirely new to him, yet, again, like the road with the bungalows, this too looked vaguely familiar.

Arthur screwed his eyes up in concentration, looking for landmarks and reference points that would confirm his whereabouts.

Then it suddenly came to him, the stretch of motorway that was spread out, below, was the very place where his beloved signal box had once stood. He was now looking at the very place where he had worked all those years ago, back in the nineteen sixties. This was what he had set out to find, and now here, in front of him, was the very site where the steam trains had rumbled and clanked and hissed their way along the Western Valley railway all those many years ago.

Shielding his eyes from the sunlight, Arthur followed the motorway's course towards the distant horizon, his heart thumping as he recalled the railway and its lines which had run parallel with the base of the hill, just as the motorway now did, heading East towards Newport and the Bristol Channel, and, northwards, towards Risca, and the Western Valley.

This has got to be the place. He pointed the pipe stem towards a nearby lamp post, which stood on the motorway's hard shoulder. *Yes, that's where the railway ran, and there,* he nodded at the lamp post, *is where the signal box would have stood.*

The old man was now back in time, seeing it as it was in his youth, back in the days when a four-track railway ran through the heart of the small town instead of the present-day six-lane highway.

Arthur shifted his gaze from the motorway to an area, further over, nearer the river, to the site where the power station's huge cooling towers had once cast their shadows over the seemingly, endless rows of attendant railway sidings. Now, a supermarket, along with its acres of car parking space and obligatory filling station, occupied the land. Arthur stared at the strings of bunting that hung limply between coloured poles on the supermarket's vast expanse of roof, which stood out like an island, in a sea of sprawling Mock-Tudor semis, with obligatory Cypress Leylandii trees and gaily painted carports.

Raising his eyes, Arthur followed the natural rise of the land that lay beyond the supermarket and the distant river. *At least they haven't built on the Graig yet,* he thought, recognising the hill at once.

Chapter Two
Church Forge

The Graig hill was just as he had remembered it, not really high enough to qualify as a mountain, yet stark and angular, its midriff covered with a thick, dark belt of fir trees, which gradually became sparser the higher up its sides one looked, eventually giving way to an area of more lightly coloured gorse, which covered the head and shoulders of its craggy peak. The fir trees partly obscured a ribbon of road that zigzagged up its steep flanks to the summit, where it disappeared from sight as it tipped over the hill's crest into the next valley.

At the base of the hill the River Ebbw sparkled and frothed its way along the valley floor, on its journey down to the coast. His eyes still shielded from the bright sunlight, Arthur followed the river's progress across the distant fields until it disappeared from sight behind the supermarket and the attendant housing estate.

Removing the unlit pipe from his mouth, he nodded with satisfaction, for now, he knew exactly where he was.

A single speck of light, reflecting off a car windscreen, caught his attention, it was high up on the Graig. Arthur shielded his eyes again and stared up at the rugged hill, watching the vehicle as it zigzagged its way slowly upwards, painstakingly negotiating every twist and turn of the narrow lane that led to Church forge village, on the other side of the hill.

"Bloody Nora," Arthur exclaimed, "Church Forge, how could I not remember Church Forge?" He pulled at an ear lobe, his face screwed up in annoyance. *I know its forty odd years ago, but, Bloody Hell! how could I forget the very village where I started out as a signalman, that's bloody unforgivable.*

Staring at the hill, yet not seeing it, his brow furrowed, the old man tried desperately to get his memory banks back in working order. Gradually, recollections of that era began to return, bringing with them images of the village and its assortment of cottages that clustered around the church and the post office.

Arthur bit hard on the pipe stem, as he savoured every bit of information that was being reprised, his eyes sparkling.

Removing the pipe stem, he pointed with it towards the Graig, now in his mind's eye, the other side of the hill and Church Forge village, as it was in 1958.

Arthur pictured the winding country road that bisected the village, separating the post office, church and school and the scattering of thatched cottages, from the Church Forge Arms, on the other side of the road, next to which, almost obscured by an enormous oak tree, stood a small, ivy-clad, grey Presbyterian chapel, its tiny, walled burial ground, overlooking the railway, which ran at its rear.

At this point, he remembered, the road widened, and ran parallel with the railway tracks, before turning South East, towards Newport and the Bristol Channel, some fifteen miles further down the valley. Here, the railway line snaked left to the North West, away from the road, before eventually turning eastwards, rounding Bass Alton hill in a long gentle two mile curving slope, which took it past the neighbouring village and on towards the coast.

In the triangle that separated the road and the railway, stood the railway station with its two redundant platforms, both overgrown and neglected since its closure in the late nineteen forties. At the end of the down platform, stood the tiny, ten-foot square, signal box, which was still in operation; although, five years later, it would be considered expendable, as it, and the line to Trethomas, became the latest victims of the Beeching Axe.

By then, Arthur had transferred away from the sleepy hamlet and its tiny signal box, back to the more comforting and familiar territory of dockland, Newport.

Initially, he had never been entirely comfortable working at Church Forge Sidings, it being in the middle of the countryside, miles away from his preferred urban environment. But, in those days, one had to take what was on offer, and a job as a signalman, when it occurred, was much sought after, and readily accepted. *You had to start somewhere,* he argued, *and Church Forge just happened to be my somewhere.*

Arthur remembered how he had stood in the doorway of the tiny signal cabin having just arrived, ready to begin his spell of learning duty on that first day at Church Forge Sidings. Trying not to show his disappointment, he had surveyed the cramped, musty interior of the ancient lineside cabin, noting with dismay, how it lacked even the usual necessary amenities, such as, electricity and piped water.

The lighting, he recalled, was provided by a large, brass oil lamp that hung from the ceiling, and the water supply came in the shape of a two-gallon, galvanised container, complete with a tap, which, apparently, was to provide the occupants with water for their eight-hour shift. The furniture department sported a handmade wooden armchair, with a homemade cushion, which had seen better days. The chair's uneven, knotted back, which was pressed against the door of a lamp locker, left just enough room for a normal sized person to stretch one's legs towards the black-leaded fire grate, whose ashy bars contained smouldering coals.

Arthur shook his head and grinned. *Oh Yeah, Church Forge Sidings signal box had certainly boasted all the mod cons.*

The Great Western Railway, or its successor, British Railways, had not got around to installing electricity in many of the isolated country signal boxes, and, Church Forge Sidings was no exception. The only source of electrical power came from an array of batteries, housed in the ground floor compartment, which only provided the power for the telegraph system. The nearest piped water was a brass tap, on the outside wall of the disused public toilet, which mouldered at the end of the up platform, where each unfortunate occupant of the signal box would have had to fill the container and then struggle back, along the platform, with it, its metal handle cutting into the palms of the hands, each step promising an impending hernia.

He shook his head. *Kids today; they don't know they're bloody well born.* He shook his head again. *What was I then? A wet-behind-the-ears, eighteen-year-old, town boy, who suddenly found himself in charge of a signal box miles from his dockland home, in the middle of the bloody countryside. Harold sodding Macmillan was right, 'we never had it so good.'*

Arthur did concede, however, that during the day, especially in the spring and in the summer months; life in the little cabin was not all that bad, in fact, more than acceptable, for, in between the couple of trains an hour, that kept him occupied, he would stand in the open window, surveying the village life, as it went about its business. Occasionally, maybe once a week, he would go out onto the down platform and tend to the irises that he had rescued from the clutches of the brambles and nettles, in what had once been the platform's flowerbed. He even scattered the contents of a packet of marigold seeds around the edges of the newly resurrected patch of earth, but had missed out on seeing the results of his labours, for, by then, he had moved on to another signal box.

The old man rubbed his hands, savouring the feelings that memories of those summer days brought forth. *Yeah, summertime at the old sidings box was not too bad, come to think of it, and the autumn, that too, was ok,* he conceded. It was when the nights started to draw in, when it became colder and darker, and very often wet, that was when Church Forge showed its other face. *That's when it all started to go downhill,* he recalled.

After midnight, was generally the worst time, when the village had gone to bed, and put out its lights, that was when the surrounding countryside took over, becoming, in a trice, a pitch-black place, made of the stuff of nightmares.

At least, that's how it appeared to that young, naïve town boy, as he sampled his first few weeks on the night shift.

With the last customer long gone from the Church Forge Arms, and the lights from the cottages, finally extinguished, Arthur would be sitting in the rickety, armchair full of foreboding, peering anxiously into the night, expecting the worst, every time the sound of a barking fox, or the hoot of an owl, came from the nearby woods.

Sheepishly, he remembered how he would lock the front door and latch the windows after the passing of the last down train, the One Thirty, Hengoed to Newport.

Once it had clanked and hissed passed, on its way to the docks, he would watch the red taillight disappear around the bend, then, with a sigh, he would bank up the fire and sit back in the wooden armchair, hoping that a book, and the sounds of Ella or Kenton, courtesy of the Voice-Of-America, crackling out of his battered, Dansette radio, would take his mind off the lonely, silent hours to come.

Some, two and a half uneventful hours later, the silence would be broken by the bell code from the next signal box, telling him that the three- forty-five trainload of empties, from Maesglas, was on its way, which would break the spell and restore his flagging spirits. He would then set the signals to go, and wait, expectantly, peering into the darkness, for the first sight of the oncoming train's headlights and the welcoming hiss of steam, and the grunts, from the labouring locomotive. Soon, the noise of the engine, and the clank and rattle of the following wagons, would be echoing off the station building's walls, filling the night with sound, dispelling the silence of the past three hours.

With normal activity resumed, he would then bank up the fire again, make himself a cup of tea, and watch for the first streaks of dawn to appear on the horizon.

"Thank God for tea and coal," he murmured. "They saw me through more than one winter, especially at Church Forge. My God, it could get cold up that valley, you needed that bloody coal fire, that's for sure." He gave a deep chortle. He then looked around with embarrassment, thinking that he might have been overheard.

Seeing that he was still alone, he once again delved into the archives, and brought forth the memory of his first winter as a signalman, that memorable February at Church Forge, when there was not just a blizzard to contend with, there was also Buddy Holly's double.

Chapter Three
Buddy

It was February the fourth, 1959, five thirty in the morning and it was bitterly cold. Arthur and Dai Marshall sat, side by side, shivering on an unheated, driverless, single-decker bus, which was parked in the main street of Newport. They both stared gravely ahead, silent, their breath on the air.

On Arthur's lap lay an unopened Daily newspaper; across the front page was the banner headline: ROCK STARS PERISH IN TERROR PLANE PLUNGE!

Sitting there, tight-lipped, dumbstruck, disbelief showed on their eighteen-year-old-faces. Their heroes, rock and roll giants, Buddy Holly, Ritchie Valens and J P Richardson, the Big Bopper, were all dead, killed in an air crash, somewhere in the United States, wiped out, no longer a part of their young lives.

The shell-shocked look on their faces told all, that the impact of such a disastrous event was going to take some time to sink in and, even longer to get over.

"We're going to have to have a two-minute silence in the King Billy, tonight, Arth'," said Dai, his teeth chattering, desperately trying to think of something to say that was appropriate to the occasion, his lips blue from the cold.

Arthur nodded dumbly his eyes transfixed on the headlines of the newspaper and, as his brain was in neutral, all that he could think of saying was, "Chantilly Lace."

"What do you mean, Chantilly Lace?" Dai's face had taken on a strange, manic-looking expression. "Why'd you say that, for Christ's sake?"

Arthur shrugged and shook his head, desperately trying to find a suitable explanation. "It was just one of my favourites, that's all," he added lamely.

Dai nodded, "Yeah, mine too," he said, without much conviction,

Arthur racked his brains, trying desperately to come up with something deeply meaningful and profound, something that would set the right tone for the occasion.

"Why wait until tonight, what's wrong with two minutes silence now? I reckon that's what we ought to have, as a sort of mark of respect, like, that's what the boys would want. What do you think?"

Dai blew on his hands. "Yeah, why not," he replied, without any enthusiasm, wishing that he'd never brought it up, in the first place.

"Orright," said Arthur, "let's do it, then." He looked at his watch. "Two minutes, when I give the signal, then, ok?"

Dai nodded gravely, wishing that he were still in his cosy, warm bed, and not on some bloody freezing bus, where he had to hold his breath for two minutes.

Arthur lifted his hand, then, dropped it. "Now," he said, and they both stared grimly ahead, tight-lipped.

After, what he considered to be about the right length of time, Arthur checked his watch, raised his hand again, and dropped it a second time. "Ok, time's up."

Dai's breath came out with a whoosh, the vapour hurtling down the bus. "Jeez," he gasped, "I hope Presley don't pop his clogs, I'll bloody well burst."

Arthur looked at him incredulously. "You haven't been holding your sodding breath, have you, you dull bugger?"

"Only for the first minute and a bit," admitted Dai. "I couldn't manage the full two."

"Two minutes silence means just that, not holding your sodding breath, you soft get." Arthur gave Dai a withering look and blew on his frozen hands and stuffed them into his trouser pockets. "Where the bloody hell has that Driver got to?" he complained. Arthur transferred a hand to his jacket pocket and brought out a cigarette packet. "Ciggy?" he said, offering the packet to Dai.

"Cheers," said Dai, who took one and lit up, drawing in a lungful of smoke.

Arthur cupped his hands around the flame of the match and lit his own cigarette, at the same time getting some of its sparse warmth from the match to his numb hands.

"Here they are now," said Dai indicating with a thumb as the two uniformed figures of the driver and the conductor emerged from the town arcade and ambled along towards the bus.

Arthur transferred his cupped hands from the now dead match to the glowing end of his cigarette. "About sodding time, too, I'm bloody perished."

The crew clambered aboard the bus.

The driver was middle-aged, short and fat and sported a waxed moustache, his chest wheezed as he climbed in behind the steering wheel, and the seat groaned as he lowered his bulk onto it, an inch of ash dropped, unnoticed, from his cigarette onto his trousers as he engaged the gears and let out the clutch. The bus lurched away, throwing Arthur and Dai against the back of the seat in front of them.

"Oy, Stirling bloody Moss, take it friggin' easy, will you," yelled Dai, rubbing his elbow.

The conductor, who stood at the front end of the swaying bus, disregarded the complaints, his attention firmly focused on the intricacies of his ticket machine, which hung from his skinny neck on a leather strap, he turned a knurled wheel on the side of the machine and the clicking of a ratchet sounded, he then pressed a lever several times, producing more mechanical clicks. Apparently satisfied that everything was in working order, he took a final drag on his cigarette, nipped off the end, and put the dead butt behind his ear, where it disappeared into the greasy undergrowth that curled out from under his cap, he then staggered down the swaying aisle. The youth appeared to be about sixteen years old and was painfully thin, a growth of fine down sprouted from his acne-marked chin and a Teddy-Boy style curl hung out from under the peak of his cap like an elephant's trunk, it flexed like a spring with each movement of the bus.

"Fares please," he said in an adenoidal voice.

"Return to Bedwas," said Dai offering up a ten-shilling note.

"Aint you got any less, Butt?" the conductor grimaced, the greasy coil of hair flexing.

"Sorry Taff, this is it," Dai tapped at his pockets as if to prove the veracity of his statement.

"Jeez," complained the youth, "I'm low on change, this morning, this being the first trip, like."

"I'll get them," said Arthur offering up a half crown piece. "That'll be a return to Bass Alton and a return to Church Forge, orright?"

"Return Bass Alton, return Church Forge," the adenoids yodelled, as the conductor cranked the handle on his machine, which spewed out two strips of yellow paper. "Two and thruppence, ta." He held out his hand and Arthur passed him the half crown.

The acned conductor delved inside the leather moneybag and extracted three pennies, which he handed to Arthur.

"Did you hear about the Big Bopper and Buddy Holly, then?" he said, lifting the peak of his cap and scratching at the greasy thatch beneath. "According to the news, this morning, they both snuffed it in a plane crash, yesterday, in the States."

The casual way that he referred to America was obviously meant to convey to the listener that he was a well-seasoned traveller.

Unimpressed, Arthur gave him a withering look. "Yeah, we heard," he replied, taking the tickets and the change, dismissing him.

The conductor sniffed with disdain, hitched the strap of his moneybag higher up his bony shoulder and staggered back up the swaying aisle.

"Prick!" said Dai, grimacing.

Arthur turned to Dai. "There's going to be a right old atmosphere in the King's, tonight, it'll be misery all bloody night, I can see."

Dai nodded and he dropped his cigarette onto the floor and ground it with a heel.

"Yeah, well, what can you expect? Buddy was well thought of, wasn't he? It's only natural that there'll be a bit of a mood about the place," he blew on his hands and thrust them into his pockets. "I'll pay you back the fare, tonight, at the King's, ok?" His teeth chattered.

Arthur nodded, "That's always assuming that we get back home today," he pointed at the windscreen of the bus, where countless large snowflakes were peppering it.

The driver activated the wipers and the glistening flakes spread across the glass in smears, before forming a crystallised line, at the edge of the windscreen.

"That's all we bloody well need," said Dai with disgust. "This is going to balls things up, good and proper, I can't wait to bloody well get to work."

They both stared gloomily out of the window at the swathe of swirling flakes that was being highlighted by the yellow halos of the streetlights. Arthur lit another cigarette and cupped his hands around it, dismay showing on his face. Next to fog, snow was what most signalmen dreaded; he had a feeling that the next few hours were going to be a right pain-in-the-arse.

The motor roared and the differential whined while the windscreen wipers thwacked in time with the swishing tyres. Snow was beginning to cling onto the windward side of telegraph poles and lampposts, while corners of ledges and sills were filling with it. By the time that the bus had reached Bass Alton Station, twenty minutes later, snow was settling readily on roofs and pavements.

Dai got off the bus, turned up his coat collar and ran, head down, towards the station's side entrance, where he paused, turned, waved and then disappeared through a door marked, BR STAFF.

Five stops beyond, and fifteen minutes later, Arthur got off the bus and crossed the road, bending into the wind, as he made his way towards the gate, that led to the disused up platform of Church Forge Halt.

The bus roared off, throwing dirty snow against the front gate of the chapel.

Arthur closed the gate behind him and padded through the snow along the platform towards the Church Forge sidings signal box, its darkened shape looming out of the half-light of the snow filled dawn.

The wind whistled along the empty platform, sending a barrage of white flakes slanting in, targeting the front of his British Railways overcoat. Minute pieces of ice, mixed in with the snowflakes, stung his face as he crossed the line towards the little trackside cabin.

Arthur climbed the steps to the porch, where he stamped the snow from his shoes and brushed the film of white from his uniform, and unlocked the door.

Once inside the gloomy cabin, he felt for the chain that hung from the ceiling, pulled at it, and lowered the suspended oil lamp down to head height, where his numbed fingers fumbled for the lamp's glass funnel, which he lifted up. Striking a match, he held it to the lamp's oil-soaked wick, which immediately began burning, and as he dropped the funnel back into place, it glowed brightly as it leaped up the glass, lighting the interior of the signal box with a mellow glow, transforming it, with the pretence of warmth.

Arthur cupped his hands around the glass for several seconds until they were warm enough to allow him to get on with the business of getting the box ready for the day's work schedule.

He hauled on the chain and the lamp ascended back up towards the ceiling, beyond head height.

Moving to the block instruments that were on the shelf above the lever frame, Arthur tapped out the signal-box-open code, on the telegraph button, to the nearest adjacent signal boxes, then set all of the signals, under his control, back to their danger positions, and waited for a response.

Within a matter of moments, the bells, on the shelf rang out, as the nearest signal boxes on either side, in each direction, acknowledged his opening code.

"Well, at least someone else has made it into work, then," he said to himself as he blew on his numbed hands and set about lighting the fire in order to get a brew of tea on the go.

Chapter Four
Snowfall

Forty minutes later the fire was going well and the kettle was singing away on the hob like a contented pet, its lid rattling.

It was still snowing, the seemingly unending fall of large flakes, stretching like a grey curtain as far as the eye could see.

For the first time that morning, Arthur felt reasonably warm and almost comfortable, standing with his back to the fire, warming his backside, he drew on a cigarette and studied the surrounding countryside, just about able to make out, through the swathe of swirling flakes, the ghostly shapes of the nearby houses and the tops of the headstones in the churchyard.

He rubbed clear a patch in the condensation on the window and looked towards where the main line was once visible. *There won't be anything moving along there for a while,* he observed.

He was proved right, for four hours later, although the wind had dropped and the snowflakes were now only gently falling vertically, rather than being blown horizontally, not a wheel had turned. Locomotives were either, still snowbound in their sheds, or their crews were snowbound in their homes. Whatever; not a carriage was to be seen, not a whistle to be heard, nothing had moved all morning, the landscape was white and eerily silent.

Even Jethro, the Bull Mastiff from the village post office, was conspicuous by its absence, having failed to call for his usual pee on the iris bed.

Arthur, standing framed in the window, a cup of tea in one hand, and a smouldering cigarette in the other, surveyed the landscape. Nearly a foot of snow covered both platforms in a smooth, unmarked layer, which continued on over the coal sidings and beyond, in a great, white cloak, broken only by the protruding tops of the rusty buffers, and the skeletal top half of the Yew hedge that bordered the lines.

Arthur drew on his cigarette and looked casually towards the up line, in the direction of Trethomas, then he did a double take, as he spied a lone figure in the distance slowly lumbering through the white, virgin snow leaving behind a churned-up trail in his wake. Arthur eyes strained to make out the slowly approaching individual.

"Who the bloody hell is this plonker?" he muttered, as he watched the hooded shape's strides, which carefully matched the distance between the hidden sleepers, each foot's imprint revealing the blackened, wooden surfaces, as he made his approach.

Rubbing at the window with a sleeve, Arthur studied the figure, as it progressed nearer to his viewing point, the features, beneath the cowl, now vaguely visible.

Suddenly Arthur's heart jumped in his chest and he gasped with shock, dumbfounded. "Hell's Bloody Bells, it's the ghost of Buddy Holly!" he croaked, irrationally, a cold shiver running through his body, while the hairs on the back of his neck stood to attention.

The tall, slim figure, that approached, had a pale face with dark, brooding eyes that stared out of a pair of thick, black-framed spectacles with snow-spattered lenses. Arthur took a nervous pull at his cigarette, and it trembled between his fingers, while the cup, in his other hand, which had become frozen at a crazy angle, began slowly depositing a small dribble of tea onto the toe of his boot.

"Shit!" he hissed, coming out of his trance and shaking his foot, throwing the remains of the cigarette into the fire and the dregs of the teacup into the coal bucket, Arthur grabbed a lever cloth and angrily rubbed it across the defiled boot. "C'mon get a grip, Tanner. For Chrissakes, you soft sod," he murmured, sheepishly grinning at the initial reaction that the Buddy Holly look-alike had caused.

Arthur turned back to the patch in the condensation and took another look at the bespectacled stranger, who had, by now, slowly crunched his way through the white crust, and had nearly reached the signal box.

Arthur rubbed a hand across his face and, shamefaced, said to himself, "Fair play, he's the bloody spit of Buddy Holly!"

Still embarrassed, he tried to rationalise his earlier moment of shock. *Reading all that stuff about Buddy, in the paper, this morning, and now, seeing his sodding double coming down the main line, jeez, that's enough to make anyone crap himself,* he grinned self-consciously, but the nagging doubts remained. *Ten to one he speaks with a Texas accent,* said an inner voice.

He laughed out loud at the absurdity of the situation, yet, inwardly, he was still quite wary, not being that ready to dismiss the notion entirely.

Arthur watched the hooded figure as it moved into the shadow of the signal box, and slowly ascended to the top of the outside stairs, where the stranger stamped the snow from his Wellington boots and knocked on the front door, opened it and walked in.

"Orright Butt," said Buddy's double, "what poxy weather, ain't it! I'm frozen to the bloody marrow, me." He patted his white outer garment and a shower of snow fell to the floor and became a puddle, the garment now revealing itself as a grey duffel coat. Buddy pushed the hood off his head. "Sorry to bother you, like, but I was supposed to be down at Bass Alton station forty minutes ago, but, because of the snow, and the like, I've been delayed a bit, so d'yer mind if I used your 'phone a sec?"

Arthur pointed to the receiver on the wall. "Help yourself, although you'll be lucky if you get through. I don't suppose Reg, the station clerk, has managed to get there yet, and as there ain't likely to be any buses or trains down to Bass Alton for a while, I wouldn't bank on getting down there much before noon."

Buddy's double warmed his hands at the fire then he turned around and lifted his duffel coat to allow the heat to get to his rear end. "I'm not going there to catch a train," he explained. "I'm going down there to work, I'm supposed to be reporting for duty at the station master's office, today. It's my first shift down there, I'm the new porter, see?"

Arthur nodded, "Right, now I come to think of it that does ring a bell, I remember Dai saying, last week, something or the other about a new porter starting. So, you're him, then?"

Arthur held out his hand. "I'm Arthur Tanner how're you doing?"

"Orright, Butt," said Buddy, grasping Arthur's hand, his eyes looking beyond Arthur, in dismay, at the fine curtain of flakes that was still descending. "I ought to be down at Bass Alton Station by now, the powers that be will be wondering where the bloody hell I've got to," said Buddy, biting his lip in consternation, his eyes still fixed upon the snow that covered the surrounding countryside.

"I wouldn't worry," said Arthur over his shoulder as he stooped to poke the fire. "There's not going to be any bugger down there, for a while, anyway, apart from Dai Marshall, and maybe the booking clerk." He dropped the poker back onto the fender with a clang and flopped back into the armchair, stretched his legs out and rested his feet against a lever. "Unless there's a rapid thaw, I'll be surprised if anybody else manages to make it down there before lunch time," said Arthur, "especially the Station Master, Charlie Protheroe, he lives on the other side of Caerphilly, and he has a fair old way to travel, so I wouldn't bet on seeing him today."

Buddy's double nodded. "Aye well, you may be right, but I still think that I'd better give them a ring, all the same, just to let them know that I'm trying to get there," he gestured towards the telephone. "So I'll give them a ring if that's orright."

"Sure, help yourself," Arthur repeated. "The number for the station booking office is three one three, just crank the handle on the side of the phone that number of times."

The stranger turned the handle as instructed and lifted the handset to his ear. After several seconds there came a response. "Hello, is that Bass Alton station? This is Clive Stark, yes, that's right, Clive Stark. I'm supposed to be reporting for duty down there this morning." Clive chewed at a thumbnail while the person at the other end of the line, digested the information.

"Yeah, that's right, this morning," Clive continued, "but there's no way I'm going to get down there yet, not unless the snow starts to melt," he paused and looked out of the window. "I'll give it half an hour or so, and have a shot at getting down there then. You what?" Clive pushed the black-framed spectacles higher up the bridge of his nose as he concentrated on every word from the speaker on the other end of the line. "I'm phoning from Church Forge sidings signal box, yes, Church Forge," he repeated. "I've been here about ten minutes," he shook his head. "No, I walked down from Bedwas Yard, it wasn't too bad then." The black-framed spectacles were once again pushed back up the bridge of Clive's nose. "Anyway, as I said, I'll give it, maybe a half an hour, and if the snow starts to melt, I'll start to make my way down to you, OK? Yeah. Orright then, see you in a bit, tarrar." Clive replaced the receiver and turned to Arthur. "You were right, then, the station master hasn't got there yet, but I'm going to have a go at getting down there, anyway."

"It's a couple of miles, mind," said Arthur. "You'd be better off hanging on for a while, it's bound to ease off soon." He peered through the side window, it was still snowing, but the flakes were miniscule compared to earlier on. "It looks like it's almost stopped, but I'd still hang on for a while, if I were you," Arthur advised.

Clive Stark stared out at the snow that covered the down platform and nodded. "Yeah, I think you'm right there, Taff." He sat down on the footlocker and delved inside his jacket. After much searching, he brought out a brown, leather pouch, from which he extracted several pinches of golden tobacco, which he spread evenly along the length of cigarette paper before rolling them between thumb and forefinger.

"Still, can't be helped, can it?" Clive said, applying his tongue to the gummed strip of paper. "I've done my best to get through to the station, can't do no more, can I?" Smoothing the newly formed cigarette roughly into a tube shape, Clive stuck it in the corner of his mouth. "You haven't got a light on you, I don't suppose?"

Arthur picked a paper spill from out of the coal bucket and offered it to Clive. "Here," he said handing it over. "Light it from the fire."

Clive took the spill and lit it, holding the flame to the end of the misshapen cigarette, which he puffed into life. "Ta," he said, knocking out the spill and dropping it back into the bucket.

Taking a big draw on the cigarette, Clive blew out the smoke in a long, swirling stream of greyish blue.

"Whereabouts are you from, then, Clive?" Arthur leaned forward in his chair. "It is Clive, isn't it?"

"Yeah, that's right, Clive, Clive Stark," the bespectacled stranger replied, blowing on the end of his cigarette, making it glow. "Pengam, me, not far from the station sidings, nice and handy for work, see."

"How come you've come down here to work, then?" asked Arthur. "Don't you like working up that part of the valley, then?"

"Aye its orright, I suppose," Clive grimaced and he shrugged his shoulders. "I just wanted a change, and it's a bit more money."

"Hey, I hope that you don't think I'm being nosy," said Arthur. "I just thought that travelling down to Bass Alton would be a bit of a pain in the arse, seeing as how it's that much farther for you to come, like."

"No." Clive shook his head and took a last long drag on his cigarette before throwing it into the fire. "I don't mind the extra walk, walking is good exercise, ain't it?"

"Better you than me," grinned Arthur. "It might be good for you, but it's still a hell of a walk, that's for sure."

"Oh, it's not too bad," said Clive. "Although the going was a bit of a sod this morning."

"You didn't bloody walk all the way down the line this morning, did you?" asked Arthur, looking astonished.

"No, I came down the main road, most of the way," replied Clive. "I only walked down the track for about two hundred yards. I came through where the fence is broken."

"I didn't know there was a break in the fence," Arthur said, looking in the direction from where Clive had come. "Whereabouts did you say it was?"

Clive waved a hand in the general direction of the up line. "Oh, about two, three hundred yards up the line, near the down distant-signal, the weight of the snow probably brought it down."

Arthur nodded and made a note in the train register. "I'll have to remember to report that or we'll have bloody sheep all over the sodding line."

Clive rose to his feet and looked at the clock. It told him that it was quarter to eleven. "I think I'll make a move. It looks like it won't be long before it'll turn to sleet." He did up the toggles on his duffel coat and moved towards the door.

"You be careful out there, now," warned Arthur. "You'll not be able to tell the sleepers from the permanent way in this little lot," he indicated at the snow with a thumb. "It's got to be at least a foot deep out there, you'll go arse over tip, if you're not careful."

Clive put up his hood. "I'll be orright, me, I'm used to snow, spent six months winter training in Norway, so you don't have to worry about me." He opened the door and strode through.

A blast of cold air hit Arthur in the face as he got to his feet and watched Clive make his way slowly down the stairs.

"See yer," Clive called over his shoulder, as he started to crunch his way along the down platform.

"Hey! Clive," Arthur called after him.

Clive stopped by the iris bed and turned around. "What's up?"

"What were you doing in Norway, then?" Arthur asked, suspicion showing in his eyes.

Clive gave a wink and tapped the side of his nose. "Can't say, but if you were to think SAS, I couldn't argue." He thrust his hands into the duffel coat's pockets and continued on his way, carefully treading through the virgin snow.

Arthur looked mystified. "Oh, right then," he murmured, then, as he about to close the door, a new question occurred to him. He called again to the duffle-coated figure. "Oy, Clive, one more thing."

"What's up, now?" Clive stopped and turned slowly around, suspicion showing in the eyes behind the black-rimmed spectacles.

"Nothing's up," Arthur shook his head. "It's just that I wondered how often you get mistaken for Buddy Holly, that's all."

Clive frowned. "Who's Buddy Holly?" he called back, apprehensively.

Arthur let out a hoot. "What do you mean, who's Buddy Holly?" he said, staring at Clive in disbelief. "Buddy bloody Holly, you know, the rock star who was killed in an air crash, yesterday, are you pulling my plonker, or what?"

The frown stayed on Clive's anxious face. "I'm sorry, I don't understand," he shouted, from the end of the down platform.

Arthur was starting to shiver and wanting to return to the comfort of the warm, little cabin, dismissed thoughts of an explanation. "Never mind, just watch your step, orright?"

"Yeah, cheers," shouted Clive, relief showing on his face and he waved and turned back to continue his trek down the track towards Bedwas Station.

Arthur closed the door and made for the fire, arms outstretched seeking the heat. "What a bloody toy," he said to himself, laughing aloud. "Who's Buddy Holly, for Chrissakes, that's the bloody best one, yet."

He scraped at the bottom bars of the fire with the poker, removing the build-up of ash.

Wait 'till I tell Dai, that'll crack him up, who's Buddy Holly.

Arthur added another shovel of coal to the fire, wiped his hands on his trousers and then he settled down in the armchair, lighting up a cigarette and opening the newspaper.

Chapter Five
Snowplough

Twenty minutes later the telegraph, from the next signal box, up the line, chattered out the call-attention code, shattering the peace.

"Bloody hell! Signs of life," said Arthur getting to his feet. "Wonders will never bloody cease."

Moving to the telegraph control, Arthur tapped out an acknowledgement, and a reply code came back, telling him that a locomotive and a brake-van was ready to make its way down the main line from Pengam Sidings. Arthur tapped in the acceptance code, which would allow it onto his section, and then signalled it on to the next box down the line, which also replied with an acceptance code and Arthur lowered the signals.

The telephone rang. Arthur threw the stub of the cigarette into the fire and picked up the receiver. "Church Forge," he said.

"Hello Taff, how's it going, then?" It was Ron Scott, the signalman from the Pengam sidings signal box, calling. "I hope you haven't been throwing snowballs at the schoolgirls down there," Ron said laughingly down the telephone line.

"Schoolgirls?" Arthur said with feigned innocence. "You're bloody joking, aren't you? I haven't seen hide or hair of anyone, all morning, never mind bloody schoolgirls." He paused, "No, I lie, Ron, there was some plonker who nearly gave me a heart attack, when he walked into the box, earlier on."

"Who was that, then, Butt?" asked Ron.

"Clive Stark," replied Arthur. "Supposed to be on his way down to Bedwas station, said he was starting down there today."

Ron let out a hoot of delight. "Starky! You've had Starky down there and survived? Arth' if you only knew how close you were to coming a bloody cropper."

"What'yer on about, you tosser?" Arthur gave a half laugh into the telephone. "He seemed to me to be a reasonable sort of fellah. Although, mind you, when he walked in on me this morning, dressed like a sodding mad monk, he didn't seem so bloody reasonable. What's up with him, then?"

"What's up with him? What's up with him?" Ron sounded incredulous. "He's a friggin' disaster area that's what."

"How come?" Arthur asked.

Ron guffawed down the telephone. "You'd never bloody believe it Arth', he's only been working down in Pengam yard, just this last three months, and he's caused enough bloody mayhem for a lifetime."

"Why, what did he do, then?" Arthur was beginning to sound interested.

"You might well ask, old son," said Ron with a chortle. "The first week that he began on the night shift, right? He only goes and sends a coal wagon down the wrong siding, don't he?"

"Marvellous!" said Arthur sarcastically. "That cocked things up, no doubt?"

"It did more than cock things up," Ron laughed. "He sent it down the same siding that Archie Jenkins's brake van was in, didn't he?"

"Bloody hell fire, what happened?" Arthur chortled.

"I'll tell you what happened. Archie Jenkins was inside the bloody thing, wasn't he?"

Before Arthur could ask, Ron continued. "The wagon came down the siding about ten miles an hour and buffered-up to the brake van with a fair old bang, I can tell you."

"Jeez! Old Archie wasn't hurt, was he?" asked Arthur, concern in his voice.

"No, Archie was all right, bit shook up, like," replied Ron. "The biggest problem was that the collision knocked over Archie's tea-can, spilling bloody tea all over his trousers and soaking his log sheets, it took two of the shunters and a lamp man to drag Archie off bloody Starky." Ron continued, between snorts, "And that's not all, last Monday week, really put the tin hat on it, didn't it?"

"Why, what happened then?" gasped Arthur weakly, holding his aching ribs.

Ron gave a hoot. "Well, it's just after six and he's on his first spell of mornings at the West sidings, and it's his turn to light the fire in the shunters' cabin. So, what's the problem? I hear you say. Well, according to Dougie Johnson, who is watching Starky preparing the fire, you know, putting in the sticks and the cotton waste, then the coal, on top, last."

Arthur nodded. "Yeah, then what?"

"Well," replies Ron, "Dougie, satisfied that Starky knows what he's doing, leaves him to it, just as he's putting a match to the cotton waste. What Dougie didn't know, and what, we were all to learn later, was that when Starky picked up the handful of cotton waste, there were two fog warning detonators caught up inside."

"Oh, jeez," said Arthur. "What happened, then?"

"Well according to Dougie, Starky said that he lit the cotton waste, making sure that it and the sticks had caught, then he went outside to fill the kettle from the tap by the Guard's cabin. In the meantime, the sticks and the paraffin-soaked cotton waste must have been going well and truly."

Arthur tried hard to contain his laughter. "Jeez, don't tell me, he set fire to the mess hut?"

"He did better than that, Butt," said Ron. "The bloody place blew to smithereens, didn't it? The heat from the burning sticks soon got to the detonators and it wasn't too long before they exploded with such a God Almighty bang that it was heard at the other end of the yard. Anyway, to cut a long story short, the blast blew out the front of the fireplace, sending it through the wall of the cabin onto Mostyn Rees's cabbage patch, buggering up his prize Savoy in the process. The rest of the force of the explosion went straight up the chimney and blew a hole in the bloody roof, sending slates across to number three siding, it was bloody bedlam, people were running around like scalded bloody cats. There was soot and slates and dust flying about everywhere."

"What about Clive?" Arthur snorted.

"Lucky little sod escaped unharmed," replied Ron. "They found him lying by the bike shed, black as Al bloody Jolson, unharmed apart from the peak of his cap, which had melted."

"Stop, for Chrissakes, no more," pleaded Arthur, holding his sides. "I can't handle any more."

"You can laugh," said Ron, seriousness creeping into his voice. "It was no bloody laugh at the time, I can tell you, apart from the fact that some bugger could've been seriously hurt, all the sodding Christmas club money went up in smoke."

"What do you mean, went up in smoke?" asked Arthur.

"Charlie Tonks the sports and social rep' collects a pound a man, per week, for the Christmastime pay out, many of the yards do it," Ron explained.

"Yeah, that's right," said Arthur. "We got a similar sort of thing down at Bedwas station."

"That's right," replied Ron. "Well Charlie must have had at least a hundred pounds of Christmas club money stashed in his locker when the bloody hut blew up."

"Christ didn't they find any of it, then?"

"Not a bloody bean," said Ron. "Everything was burnt to a sodding cinder. The only thing that they found was the brass clock, and that was as flat as a bloody pancake."

"Bloody rotate!" exclaimed Arthur. "There must have been bloody murder up there, then. I'm surprised they didn't sodding well lynch the bugger?"

"They came bloody well close to it, I can tell you," laughed Ron. "The yard master called a meeting of the men and pointed out, that although Stark had lit the fire, and should have been more careful with the cotton waste and all, it wasn't he who had put the waste on top of the fog detonators, so it would be completely unfair to blame him totally."

"I suppose so," said Arthur doubtfully.

"Anyway," said Ron, "after much umming and arring, all the men agreed that it was just a bit of bad luck that old Starky went and picked up those detonators with the cotton waste. So, it really was down to whoever had stuck the waste there, in the first place, that's where the blame lay for the cause of the explosion, the fire and the Christmas club money going up in smoke. Of course, nobody would admit to being anywhere near the cotton waste, would they? So, the matter has been dropped."

"Well, I hope to God that he doesn't blow up our bloody Christmas money or he'll wish he'd never left bloody Pengam, that's all," replied Arthur.

"Don't say that you haven't been warned Arth', this boy is dynamite," Ron let out a manic cackle, "and now the bloody idiot has transferred down to Bass Alton, and the best of bloody British, an' all."

Arthur snorted with derision and then he said, with a slightly steadier voice. "Yeah, well we'll see, anyway, enough of sodding Stark. What the bloody hell do you want, anyhow?"

"What do you mean, what do I want?" replied Ron.

"Well, you were the one who rang me, you Tit," Arthur laughed.

"Oh aye, that's right," said Ron. "I almost forgot, the light engine and van, that's on its way down to you? It's got a snow-plough-blade on the front and it's going to clear the line down as far as Bass Alton, then turn on the Trethomas triangle and come back up the valley and clear the line as far as Hengoed Halt. Will you pass on the message Arth', orright?"

"Yeah, sure." said Arthur. "Will do."

"Once the engine has cleared the section," said Ron, "there will be a passenger train coming down, which will be the eleven o'clock Machen to Newport, that'll be following on down in about a quarter of an hour, ok?"

"Okey Dokey, my son," said Arthur. "Thanks for that, I'll speak to you again."

"Cheers, Arth'" said Ron and the telephone went silent.

Arthur put the mouthpiece onto its hook and looked out at the surrounding countryside. The snowflakes were, by now, decidedly smaller, almost sleet. *With a bit of luck this lot will turn to rain before too long,* he thought.

Arthur looked towards the up line, in the direction of Pengam, hoping to see the oncoming snow plough, but there was no sign of it, so he removed the kettle from the hob and set about filling it from the galvanized water container that stood on its metal stand in the corner by the lamp locker. As Arthur bent to turn the tap, he caught sight of a folded-up piece of paper under the bench that was below the wall-mounted telephone.

He picked it up and was about to unfold it, when a whistle sounded and the snowplough crawled into sight.

Arthur tossed the piece of paper onto the desk and turned his attention towards the distant locomotive, watching its plough as it churned up the fresh snow and turned it into dirty, irregular lumps at the side of the down line.

The driver gave a cock's crow on the whistle of the engine and brought it to a halt outside the cabin. Arthur opened a window and leaned on the safety bar feeling the heat from the locomotive's boiler wafting over him, the smell of steam, smoke and hot oil filled the air.

"We're going as far as Bass Alton, then turning on the Trethomas triangle, OK?" the driver bellowed, which was audible over the escaping steam that screamed from the engine's ejectors.

"Yeah, you're cleared through to the station," Arthur bellowed back, giving the thumbs-up sign.

The driver acknowledged Arthur, sounded the whistle and yanked the regulator up a notch.

The tank engine let out a whoosh of steam and slowly moved off in the direction of Bass Alton station.

Arthur watched it clank away, hurling aside the snow in its path, until it disappeared out of sight around the bend. He closed the window and signalled the snowplough out of the section and restored the signals to their on-positions.

Flopping back into the armchair, Arthur picked up the newspaper again. "Now, where was I?" he said turning the pages.

The telephone bell shrilled. "Aw, for Christ's sake," he muttered, throwing the newspaper back onto the chair. "What the bloody hell now." He got up and crossed to the telephone and lifted the handset. "Church Forge," he said testily.

"Do you want the good news first or the bad?" It was Dai Marshall.

"Marshall, you Git, what do you want?" Arthur smiled into the handset. "What the bloody hell has made you surface? What woke you up, then?"

Dai ignored Arthur's taunts. "Why don't you listen, you miserable sod. I said I've got some good news and some bad, which do you want first?"

"Orright, Smartass, give me the good, then," replied Arthur.

"Right then," said Dai. "You'll be pleased to know that the buses should be running between Pengam and Newport as normal by about one o'clock."

"Great! So, what's the bad news, then?" asked Arthur suspiciously.

"Buddy Holly's losing weight," Dai cackled maniacally.

"You are bloody sick, Marshall," said Arthur in disgust. "There's something wrong with you, you bloody tosser." Arthur strove to keep his voice at a serious level. "That's going to be the first thing on the Western Movies Club agenda tonight. I'm going to propose that you buy the first three rounds as punishment for being such a sick plonker, and for bringing shame on the name of the club and its members. You're definitely in the cacky, Son, good and proper."

"Aw, not three rounds," whined Dai theatrically. "You wouldn't do that to a mate, would you? Not three pints, please, I apologize, I take it all back. Besides, I've only got a couple of quid to last me until payday," his voice cracked and he broke into a laugh.

"You'll not get away that lightly, you pervert," said Arthur severely. "You sick prick, you're dead wrong, anyway, not only is Buddy not losing weight, but he's alive and well and is down with you lot at Bass Alton, right now, to see the station master."

"So, you've finally flipped, have you?" Dai chortled. "I knew you weren't far off the brink, and now, you've finally dropped off the edge."

"No, I'm serious," said Arthur. "He's down there with you, now."

"Ok, you've got me," Dai gave an exaggerated sigh. "I give in, what the bloody hell are you on about?"

"Buddy Holly!" Arthur yelled down the telephone. "He was here this morning, I spoke to him personally, honest," Arthur fought to keep his voice serious.

"I knew this morning's news had upset you, Arth', but I didn't realize that you'd completely flipped? I hate to have to tell you this, Arthur Boy, but Buddy Holly is no more, I'm sorry to say. Not only is he no longer of this planet, he is not in with the gaffer, either, *there's nobody here but us chickens,*" Dai sang down the line.

"What about Clive, then? Clive Stark isn't he with you?" said Arthur, now more serious.

"Who the bloody hell is Clive Stark, when he's home?" Dai laughed. "Look, I know I was out of order with that sick joke, but you're not going to get one over on me with a Clive what's-his-face story, you'll have to get out of bed earlier to catch me, old Son. I don't care whether you saw Buddy Holly, Marylyn Monroe, or whoever, this morning, there's no way I'm falling for one, of your tricks, Butt."

"Hey, I'm not bloody joking, Dai, honest," Arthur's voice had taken on a more serious tone. "This bloke, Clive Stark, at least that's what he said his name was, he was here this morning, I swear to God, he was, and, he was the bloody spitting image of Buddy. Scared the shit out of me when he came into the box, he was wearing a duffel coat which was covered in snow, looking like a monk or something, gave me a right sodding shock, I can tell you."

Dai groaned. "Do me a favour, Arth', will you, eh? I've already apologised for the Buddy joke, so, no more ghosts and bloody ghoulies, is it?"

"Honest to God, Dai, I'm not kidding, this plonker Clive is for real, honest. He's supposed to be down there with you. He ought to be there by now."

"What do you mean down with me? There's no bugger else down here except the booking clerk."

"You're joking!" exclaimed Arthur. "Clive left here about an hour ago, on his way down to Bass Alton station to see the old-man, he said that he was supposed to be starting down there today, portering, he's bound to be down there by now?"

"Well he bloody well ain't, and that's that, Butty," Dai replied.

"No kidding, now Dai," Arthur's voice had taken on a serious edge. "Are you sure that he's not there, maybe he's been and gone or something?"

Dai noted the new tone to Arthur's voice. "I'm almost positive, Arth', but hang on, I'll go and check with the booking clerk, downstairs."

"Orright, but don't be too long," warned Arthur. "I don't like the way this is beginning to turn out."

"Ok, I won't be a sec," said Dai leaving the phone.

Arthur heard the handset being put down and the sound of Dai walking away from the telephone, across to the door.

The call-attention signal bell sounded and Arthur left the telephone in order to answer it. The code for a passenger train rang out. Arthur acknowledged it and went back to the telephone.

Another bell informed him that the snowplough had now cleared Bass Alton North, the next section down the line.

Arthur put the telephone earpiece back onto the desktop again, and signalled the passenger train forward. The Bass Alton North signalman signalled his acceptance of the passenger train onto his section of the line and Arthur set about adjusting the signals to go, before returning to the telephone, where he waited for Dai's response.

Half a minute later Dai returned. "No, I was right," he said. "Barry, the clerk, can't remember him. He's been taking telephone inquiries all morning about the train service, but he's not seen anyone in person, and there are only two sets of footprints along the platform, and they're both mine."

"Oh, bloody hell," groaned Arthur, "that puts the bloody tin hat on it, that does."

"Don't be so bloody soft, you daft bugger," said Dai. "It's not your fault that this arsehole, Stark, has gone missing, so he's gone and got himself lost. For Chrissakes, balls to him, that's what I say, Jeez! He could be any bloody where by now, so forget the stupid sod, Arth', it's not your bloody problem."

"Bullshit!" Arthur barked down the telephone, "of course it's my sodding problem, I should have stopped the bloody pillock from going down the line to Bass Alton, in the first place, at least until the snow had melted. Christ! When he left here it was still snowing. Ok, I know that it had practically stopped, but, nevertheless, he was still walking down the bloody main line, not knowing that there was a frigging great snow plough on its way down behind him."

"Oh shit," said Dai quietly. "I see what you mean, Butt. What're we going to do about it, then?"

"Well, the first thing you do is get on to Lewis Griffiths at Bass Alton South and get him to stop that bloody snow-plough and get it examined. If there's no sign of a hit, then he will have to instruct the driver and the fireman to examine the line between Bass Alton South and you at Bass Alton Station."

"What about the stretch between you and the North box, that'll have to be searched, as well, won't it?"

"Leave that to me," replied Arthur. "There's a passenger train on its way down from Pengam. I will stop it and get the crew to examine the stretch of line down between here and the North box."

A whistle sounded in the distance. "That's it coming now, so we'd better shift our arses and get on with it, orright?"

"Hang on a minute, Arth'. What if nothing is found, what then?"

"Then we call the police," said Arthur replacing the receiver.

He put the signals back to the danger position and waited for the passenger train, red flag to hand.

Chapter Six
Detection

Forty minutes later, the line down to Bass Alton station had been examined and found to be clear. The station master, who had finally made it to Bedwas, took charge of the situation and promptly telephoned the police, who set about examining the line and its surrounding undergrowth.

By twelve forty-five, the sleet had turned to rain and had almost stopped. The wind too, had eased and road traffic was once again moving along the main Bedwas to Pengam road. Arthur leaned on the window-bar and surveyed the scene.

The village had woken from its slumbering, the snow sparkled beneath the sun's rays and the sound of scraping shovels echoed across the main road, along with excited children's voices coming from the direction of the village school. Arthur spotted a snowball sailing through the air.

"Little Bastards!" he said, sliding the window shut and slumping back into the chair.

Picking up a paper spill from the coal bucket, Arthur lit it from the glowing coals in the fire grate and ignited a cigarette.

The sound of the platform gate closing brought him upright and he looked towards the up platform. Striding through the crisp, packed layer of snow were two policemen, their breath showing on the air like plumes of smoke. They crossed the line and headed towards the Church Forge signal box, leaving behind a trail of dirty grey footprints in the crisp snow.

Arthur crossed to the door and held it open; he nodded and flicked ash from the end of his cigarette over the balcony rail onto the jumble of dirty snow beneath.

"Good morning, Sir," said the taller of the two, who pointed to his companion. "This is Constable Durning, and I'm Sergeant Phillips, we are from the Bedwas police station," he extended his hand to Arthur. "No doubt you know why we are here?"

Arthur nodded and shook the Sergeant's hand. "It's about that plonker Stark, isn't it? Have you found the git, then?"

The policemen entered the porch and they wiped their feet on the coconut mat, removing their helmets at the same time.

"Yes, Mr Stark," mused the taller of the two as he started to undo the buttons on his navy-blue regulation mackintosh. "Yes, we have come about Mr Stark, and no, we have not found him yet. I am hoping that you might be able to provide us with some answers that may shed some light on this whole affair and help us clear up this business of the mysterious Mr stark and his apparent disappearance."

"He's still missing, then?" said Arthur, gesturing to the hard, backless bench, beneath the side window. "Have a seat."

"Thank you, but no," said the sergeant. "We'll stand if it's all the same to you." He delved into the depths of his jacket pocket and extracted a small, black notebook and a packet of whiffs. Flicking open the top of the whiff packet with a thumbnail, the Sergeant extracted a whiff with his mouth, he bent towards the coal bucket. "May I," he said gesturing to the paper spills.

"Yeah, help yourself," said Arthur.

The sergeant lit up and began flicking through his notebook. "So, let's see." He flicked a page back and forth between his fingers.

Arthur remembered seeing Broderick Crawford doing a similar sort of thing on TV's Highway Patrol.

Constable Durning, not to be outdone, brought out his own notebook, licked the point of his pencil and stood poised, ready to record Arthur's every word.

The sergeant looked up from his notebook. "Yes, he's still missing." He turned his attention back to the notebook. "Yes, that's right, Clive Stark." He looked up, from his notebook, apparently content that his memory and his notes tallied. "How long have you known this Clive Stark, then?" asked the sergeant.

"I don't know him," replied Arthur.

The sergeant looked up from studying the glowing end of his whiff, surprise in his eyes. "Oh?"

"Yeah, that's right," said Arthur. "This morning was the first, and the last time that I've clapped eyes on the bloody idiot."

"So how did you know who he was? Did he introduce himself to you, then?" inquired Sergeant Phillips casually.

"No, not really," answered Arthur. "He gave his name over the 'phone, when he was speaking to someone down at the station, that was when I got to know who he was."

"I see," the sergeant's face took on a somewhat pensive expression and he stroked at his cheek, as though checking to see whether this morning's shave had been a complete success.

"Now, what time did this Mister Stark arrive here?"

Arthur scratched his head. "As far as I can remember he got here about ten-ish."

The sergeant nodded and turned to the constable. "You're taking this all down, Durning, I trust?"

Constable Durning licked the point of his pencil again and nodded, "Yes Sarge' all down verb ate um."

Sergeant Phillips drew on his whiff. "Ok, so he got here about ten? Then what?"

"Then nothing," Arthur shrugged his shoulders. "After he'd 'phoned the station, he sat down, there," he pointed to the bench beneath the window. "He rolled himself a fag and had a smoke while he waited for the snow to ease up, then after about a quarter of an hour, he buggered off down the track towards Bass Alton station."

The constable's face had taken on a manic expression as his pencil raced across the page.

"So, he made his way down the track there," the sergeant gestured with his whiff, "down to Bass Alton station, is that correct, Sir?"

"That's it," said Arthur. "He went along the down platform then on to the down line, that's when I lost sight of him." He pointed towards the disused platform. "That's where his footprints were before the snow-plough churned up all the snow and covered them up."

The policemen stared out at the line of dirty-grey lumps that adorned the down platform. Sergeant Phillips screwed up his eyes in concentration, and stared at the soiled lumps, almost as if he expected the soiled snow to reveal clues of great and startling importance, which would, not only solve the mystery of the disappearance of Clive Stark, but, would also enable them to close the case and to get across to the local for a quick pie and a pint before returning in triumph to Bedwas police station.

The sergeant turned slowly back and stared into the fire. "So you didn't know this Mr Stark prior to this morning, then?"

"No, I told you. I didn't know him from bloody Adam."

"Ok, Mr Tanner, so can you give us a description, then?"

"That's easy," Arthur grinned. "He was the bloody spit of Buddy Holly."

The sergeant looked at Arthur, his eyes narrowing. "Buddy Holly?"

The constable's hand, complete with pencil, seemed to be in a state of suspended animation.

Sergeant Phillips stared down at the toecaps of his shiny boots. "Can you be a bit more specific, Sir?"

"How more specific?" asked Arthur, frowning. "Buddy Holly is Buddy Holly, how more specific can you get?"

"With respect Sir," the sergeant's voice had taken on a more formal tone. "If you said that it was the Duke of Edinburgh, I would still need a formal description. It's no good you telling me that the chap looked like the Duke of Edinburgh when, in fact he was Winston Churchill, do you see my point, Sir?"

"Yeah, I can see what you're getting at," said Arthur conceding the point. "Sorry, I just assumed that everybody knew what Buddy Holly looked like, especially after what happened yesterday."

The sergeant raised his eyebrows. "Yesterday, what happened yesterday?"

"He was killed in an air crash, wasn't he? It was in all the papers this morning," Arthur picked up the newspaper from the table and showed them the headlines. "Killed, along with the Big Bopper and Ritchie Valens, see, it's on the front page."

The sergeant pursed his lips. "Yes," he said; slowly letting out the word like a sigh, along with a stream of blue tobacco smoke. "I seem to recall somebody mentioning the fact at the station this morning." He threw the butt of his cigar into the fire. "Bit of a coincidence, though, don't you think? Mister Tanner?"

"What do you mean, coincidence?" asked Arthur frowning.

The sergeant scratched at his chin. "Well, look at it like this, Sir, there's this pop-star character, who gets himself killed last night, and within a matter of hours, after the news release, his doppelganger turns up in the middle of a small Welsh village, in the middle of a blizzard and promptly proceeds to disappear." Sergeant Phillips shrugged his shoulders and looked out of the window at the surrounding countryside before slowly turning back and fixing Arthur with his penetrating gaze. "Nobody else, apparently, has seen hide, nor hair of our, Mister Stark, since. Don't you think that just a wee bit odd, all things considered?" The sergeant's eyebrows arched upwards with the question.

Arthur glared at the sergeant. "Are you calling me a bloody liar or something? Do you reckon that I've made all of this up, like?"

"No Sir, but you have to admit that it all looks a little odd. Don't you think?"

"Well, yes, I suppose it does," Arthur conceded, "but it's all true, what I've been telling you, honest."

"I'm sure that you are right, Mister Tanner, but you must appreciate our position," the sergeant replied. "A person has been reported as missing and we are here to try and establish the facts as they stand, and, bearing in mind that you are the only person to have met Mister Stark, this morning, as far as we know. You have to appreciate that, before we can extend our inquiries, we have to establish that this person actually existed. Then we can declare him officially missing. Do you see what I'm getting at?"

Arthur nodded, "I see your point right enough, but I can only keep repeating that what I've been telling you, is the truth."

"I'm sure that you're right, Mister Tanner, so bear with me for a few minutes longer, and I'm sure that we'll get this matter all sorted to everybody's satisfaction, OK?"

"Yeah, orright," replied Arthur, busying himself by piling more coal on the fire. Sergeant Phillips, in the meantime, consulted the constable's notebook, licking his thumb and flicking each page up and over the spiral binding.

He closed the book and passed it back to the Constable. "Right, Mister Tanner, you've given us a pretty good timetable of Mister Stark's movements this morning. Now, what we need from you is an accurate description of him."

The Constable licked his pencil point in anticipation.

"Ok." Arthur scratched his head. "Well, as I said earlier, he was the spit of Buddy Holly." He held up his hands. "Ok, ok, I know you want more than just that, well, let's see," he pulled at his lower lip while he tried to remember Clive Stark, as he appeared earlier that morning. "First of all," Arthur said, "he wore a knee-length grey duffel coat, with a hood and those bone things instead of buttons, you know like Jack Hawkins wore in the Cruel Sea?"

"Toggles," the sergeant said.

"Yeah, toggles," nodded Arthur, "that's it, toggles." He nodded again. "That's right, I can see that coat now; it was covered with snow. From a distance he looked like a sodding monk, scared the shit out of me, I can tell you."

The constable coughed and studied his pencil.

"Yes, I'm sure it must have done," said the sergeant, rubbing his chin and staring at a curious green-blue flame that was emanating from a piece of coal that burned in the grate.

"Anyway," Arthur continued. "When he pulled back the hood, I could see that he had black hair, very black it was, so were his eyes, they were black as well, and so were his glasses. As a matter of fact, I remember thinking at the time, how his hair and his eyes and his glasses were all identical in colour, really weird, like, especially as he had such a pale face. They really stood out, those glasses and the eyes behind them."

"Thank you, Mister Tanner I think we've got the picture," said the sergeant, looking at the toecaps of his boots, a pained expression in his eyes. "What about the rest of his clothes? Gloves, shoes, trousers, what can you tell us about those?"

"Not a lot," shrugged Arthur. "The trousers were dark, as far as I can remember." He scratched at his head. "I haven't got a clue about his shoes, and I don't think that he had any gloves on. No, he didn't," Arthur smacked his hands together in triumph. "I remember now, he came into the signal-box blowing into his cupped hands, yeah, that's it, and he wasn't wearing shoes, either, he had wellies on."

"Right," the sergeant looked up from his boots and studied the brass oil lamp that hung above his head. "Ok, what have we got, then Constable?"

Before the constable could open his mouth to reply, the sergeant held out his splayed fingers and began counting off on them. "One, we know what the chap looked like. Two, we know when he arrived here, and we know what time he left. Now, we've checked with the yard master at Pengam, and he has confirmed that Mister Stark was supposed to start today at Bass Alton Station. We have also obtained a description of Mister Stark and it more or less tallies with yours, Mister Tanner."

"He didn't mention Buddy Holly of course," the sergeant said, dryly, "but his description bore marked similarities to yours."

Turning his attention back to his notebook, Sergeant Phillips flicked back through the pages. "Now is there anything else that you can think of that may help us in our inquiries, anything at all."

Arthur slowly shook his head. "No, that's about it really. I honestly can't think of anything else."

A telegraph bell sounded, interrupting his thoughts, and Arthur got out of his seat and answered it. The bell rattled out the code that told Arthur that the engine with the snowplough was on its way back up the valley. He accepted it onto his section and signalled it on to the next signal-box and set the signals at all clear.

Walking across to the desk, to book down the train's details, Arthur, discovered the folded-up piece of paper on top of the train-register. The piece of paper that he had picked up from the floor earlier. "Hang on, how about this, then," he brandished the paper.

"What have you got there, Mr. Tanner?"

"Sorry," said Arthur. "I'd forgotten all about it. I found it this morning below the telephone, after Stark had left. I suppose he must have dropped it."

"What is it?" asked the sergeant holding out his hand. "Let's see."

Arthur passed it over. "I don't know, I didn't look."

The sergeant unfolded the paper and read silently, then looking up from the paper, he said, "How old would you say this Mr Stark was?"

Arthur shrugged. "Seventeen, or eighteen maybe, certainly no more than eighteen. Why is that?"

"Well, according to this letter, our Mister Stark here, is an ex naval officer of some standing." The sergeant allowed himself half a smile.

"Naval officer!" Arthur laughed out loud. "I've never heard such a load of old bollocks in my life," he snorted. "Naval officer? Navy cadets, more like. I bet the nearest he's ever got to a ship was on the boating lake at Roath Park in Cardiff."

The sergeant managed another small grin. "Well, according to this letter, not only is our friend Mister Stark a prominent Pengam businessperson, but he is also a Commander in the RNVR."

"What the bloody hell is that, when it's about?" said Arthur, nonplussed.

"The RNVR, Mister Tanner, is the Royal Naval Volunteer Reserve."

"Oh!" Arthur said, none the wiser. "That's probably where he learned his explosive skills," he sniggered.

"What explosive skills would they be?" asked the sergeant sharply.

Arthur shrugged. "None, really, just joking, that's all."

"Why would you joke about something like that. Is there something that you haven't told us, then?" the sergeant's face remained expressionless; but the eyes had narrowed and taken on a glittering appearance.

Arthur shrugged again. "No, it was just something that Ron Scott told me this morning."

"Who's Ron Scott?" asked the Sergeant.

"He's the signalman in the next box up the line," Arthur indicated with a thumb.

"What did he have to say about our Mister Stark, then?" inquired the sergeant, now very attentive.

"Aw, he only happened to mention as how Stark had blown up the shunters cabin in Pengam yard."

The sergeant looked at Arthur incredulously. "Blown up, how do you mean, blown up?"

Arthur shrugged. "Ron said it was an accident, it wasn't really Stark's fault."

"What wasn't?" the sergeant was starting to look exasperated.

"The explosion," said Arthur.

The Sergeant held up his hands. "OK, OK, Mister Tanner just tell us what Mister Scott told you, all right?"

Arthur nodded, sat down and proceeded to relate the tale of Clive Stark and the shunters' cabin, word for word, as, he had been told, by Ron Scott.

The sergeant crossed his legs, folded his arms and leaned against the doorjamb, listening in fascination.

"Anyway," said Arthur, concluding his story, "by the time the fire brigade had got there, there was bugger all left. The whole lot had been burnt to the ground, everything, chairs, table, lockers, money, everything."

The sergeant straightened up, his face expressionless, his jaw set. "What money?" he asked quietly.

"The Christmas club fund that Charlie Tonks kept in his locker," replied Arthur.

"In the cabin that caught fire?" the Sergeant said, his jaw set.

"Yeah," nodded Arthur. "It was the locker in the corner of the cabin. According to Ron, they reckoned that there must have been a hundred quid in there."

The sergeant gave the constable a meaningful look. "Oh, really," he said, shaking his head and gazing across the lines towards the village. "And it was all burnt to a crisp? Not a fragment left to be recognized, of course?"

Arthur shrugged. "I can only tell you what Ron told me; I don't know any more than that."

The sergeant brought his attention back to the note. "Well Commander Stark, I think you and I are going to have a little natter about one or two things." He folded up the letter and put it inside his notebook. "Right Constable, I think our work is done, here, we won't take up any more of your time Mister Tanner." He held out his hand and Arthur shook it. "Thank you for your help, if there is anything else that we may need to ask you, I'll give you a telephone call, OK?"

"Yeah, cheers," said Arthur opening the door for them.

The two policemen made their way down the steps.

A whistle sounded and the snowplough came into sight, steam whooshing from its cylinders.

"Watch out for the engine on the up line," warned Arthur.

The two policemen acknowledge his advice with a wave and scuttled across the line to the opposite platform and disappeared through the gate at the end.

The snowplough chugged passed, slowly pushing aside the slushy snow onto the up platform.

The driver waved and Arthur waved back. He looked at the clock; it was ten past one.

Thirty-five minutes later, to Arthur's relief, Tommy Ackroyd, came into sight, cycling through the melting snow along the up platform.

He arrived at its end, shouldered his bike and carried it across the tracks and parked it against the side of the signal box stairs.

"Orright Arth'?" he said as he entered the cabin.

"I am, now that you've arrived," said Arthur, taking down his coat from the wall-peg. "I'll be bloody glad to get out from here, that's for sure."

"Why, what's up, then?"

Arthur related the morning's happenings to Tommy.

"He sounds a right bloody tosser, this Starkie," said Tommy scratching at his crotch. "The sooner they give him the elbow, the bloody better, eh?"

"Yeah, well, to be fair we don't know what's happening with him, do we?" said Arthur, in Clive's defence. "I mean, the poor bugger could be lying somewhere along the track fatally injured, for all we know, couldn't he?"

Tommy shrugged. "Aye, I suppose so." He took his haversack from his shoulders and dropped it onto the desktop. "We'll soon be told, one way or the other, I expect."

Arthur nodded. "Anyway, there's not much doing, at the moment. A snowplough that went down to Bass Alton, has come back up and is on its way to Pengam sidings. There's been one passenger train down, so far, and that's just about it, Tom."

"Ok." Tommy nodded. "Things will soon be back to normal, I expect. According to the news, this snow is moving away east and there's heavy rain coming in this afternoon, so it'll probably all be gone by teatime."

Arthur hitched his bag over his shoulder. "Aye, well let's hope so." He opened the door and started down the stairs. "See you tomorrow, Tom."

"Cheers," said Tom closing the door behind him.

Chapter Seven
Starkers

Arthur made his way through the slush along the platform and on out through the gate onto the main road at the front of the station building. He looked at his watch, the bus wasn't due for another five minutes so he lit up a cigarette and leaned against a telegraph pole, and casually scanned the surrounding countryside.

Everything seemed to be dripping with melting snow. Gutters were oozing with a slow-running gruel-like mixture of dirty, half-melted snow and road dirt. Down pipes gushed, sinks gurgled.

A slab of snow released itself from the roof of a nearby house, slid off the edge and thundered onto the freshly cleaned pavement. The door of the house opened, and a balding head looked out at the pile of snow splattered across the front pavement.

"Bollocks to it," he shouted and went back inside, slamming the door behind him.

Arthur grinned and flicked his dog-end into the gutter, where it slowly sailed along with the other detritus, bound for the sink and the sewers.

A police car emerged slowly from the Church Forge Arm's car park and made its way down the road towards Arthur.

Oh aye, here comes Bedwas's finest, been investigating the local brew, have we?

The car pulled up alongside Arthur and the window was wound down. Sergeant Phillips poked his head out of the open window.

"Ah! Mr Tanner, what a bit of good luck to catch you before your bus has got here."

"Yeah, it's due any minute," Arthur looked up the road, as if to confirm his statement.

"Right, well before it gets here," said the sergeant, "would you be so kind as to look into the back of the car and tell us if you recognise the specimen slumped next to the constable."

The Constable lowered the window and Arthur looked in. There, sprawled half across the seat and half on the floor of the car was Clive Stark, eyes closed, mouth agape, snoring.

"Jeez, it's Starky," said Arthur, incredulously. "Is he pissed, then?"

"As the proverbial parrot, sir," replied the sergeant looking in the mirror at the crumpled figure in the back seat. "Is this the person who visited you in your signal-box this morning?"

Arthur nodded.

"Is this the person who identified himself over the 'phone as Clive Stark and subsequently left your signal box and started down the line towards Bedwas?" asked the sergeant, now in official mode.

"Yeah, that's him," confirmed Arthur. "What's going on for Chrissakes?"

The sergeant beckoned with a thumb. "Apparently our friend here, decided, having walked a hundred yards or so down the line, that he had a toothache coming on, and that he should repair to the nearest hostelry for treatment."

Arthur was flabbergasted. "Do you mean to tell me that all the time that we were crapping ourselves about bodies on the line and that, that this twat was in the Church Forge Arms pissing it up?"

"I couldn't have put it better myself, sir," said the sergeant, managing a wry smile. "According to the Landlord, our friend here consumed the best part of a bottle of crème-de-menthe, which apparently did the business as far as his toothache was concerned, because he then had three pints of cider, a bag of Bovril flavoured crisps and two pickled eggs, the result of all of that intake can now be seen slumped on some of the back seat."

"The bastard! I hope you lock him up and throw away the key," Arthur said savagely.

"That, of course will be at the discretion of the court," said the sergeant. "In the meantime, he will be spending the next twenty-four hours as a guest of Her Majesty in a first-class suite at the Bass Alton police station."

Arthur gave a nasty cackle. "Too bloody right, an all." A red and white bus came in to view and Arthur stuck out a hand. "Here's my bus, I got to go, orright?"

"Certainly, Mister Tanner," Sergeant Phillips smiled, "and thank you, once again for your help. You will no doubt be hearing from us in the ensuing weeks. Thank you again," he repeated.

He wound up the window and the car sped away.

Arthur waved goodbye and climbed the steps of the bus.

The door clanged shut and the bus lurched forward, sending Arthur staggering down the swaying aisle until he sat down heavily on the nearest available seat.

He settled himself, lit up a cigarette and gazed through the misted-over window at the passing countryside, while the bus driver wrestled with the gears until bus picked up speed and hissed along the main road. Arthur continued to stare at the patchwork of snow that still covered the nearby fields, listening to the wheels of the bus swish as they flattened the remaining slush, sending it spraying onto the pavement in front of the Church Forge Arms.

He glanced back at the passing pub and shook his head in disbelief, anger and disgust welling up in him, as he was reminded of Clive and the morning's episode.

He turned back to the fields and drew on his cigarette. *To think that, that bloody plonker was in there, all that time, while we were wetting ourselves, imagining that he was out there, somewhere on the tracks, a mangled bloody heap. I hope the bastard gets all he bleeding well deserves, he thought viciously.*

"So, how's your Mister Stark getting on, then? No bother, I hope?" A woman's voice inquired from the back of the bus.

"Bother? No fear, the last thing he is, is a bother, he's a lovely man, best lodger that I've ever had, for sure."

Arthur ears pricked up on hearing the word Stark, he turned his head slightly to one side so as to get a clearer reception of the conversation.

"Yes, I must say it's a real pleasure to have a man about the house again, especially Clive, he's so clean and quiet, you'd scarcely know he was there sometimes, and do you know he never leaves a scrap on his plate, and the loo is a joy to behold, never a wet seat, not like my dear departed Arnold, God love him." The woman gave a low reverential cough and continued, "And his room? spotless, not a thing ever out of place. Take the samples of cleaning materials that he has stacked up on the ottoman, gleaming they are, not a speck of dust to be seen, cleans them religiously every day, does Mister Stark. 'That's how they will look when they go on the shelf, Missus Evans,' he says. 'Presentation is everything in my business'."

"What! Is he a traveller, then?" asked her companion.

"Traveller, no fear! Mister Stark is a businessman, import-export," the first woman replied. 'Import and export, Missus Evans,' he said, when I asked him for his particulars, before I took him in. 'I'm still in the process of finalising contracts,' Clive said. 'You know how it is in business? It all takes time.' Yes, I replied," the first woman explained. "They said the self-same thing on World in Action the other week, what with the strength of the dollar and, that there, balance of payments thing. 'Yes, you're quite right there, Missus Evans,' he said. 'I can see that you have a good grasp of the economic climate'. Well I was really pleased, I can tell you, it's not often we get paid any compliments, these days, not so?" said Mrs Evans loudly to the rest of the passengers.

The second woman replied. "So, if all this stuff, up in his room, is unsold, how is he making any money, then?"

Missus Evans lowered her voice a notch and Arthur strained his ears.

"Well seeing as how he's still sorting out the business side of things, he's gone and taken a temporary post with British Railways," Mrs Evans said lowering her voice.

"The railways," the other woman sneered. "Doing what, for instance?"

"A job in admin, he said," explained Mrs Evans. "What, an office job?" I said. "He just smiled one of those knowing smiles of his. Mr Stark didn't have to say any more, I just knew. I mean, where else would Clive work, what with him being so educated and with such a military background. He's probably in charge of the wages and invoices and the like."

The second woman sniffed, "Well, Missus Protheroe's boy, Dennis, works in the office, up at Bargoed Station, and I've never heard her mention invoices or wages, he just issues tickets, that's all."

"Well I can only tell you what he told me, can't I?" Missus Evans retorted sharply. "Besides, he's bound to have a good position, I mean, he'd only been with me a fortnight, when he says, 'Missus Evans, as I'm likely to be here for a while, so I'd like to pay you for my room, three months in advance, what do you reckon'? Well you could have bowled me over, and before I could reply, he took out this wad of notes and peeled off a dozen pound notes from it. 'Here, he says, thrusting them into my hand, 'will that cover it, then?' Well I was flabbergasted, I can tell you, I just looked at the notes and I could feel myself filling up, so I just squeezed his hand and nodded."

Arthur wondered if she was dabbing at her eyes with a handkerchief but he resisted the temptation to turn and look.

"Later on, after tea," Mrs Evans continued, "when I was more myself again, I said to him, "Mister Stark, I said, you're wonderful. You can stay as long as it suits you. He helped himself to another jam tart and said 'that's orright, then'."

"How come he had all that money if he hasn't sold anything yet?" asked the other woman suspiciously.

"Well, I'll tell you," answered Mrs Evans, tartly, "when he saw me looking goggled-eyed at all that money, he said, 'this is my working capital, Missus Evans, this is helping me build up my stock, see? It's the gratuity that I was given when I left the Royal Navy'. No need to explain, Mister Stark, I said, I'm sure you deserve every penny, serving your country like you did."

The other woman said pointedly, "I didn't know that he was in the forces, then?"

"Well, he doesn't mention it that much," said Mrs Evans. "Although, once, he did say, 'South China Waters, monitoring the commies, but keep that to yourself, if you don't mind, it's still classified'. Well naturally, I told him that my lips were sealed and that he could rely on me. Mum's the word, Mister Stark, I said. It'll be our little secret, so not a peep orright Agnes?"

"You know me, Katherine," said Agnes, "not a word will pass my lips."

"I knew that I could rely on you," said Katherine Evans.

Agnes lowered her voice a notch. "What rank was he, then?"

"He never said," Missus Evans answered. "But one day, I happened to be in his room, making sure that it was tidy, you understand."

"Of course, well you would, wouldn't you?" said Agnes.

"Well," said Katherine, "I was just straightening up the things on his bedside table, you know, his alarm clock and that, when I noticed this envelope sticking out from the middle of a book that was next to the clock. I picked up the book, to give it a quick dust, the Perfumed Garden, it was called. I like a man that's keen on flowers and such, don't you?"

"Yes, I think it's very important for a man to show an interest in his garden," replied Agnes, "not like our Meredith, who spends all day on his backside studying the horses."

"Anyway," continued Missus Evans, "I saw this envelope half sticking out from the book so I eased it up a bit so that I could see who it was addressed to and guess what?" before the other woman could answer, she raced on. "Commander Stark. RNVR, it said, and it was addressed to my house, what about that, then?"

"Well, I'll be," said Agnes, suitably impressed, "it just goes to show, you just don't know who's in our midst, do you?"

"Bloody hells, bloody bells!" Arthur yelled out as the burning stub of his cigarette made contact with his fingers. He dropped it onto the floor and squashed it with a heel. "Buggeration!" He sucked at the injured digit.

The conversation at the back of the bus stopped and he looked around sheepishly. "Sorry, ladies, burnt my finger, didn't I?" He held up the inflamed finger, for their inspection.

"You ought to be more careful what you do with your cigarettes, in future, then, isn't it?" said Katherine Evans, scowling at him.

He turned back to face the front and sucked at his stinging finger. An angry looking blister had formed just below the first joint.

"Bass Alton," called the driver and the bus slowed and pulled into the kerbside.

The two ladies shuffled up the aisle, past Arthur, on their way to the exit.

One, whom he took to be Agnes, wore a brown check coat with enormous green buttons. She carried a black shopping bag over an arm, and on her head she sported a green rain hood, from the corner of which, peeked a pink plastic hair-roller.

The second woman, whom he assumed to be Missus Evans, wore a purple turban with a bright orange butterfly brooch pinned to the front like a cap badge. Her tan mackintosh strained at the buttons across her ample stomach, which was partially obscured by a brown leather shopping bag that hung from the crook of her arm and an umbrella, with a wooden, painted duck head handle that hung from the other arm.

Slowly, the pair stepped down from the bus onto the pavement.

Agnes turned to her companion. "You still haven't told me what your Mister Stark looks like have you? Tall and handsome, I bet?"

Mrs Evans lowered her bulk onto the pavement. "No, that's right, I haven't, have I," she said, rubbing her hands down her mackintosh front, in an effort to rid it of its creases. "Well, he's the dead spit of Buddy Holly."

Chapter Eight
Clubbers

Arthur continued to stare at the tree-lined flanks of the Graig while Church Forge and Buddy Holly gradually slipped back into his subconscious. Finally, he lowered his gaze with a sigh and a nonplussed shake of the head.

An angry bee dive-bombed him, he swatted at it testily, unhappy at the interruption.

Shaking his head again, Arthur returned to the era of his youth. *Nineteen-fifty-nine, jeez, that was forty-five years ago.* He folded his arms and gazed at the distant river. *I can just see me now, as I was then, a skinny, nineteen-year-old, wearing the uniform of the day, jeans with fifteen-inch bottoms, baseball boots, a zip-up jacket, a D.A and a face suffering an acne attack. James Dean, Monmouthshire style,* he grinned. *We really thought that we were the kiddies then, men-of-the-world, drinking, rock-and-rolling, pulling the birds, each of us trying to outdo the others with our wild claims of supposedly, changing girlfriends more often than we changed our socks, a new one every week. Kiddies,* the old man laughed silently, *What a load of bullshit! Bloody kidders, more like.*

None of it ever happened, of course, it was all part of growing up, seeking to be a man before the body and the brain were ready.

Several years later, in the sixties, when the arrival of the pill and the mini skirt, gradually changed attitudes and allowed for a little less stringency in the illicit sex department. The self-deluding myth, propagated by the popular press, that, drugs, sex and rock 'n' roll, was occupying every waking moment of the youth of the western world, was just that, a myth. Most teenagers in the small, provincial towns of Great Britain were no more sexually experienced than were their counterparts of twenty years earlier. The eye-opening headlines in the popular press were not having any lasting effect, at least, not in Newport, at that time.

For the majority of the youth of the town, the only drugs that they had any experience of, apart from penicillin, were cigarettes and booze.

Sex was still very much a closed book for many of them, and although the Hollywood youth culture of the sixties, had slowly filtered down to other parts of the western world, the teenage populace of darkest Monmouthshire, were still very backward in coming forward.

So to imagine, that, several years earlier, the Thursday Regulars of the King William IV, would have been sophisticated, roistering, rollicking Romeos, who lived the good life, in every sense, was a fable.

A load of old bollocks, he grinned to himself.

In the days of the late fifties, an ungainly fumble with a bra strap in the back row of the Olympia usually proved to be the pinnacle of any sexual foray for many of the town's teenagers. Suffice to say, that, the inside of a pair of M & S knickers was very much uncharted territory for most of them, although, this, of course, was never admitted.

Even though sex was frequently on the agenda, and always treated as commonplace, especially after a few pints, such encounters were in reality, rare, the world of Carnaby Street, cannabis and the Swinging Sixties was still years away, and, even then, for most, were restricted to the big cities.

In any event, by then, most of the Thursday-Night-regulars were married or involved in longstanding relationships, so, they had had to discover sex the hard way.

In practical terms then, the combination, of sex and drugs, never happened, not for Arthur and the Western Movie Club regulars, despite all the later claims.

Rock 'n' roll, on the other hand, was in abundant supply, every church-hall, youth club, scout hut and redundant cinema offered the twice-weekly opportunity of dancing to the latest American hit records, and it was thanks, mainly to the likes of Radio Luxembourg and Jack Jackson's Record-Round-up, that British youth in general, and the King-Billy-Regulars, in particular, were kept up to date on the latest news, as to who was who, and what was what on the pop record scene.

Record shops had never been so busy, the rock 'n' roll business was booming, and for Arthur, Dai and the gang, the regular Thursday evening drinking session, at the King Billy, became a hotbed of the latest in all things rock 'n' roll, so much so, that during one drunken session, the Western Movie Club was born.

The sodding Western Movie Club. Arthur shook his head and snorted with derision. *Only an ignorant, drunken bunch of bums, like us, would have come up with such an idiotic, bloody name as the Western Movie Club.* Scratching at his head, Arthur mused on the origin of the name. *Why western movie?*

Staring out across the valley, not seeing, the old man searched the dusty cobwebbed archives of his mind until it eventually came to him. The Western movie, or, to be more precise, Western movies, was the title of a top-twenty hit record, by a group called the Olympics, Arthur recalled. And, for some unaccountable reason, it had become the flavour of the month, with the Thursday night crowd towards the back end of 1958.

Arthur had now put his time machine into reverse, and he was now back in the King's Billy on an evening in November, 1958 …

Dai suddenly lurched to his feet, held his pint pot aloft, and slurred, "Here's to Thursdays and to Western movies." Arthur and the rest of the boys responded drunkenly to the toast. "Western Movies."

All, that is, except Ronnie Cox, who slurred, "The cowboy club," which was greeted with loud guffaws of derision and vee signs from the assembled drinkers.

Arthur held up his hand to quell the laughter. "Ronnie, you've cracked it," he said slapping him on the back, causing Ronnie to slop beer onto his new red, drainpipe trousers. Arthur raised his glass. "Lads, I give you, the Western Movie Club," he said getting to his feet.

This was unanimously, received by the assembled gang, who with loud, boozy acclaim, stood, as a man, pint glasses raised, until hurriedly sitting back down, sheepishly, when the landlord told them to keep the noise down or they would be toasting each other outside in the street.

Arthur waited for the landlord to move to the other end of the bar, to tend to a new customer, then he raised his glass and whispered. "The Western Movie Club." The Thursday nighters, responded, silently raising their glasses in acknowledgement, grinning.

So, the club was born, and, even though it did not have any officers or committee members, or a constitution, or subscriptions, the Western Movie Club had come into being.

Apart from the name, it had nothing of any substance that could qualify it as a club, and the name really, only served as an identifier for their Thursday night meets in the King William IV's smoke room.

Neither Arthur nor the rest of Western movie clubbers could see that the, so called club, was no more than just a collective noun for a group of acne-faced, teenagers, who used the epithet as an opportunity to get legless.

To the uninitiated, of course, none of the Thursday night's ritual would have made any sense, and, at the time, if one were to admit it, it did not make much sense to any of the members, either.

Now, some forty odd years on, Arthur found the whole idea completely absurd. He shook his head. *Cripes, what wouldn't I give to be eighteen years old and absurd again?*

Absurd or not, the pretend club prevailed, and, for a couple of years the eleven original members, met every Thursday in the King Billy's smoke-room, where they discussed such important topical issues, as, who would Newport County be drawn against in the third round of the F.A. Cup. Would Elvis still be at number one in the charts by the New Year, and how many more 'members' would they allow to swell their ranks over the coming weeks, leading up to Christmas.

Come the following January, their local soccer team, Newport County, had been drawn away, against, and severely beaten by, Tottenham Hotspur.

To everybody's astonishment, Johnny Tillotson was number one in the charts, and, to rub salt in their wounds, membership of the Western Movie Club had plummeted to just eight.

A year later, they were down to just four regulars, Arthur, Dai Marshall and the two Cox brothers, Ronnie and Danny, and, for the next twelve months, the four of them continued their Thursday soirees in the smoke room of the King Billy, where the issues of the day still centred on sport, girls and rock 'n' roll.

Nothing much had changed; Newport County was still fighting relegation, the Beatles were still undiscovered, and Elvis still ruled, sex, of course, was still a scarce commodity.

During that late summer and early autumn, the one issue that helped relieve the boredom and held their attention longer than most, was that of Jerry Jenkins, who they later came to dub the Rock 'n' Roll King of Risca.

Chapter Nine
Badgeman

Arthur had recently transferred from the Mill Street goods yard signal-box, in Newport, to the Gwent Junction, signal box, Rogerstown.

It was his third week there, and his first week on the morning shift, and during a lull in train movements, he gazed dreamily out at the surrounding countryside, the perennial cigarette smouldering between his stained fingers.

The September sun slanted in through the signal box windows and dust motes danced in its shafts of light, steel tracks snaked away into the distance, gleaming like streams of molten larva.

A telegraph bell chattered out a bell code, breaking through his reverie. He went to the telegraph and returned the code that accepted the train into his section, then, moved along the lever-frame, busying himself with the task of moving points and lowering signals for the train to continue its journey onto the section ahead.

Two minutes later, a shrill whistle announced the approach of the expected down branch passenger train, the nine thirty Brynmawr to Newport. The two-carriage train, swayed around the bend, into sight, its locomotive wheezing and clanking, steam and smoke spinning away into the bright morning sky.

The driver waved from the cab as the train hissed past the signal box. Arthur leaned on a lever and acknowledged the driver's hello while he watched the train's two, old third-class carriages rock and clatter over the points. They were empty, save for one lone passenger who leaned out of one of the windows of the second coach. He was completely bald and wore an ex-army greatcoat with the collar turned up, like a gangster in a B movie.

Inside the collar, around his bulging, white neck, was tied a fluffy, pale pink, chiffon scarf. In his hand, he held out a stopwatch at arm's length while the index finger of the other hand explored the interior of one of his nostrils, both of his eyes were closed, as though in prayer.

Arthur lit another cigarette and watched the two carriages and, the baldhead, disappear down the track in the direction of Newport. He shook his head in disbelief, "

Twat, he said to himself as he closed the window, drowning out the noise of the departing train.

Another bell told him that an engine and brake van was on its way from the Rogerstown marshalling yard, for shunting duties at the nearby power station. Two minutes later it crawled into view. Arthur changed the points, lowered a signal and the tank engine puffed slowly into the power station sidings and came to a halt in a cloud of steam, opposite the signal box.

The guard climbed down from the brake van, ducked under the buffers and unhooked the engine from the brake van, then, ducking back out from under the buffers, he beckoned the driver to move the engine forward. With one deft, practiced move, he then climbed onto the steps, on the side of the engine's cab, and balanced there, precariously as the locomotive moved slowly away in a cloud of smoke and steam to commence its spell of shunting duties.

The guard sported a bright, ginger moustache, which sprouted below a pair of horned-rimmed spectacles, one of the sides, of which, was temporarily repaired with sticking plaster; he turned and waved to Arthur.

Arthur waved back, put the signal back to danger, readjusted the points, and then sat down on the bench and picked up the morning paper.

The front page told him that the U S polls had Nixon and John Kennedy neck and neck in the race to the White House.

"Balls to Nixon," he muttered. "What about the Sunderland and Spurs match?"

The sound of a hammer striking wagon wheels rang out, disturbing the temporary peace of the autumn morning. Arthur folded the newspaper, placed it on the desk, and got to his feet, stretched and peered towards the source of the noise.

At the far end of the sidings, silhouetted against the strong morning sun, stood a crooked little figure, bearing a strong resemblance to a malevolent dwarf of Grimm's fairy tales fame.

Arthur watched the figure shuffle along the power station sidings, hitting the wheels of the wagons, then shouldering the hammer after every swing and stopping to listen intently to each resulting ring.

The rattle of the kettle's lid took Arthur's attention away from the window and he rose and went to the pot-bellied stove, where the black cast-iron vessel steamed and hissed. Lifting the kettle, he poured boiling water into the waiting teapot and returned the kettle to the top of the stove.

Arthur gave the contents of the teapot a stir, then carried the pot across to a small table, and sat down on a hard, wooden bench, cup, spoon and bag of sugar, ready for the pouring.

The chimes from the tapping of the wagon wheels were getting louder, drowning out the kettle, which had resumed its song, on the pot-bellied stove.

Arthur let the tea brew for a while then poured out a cupful and carefully sipped at the scalding, orange liquid.

From right outside the signal box came the crunching of feet on chippings, followed closely by the sounds of the downstairs door being opened, and then closed.

A discordant whistle accompanied the footfalls on the stairs and into view came a potato-shaped head, with lank, shoulder-length hair, hanging over the owner's ears, a large bald spot, the head's crowning glory.

It was the dwarf-from-the-sidings

As more of the ascending figure came into sight, Arthur was regaled by the array of metal and plastic badges that festooned the lapels of the wheel-tapper's British Railways overcoat.

There were badges, of every description, army and air force badges, train-shaped badges, bus-shaped badges, a Golly badge advertising marmalade, a Rupert Bear badge, and a Dan Dare badge, you name it; he had a badge for it.

An elastic belt, with a snake-like clasp, held up his trousers.

"Orright, Butt?" he said, displaying a mouthful of multicoloured teeth. "You're new here, ain't you?"

"Yeah," replied Arthur, setting down the cup. "Been here a fortnight, this is my first week of mornings, I'm Arthur Tanner," he said, gesturing towards himself.

"Yeah, I thought I hadn't seen you before," grinned the man with the badges. "I'm Jerry, the wagon-examiner from down the yard. I'm usually up this way once a week or so, depending, like." He rested his hammer against a lamp locker. "I generally pop in and say hya to the signalman when I'm up this way, have a bit of a natter, like."

Arthur picked up the teapot and gestured with it. "I've just made a brew, fancy a cup?"

"Aye, ta, I wouldn't say no to a cuppa," said Jerry, pulling out a battered tin from within the depths of his B.R. jacket. He extracted a misshapen, hand-rolled cigarette from it and stuck it in the side of his mouth, lit it and blew out a cloud of smoke.

"Grab a seat," Arthur beckoned towards a wooden stool that stood in a corner besides a fire bucket.

"Cheers," said Jerry, promptly sitting down and accepting the proffered cup of steaming liquid. He blew on its surface and took a sip. "Cheers," he said again.

Arthur studied the array of badges that festooned the wagon-examiner's coat lapels. One stood out from the rest. It featured a miniature red and gold guitar with two initial J's on each side of the guitar's neck; Arthur pointed to it.

"What're the J's for, then? Jimmy Jones, Janice Joplin, Jimmy Jewel, Jessie James?" he offered, jokingly.

"Jerry Jenkins," said the wheel-tapper, fingering the badge proudly.

"Who?" frowned, Arthur, looking puzzled.

"Jerry Jenkins," repeated the wheel-tapper.

"You've got me there," said Arthur, shaking his head. "I thought I was well up on the pop scene, but I can't say I've heard of him. What's one of his records, then?"

"No Butt, JJ is me," Jerry pointed to himself with a thumb and flicked the mangled butt of his cigarette into the fire bucket.

"Oh, so you're Jerry Jenkins?" Arthur feigned surprise.

"Yeah," said the wheel-tapper, a crooked grin on his face. "Jerry Jenkins and the Five Erlys, see?"

Arthur looked at him in amazement. "What, you're a musician? You've got a group?" he asked incredulously, feeling a smile tweaking at the corners of his mouth.

"Yeah," replied Jerry. "We're one of the valley's top outfits, we are, and, we're thinking of cutting a disc soon."

Arthur passed a hand across the grin, as though checking to see if he needed a shave. He then turned away and looked out of the window, giving the impression that he was checking on the shunting movements in the power station sidings.

Who is this plonker? he asked himself. *I have met some idiots over the years, but this bonehead takes the bloody cake.*

Arthur turned back to Jerry, fighting the impending grin, biting at his bottom lip. "A disc, wow that's really exciting. What are you going to use for the A side?" His voice had risen by half an octave so he faked a clearing-the-throat type noise, to try and bring it under control before the threatening laughter took over.

"The, what side?" asked Jerry nonplussed.

"The A side," Arthur rubbed at his face again and pulled on an earlobe. "You know, the main song, the one that's going to be the main song on the record?"

"Oh!" a look of recognition crept over Jerry's face. "The main song, oh yeah, the main song, well we thought we'd go for White Heather."

Seeing the look of perplexity on Arthur's face, he said, "You know, White Heather, Bing's big hit." He then emitted a strained, adenoidal wail, which Arthur took to be a snatch of the forthcoming hit.

"You can't resist White-Heather," came the discordant warble, *"chocolate and toffee, they're..."*

"Hang on," Arthur cut in; his voice was back to soprano again, "that's an advert!"

"Now it is, for sure," Jerry replied scornfully, "but not when Bing sang it originally."

"Ahem, ahum," Arthur fought with his voice box again, trying desperately to control the mirth that was threatening to gush out beyond his teeth and fill the signal box with uncontrolled laughter.

He grabbed his cup, walked quickly to the window and threw the slops out onto the tracks.

Staring at the spread of cold tea on the wooden sleepers below, he fought to hold back the great bubble of laughter that was threatening to burst forth. He took a deep breath, held it for about ten seconds, then slowly exhaled.

It seemed to have done the trick, so he turned back to Jerry and smiled. "If you've finished with your cup, I'll put it in the sink ready for washing?"

"Yeah, ta," said Jerry handing the cup to Arthur.

"Why, the Erlys?" Arthur asked over his shoulder as he washed up the cups, thinking, *This is going to be good,* then instantly regretting having asked the question.

"Well it's like this, Butt, see," explained Jerry, holding up his hand and counting off, on the splayed fingers. "There's the big five, OK? Number one is The King of course, Elvis?"

Arthur nodded. "Of course."

"Then there's the Killer, Jerry Lee Lewis, he's gotta be number two."

"Mustn't forget the Killer," agreed Arthur.

Jerry continued. "Number three is Chuck Berry, and four is the Fat Man, Fats Domino."

Arthur nodded.

"And then, there's Buddy Holly at five," Jerry continued to hold up the splayed fingers. "Now, that's the big five, as I said, but there are others who are just as big, see."

Arthur could not see, or care, come to that, but he shrugged his shoulders and he forced a thin smile.

"There's the Everly Brothers, Carl Perkins, Gene Vincent, Eddie Cochrane, Bill Haley, they're all good, but they're not the big five, OK?"

Arthur shrugged. "Yeah, all right." His patience was beginning to grow increasingly thin.

Jerry continued his explanation. "Well, if you take Eastern Valley from Everly then you're left with Erly, get it?"

Arthur was doing his best to understand the workings of the misshapen little gnome's mind, but it was a struggle.

Jerry could see by Arthur's puzzled expression that he was not making himself entirely clear.

"Now, take the Everly Brothers, right?" he explained patiently. "The Everly's, OK? Now, take away Eastern Valley, E.V., OK? E.V., Eastern Valley, you get it, then?"

Arthur nodded. His eyes were beginning to glaze over.

"Now you're left with erly, see?" said Jerry.

Arthur nodded automatically.

"That makes the big five plus the Everlys without the Eastern Valley." Jerry folded his arms, and with a self-satisfied look upon his face, he said, "Good ain't it?"

Arthur sat down and lit up a cigarette, feeling as if he had been, hit about the head with a blunt instrument. He took a drag at his cigarette, and, with a sigh, said, "Why leave out the E.V. then?"

"Eastern Valley," corrected Jerry.

"Ok, Eastern Valley," Arthur said between gritted teeth. "Why leave off Eastern Valley?"

"Because," said Jerry triumphantly, "this is the Western Valley and we're a Western Valley group, see?"

"Of course, how bloody stupid of me," Arthur tossed his head in mock disgust at himself. "You must think I'm a right pillock."

Jerry shook his head. "Easy mistake to make," he magnanimously said. "You can't be expected to know the same as me about show business, can you? I mean, we've been semi pro now for close on three months."

Arthur nodded, barely able to contain himself from crossing the signal-box floor, grabbing the ugly little sod by the throat and shaking him, like a Jack Russell would, a rat. Instead he bit his lip, and tried to think good thoughts, which was not having much success, however, for, the ridiculousness of their conversation, was becoming all too much for him, and he was having great trouble trying to contain himself.

Just as he was about to tell the lying Jerry what a bore he was, and how he could bugger off, a telegraph bell sounded, signalling that a train was on the way.

The tension was broken and the irritation that had built up inside, quickly drained from him. He got up, much relieved, and sent an acknowledgement code to the signalman in the next signal box at Tyn-y-cwm and then set about changing the points.

"Aye, its time I went and did a bit, I suppose," said Jerry picking up his hammer. "I'll see you next time I'm up this way, orright?" he waved and quickly disappeared down the stairs.

"Yeah, cheers," a relieved Arthur shouted after him. "See you!"

Boots crunching on chippings followed the sound of the front door closing, and a few moments later, Jerry's crooked figure came into view as he crossed the line towards the sidings, where the sounds of the shunting of wagons, filled the air.

He ducked nimbly under the buffers of the nearest coal wagon and disappeared from view.

Soon the morning was alive with the combined percussion of a hammer hitting wagon wheels and the rattle and clang of the wagons being shunted into their designated sidings.

Arthur stood in the open window, listening to the chimes of steel on steel, until the clanking and hissing of the approaching passenger train drowned them out.

Chapter Ten
Gigs

Three weeks later, when Arthur was back on the day shift, Jerry Jenkins came on the scene again.

With miraculous timing, the would-be, Rock 'n' Roll King of Risca, emerged from the sidings just as the kettle on the pot-bellied stove began to hiss and rattle.

Arthur shook his head in disbelief and got another cup from the cupboard.

The downstairs door slammed shut and Jerry's bald patch appeared above the banister. "Orright Butt?" he grinned, displaying a multi-coloured set of teeth.

Arthur cringed and turned his attention back to the teapot and the freshly brewed liquid. "Cuppa, Jerry?"

"Ta, that would go down a treat right now," he said, placing his long-handled hammer against the lamp locker and sitting down on the small stool. He briskly rubbed the palms of his hands together, in obvious delight. "What a gig we had last night, then?" he said excitedly, accepting the cup of scalding liquid from Arthur.

Arthur feigned puzzlement. "Gig? what's that then?"

Jerry fought to find an alternative word, which Arthur would be likely to understand. "Aw, whatyer call it, you know, when the group plays on the stage."

"What the Five Erlys?" Arthur blew on his tea.

"Yeah, of course, the Five Erlys," said Jerry disdainfully.

"Oh! You mean, a booking. Sorry I thought you were talking about a sort of cart," replied Arthur trying to keep a straight face.

Jerry stared into the orange depths of the tea, wondering what the bloody hell Arthur was saying.

He gave up the challenge and sipped at the contents of the cup, then he said, "Anyway, as I said, the joint was really jumping."

"What joint would that be, then?" asked Arthur.

"Cwmtillery Scout Hall," replied Jerry proudly. "Jeez, you should have been there, they couldn't get enough of us." He drained the cup and handed it back to Arthur. "Cheers, Butt."

"They liked you, then?" said Arthur trying not to let the smile on his face turn into a grin.

"Liked us? I should cocoa," Jerry slapped his knee in delight. "We had to fight them off."

Arthur tried to hide his embarrassment by busying himself with the business of extracting a tipped cigarette from its packet and lighting it.

Jerry, oblivious to Arthur's discomfort, extracted a battered, hand-rolled cigarette from his top pocket, lit up and continued with his monologue about the rave-up at the Cwmtillery Scout Hall.

Arthur knew that he should have kept his mouth shut, nevertheless, he asked, "Tell me about your line-up, then?"

Jerry looked nonplussed. "Yer what?" he plucked at a non-existent shred of tobacco from his lower lip.

"The line up," said Arthur. "You know, which instruments do you all play." He sighed, "Who plays what?"

"Oh! The line-up," Jerry showed his multicoloured teeth to the world and, with a touch, of what Arthur took to be artistic disdain, said flippantly, "Lead guitar, bass, rhythm, electric organ and drums."

"What do you play, then?" Arthur asked innocently, his eyes fixed upon the blue and gold ABC Minors' badge that was pinned to the bottom of Jerry's greasy lapel.

"Lead, of course," Jerry puffed out his chest like a randy, farmyard rooster.

"Plectrum or nail?" asked Arthur, remembering an article that he had once read regarding the American Guitarist, Chet Atkins.

"We got both types, Butt," answered Jerry without conviction.

Arthur buried his face in his handkerchief and blew his nose in an attempt to disguise the hoot of laughter that he was rapidly failing to suppress. He blew his nose again and regained his composure.

It was obvious to him that Jerry knew as much about music as he did about the DNA double helix structure; a subject that Arthur had read about in an article in the Reader's Digest magazine, but hadn't understood.

All that Jerry had succeeded in doing was to compound the original lie, but Arthur was not about to let him off the hook that easily. "What do you use, with the sound system then, bafflers or woofers?"

Jerry frowned at the brown linoleum and cleared his throat. "Yeah, all of that," he said wishing Arthur would change the subject.

"What sort of music do you generally play, then, Jerry?" said Arthur continuing the cross-examination.

"All sorts," said Jerry, throwing his dog-end into the fire-bucket. "You name it, Butt, and we'll play it, see."

"Like what?" asked Arthur. "Rockabilly, western swing, calypso?" He could feel his mouth beginning to pull at the edges again.

"Yeah, all of that, and the top twenty, we do all them, as well," replied Jerry, grinning, now, having got the conversation back onto familiar territory again. He dug into a pocket and extracted a crumpled piece of paper. "Here you are, look." He held out the paper towards Arthur. "We do all of these."

Arthur took the newsprint, unfolded it and read it. It was a list, of the current week's top twenty best-selling records, from the Melody Maker magazine. He scanned the list, looking for one that he could catch Jerry out with. His eyes lighted upon a current instrumental hit, by Perez Prado and his orchestra.

"What about Patricia, then? Is that one that the Erlys do?"

"For sure," replied Jerry, "that's one of our favourites."

"Who does the vocals for it, then, you?" Arthur bit his bottom lip for all that he was worth.

Jerry laughed. "Are you kidding, Boyo, I leave the singing to our drummer. He's got a voice just like Perry Como."

Arthur went to the window and opened it. His eyes were starting to water and his sides were beginning to ache from the laughter that he had been suppressing. He breathed deeply at the outside air, held it in for as long as he could then let it out with a whoosh.

He closed the window and turned back and handed the ragged piece of paper back to Jerry, then he moved to the stove and poured himself another cup of tea.

Which proved a big mistake for, as he picked up the cup of hot, strong orange liquid and sipped at it tentatively, Jerry said, with an air of authority.

"I tell you what, though, Butt, in my opinion, the Debbie Reynolds' version of High Noon is much better than the Edmondo Ross one."

A stream of hot tea sprayed across the room and Arthur rushed to the window, red-faced and spluttering, wiping at his burning lips and muttering a string of expletives.

It was a good five minutes before he was able to speak again. "Don't do that to me again, for God's sake," he said, wiping away the tears from his eyes.

"Do what to you, Butt?" Jerry looked puzzled.

"Mention High Noon, not when I'm drinking hot tea," replied Arthur wiping at his streaming eyes again and blowing his nose.

"Why is that, then Butt? Don't you like the Debbie Reynolds one?" Jerry looked mystified.

"No, no, I think Debbie's version is great, and so is Edmundo's. No, it's not that." Arthur had now regained his composure and he shook his head gravely. "No, I'm not fussed if it's Debbie, Edmundo or the Luton Girls Choir, it's the High Noon bit that gets me." He went to the window and threw the remaining tea onto the up line, then closed the window and turned to Jerry, his face set. "It's just that every time I hear that tune it reminds me of the film." He tapped the side of his head and feigned a nonplussed look. "What the hell was it called? You know?" Jerry shook his head, completely lost. "You know, the one, where all those squirmy, green Martians are attacking the army on Salisbury Plain," he shook his head in mock despair. "Oh, what the heck was it called?"

Jerry shook his head. "Dunno."

"Anyway," said Arthur, "that's what puts me off, about the song, all those horrible Martians, see?"

"Aye, you're right there, orright, Arth,'" said Jerry, now completely nonplussed.

To cover up his obvious discomfort, he patted his jacket pockets and produced a box of matches, from which, he carefully extracted a match and proceeded to probe the interior of one of his ears. After several insertions of the match, he examined it, and apparently satisfied, wiped it on his trouser leg and then put the match back in the box.

"Quatermass!" Arthur yelled, suddenly jumping to his feet.

Jerry took a step backwards, uncertainty showing in his eyes.

"Quatermass, that was the name of the film, Jerry, do you remember it?"

Jerry shuffled awkwardly from one foot to another, nodded and cleared his throat, then he said, "Yeah, that's the one." He looked at the clock. "Is that the time? I had better go and do a bit, isn't it?"

He picked up his hammer, put it on one shoulder and quickly started down the stairs. "See you, Buttie," he called over his shoulder and disappeared from view.

"Cheers, Jerry," Arthur called after him, plumping down upon the bench utterly exhausted.

He heard the sound of the front door closing and the crunching of boots on gravel. He got up from the bench and went to the window, where he watched the crooked, little figure shamble off across the sidings and duck under the buffers of a coal wagon and disappear from sight.

Arthur's smile began to fade. *He believes it all*, he thought, *that daft, little plonker really believes all that garbage that he's coming out with, the poor bastard,* not knowing that, that would be the last time that Arthur would see Jerry in the Gwent Sidings signal box.

Chapter Eleven
Thelma

That same night, Arthur related the latest Jerry Jenkins episode to members of the Western Movie Club, as they sat in a circle in the lounge bar of the King Billy in Dock Street.

"This is no bullshit, honest, he looks just like a bloody gnome," Arthur said, repeating the description of the wheel tapper that he had given to the club members, earlier that month. He took a swig from his pint pot. "He's barely five foot, got a bald head that's shaped like a spud, and he knows as much about rock music as Cedric Mathias knows about working for a living."

Arthur's audience hooted with laughter, apparently content to hear the story repeated.

"What's the little Git's name, again?" asked a slightly Drunken Dai, from across the table.

"Jerry Jenkins," replied Arthur, happy to continue repeating the tale of his encounters with Jerry Jenkins, for as long as his audience were prepared to listen. "You must have come across him in your travels, Dai?"

Dai shook his head. "Never heard of him, he's a new one on me."

Arthur looked suitably perplexed. "Well, all that I can say, is that Dinky Phillips reckons that this plonker, Jerry's, been working up the valley, in Risca, for nigh on eight or nine years, before he came down to Rogerstown yard."

Dai shook his head again and rubbed at his chin. "I've worked most of the boxes, between Newport and Cross Keys, as a relief signalman, for best part of five years, but I'm buggered if I've heard of him, Arth'," he drained his glass and let out an enormous belch. "Next time I'm up that way, I'll ask Dinky to point him out to me, OK?"

"You can't miss him, Butt. He's got a head shaped like a King Edward and a coat covered in badges," Arthur reiterated, just in case they had missed it the first, second or third time of telling.

"What sort of badges d'yer mean?" asked Ronnie Cox from behind his pint glass. "Like in the war and that?" Ronnie wasn't the sharpest knife in the drawer, which Arthur didn't mind, as it gave him a valid reason to hold court and be able to repeat the story, which looked as if it could run and run.

"What are you going on about, you bloody plonker," admonished Ronnie's brother, Danny, leaning across the table. "Didn't Arth' say, earlier, that this frigging Jerry is only about nineteen years old. What bloody war do you think he's been in, then? — You daft sod."

"You never know," Ronnie frowned and shrugged his shoulders. "He might have been a Boy Soldier or something."

"Boy Soldier? Bloody Boy's Brigade more like," said Danny, shaking his head in disgust. "What are you like? Our Ronnie eh?"

Arthur interjected, not too happy with Danny Cox stealing his thunder. "No, these are more like your civvy badges, you know? Like the ones you get given in the ABC Minor's Club, in the Olympia, on Saturday mornings."

"Oh aye," said Ronnie fishing out a cigarette and lighting it. "He sounds a right bloody star. If you ask me, a bloody nineteen-year-old walking around with a coat load of frigging badges, like some bloody schoolboy."

Arthur nodded. "Yeah, well he can't help it, he's not the full shilling, anyone can see that."

"What do reckon on all this rock bollocks that he's been coming out with, then, Arth'?" asked a semi-interested Dai.

Arthur shook his head and chewed on a thumbnail. "I don't know, that's for sure. I can't see Jerry Jenkins bopping around on some bloody stage, can you?" He took a slurp from his pint glass.

They all shook their heads in unison.

Arthur continued, "I can't see old Jerry boy rocking away, can you? Especially, up at Newbridge or Abercarn." He took another swig from his glass, wiped at his grinning mouth. "Can you imagine our boy surviving up there on knicker-night? He'd get eaten alive, some of those divorcees up at the Cwmmer Club are as randy as ten men."

Dai elbowed Ronnie Cox in the ribs. "They'd have him off that stage, and have his kecks off, before you could say knife, eh, Ron?"

Ronnie grinned and nodded dumbly, wondering what knicker night was.

Arthur got up unsteadily. "Who's having what, then?"

"Pint of SA for me, Butt," said Dai handing over his empty glass.

"Yeah, me too," said Danny Cox.

"What are you having, our Ron?"

Ronnie Cox drained the dregs from his glass and smacked his lips. "Mine's a Worthy BB, Arth'." He slid his empty glass along the table top towards Arthur and then placed an old battered tin in front of him, his forefinger and thumb delving inside and extracting shreds of dark, sweet-smelling tobacco, which he proceeded to roll in paper between his heavily stained fingers.

Arthur retrieved the empty glass and headed for the badly scratched, and, equally stained bar, which lay beneath a curtain of smoke, behind which, stood a pretty, raven-haired barmaid, who was polishing a glass on a tea towel, her heavy chest tightly packed into a bright-red satin blouse.

She stopped chewing momentarily and watched Arthur's unsteady progress towards her. She flashed a broad welcoming smile at him.

"What'll it be, then?"

"Three SA's and a Worthy BB, ta very much, Luv," he said returning her smile.

She pulled the first of the pints and placed it on the bar in front of Arthur, who lifted the glass to his lips and took a huge gulp from it, his eyes watching over the rim as the contents of the barmaid's congested blouse fought for freedom.

For God's sake give 'em some air, before they bloody well suffocate, called a small voice from inside his head. *Our Arthur, here, will give you a hand, ain't that right Arth?*

"Too right!" he said out loud.

"Pardon me?" the barmaid looked up from the pumps.

"Too tight," he said, quickly loosening his tie. "Too tight, my tie's too tight, is it me, or is it getting hot in here, all of a sudden?"

"It's the smoke, I expect, I'll put the extractor fan on, is it?" she reached up for the switch next to the optics, and turned on the fan, her bodice swelling to bursting point.

Arthur inwardly winced, half expecting to see a size thirty-nine B-cup disintegrate and come catapulting across the bar, into the smoke-filled room, causing havoc and panic amongst the drinkers, who would have been in imminent danger of decapitation, if unlucky enough to be in its flight path.

But, defying all known scientific principles, the bodice, somehow, remained intact, and, having survived the enormous internal pressures placed upon it, miraculously, returned to its normal overcrowded look.

Arthur gave a huge sigh of relief, hiccupped, and in a blinding flash of realisation, knew, that at that moment, as he stood there surveying the outline of the contents of the barmaid's generous blouse, that he was starting to become less than sober.

"You're new here, then?" said Arthur, trying to appear to be in total command of both mouth and legs. He took another pull at his pint and held out his hand. "I'm Arthur, one of the Thursday-night regulars."

Her chewing recommenced as she studied the semi-drunk youth grinning across the bar at her. "Yeah, that's right, started on Monday," she said, taking his hand in hers and shaking it. "I'm Thelma, nice to meet you, Arthur."

"Where are you from, then, Thelma? You sound more Valleys than Docks or Corporation Road, to me?"

The barmaid retrieved her hand and began wiping down the bar top. "Yeah, you're right, I'm from up the Western valley, Cwmnant, see, do you know it?"

Before Arthur could reply, he was interrupted, by Dai bellowing to him from across the room. "What's happening with those bloody pints, then? We're all gagging, over here."

Unfazed, Arthur turned slowly around, and, nonchalantly, crossing his legs, made to place an elbow on the bar, like Alan Ladd in the film, Shane. Unlike Alan Ladd, Arthur's elbow missed its mark and he stumbled forward, his shoulder crashing into the stained mahogany. Grabbing for the bar with his free hand, Arthur levered himself upright.

"Bollocks!" he said under his breath, a pained expression on his face as he fought to regain his composure. "Sorry about that, Luv, it's my knee playing me up again," he said deceitfully, through gritted teeth. He flexed his knee several times, in order to show that it was a genuine problem. "No, I think it's going to be OK, it hasn't locked on me, this time." He flexed it one more time for good measure.

"How come you've got a bad knee? What's wrong with it, then?" asked Thelma, concern showing on her face.

"Ah, it's now't, really," replied Arthur feigning a grimace. "It's an old injury that I got playing against Swindon Town in the cup, a few years ago," he lied, bringing out a cigarette and lighting it, studying her reaction over the flame.

"You're a football player, are you?" She leaned forward on her elbows. "Who'd you play for, then?"

"Used to be," he said casually, blowing a stream of blue smoke across the bar. "I played a few matches for the County, but had to retire, on account of my dodgy knee." He tapped his leg, as if to remind him that it was still there, slyly watching her out of the corner of his eye.

"You must have been good if you played for Monmouthshire," the big-busted barmaid said, admiration shining from her bright, blue eyes, her blue-black ponytail swinging across her shoulders as she shook her head in wonderment.

"No, not Monmouthshire County," responded Arthur, shaking his head as he fought back the impatience that was welling up inside him. "Newport County, not Monmouthshire, they're the Town's soccer team, they're in the Third Division South league, just missed promotion by six points, last year."

Thelma shook her head. "I have heard of them, but I'm not that well up on soccer, I'm more rugby, me."

"Yeah?" he replied, trying to keep a straight face. "Well, to each his own, I suppose." Arthur took another drag on his cigarette, while he desperately tried to conjure up another subject, away from sporting ploy, that was obviously getting him nowhere.

An irate Dai arrived at the bar, saving the situation and stopping any further discussion on the merits of soccer or rugby union.

"What the bloody hell are you doing, For Christ's sake, we're dying of bloody thirst, over there," Dai gestured towards the others.

"Sorry, Butt," said Arthur, apologising profusely. "I got carried away, like, talking to Thelma, here," he indicated with his cigarette towards the barmaid.

"Oh aye, Thelma is it?" Dai gave him an old-fashioned look and took two of the pints from the bar and headed back to the table, calling over his shoulder. "You fetch the other two on over, and bloody well hurry it up."

Muttering to himself, he dispensed the glasses to the Cox brothers, shaking his head in disgust. "Bloody Thelma."

"Yeah, Orright," Arthur called after him. "I'm coming, right." He turned back to the barmaid, the smooth look of the predatory male now on his face. "Before I go, I was wondering, when's your night off, then?" he tried to sound casual.

"I'm off on Tuesday, next week," she flicked her ponytail from her shoulder with her hand. "Why is that, then?"

"Well I was wondering how you'd fancy going out for a drink, or something, like." He looked down at his cigarette and blew absentmindedly on the end, it glowed bright red.

"You don't waste any time, do you?" she laughed. "You've only known me ten minutes and you're already giving me the chat, you're a star you are, for sure."

Arthur put on a hurt expression. "Don't get me wrong, Thelma, I'm not normally this pushy, it's just that I'll be on the afternoon shift next week, and then nights the following week, so it could be a fair while before I'm in here again. If I don't ask now, I may not get another chance for ages." He shrugged his shoulders in resignation then grinned. "You know what I mean?"

Taking a final puff from his cigarette, before stubbing it out, Arthur added, "Of course I'll understand if you say no. That's the trouble with working shifts, you don't get much chance to get to know a girl all that well." He gave a small impish grin. "So, I've got to make up for lost time, see," he shrugged. "Anyway, have a think about it, OK? In the meantime, I'd better get these drinks over to the boys or they'll have my guts for garters."

"I don't get a day off until next Tuesday," Thelma repeated, taking the ponytail in her hands and giving it a close inspection, "and I usually wash my hair, that night." She held her hair up for his inspection, knowing full well that he would say that it looked good to him, regardless of its condition.

Arthur sensed that she was beginning to waver. He scented victory in the air. "That's OK, I understand," he said turning away from the bar.

"Hang on, Arthur," she gently tugged at his sleeve.

He turned back to her, suppressing a grin of triumph, knowing that he'd cracked it.

Her eyes twinkled and she gave him a wide smile. "You take the cake, for sure." She tossed her head and tutted with mock resignation. "Oh, orright then, but I can only come out for an hour, see."

"Great!" Arthur picked up the drinks. "I'll have to get over to the lads, now, I'll see you before we go, OK?"

She nodded and began wiping down the bar top again. "Ok, but don't be too long, I might change my mind."

"Don't worry, Thelma, I'll be back before you can say knife," Arthur called back, as he weaved his way back to the table, grinning like a Cheshire cat.

"About bloody time, too," complained Ronnie Cox. "Danny here, is almost dehydering."

"Dehydrating," corrected Danny.

"Yeah, whatever," replied Ronnie. "All that bloody chatting up has lost us good drinking-up time, that's all I know, it'll be bloody 'shut tap' before you know it." He took a swig from his glass, "and I don't suppose you did any good, anyway?"

"Wrong!" said Arthur triumphantly. "As a matter of fact, Thelma and I are going out for a drink next week."

"Is she taking her guide dog and her white stick, with her?" Dai let out a huge guffaw and the rest joined in, banging their glasses on the table in a show of solidarity, causing the hubbub in the room to subside and heads to turn in their direction.

"Keep the frigging noise down, will you? You'll get us all chucked out," Arthur hissed, his jaw set firm. He picked up his glass and drained it in one long gulp, gave an enormous belch and, with a slow smile appearing, said, "Orright, you bunch of bums, d'yer know what I'm going to do now?" He rose unsteadily to his feet.

Ronnie Cox looked at Arthur with some trepidation, half-expecting trouble to break out, he shook his head.

"Just to show you what a good mate I am, regardless of all the piss that's being taken around here, I shall now get rum and blacks all round?"

"Are you paying, then?" asked Dai warily.

"Of course, I am, so yes or no, I'm only offering once," Arthur replied, jutting his jaw out, defying them to refuse.

Danny Cox passed over his empty glass. "Now you're bloody talking 'Arth', that'll, do for me."

"Yeah, me too," grinned his brother Ronnie.

"Yeah, go on then, you, jammy sod," smiled Dai.

Arthur picked up the empties and headed back to the bar, the conversation in the room, had, by now, returned to its normal shouting level.

"Same again, is it, Arth'?" Thelma reached for the empties, her blue-black ponytail swinging.

"No, they're dead. We'll have four rum and blacks this time," he pulled out a cigarette and lit it. "Now, what about next week, then?" He blew smoke at the ceiling and produced a pound note from his back pocket.

She turned back from the spirit optics. "How well do you know Cwmnant, then?" the barmaid asked, as she reached up to the top shelf where the blackcurrant cordial stood.

Arthur gazed into the bar's mirror at the reflection of Thelma's well-packed blouse, suddenly feeling the effects of the evening's drinking hitting him again. He steadied himself and forced out a passable attempt at sobriety.

"Yeah, I know it, orright, just tell me where to meet you and at what time and I'll be there, no problem."

She topped up the rums with the cordial. "I'll be at the bus stop by the clock in the square at quarter to eight, OK?" She gave another wide smile.

"Smashing, I'll be there, for sure." He was beginning to slur slightly.

"You make sure you are." She laughed a deep, throaty gurgle, "and don't be late, or else!"

"Don't you worry about that, orright?" He winked at her, turned and made his way unsteadily back towards the table. "Here we go." He dumped the glasses down on the table unceremoniously and thumped down into a chair. "Jeez, I'm beginning to feel a bit pissed." He rubbed his hand across his face, leaned back in his chair and exhaled deeply.

"A bit pissed? Judging by the way that you staggered over here, I'd say that you were well on the way, my Son." Dai grinned at Arthur and elbowed Danny in the ribs. "What d'yer reckon, Dan? Is our Arthur looking the worse for wear, or what?"

Danny's glass missed his mouth and hit his chin, rum and blackcurrant dribbled down onto his shirt collar.

"Friggin' hell, Dai, watch it, will you?" he complained, mopping at the dribbles with an off-white handkerchief.

"If you ask me, we're all getting pretty stoned," observed Ronnie, with a flash of out-of-character insight. "I don't know about you lot, but I've had my share for tonight." He tossed down the remains of his drink and got up unsteadily. "I'm off for a slash, then home for me." He scraped back his chair and headed for the door. "Are you fit, our Dan?" Ronnie called over his shoulder.

Danny blew his nose in the black currant-stained handkerchief and finishing off his drink, followed his brother across to the toilets. "Yeah, I'm right with you, Ron. You coming lads?" He called over his shoulder.

The landlord made up their minds for them by ringing an old, brass A.R.P bell, that was suspended from a gibbet next to the bar's mirror.

"Drink up now Ladies and Gents, it's well past time," he said, blowing his nose in a tea towel and picking up a crate of empty bottles. He lifted a trap door and disappeared from sight down into the cellar.

Arthur looked at the bar room clock. "If we shift ourselves, we can make the last bus and get a bag of chips at Alonzo's, is it?"

"For sure," said Dai buttoning his jacket.

"Right, c'mon, then," said Arthur, heading for the Gents. "We've got four minutes to have a slash and get to the bus station."

Having emptied their overfull bladders, the Thursday-nighters headed for the exit in a mad scramble. Arthur gave one last look back towards the bar in the hope that he'd see Thelma, but there was no sign of her.

Dai pulled at Arthur's sleeve. "Shift your arse, Arth', for Christ's sake, will you?"

They ran wildly down Market Street, heading for the bus station, shouting and cursing as they dodged in and out of the late-night crowds that were emptying out of the town centre's pubs and cinemas.

The last bus to the docks was just pulling out as en masse, they clambered onto its open platform and made their way unsteadily down the central aisle of the bus, as it lurched its way out of the bus station and headed down Dock Street towards their destination.

The Irish conductor glowered at them, saying nothing as past experiences with late-night drunks had taught him to be very cautious on occasions such as these.

Ten minutes later, having seen the Cox boys disappear off into the distance towards their own street, Arthur and Dai weaved their way along Commercial Road, each holding crumpled, vinegar-soaked newspapers that had once held, piping hot potato chips.

Dai picked out several limp, rapidly cooling chips and popped them into his mouth. "What's with this bloody barmaid, then?"

"What do you mean?" Arthur asked innocently, his mouth also full of chips.

"You know what I mean. When are you supposed to be going out with her, then?" Dai rooted around in the bottom of the paper for the last crispy remnants of the sixpenny-worth, "that's if you are taking her out, of course!"

Arthur didn't rise to the bait. He slowly crushed the vinegar-stained newspaper into a ball, held it out at arm's length, and swaying, attempted to drop kick it over a nearby lamp post. His wild kick missed, and he staggered back and sat down in the gutter with a bump.

"Shit!" he cried and grabbed at the lamppost, and, with much cursing, and a lot of effort, he heaved himself back up onto his feet.

Dai was crying with laughter.

"Go on laugh, you prick." Arthur dusted off the backside of his pants. "Just you buggers wait until next week, after I've taken her out, I'll be the one laughing, for sure."

"I can't wait," sniggered Dai.

"No, neither can I," Arthur grinned. "Anyway, balls to all that. What about tomorrow?"

"I'll be around your house about half seven, OK?" replied Dai, wiping at his eyes.

"Yeah, orright," said Arthur. "We can go and have a few pints in the Legion with Granddad and Cedric, is it?"

"Great," replied Dai. "I'll see you tomorrow then," he said staggering off across the road and turning a corner, the sound of his footsteps fading into the night.

"Cheers, Dai," Arthur called after him.

Chapter Twelve
Cwmnant

Five days later Arthur sat inside a red and white, Western-Valley bus, anxiously waiting its departure, looking at his reflection in the bus window and adjusting the Tony Curtis style curl that clung greasily to his forehead. Satisfied, he turned his attention to lighting a cigarette that he had taken out of a pack, from his jacket pocket, he blew smoke at the seat in front of him, and settled back on the blue and white vinyl.

For the fourth time since he boarded the bus, he looked at his watch. It told him that it was a minute to seven o'clock, one minute away from the scheduled departure time.

Arthur did the calculations in his head again. *Let's see, there's going to be about a forty-minute journey, before we get to Cwmnant. That'll be at twenty to eight, five minutes before I'm supposed to meet Thelma. I hope to God the bloody bus gets there on time,* he thought anxiously.

The driver, a red-faced, tubby little man, who had wisps of carrot-coloured hair sticking out from under his cap, studied his watch and started the engine. The gears meshed with a screech and the bus lurched away from the bus station and roared its way along Upper Dock Street, at what can only be described as, a moderate pace.

Arthur consulted his watch again. *Jeez, I hope his foot's not right down, or it'll be bloody midnight before we get there.* He need not have worried, for once beyond the traffic lights, by the old castle, the driver went into afterburner mode and the old bus took on a new lease of life as it sped on its way to its destination at the top of the Western Valley.

Newport and its environs were soon left behind and the steady climb up the Western Valley began in earnest.

For much of the journey Arthur stared disinterestedly out of the window at the unchanging landscape of sombre, wooded hills, and undulating meadows with their scattering of sheep.

The monotony was broken, from time to time, by the occasional village, with its strand of terraced cottages, small shops, pubs and chapels, which the bus roared through, charging along each narrow street, which had only originally been designed for horse and carts.

To Arthur, the journey seemed to be taking forever, and he looked anxiously at his wristwatch whenever the old bus stopped to take on board, or discharge its assortment of passengers. Eventually there came a fork in the road, where an attendant finger post pointed the way to Cwmnant, it informed the world that the village was one and a half miles further on. Arthur was now, the only passenger remaining on the old bus.

The driver changed down through the gears and the bus slowly passed under a railway bridge before negotiating a tight bend and commencing its grinding, bone-rattling journey up the steep, narrow, winding road that led to Cwmnant.

As the bus crawled up the hill, the whole of its interior either rattled or squeaked, its differential, joining in, sending out distress calls. Arthur turned in his seat and looked through the window, back down at the hill that they were slowly negotiating. Laid out, below in the twilight, were the lights of the villages that they had passed through earlier, necklaces of receding, orange sodium traffic lights snaking away into the distance. High above, half a moon poked out from behind the deep blue outline of Cwmnant Mountain that loomed over them.

As the old bus reached the top of the long climb, the complaining springs, the differential and the spluttering roar of the motor finally subsided, with the selection of a higher gear.

Arthur combed his hair for the seventh time, as the vehicle turned a corner, and Cwmnant Village square came into view.

"This is your stop, Butt," the driver called back to him.

"Cheers," said Arthur getting up out of his seat, feeling as though he had just completed a circuit on the figure-of-eight ride at the Porthcawl fairground.

The bus pulled up with a jerk and the Perspex-panelled door swung open with a thud. Arthur made his way towards it.

"What times are the buses from here, back to Newport, then, Taff?" he asked the driver, as he negotiated the steps down onto the pavement.

The driver lifted his cap and scratched at the dozen or so strands of sparse, ginger hair that decorated his scalp.

"Every hour, on the hour from Aberbeeg," he said replacing his cap. "That'll be quarter past, by here, orright?"

His cap had trapped some of the sandy hair, which now stuck out over his ears like wings.

Arthur acknowledged the driver with a wave. "Cheers, Butt," he called.

The Perspex door slammed shut and the bus slowly pulled away and turned out of the square, its gears once again unhappy.

Silence descended and Arthur looked about him. Sure enough, there was the clock, atop a wrought-iron support, standing on its own little concrete island in the middle of the square, just as Thelma had promised.

Opposite stood a shabby, pebble-dashed building, its faded, brown-painted woodwork, cracked and peeling. Across its facade was the faded legend, 'Cwmnant Gunner Club — Abernant Ales, Fresh from the Thirst to The Last.'

From within the bowels of the club came the muffled thud of an electronic bass guitar.

He looked at the clock and then at his watch, they both agreed, it was twenty minutes to eight.

There was no sign of Thelma.

He crossed the road towards the club and leaned against a pillar-box, lit a cigarette and took in his surroundings. The blue and violet hues of the early autumn evening had finally given way to a dark, navy blue night that now cloaked the small square, where only the dim light, from its three lamps, cast little islands of light onto the pavement.

Across, from him, on the opposite side of the square, stood a shop, its front barely visible in the meagre lamplight. On its dirty window, spelled out in crooked, multi-coloured stick-on letters, was the proclamation, **'CWMNANT BOUTIQUE & LINGERIE CAVERN'**. Underneath, in fading white-wash, was the message: **'CLOSING DOWN SALE — EVERYTHING MUST GO.'**

Everything had gone, for the shop was empty, save for a milk crate, which stood on a stool behind the dirty glass.

From its darkened doorway came a voice. "You've made it, then?"

Arthur took a pull on his cigarette and peered across at the shop. The large-busted figure of Thelma emerged from its doorway and crossed the square, her blue-black ponytail swinging across the shoulders of a dark blue mackintosh, which strained across her enormous chest.

"Course I did, said I would, didn't I," replied Arthur, a wide grin on his face.

She stopped before him, taking in the black and white houndstooth jacket and the emerald-green shirt that he was wearing.

"My, ain't you the bees knees, then?" She gave him a wide smile.

"Glad you like it," he grinned. "You look pretty good yourself."

"Ta." She gave him the demure treatment by momentarily lowering her eyelids. "Shall we go, then?"

"Yeah, I guess." He looked around the small square. "Like where, for instance?"

She pointed to the scruffy, pebble-dashed facade of the club. "In the Gunner's, over by there, they've got the best rock music in the valley, see."

She linked arms with him and led him towards a set of faded, brown doors that were next to the pub's main entrance.

He inwardly groaned. *This is going to be a bloody wow.*

She read his thoughts. "C'mon, you'll love it. Honest."

"I'll bet." He threw away the smouldering cigarette stub and followed her through the doors into a dingy brown-papered passageway.

"Up here." Thelma, indicated towards a brown-painted flight of stairs. "It's the door on the first landing," she said, looking back at him as she began her ascent.

Christ! How big is this bloody pub, anyway? he thought, peering up the gloomy, lino'-covered stairs as he started up after her.

She opened the brown-painted door at the top of the stairs and stepped into a long, similarly lino'— covered passage.

"This is not the pub, really," she said, turning back to him, indicating the passage walls. "This is the way into what used to be the old territorial-army drill hall, which is next door to the pub. It's all one, now, of course and the club part of the pub is at the end of this passage. It's all the Gunner's of course, but this part is called Cannons." She gave a chuckle. "Cannons and Gunners, get it?"

He got it.

"I expect half the bloody South Wales borderers are in there, bopping, then, is it?" he said.

She gave him a puzzled look. "Why do you say that, then?"

"Only a joke, see." He explained, "What with all that army stuff, guns and the like, you know?" He gave her a half-hearted grin.

She gave his arm a friendly punch. "What are you like, you daft ha'p'orth?" She put her arm through his and they walked arm in arm toward the far door, the music, getting ever louder as they approached. Arthur opened the far door for her and the sound hit them.

A nasal voice was giving *Twenty-Flight-Rock* the treatment.

Holding his hands to his ears, Arthur inwardly cursed. *Christ all bloody mighty.* His ears jarred, by the god-awful singing.

"Too loud, is it?" Thelma yelled.

He shook his head. "No, just took me by surprise that's all," he lied.

Arthur looked around him; they were on a small balcony that overlooked a long, narrow dance floor. A central staircase led down from the middle of the balcony to the back of the hall.

At the top of the stairs, sitting on a deck chair, behind a rickety bamboo table, was a wrinkled old lady, wearing lace mittens. She held out a hand. "That'll be two bob, luv," she said, ripping two tickets from a roll and handing them to Arthur.

Delving into a trouser pocket, he extracted some loose change.

"Cheers," said Arthur, offering up a half a crown and taking the tickets. "Is there a cloak room around here, anywhere."

The old lady indicated over her shoulder with a gnarled thumb. "Over in the corner, by there," she said, pointing to a rack full of coats. "Mind you, you'll be lucky to find a space, it will be full," she added.

Arthur peered into the gloom towards the back of the balcony, a dressmaker's rack was standing against the far wall and it was full.

"Cheers," Arthur repeated, with not too much enthusiasm. He turned to Thelma. "Give us your mac, Thelm', I'll see if I can make some room for it."

"Ta, Arth'," she said, disrobing and handing him her raincoat, revealing, in the process, her mighty chest, which was cocooned in a sequin top, that left little to the imagination.

Hello again, you two, you're looking as good as ever. Arthur silently greeted the bosom as he took the coat and crossed to the rack, where he forced open a space and hung up Thelma's coat.

They then went arm in arm down the stairs and stopped at the bottom, surveying the scene before them, before moving to one side, away from the dance-floor, where they stood and watched the scores of couples who were gyrating to the strains of *Sweet-Little-Sixteen*, which that was being blasted out by a four-piece group of musicians, at the far end of the hall.

Above the dancers, a facetted, silver ball slowly revolved, its mirrored surface reflecting multicoloured spears of light down onto the shoulders of the sweaty, spinning bodies.

"C'mon, let's jive." She pulled him onto the dancefloor where they were quickly swallowed up by a maelstrom of whirling arms and legs.

Thelma proved to be a good dancer and she followed his every move as if they had been dancing together all of their lives.

They jived non-stop to a succession of rock tunes for about twenty minutes.

Arthur grudgingly had to admit that, regardless of his sweat-soaked shirt and the apparent lack of oxygen in the hall, he was having a great time.

Finally, his lungs were saved, when the group slowed things down and began playing a series of slow, smoochy numbers.

Arthur pulled Thelma to him and they swayed on the spot while the band's bass player gave a nasal rendition of, *It's-All-In-The- Game*.

It's all in the bloody chest, more like observed the little voice inside Arthur's head, as Thelma's mighty bosom pressed into him.

For fifteen ecstatic minutes those glorious orbs massaged his shirtfront as he and Thelma swayed together, barely moving from the spot, until an ear-piercing, electronic screech of feed-back from the loudspeakers brought his joy to a sudden end. The slow, seductive tempo of *Mister-Blue* came to an end, and was quickly followed by a blast of sound, which heralded the start of yet another of the band's fast rock numbers, during which, an adenoidal voice told the listeners of a *Brand-New-Cadillac*.

The boom from the bass guitar joined in unholy matrimony with the high-pitched riffs of the lead guitar and suddenly scores of bodies became unglued and began whirling and cavorting crazily across the dance floor. Thelma swung away from him and switched back into jiving mode. Arthur, feeling somewhat cheated, reluctantly followed her lead, and for another fifteen minutes, legs and lungs, were, once again put to the test.

Eventually, the group finally ground to a halt, seconds before Arthur would have been forced to do likewise.

The lead singer mumbled something into the microphone.

Arthur only caught the words, break and minutes, which he took to be the cue for group's beer break.

"Jeez," Arthur gasped. "I've got to admit, they're not a bad little group." He mopped at his brow with a handkerchief. "Are they local, or what?"

"Yeah, that's right," said Thelma over her shoulder as she led him back off the dance floor. "Rory Stone and the Diamonds, ain't they great?"

"Yeah, great." Arthur suppressed a grin. *Rory friggin' Stone,* he thought. *What a bloody laugh.*

She put her arm through his. "I went to the same school as Rory. He lives just up the road from my gran, in Abercarn."

"I bet he got the piss taken out of him in school, with a name like bloody Rory?" he laughed.

She gave Arthur a puzzled look. "No, that's not his proper name, see, that's his stage name, like, his real name is Byron Watkins, drives a crane down at the wire works in Cwmmer."

Arthur tried to focus on her words, feigning a look of interest. "Yeah, well, as I said, they aren't half bad, fair play." He mopped his forehead again. "Are there many other groups from around here, or is this the only one?"

She shrugged. "No, there are one or two that sometimes play up here, but it's mainly Rory's group up here at the Gunner's. They're our favourites, see," she added.

"Does Jerry Jenkins and the Five Erlys ever play up this way, then?" Arthur asked, already knowing the answer.

"Jerry who?" She frowned and shook her head, her ponytail swishing across the sequins on her shoulders. "Can't say I've ever heard of them, whereabouts are they from, then?"

"From…" Arthur stopped in mid-sentence. A great howl of laughter had gone up from near the stage, interrupting his flow. He craned his neck and looked over the heads of the couples in front of him, hoping to see just what all the fuss was about.

There, making his way unsteadily up the steps, leading to the stage, was the misshapen figure of Jerry Jenkins, carrying a tray loaded down with glasses of beer.

Arthur studied Jerry's progress, seeing the beer slopping onto the tray with each erratic step, while the band clapped and laughed at his unsteady progress. The tail of his shirt was hanging out of his trousers.

Anger swept over Arthur as he listened to the howls of derision and the hoots of laughter that swept through the hall. He suppressed a strong urge to rush up to the stage and to drag Jerry down from there, but he did nothing. He just continued to stand there, listening to the people around him, braying and applauding, and hating himself, having to admit to having been just like them.

Thelma giggled at Jerry's bumbling efforts, while Arthur did his best to feign disinterest. "Who is that up there?" he asked, indicating Jerry. "Is he in the group, then?"

Thelma gave a hoot of laughter. "Don't be daft, Mun, for God's sake! Rory wouldn't have that little creep in the band. All he's good for, is fetching and carrying, that's all."

She somehow sensed his discomfort. "Hey, what's wrong, then, you've gone all quiet?"

Arthur gave her a small smile. "Nothing," he shrugged. "I was just thinking, as how that bloke up there, on the stage, looks a lot like someone that I used to work with, that's all."

She squeezed his arm. "Well that's all right then, isn't it?"

"Yeah," he replied and then he said absentmindedly. "Who is he, anyway?"

"Search me." She shook her head and her ponytail swished back and forth. "I haven't a clue, all I know, is that the boys in the group call him

Quazzy." She dug Arthur playfully in the ribs. "You know, like that hunchback bloke in the films."

Arthur felt a tug on his sleeve.

"Always good for a laugh, is Quazzy," said a voice. Arthur turned towards the source of the statement.

A burly, greasy-haired youth stood there, grinning widely.

"Is that right?" said Arthur forcing half a smile.

"Yeah, he's a toy, for sure," said the youth, passing his hand over his greasy head. "You should've been here last week, what a laugh, Rory and the boys got him pissed on cider and then gave him half a crown to sing up on the stage during their break." He gave Arthur a friendly punch on the arm. "He brought the friggin' house down, didn't he?"

"Yeah? What happened, then?" asked Arthur, through gritted teeth.

The oily-haired youth gave a snort. "He only sang that advert, White Heather, didn't he?"

Arthur's fixed smile was getting thinner by the second. "What the one on the telly?"

"Yeah that's the one. What a prick, eh?"

Arthur came very close to giving greasy-hair a thick lip but thought better of it. *One wrong move, up here and I'll have half the bloody Western Valley giving me a good kicking,* he concluded.

"Yeah," he replied to the Youth and turned to Thelma. "I wouldn't say no to a pint, right now. How about you?"

"All right, Arth', let's go into the bar, is it?" she replied.

"Great, lead on," he turned to greasy-head. "We're off for a pint, see you!"

"Aye, see you, Butt." The youth nodded and then turned his attention back to a blonde with the beehive hairdo and the black moons and stars on her stockings.

Chapter Thirteen
Trouble

Thelma led Arthur across the dance floor towards a door, which bore the faded gold coloured legend, BAR AND TOILETS.

"Through here's the bar of the Gunner's." She opened the door and they entered another brown-painted passage, shorter than the previous one, but equally drab. Halfway along, there was another brown door, with the word **TOILETS** above its frame, the flushing of a cistern, from within, confirmed it.

At the end of the passage was a pink door with the word, **BAR,** imprinted on it.

They must have run out of brown paint, thought Arthur, opening it for Thelma and following her through into the room that was in the pub half of the building.

The Gunner's Bar proved to be long and narrow, and the small group of couples, standing at the drab bar, seemed to fill it.

A curtain of blue-grey tobacco smoke clung to the ceiling like an enormous cobweb. It billowed in the draught as Arthur closed the door behind him.

Above the bar was a succession of small shields, bearing, what appeared to be regimental insignia. Similarly, above each of the two doors of the room were flat, plywood shields with depictions of cannons in hand-painted, peeling gold paint, on them. From one, hung the remnant of a silver and blue Christmas garland.

Across the room, opposite the bar, was a black-leaded fireplace with a glowing glass fibre log in the maw of its blackened, chimney breast, above which, was an uneven, and equally blackened, wooden mantelpiece. On the wall above was a curled, pink notice, which urged the clientele to come along on Saturday nights to see Hopkin Evans and his organ.

Hanging from the two sidewalls were quasi-military banners, which flapped every time the door to the bar was opened and closed.

Arthur looked back at Thelma. "What are you having to drink, then, Thelm'?" he said, leaning on the bar brandishing a ten-shilling note.

"Can I have a gin and orange, Arth'?"

"Sure," he said magnanimously. "Have whatever you fancy!" He shot her a grin and she lowered her eyes demurely, a red tinge on her cheeks.

With all the military flags and the shields adorning the walls of the bar, Arthur had half expected the barman to be a square-shouldered, moustachioed ex-NCO with clipped speech and highly polished toecaps to his civvy shoes.

He was wrong on every count, what shuffled into view was a short and scrawny individual who answered to the name of Tommy. Tommy sported a short-sleeved Fair Isle pullover over an open-necked shirt that hung loosely from his bony shoulders. The pullover stopped short of the waistband of his trousers by a couple of inches, which proved unfortunate, as the bottom button on his shirt was missing, thus affording the viewer the unwelcome sight of a revolting patch of flaccid, hairy stomach. On his feet he sported dirty, grey plimsolls.

"What can I get you, then?" asked Tommy, his dentures clicking.

"Gin and orange and a pint of Best, ta." Arthur placed the ten-shilling note on the bar. "Oh! And give us ten Senior Service, while you're at it."

Tommy clicked his dentures while he pulled the pint. He placed the drinks on the bar.

"That'll be four and a penny."

Arthur delved into his pocket for loose change. "I've got the odd penny here, if that'll help?"

Tommy took the penny and placed the money into the open drawer of the till, closed it with an elbow and turned to Arthur and counted out six shillings onto the bar.

"That's six-bob change, OK?" He clicked his teeth and shuffled off to the other end of the bar, without waiting for an acknowledgement.

Arthur lifted the glass to his lips and took a pull at the beer.

"Cheers," he called after him, wiping his mouth on his hand and grinning. "He doesn't look much like a Sergeant Major, to me."

"You what?" Thelma gave him a puzzled look.

Arthur gestured towards the barman. "Charlie boy, there, I was half expecting to see an ex-Welsh guardsman behind the bar, not him."

"Why do you say that, Mun?" asked Thelma, taking a delicate sip from her glass.

Arthur gestured at the walls. "What with the flags and all this other military stuff around here, I somehow half expected the barman to be ex-army, you know?"

"Who Tommy? You must be joking. The nearest he's ever been to the army is the Sally Anne in Alma Street, where he gets a free cuppa and a bun on Tuesdays." She gave a sneer. "The only way he'd get in the guards is as the goat, he must be the ugliest man around!" She gave a nasty, little snigger. "Apart from Quazzy, in there, of course," she said, pointing towards the dance hall.

Arthur took out a cigarette, lit it and studied the blue, grey smoke as it curled towards the ceiling, joining the other eddies. The sight of the crooked, little figure of Jerry slopping beer as he negotiated the steps of the stage had stayed with him, and the mocking jeers of the dancers were still ringing in his ears.

"A penny for them." Thelma touched his arm.

"You what?" Arthur frowned.

"Your thoughts, you know? A penny for them."

"Oh! Right, I get you, now." He took a drag on his cigarette and a deep gulp from his pint glass. "My thoughts, is it?" He gave her a thin smile. "Well I was just thinking, that I'm bloody glad that I wasn't the one having to carry the beer for the group, back there." He indicated with a nod in the direction of the dance hall. "I think if I had been me up there, having the piss taken out of me, then Mister Rory bloody Stone would have had his guitar shoved where the sun don't shine."

"Don't be daft, Mun." Her face had a hard edge to it. "It's only a bit of fun, like." She took a gulp of her gin and orange. "It goes on all the time, and, besides, Quazzy wouldn't be here week in week out if he didn't like it, would he?"

Arthur couldn't argue with that, but he still felt uncomfortable about the whole unsavoury episode. He nodded. "I guess you're right, Thelma," he replied woodenly.

He drank up the rest of his beer and looked around the room. The drab-flags hung listlessly from their greasy poles. The false log in the grate had stopped glowing.

Most of the drinkers were starting to drift back into the dance hall. "I'm having another. How about you, Thelm'?" asked Arthur placing the empty glass back on the bar.

"No, I'm all right with this one, ta very much," she replied without looking up from her close inspection of her coral nails.

Arthur tapped his empty glass on the bar. "Same again Tommy boy." He waved the empty in the direction of the barman.

Tommy shuffled back to the pumps. "Pint of stunner, was it?" His teeth clicked.

"No, I'll stick to the best bitter, ta," replied Arthur.

"Anything for the lady?" The dentures clicked once more.

"No just the pint," said Arthur placing a half crown on the bar.

He picked up the fresh pint and took a long pull from it. "You sure I can't get you another drink?" he asked Thelma.

The door to the bar banged open, pre-empting her reply, causing the tobacco smoke to swirl and the flags to flap excitedly.

"Give us a pint of stunner, Tom. I'm frigging gasping," said the voice of the newcomer.

Arthur looked up from his drink in its direction. It belonged to the greasy-haired youth from the dance floor.

"Orright Butt?" asked the youth and slurped at his newly poured pint.

"Yeah, and you?" Arthur replied without a smile.

The tall youth mopped his brow with a sleeve. "Jeez it's bloody baking in that hall, I was bloody glad to get out from there."

"Why didn't you come out earlier, then?" Arthur asked without interest.

"I had to wait for the band to start their antics, didn't I? They always spend at least five minutes taking the piss out of Quazzy before starting the second half, can't miss that, can you?"

"Yeah I can miss it," replied Arthur through clenched teeth. "As a matter of fact, if I missed the whole frigging lot of you bunch of bums, I wouldn't spill a bloody tear." He put his pint on the bar in anticipation of a reaction.

The tall youth looked nonplussed for brief moment, then it dawned on him that Arthur wasn't joking. "What's up with you, then Mun? You a mate of Quazzy's or something?"

"Never mind what I am." Arthur's voice had taken on a hard edge. "Don't any of you bloody Taffs know the bloody bloke's real name, for Christ's sake? He's a human being, not a bloody animal."

"He is a bloody mate, isn't he?" The youth poked a finger at Arthur's chest. "What are you some kind of head banger, or what?"

That's when Arthur hit him.

The youth staggered backwards and sat down heavily in the fire grate, demolishing the false log, blood pouring from his nose and from the corner of his mouth.

Arthur, ready to defend himself, expected the youth to get up and rush at him; but instead the youth just mouthed a string of obscenities and hurried out of the room, heading for the dance hall.

"Well that takes the bleeding cake, that does," said Thelma. "You come up here, bloody *Jack-the-Lad* from the big city, thinking you're the bloody kiddy. All you've done is criticise us all night, and now, you go and hit Gareth Thomas on the nose. What sort of plonker are you, anyway?"

Arthur shrugged with disdain. "He had it coming, the prick."

"Yeah, well you'll have it bloody coming too, once his brothers in the dance hall hear about it. I'm surprised they're not already in here, sorting you out."

Arthur groaned inwardly. *That's all I bloody well need, a good hammering from a bunch of valley hillbillies.*

He assumed an air of false nonchalance, and said, "In that case I'm not hanging about to find out." He hastily gulped down the remainder of his beer. "Can I get out to the square through there?" He indicated towards a door in the far corner of the bar.

She shook her head, angrily. "That's for me to know and for you to find out, Butt," she said contemptuously as she turned on her heel and walked out of the room, the door banging loudly behind her.

Chapter Fourteen
Escape

Arthur was already at the far door by the time Thelma had disappeared through the doorway leading to the dance hall. He wrenched at its handle and the door swung open, revealing a small porch with an outer door, which he opened gingerly and peered warily out into the square.

It was dark and empty, nothing moved except for a torn chocolate wrapper that was skidding along a gutter with the help of the light breeze that also flicked at his hair.

He quickly closed the outer door behind him and looked about, his mind working overtime, as to what his next move should be.

Where now, for Christ's sake, he thought. *If I stay in the square, they're bound to spot me.* He looked around, desperately seeking a hiding place that would keep him out of harm's way until the next bus was due.

He studied the brown door that was a couple of yards away from the pub door. It was the door that he and Thelma had entered earlier on that evening, the door that eventually led to the dance hall.

"What the hell," he muttered, quickly heading for it. "This'll be the last place they'll expect me to be." He reached the door, silently opened it and entered the passageway. *Fingers crossed anyway*, he thought, as he gently closed the door behind him.

Voices came from the direction of the square.

"Oh, bloody hell!" gasped Arthur and he began running on tiptoe up the passage to the stairs, which he took two at a time, until he had reached the landing and the door at the top, which he slowly opened, cautiously peering into the long passageway.

It was deserted.

A quarter of the way along the passage Arthur spotted a side door, which he reached in a matter of a few strides. He examined the faded legend that was spelled out across the door's front panel, 'Comitt Roo' read the peeling notice.

Committee Room, I don't remember seeing this door, when we passed down this corridor before. He tried the handle. It turned, and, to his surprise, it opened readily. Arthur peered apprehensively around the half-opened door into the darkened room, listening attentively.

Hearing nothing, and sensing that it was empty, he cautiously entered the room, quietly closed the door, and stood with his back against the wall, his heart hammering away inside his chest, as he listened for any sounds coming from the passageway, his ear pressed against the door panel.

All was quiet, and he let out a huge sigh of relief and gradually his panic attack began to subside.

Arthur felt along the wall for a light switch, found one and flicked it down. Surprisingly, the light came on and its low powered beam revealed a long, narrow room, which was empty, except for a solitary grey, filing cabinet that stood decaying in the far corner. It was obvious that the room had been unused for some time, for it had that flat, metallic musty smell, that told of dampness and neglect.

He studied the door, hoping that there was some means of locking it from the inside, but there was no catch on the lock that he could activate, and no inside bolt either.

"Balls," he muttered with disappointment. "I can't stay in here, with an unlocked door, that would be asking for trouble." Grasping the door handle, Arthur turned and looked back at the room, hoping for some inspiration that might save him, then, he did a double take. "That's a door over there," he murmured, staring across to the far corner of the room.

Arthur slowly opened the committee room door a couple of inches and listened intently, his ear to the crack. All was quiet. Except for the distant, muffled throb of a bass guitar.

He quietly closed the door and made his way silently across the room to inspect his newly found discovery, his spirits lifted by the possibility of another means of escape. Sure enough, next to the filing cabinet, encrusted with years of accumulated dirt and dust and rust, was a metal door, which proved to be an old emergency exit, complete with a crashbar which, when activated, would have, in its heyday, allowed the door to open outwards.

Arthur rubbed his hand over the door's cobwebbed surface, leaving a path in the grime and rust. The door was so dirty that it was little wonder that he'd almost missed seeing it. He pushed hopefully at the bar, it was jammed solid.

"Bastard!" he mouthed his disappointment. "I bet the bloody thing hasn't been used since the old King died." He crossed back to the committee room door again, opened it and peered into the corridor and listened, all was silent and, the corridor was still deserted.

He quietly closed the door behind him, ran across the room and aimed a kick at the crash-bar, which squealed but remained unmoved. He tried again, the squeal was louder and the bar moved a fraction of an inch. Throwing caution to the wind, Arthur kicked at the bar once more, again it gave a squeal, and again, there was more movement, then, for a fourth time, he kicked desperately at the bar, which groaned and then slowly dropped forward with a clank.

Spurred by his success, Arthur pushed frantically at the door, but, like the crash bar, age had jammed it solidly shut. Undaunted, he put his shoulder to it and pushed with all of the strength that he could muster. The door slowly started to open, complaining with a frightful squeal, which he felt sure, the whole of the village would be hearing.

Taking a deep breath, Arthur pushed at the metal emergency exit a second time, it groaned loudly and gave about eight inches, which was just wide enough for him to squeeze through.

Cold air greeted him, along with feelings of elation and relief, which were short-lived.

"Bollocks," he mouthed, through gritted teeth. "The bloody light's still on in the committee room." He sucked in his stomach and squeezed back through the narrow gap into the room, which he quickly crossed and turned off the light, before carefully making his way, through the gloom back towards the gap, which he squeezed through a second time.

He couldn't close the door behind him, it was unyielding, and, by now, his strength was rapidly ebbing.

Ah well, stuff it. He shrugged his shoulders resignedly and turned and peered into the gloom.

Arthur found himself standing on a metal landing, at the top of a flight of metal steps that sloped away into the darkness.

Not a sound disturbed the night, except for the muffled beat of the music, coming from within the bowels of the building.

He sighed with relief, and taking in a gulp of the night air, he waited until his eyes had grown more accustomed to the darkness, then he slowly made his way down the stairs, testing each one carefully before allowing his full weight upon it.

At the bottom he found himself in a tiny courtyard that was surrounded on all sides by brick walls.

"Shit!" he said out loud. *No wonder the bloody emergency exit was so bloody stiff, it probably hasn't been used since they bricked up this end of the yard.*

He looked around in desperation, the wall behind the stairs was the lowest of the four; but the only problem was that the stairs themselves blocked his way to it.

Go for it, said a tiny voice in his head, and letting out a sigh of exasperation, Arthur reluctantly climbed back up to the top of the stairs, where he mounted the handrail, climbed over it, and edged his way along the rim of the metal landing, his stomach pressed against the handrail, both of his hands gripping the metal rail.

"Ah well, shit or bust," he said through gritted teeth, and he lowered himself from the landing, until he swung by his arms from its metal rim. Then, reaching out with his legs, Arthur felt for the top of the wall, until they made contact with the brickwork, then he let his feet come to rest upon the top of the wall.

Steadying himself, he gradually let go of the metal rim, one hand at a time, until he stood swaying precariously on the wall's narrow top, then, slowly bending his knees, Arthur gingerly placed them, one at a time, onto the top of the wall, until he was in a kneeling position. He then quickly grasped at the rough brickwork, turned and swung his legs over the wall and sat down heavily on its top.

"Jeez," he gasped, holding his head in his hands. *What a bloody nightmare.*

He didn't know how long he had been sitting unsteadily on top of the wall, but it seemed like forever, but he had to force himself to wait, until his heart had stopped racing, and normality had more or less returned.

Right, let's make a bloody move, is it? said a little voice in his head, and he turned and edged his way, belly-down, over the wall until he hung by his fingertips.

Then he let go and dropped into the unknown darkness below, bracing himself for the impact.

It came almost instantly, and he hit the floor and toppled over onto his backside. "Bloody Nora," he said through gritted teeth, feeling the effects of the six-foot drop on his legs and buttocks.

Trying to dismiss the pain, Arthur quickly got to his feet, rubbing at his backside, which felt as if a horse had kicked it. He took a few tentative steps, flexing both knees, testing for any lasting damage. His body seemed to be hurting all over, but nothing appeared to have been broken, and he seemed to have movement in all parts.

Dusting himself down, he peered into the gloom. He was now in a much larger yard, which was half full of empty beer barrels and crates of empty beer bottles; it was the Gunners Club's delivery area.

Arthur peered across to the far end of the yard, where he could just make out the faint outline of a wooden gate. He quickly crossed the yard to it. More disappointment swept over him, the gate was secured with a chain and a padlock.

"Oh well, here we go again," he muttered, now, no longer too concerned about personal injury, but more about escape.

Launching himself forward, Arthur leapt at the gate, his hands seeking for the top of it while his feet thrust against the wooden cross-members. His hands grasped at the top of the gate, and he levered himself up, one foot pressing down on the top of the gate's metal latch, while his other foot found the middle cross-member. He hauled himself up and, hooking one leg over the top of the gate, turned onto his belly and allowed himself to briefly hang by his hands, before quickly dropping down the other side, this time, landing on his feet.

Arthur stayed where he had landed and slowly collected his thoughts, as he gulped in air, his back to the wooden gate.

Looking about him, Arthur could see that he was in a dimly lit, cobbled lane, which appeared to run parallel with the village square at the front of the Gunners Club.

This must run parallel with the square, he mused. *So, there's bound to be a way out along here, somewhere.*

He moved silently up the lane on tiptoe.

Some thirty yards further on, the lane turned sharply to the left, towards the square. Arthur edged his way silently to the corner of the lane and slowly peered around it. Ten yards in front of him, was the Village Square, just as he had hoped.

Taking a deep breath, he tiptoed to the corner, where the lane met the village square, and, with his back pressed against the wall, strained his ears for any sound.

From not too far away came the muffled sounds of several voices.

Arthur got down on his hands and knees and peered around the corner at ankle level, a trick he'd been taught during a brief spell in the 18th Troop of the Dock-Street Boy Scouts.

He slowly edged his face around the corner and studied the group of people who were standing outside the Gunners Club.

"Listen, it's only about twenty minutes since that git legged it, the bastard can't be that far away," a harsh, nasal voice pointed out.

"Well, he's not in the bloody square, that's for sure," said another. "Gareth and me have searched all around, no sign."

A female voice joined in, it was Thelma's. "If you lot are looking for the Bloke who was in the bar with me, then you're wasting your time, he's long gone."

"You've got a bloody nerve, showing your face here, after what your friggin' boyfriend went and done," a nasal voice snarled at her.

"He's not my bloody boyfriend, see," she snarled back at him. "Tonight, was the first time I've been out with him. I didn't know what he was going to be like, did I? For Christ's sake." She spat the words out at him.

"Yeah, orright, then," conceded the voice, grudgingly. "But how'd you know he's long gone?"

"Because he came up here in a car, that's how," she lied, pointing across the village square. "It was a black Standard Vanguard, he parked it over there by the chapel."

"How the bloody hell d'yer know that, then?" asked another of the group.

"Because he told me, that's how," Thelma retorted angrily.

"Well it ain't there now," said a second nasal voice. "So he must be long gone, isn't it?"

"Yeah, it looks like," agreed nasal voice number one. "Let's get back to the bloody dance, that bleeder's probably in Risca, by now."

One by one the members of the gang of locals slowly made their way back into the bar of the Cwmnant Gunners Club.

Arthur slowly got to his feet and let out a sigh of relief. "Good on you, Thelm'. You saved my bloody bacon, there," he muttered.

He looked at his watch it showed twenty past nine. He grimaced, knowing that if he had either missed the bus, in which case he had another hour to wait, or, if his luck was in, it was five minutes late. Arthur didn't relish the thought of another hour in hiding, so he crossed his fingers and hoped that the bus was running late.

Keeping in as close to the walls as possible, he slowly made his way around the perimeter of the square until he reached the doorway of the disused shop, where he happily melted into the shadows and waited.

A further five minutes had elapsed and there was no sign of the bus.

"Oh Shit!" he groaned. *If that bloody bus has gone, then I'm right in cack street.* He looked around the square. *I'll give it five more minutes then I'll just have to start hoofing it down the bloody road. There's no way I'm hanging about here, for another hour.* Walking back to the nearest village was not a prospect that he relished, but anything was better than staying put and risking a hammering from the local *Mafiosi.*

He checked out the square once more and, just as he was about to dash across it to freedom, there came the familiar sounds of a grating gearbox, and the squeaking of ancient suspension, followed by the emergence into the square of the old grey and red bus.

Chapter Fifteen
Homeward

Arthur dashed from the shop doorway into the road yelling and waving frantically at the bus driver, who jammed on the brakes. The bus ground to a halt and the door clanked open.

"I thought I'd missed you," Arthur gasped to the driver as he hauled himself up to the top of the steps, with one hand while, at the same time, searching feverishly through his pockets for his return ticket, with the other. "Bloody ticket! I know it's here somewhere, he panted."

"That's orright, Butt, I remember you from the up journey. You go and grab yourself a seat," said the driver, adjusting his hat and letting in the clutch at the same time, the gearbox once again complaining.

"Cheers," Arthur gasped, and he headed down the lurching aisle, towards the nearest seat, the door slamming shut behind him as the bus bounced and sped across the square, its springs groaning.

Arthur flopped down onto the scuffed, blue vinyl seat and let out a huge sigh of relief, and he looked back, through the window, at the fast disappearing, still deserted square.

The bus slowly negotiated the tight turn out of Cwmnant Village Square and started its journey on the long steep descent back towards the twinkling lights of the distant villages that were spread out along the valley floor below.

"Been waiting long, then?" the driver yelled over his shoulder, trying to make himself heard above the roar of the engine.

"No, I'd only just got there as you arrived," Arthur replied, as he tried, with shaking hands, to apply a lighted match to a cigarette.

"You were lucky, then, son," shouted the driver. "If it hadn't been for sheep on the road at Pontywaun, we'd have been long gone. As it is, we are running a quarter of an hour late, so you're lucky," he repeated, blowing his nose into a khaki handkerchief and inspecting the result, while at the same time, wrestling single-handedly with the steering wheel.

"Thank God for sheep, then," replied Arthur, blowing smoke at the ceiling.

"Aye well, not to worry," the driver yelled. "We don't get too many pick-ups on the way down the valley at this time of night, so we'll soon make up the difference."

"Right," Arthur replied and they both lapsed into silence, happy at not having to strain their respective voice boxes over the howling engine.

Arthur turned to look out of the window, and saw, to his horror, his reflection in the window's glass. It looked as if he'd been in a battle, and lost. His hair stuck out at all angles like a clown's and was a complete mess. A long streak of dirt was spread across his nose and cheek, and a smear of something decidedly unpleasant adorned the right-hand lapel and shoulder of his jacket. He cursed under his breath and got out his handkerchief and set about trying to clean himself up, spitting on it and furiously scrubbing at his face.

He stopped and peered again at his reflection, using the window as a mirror, his onslaught with the handkerchief had had some effect, his face now looked reasonably clean.

Satisfied that it would pass muster, he set about attacking the smear on the jacket, which took another five minutes of vigorous rubbing, before; it too, became fairly presentable. He inspected the well-soiled handkerchief, to see the results of his labours. Whatever the substance was, it was odourless, and appeared to be harmless, so he guessed that it hadn't emanated from an animal's rear end. Much relieved, he pushed the handkerchief back into his pocket and settled back in the seat.

He took a long pull at his cigarette and flicked the ash from its end. The ash landed on the knee of his trousers, and he lifted his leg to blow the ash away, only to find more disasters.

"Oh shit!" he groaned, on seeing his knee protruding through a jagged gash in the cloth.

"What's that Butt?" the driver yelled at him.

"Nothing," Arthur yelled back. "My leg has gone to sleep, that's all."

"Wriggle your toes about, that'll sort it out," advised the driver.

"Yeah, right. I'll do that," Arthur replied wearily.

They both fell silent again and Arthur set about inspecting the rest of his clothes.

It was a horror story.

As well as the rip in the knee of his trousers, a large, irregular flap of material poked up where there had once been a jacket button, and across the jacket's left elbow was another ragged tear. Whatever had snagged it had done a good job, for it had also shredded the lining and the shirtsleeve underneath.

He tried to tuck the flaps out of sight but with little success, so he dismissed the thought of them and set about combing his knotted hair.

As he dragged the comb through the greasy locks, he could feel his hand throbbing. He inspected the palm; across it was a pattern of tiny criss-cross cuts and scrapes. He looked at the other hand; two of the knuckles were swollen and were an angry red.

All in all, I would say that I got off pretty lightly, everything considered. He snorted and grinned. *Well at least I didn't get a good hammering, anyway.* He let out a huge guffaw, as the absurdity of it all hit him. "Christ! What a frigging night," he burbled. Tears of laughter began running down his cheeks, releasing from him, some of the tension of the last half an hour.

"You still having trouble with that leg, then?" the driver yelled his concern.

"No, it's OK now," Arthur's voice had risen an octave. "It's just coming back to life." He fished out his handkerchief again and blew his nose in it and looked at it critically. "That'll take some bloody washing," he wailed, pressing the soiled handkerchief against his mouth in an effort to suppress the hoots of laughter that were bursting forth. His sides heaved and he held them, trying to alleviate the pain that was almost bending him double.

Slowly the laughter subsided, and, as the bus careered down the steep mountain road, and the lights from the villages drew ever nearer, he slumped down in his seat exhausted, his sides aching and his eyes burning.

The driver was proved to be right about the pick-ups on the way down, or rather the lack of them, the first, not coming until they had sped through three deserted villages.

The fourth also seemed deserted, and the roar from the bus's motor echoed off the walls of its narrow, empty main street, rattling the

116

windows of the adjacent shops and houses. The driver changed gear and applied the brakes, jerking Arthur into an upright position.

They had stopped outside a small chapel and the door of the bus clanked open.

"Good evening Missus Watkins," said the driver, doffing his cap. "Bingo tonight, was it?"

A little old lady, carrying a bundle, wrapped in a tartan shawl, slowly mounted the steps.

"For sure," she replied, using her free hand to pull herself to the top step. "We won the flier on the fifth house, two pounds five and six."

"Well, that's good then, isn't it?" said the driver, sounding well pleased. "I bet your Randolph enjoyed himself, then?"

"Yes, he loves his bingo, does our Randolph," she replied, thumping down into the seat opposite Arthur.

"You orright, Missus Watkins? Sing out when you're settled," the driver called as he let in the clutch.

"Yes, ta, driver," she replied. "Off you go, then."

"Right, hold tight," said the driver and the bus lurched away from the kerb, and roared on into the night.

"You going to Newport, then?" the old lady asked, leaning towards Arthur, a blast of extra strong mint hitting him in the face.

"Yes, that's right," he nodded. "I'm on my way home from Cwmnant."

"Cwmnant," she half shouted. "Nobody in their right mind would want to go to Cwmnant; the place is full of arseholes."

Before Arthur could reply the driver cut in. "Now Missus Watkins, there's no need for that sort of language, is there?"

She ignored him and, having dismissed Cwmnant, continued. "I hear there are quite a few bingo halls in Newport, is that right?"

Arthur bit his lip to check the grin that was starting to pluck at the edges of his mouth. "Yes, quite a few."

"I'll have to treat our Randolph, here, to a trip down to the big city one day. He loves his bingo, does Randolph, don't you love?" She opened the shawl slightly and revealed the contented face of a smug, well-fed tabby cat, which was fast asleep.

Arthur was almost speechless and all that he could think of saying, was, "How did he get the name, Randolph, then?"

"He was my late husband's favourite, see," she replied. "He never missed one of Randolph Scott's pictures, did my Denzil, well, not when he was alive, anyway." She pulled the shawl closer around the cat. "After they buried him, the lads from the colliery brought me a kitten from the lamp store." She nodded at the sleeping bundle. "So, I named him Randolph in memory of my dear departed Denzil, that's right isn't it my precious?" She kissed the bundle fondly.

"Yeah, I'm sure your husband would have loved that," said Arthur, forcing a smile.

The gearbox intervened. "Here's your house, now, Missus Watkins," the driver yelled. "It's the green and white one, isn't it?"

"That's right, driver, the third down from the Co-op."

The bus pulled up with a jerk and the springs groaned, as the door clanked open and the driver got up from his seat to assist the old lady down the steps.

"Take care, now luv," he said, adjusting his cap, while he waited until she had opened the front door of her house, and let herself in.

Smiling, he shook his head and climbed back into the driving seat and let in the clutch. With a howl the bus lurched forward and headed on into the darkness.

"Nice old girl," yelled the driver, double-declutching. "Catches this bus twice a week, for the bingo, like, always has her cat with her." He chuckled and shouted something else, but it was lost as the roar of the motor swallowed it.

"Yeah, lovely," acknowledged Arthur, who, by now had settled back in his seat and was watching the terraced houses flash by through half closed eyes, his chin gradually sinking down onto his chest as he drifted off into a fitful sleep.

Twenty minutes later the brakes squealed, and the bus lurched to a halt, throwing Arthur forward against the back of the seat in front of him.

"Christ almighty!" he yelled as he hit his elbow against the chromium-plated handrail, in front of him.

"Sorry, Butt," yelled the driver. "The bloody lights turned to red just as I was on top of 'em."

Arthur rubbed at the elbow and peered out of the window. "Where are we, anyway?"

"Just coming up to Barrack Hill, on the outskirts of Newport. We'll be in the town centre in a couple of minutes."

The traffic lights turned to green and the bus roared away.

Arthur stretched and rubbed at his tired eyes. He felt awful. His back ached, his mouth was dry as dust and two of his knuckles on his right hand, were swollen and throbbing.

"Drop me off by the castle, will you, driver?" he yelled, combing at his hair, again, using the window as a mirror, as he tried to make himself more presentable, for when he was to get off the bus.

"Yeah, no problem, Butt," the driver yelled.

Two minutes later Arthur stood on the pavement, by the ruins of the town's medieval castle, watching the back of the bus disappear down Dock Street.

"What now?" he muttered, looking around him. "It's too early to go home, besides, if I arrive looking like this, our Mam will give me a right old bollockin'."

Anyway, he inwardly argued. *I'm gagging for a pint.*

Arthur made his way along Canal Terrace, avoiding High Street and Dock Street and all of the other usual haunts, where he knew he was bound to run into some of his mates. Which was the last thing he wanted, right at that moment, for there was no way that he was going to allow himself to be seen in the state that he was in, he'd end up a laughingstock.

Jeez, if they see me looking like this, I'll never live it down. Bloody Dai would have a field day.

So, wisely, he kept to the back streets, following the terraced, back-to-back houses, that sprawled along, running parallel with, and adjacent to, the town's river, whose all-pervading smell of sour mud, salt water and untreated sewage invaded his nostrils, reminding him that it was only a stone's-throw away.

Turning into a dimly lit cobbled lane, Arthur crossed to the other side and looked up at the lane's nameplate, that adorned the side of the first of the terraced houses.

"Granville Place," he muttered, reading the well-worn words on the nineteenth century cast-iron plate. He rubbed at his chin. *Granville Place,* he thought, vaguely recognising the name. *As I recall, there used to be a pub somewhere around here, where Grandad used to drink, from time to time.*

"Yeah, that's right," he said to himself. "I remember coming along here with him for an illicit, under-age pint, a few years ago."

His memory didn't let him down, for, jutting out from the upper story of a building, a hundred yards away, was a weathered pub sign.

He reached it and peered up into the gloom at it. "Of course, the Rose and Crown," he muttered, recognising the public house, as the place where he and his grandfather, and one or two others, had rounded off an evening on the town, getting more than the worse for wear in the process.

He pushed at the drab, green door and entered the pub, whose interior, although not immediately recognisable, looked all too familiar. It could have been any one of a dozen other back-street pubs that were scattered between the river, the railway and the canal. Arthur looked around the pub, which comprised just one small, gloomy room, where dust clung tenaciously to the picture rails and the parchment lampshades.

At the far end of the room two old men sat side-by-side on a dusty, dark-pink settle, the padded seats of which, had seen better days. Each old man appeared to be frozen in time, with pint pots halfway to their open mouths, their dull eyes staring ahead at nothing in particular.

In the middle of the room, four men sat, around an oblong wooden table, engrossed in a game of five-card Don, a pile of coppers in the middle of its scratched surface, comprising the kitty.

Behind the bar, sat the landlord, perched on one buttock on a high stool, reading the Evening Argus. The bored expression on his face showed that it was a slow-news day, as well as the usual slow, pub trading day. He looked up from his paper, surprised to see another customer.

"What's it to be, then?" he said, eyeing Arthur's clothes suspiciously.

Arthur surveyed the pumps. "I'll try a pint of Hobby Horse, ta."

The barman pulled the pump-handle with a long, easy stroke that came from years of drawing pints.

"There you go," he said, putting the brimming glass on the bar. "That'll be eleven pence, ta."

Arthur slid a shilling across the bar and picked up the glass and took a long, slow swallow, before letting out a sigh of relief.

"Jeez, that's a cracking pint, that is," he said, wiping his hand across his lips. "I'll have to call in here more often, for sure."

"This is your first time in here, then?" The barman folded the newspaper and put it away, under the bar.

"I'm not sure," Arthur took another long swallow. "Although I've got an idea that I came in here with my grandfather a few years ago."

He decided to play it cagey, just in case there had been a bit of bother that night, which he may have forgotten.

"Who would that be, then?" asked the barman.

Arthur took out a cigarette and lit up. "Jack Baxter," he said, blowing smoke at the ceiling. "Lives the other side of the canal, down by the railway, I expect you've heard of him, most people have."

"Jack Baxter," the barman snorted. "Have I heard of him, be buggered." He poured himself a half of Hobbyhorse, sat back on the stool and sipped at it. "Have I heard of the old sod? Christ! We worked together at Lysaght's steel works for years, on the cold-rolls." He took another sip. "Mind you, I haven't seen old Jack for a few years, now, I bet he's well into his sixties, for sure."

"Sixty-six, last May." Arthur finished off the rest of his beer and smacked his lips. "I'll try another pint of that Hobbyhorse, that was a tasty pint, orright."

"On me, this time, Lad," said the barman pulling the pint. "If you're Jack bloody Baxter's grandson then you deserve a pint." He gave a huge guffaw and looked around the room for support.

The sudden noise brought to life one of the old men at the far end of the room, breaking his reverie. He got up unsteadily and made his way towards the bar, the empty pint pot shaking in his hand.

A chair scraped back and one of the Don players stood up. "It's my shout, same again, is it, lads?" They all nodded.

Arthur stood up. "Where's the Gent's, then?"

"Out the back, through that door there," said the barman pointing at a door in the corner, next to the dartboard.

"Cheers," said Arthur and he left the bar and crossed the room, passing the old man and the Don-player as they arrived at the bar together.

"Bloody Nora," complained the barman. "I've barely sat down, when, suddenly I've got a bloody rush on my hands."

"Barely sat down, my arse!" The old man placed the empty pint pot on the bar, and it played a quiet tattoo on its smeared surface.

"You've been reading that sodding Argus for the last half hour, ain't that right, Arnold?"

The card-player nodded. "Yeah, bloody right you're there, Tom." He rapped a half crown on the bar. "Let's have four pints of whoosh and be sharpish about it, OK? There's five bob to be won in that kitty before shut tap."

The barman gave him a long, hard look then broke into a grin.

"All in good time, all in good time, young Tom here is before you, so hold your horses." He pulled a pint and handed it to the old man. "There you go, you old sod, pint of George's, that's right, ain't it?"

"Yeah, you cheeky, young bugger," said the old man pocketing his change. "Any more of your lip and I'll get old Carney to come over and sort you out." He nodded towards the other old man, who was staring at nothing in particular, a wry grin on his face.

Arthur placed his pint glass down on a table by the door next to the dartboard. He opened the door and stepped outside into the gloom of the backyard of the pub.

"Christ! I might as well be back up the bloody valleys, at Cwmnant," he muttered, peering across the yard into the gloom, where a small, brick building was silhouetted against the skyline. Judging by the appalling stench that came from its direction, Arthur took it to be the lavatory.

He screwed up his nose in disgust. "Bugger that for a ball of chalk, this'll do right here," he muttered, and he randomly urinated into the darkness.

A light from the bedroom of the house next door came on and the small yard was suddenly semi illuminated, highlighting the result of his bladder emptying.

"Oh bloody-hell!" he said, with dismay and quickly zipped up his trousers fly and hurried back into the pub. He closed the door quietly behind him and entered the bar, hoping that the next person to go into the yard wouldn't notice the dripping saddle and the brimming saddlebag of the old black Humber bicycle, that leaned against a barrel.

Arthur collected his pint and headed for a pink-velour settle that was the twin of the one that housed the two old men. He sat down with a sigh and took another long pull at his drink.

"What a bloody day this has been," he muttered, rubbing his hand across his face as tiredness crept over him. He took out a cigarette, lit it and yawned as he watched the smoke curl upwards. A hush had descended upon the room.

The two old men in the corner had resumed their frozen positions. The card-players stared silently at the table-top before them; each engrossed in every turn of the cards.

The barman stared past the grimy curtains at the darkened street that lay beyond the smeared windowpanes, wishing he were somewhere else.

Arthur stared without seeing; he was back in Cwmnant reliving the events of that evening, memory piling upon memory until the whole episode became a jumbled mess. He pictured an old lady chasing Randolph Scott down a back alley and on out into a walled square, in the centre of which stood an old grey and red bus, rock 'n' roll emanating from its interior. Thelma stood on top of a Standard Vanguard, hands on hips, her breasts huge, like those on a saucy seaside postcard. She was looking up at the village-clock, a huge maniacal grin upon her face, as she viewed the hapless Jerry Jenkins, who was hanging from the clock-hands by his shirttail, hammer in hand, ready to strike at more wagon wheels …

"Last orders now, Gents', if you please," shouted the barman, the relief in his voice, palpable, as it broke through the room's wall of silence, ricocheting off the drab walls and the dusty light fittings.

So strident was his call that it caused both of the old men, in the corner, to look up in trepidation and the card-players to hurriedly scrape back their chairs in an effort to get a last beer in. It also ended Arthur's reverie.

He awoke and sat up with a lurch, the cigarette had almost burned down to the fingers that still gripped the handle of his glass. Arthur rubbed his hand over his face and looked at his watch, it was twenty past ten. He picked up his beer and finished it with one long swallow, before slowly getting to his feet and taking the empty glass to the bar.

"Same again, is it?" the barman asked.

"No, ta, I'm knackered, me," said Arthur, suppressing a yawn. "I'm off home."

"Well, all the best, lad," said the barman. "Say hello to Jack for me, will you?"

Arthur turned and waved. "Yeah, I will that, cheers now."

He closed the door behind him and slowly made his way towards the distant lights of the main road to the docks, leaving the gloomy little lane behind.

God! I'm tired, I'll be glad to get into bed and forget about tonight, that's for sure.

Twenty minutes later he flung his ruined clothes onto the bedroom chair and crawled into bed exhausted. Within seconds of his head touching the pillow he was asleep.

Chapter Sixteen
Mariners

During the following weeks, the episode in Cwnant, involving Jerry Jenkins, gradually faded from Arthur's thoughts, being replaced by the more pressing issues of — which team Newport County had been drawn against in the second round of the FA Cup, and which horse was going to win the Cambridgeshire Handicap.

Thelma too, had disappeared from the scene, having, according to the licensee of the King Billy, found other bar work nearer to home.

This suited Arthur just fine and it saved him much explaining to Dai and the others.

A week of afternoons, followed by a week on the night shift also helped, as it kept Arthur away from his usual haunts and spared him an inquisition from the members of the Western Movie Club.

So, when he did go back to the King Billy, it came as no great surprise, that little was made of his Cwmnant jaunt, the episode, having quickly faded from minds of the regulars, being replaced, by other more pressing topics of conversation.

On the Monday morning of the first week that Arthur was back working the morning shift, following the Cwmnant episode, there was a lull in the passing of trains that allowed him to prepare the brewing up of his mid-morning cup of tea.

As he poured out the steaming, orange brew, he was reminded of the misshapen little wagon-examiner, whose unerring appearance always seemed to coincide with the pouring of the tea.

Arthur cocked his ear, expecting to hear the sound of hammer on wheels, but all remained silent, there was no ringing of steel hitting steel that morning, and, from time to time, during the shift, he would survey the sidings for the gnome like figure of Jerry, but, without success, for, unknown to Arthur, that fateful night at Cwmnant, was to be the last time that he was ever to set eyes on Jerry Jenkins again.

In fact, it was to be another three months, before he was reminded of Jerry Jenkins and the Cwmnant affair.

Arthur sat on the hard, ex GWR bench reading the daily paper. The mid-morning autumn sun filtered through the signal-box windows and reflected off the gleaming levers and the polished linoleum floor.

As usual, Arthur started with the sports news, on the back page, so it was nearly half an hour before he got to the front page and its banner headline:

RISCA MAN CHARGED WITH MURDER.

Arthur read the article in disbelief. The Monmouthshire police force had apparently arrested a Risca man, one, Jellicoe Jenkins, for the murder of a second hand goods dealer, William Evans, who, it appeared, had been bludgeoned to death in his shop, in Risca High Street, by a man wielding a blunt instrument, literally, for it turned out that the instrument in question, was a second hand Stratocaster guitar. The attack had taken place at around about noon, when the shop was at its busiest, and so most of its shoppers had witnessed Jellicoe running from the shop, wild-eyed, in a state of panic.

Therefore, identification of the accused, proved to be pretty much a straightforward affair; each witness remembering the Max Wall hairstyle and the dozens of badges that adorned the lapels of the fleeing man's railway jacket. Fingerprints, matching those of the arrested man, had been found on the neck of the guitar. It appeared to be an open and shut case.

Arthur was staggered. He was shell-shocked, and for the remainder of the shift, he went about his work on autopilot.

It was not until the following Thursday, when he was at the marshalling yard collecting his pay, that he got the full story from a reluctant Dinky Phillips, the yard's head shunter.

"Orright, Arth'"? yelled Dinky, as he cycled past, deftly negotiating a sidings hand point.

"Hey! Dinky," Arthur called after him. "Hang on a minute."

Dinky pulled up sharply, the skidding tyres sending ash flying from the path against the wheels of a nearby, empty cattle wagon. He dismounted and waited for Arthur to catch him up.

"What's up, then, Arth'? What are you after now?" he asked, suspiciously.

Arthur shook his head. "Nothing, honest, just a bit of info, that's all." He grinned. "Don't worry, you old bugger, I'm not after your bloody money," said Arthur digging the head shunter playfully in the ribs with an elbow.

"Go on, then, ask away," Dinky said, eyeing Arthur suspiciously.

"Is that right what I've been hearing about Jerry Jenkins?" Arthur asked. "Word has it that he's been had up for murder?"

Dinky slowly removed his cap and scratched at a bald spot. "Yeah, that's right, poor sod," he replied with feeling.

"According to the paper, his name was Jellicoe. How come? I always called him Jerry," said Arthur quizzically.

Dinky's face had taken on a set expression. "No, he never liked the name Jellicoe, on account of his father and that," Dinky said as a matter of fact, and made to get back on his bike.

"Hang on Dink, on account of his father and what?"

Dinky turned back reluctantly and faced Arthur. "Well, it was his father, Nuffield who gave him the name Jellicoe, see. Nuffield was very keen on things nautical, was Nuffield, so he named him after the famous Admiral, Jellicoe."

"Nuffield, bloody Nuffield," snorted Arthur, giving a hoot of laughter. "What sort of name is that for Christ's sake?"

Dinky looked slightly miffed. "There's no need to laugh, I see nothing wrong with the name Nuffield, just because it sounds a bit posh don't mean to say that there's anything wrong with it." He blew his nose on a khaki handkerchief and examined the contents. "As a matter of fact I quite like a posh name, myself, my Aunty Gladys once had a macaw named Dexter, that was posh, but I liked it, Butt." He thrust his chin out belligerently, defying Arthur to contradict him.

Arthur looked shame-faced. "Yeah, you're right there, Dink'," he conceded, slightly taken aback by the head shunter's sudden outburst. He assumed a straight face. "Sorry I didn't mean nothing by it, except, it just struck me as being a bit unusual, that's all."

"Yeah, well," replied Dinky, somewhat mollified. "Nuffield was a bit of an unusual sort of person," he said mysteriously.

"Well, why Jerry, and not Jellicoe? Didn't he share his father's liking for things nautical, then?" Arthur asked, still mystified.

"You must be bloody joking," barked Dinky angrily. "That Nuffield was a right bastard."

"How come?" asked Arthur.

"He only up and left the mother, just six months after baby Jellicoe was born, didn't he?" Dinky snarled.

"What happened then, Dink'," asked Arthur. "How come Nuffield buggered off, then?"

Dinky cocked his leg back over the crossbar, his face set.

"He ran off to Droitwich with an Able Seaman named Brendan, and has never been heard of from that day to this, so now you bloody well know, don't you," he said through gritted teeth and rode off down the siding, ringing his bell furiously at an approaching innocent shunter.

Arthur stared after him open-mouthed, not knowing whether to laugh or to cry.

Chapter Seventeen
Observations

The old man pursed his lips and stared off into the distance. *I wonder what ever happened to that poor sod, Jerry?*

He removed the empty pipe from between his teeth, and examined the interior of the bowl, probing the depths with his little finger. He withdrew it and inspected the charcoal-stained digit, declaring to himself. "The poor bastard ended up getting life, didn't he?"

He tapped the pipe bowl on the heel of his palm, before returning the pipe to the corner of his mouth, his teeth clamping shut on the stem.

He's probably out by now and has taken up bell ringing or something equally stupid, he concluded, dismissing Jerry.

His shifted his gaze, from where, the down main railway line had once been, back to the sprawling mass of semi-detached houses that lay beyond the supermarket; the unfortunate wheel tapper now consigned to his mind's recycled bin.

A series of clouds scudded across the valley, passing in front of the sun, their shadows, racing over the Graig, turning the craggy hill's summer countenance to a sombre grey.

The change that had come over the valley was so rapid and dramatic, that for a brief moment one could have easily mistaken it for winter.

Although the moment was fleeting, and the hill soon became bright with summer sun again, the sudden darkening of the sky had struck a chord deep within his memory, and in a trice, he had resurrected another episode from the annals of his youth.

That month there had been ten days of continuous hard frosts and bitter, clinging fogs. The old man could clearly remember, as a youth, looking out of the signal-box window and seeing the final traces of the early morning fog on the point of dispersing, revealing a heavy covering of frost, that was spread out as far as the eye could see, revealing the landscape as a glistening, unreal world, where everything sparkled.

Even the hard-core beneath the tracks had been transformed into twinkling chunks of white marble, and the normally blackened, sleepers gleamed like iced cake, while Marquisette encrusted signal posts glittered in the weak winter sunlight.

The whole twinkling scene reminded him of the Christmas grotto in the toy department, of Unwins and Isaac in Griffin Street, which beguiled the local children of Newport from early November, through to the New Year.

He smugly surveyed the wintry scene from within his glass cocoon, his back to the pot-bellied stove, revelling in the heat that played upon the backside of his heavy serge British Railways trousers, the polished linoleum floor mirroring the stove's flickering flames.

He yawned and stretched. *No doubt, granddad will have something to say about the weather, in the Legion tonight,* he thought.

He was later to be proven right.

That evening Arthur sat in the British Legion watching his grandfather, whose bright-blue, intelligent eyes, set in a weather-beaten, pugnacious face, closely studied his audience, who sat on the other side of the blue-grey smoke that issued from the Capstan full-strength cigarette that was clamped in a jaw set ready for an argument.

"The bloody bronchitis patch, that's what it is," Granddad said, stabbing a finger in the direction of Cedric, Dai and Arthur, "and it don't come by accident either." He cleared his throat and took a swallow of the brown ale and bitter mix and continued his observations. "You can bet your boots that it was sent to vex us by that great Architect in the sky," he pointed towards the nicotine stained ceiling and a dozen pairs of eyes looked upwards.

"Just like those plagues in the Bible," he pointed out.

Ernie Podmore's gaze left the ceiling and he looked back down at his dominoes.

"Is that the same Architect who designed the new bogs in Bridge Street?" he said from a nearby table, letting out a huge guffaw.

Granddad's eyes narrowed and he looked menacingly through the blue haze towards Ernie Podmore's table, but Ernie had turned back to his opponent and was leaning menacingly towards him, domino raised in dramatic fashion.

"Blank three, yer bugger," he yelled, his hairy nostrils flaring. "Get out of that then, our Merv."

Mervyn, his opponent, wiped the lenses of his spectacles on his sleeve and hooked the wire frames back around his ears.

"I knew you had that friggin' blank three," he complained.

Ernie Podmore grinned.

Dai, Arthur and Cedric brought their attention back from the ceiling and looked expectantly across the table for more of granddad's homespun philosophy.

Arthur's grandfather made a mental note that he owed Ernie, bloody Podmore one, and resumed his diatribe. "Have you noticed, it's always this time of year?" he continued, looking around for confirmation, "that, no sooner have you got 'round to putting the Christmas trimmings back under the stairs for another year, when wham! Down comes the bloody fog, and as sure as eggs, it'll be in that gap that's between the New Year and the Grand National. Just when a man needs a dose of horse racing, and the telling thoughts of Raymond Glendenning along with the soccer results on the wireless on Saturday afternoons, in order to stimulate the old grey matter."

He took a drag on his cigarette and picked a shred of tobacco from his lower lip. "But what happens? The bloody weather puts the mockers on everything, don't it?" He looked around the table again and took in the approving nods. "It's always the bloody same," he continued, before anybody else could get a word in. "Here we are, just sorting ourselves out, getting over Christmas, and suddenly its upon us, the bloody frost and fog, and what do we get for our bloody troubles?" His bushy eyebrows were raised. "Cancelled football matches, half-empty pubs, and packed-surgeries, that's what! You'd think there was some unwritten law against enjoying yourself." He stopped and took a huge slurp from his pint pot, peering over the top of his mug, as he judged the reaction of his audience, before continuing.

"Have you noticed how people don't walk normally, this time of year?" He wiped his lips on his sleeve. "Everyone always seems bent-up as they shuffle along, with misery in their eyes and plumes of steam issuing from their balaclavas."

The assembled gathering burst into laughter, even Ernie Podmore and Mervyn managed a grin, their concentration lapsing momentarily from their game of dominoes.

Cedric had a coughing fit.

Arthur's grandfather kept a straight face but was well pleased with the response to his wintry observations.

"It's my round," he said getting up from the table. "What'll it be lads?"

Chapter Eighteen
Marriage

Arthur shifted the empty briar to the other side of his mouth. *The old Sod was right,* he thought. *That's just how it used to be at that time of year, that's if you were forced to go shopping with the wife.* He shook his head, remembering the days when cars were few and far between, and the concept of the supermarket, and out of town shopping was still a thing of the future. *In those days,* he thought, *most people walked to their local shops to do their shopping, and during a cold snap, there wouldn't be a smiling male face to be seen, just an array of gloomy husbands, laden down with the week's purchases, silently trailing along behind purposeful wives, as they headed home for the delightful prospect of baked beans on toast and Cliff Michelmore on the box.*

The old man stared into the distance, his teeth still clamped onto the pipe stem; the smile had left his face.

He had finally got around to remembering and acknowledging, Avril, his wife.

Not that there is that much to remember, he confessed to himself.

It was the usual teenage story. They had met at a local dancehall, went steady for about a year, and finally married. Within six months of marrying they had moved to Rogerstown, in order to be nearer to where Arthur worked. Here, they rented a little stone-built cottage, which stood near the top of, the steep and twisty, Wern Lane, which overlooked the Village.

Although the marriage had managed to last for six years, he remembered, *it had started to go sour twelve months or so later, prior to its breakup.* He scratched at his silvery hair. *What happened? We seemed all right for a while, then, it all started to fall apart.* He rubbed a hand across his face. *Working shifts didn't help, Avril hated me being on night duty. She never liked being on her own in the cottage at night. It was so quiet, there was not that constant background noise of railways and docks that she had grown up with and had become used to hearing. Every creak of the old cottage, the wind in the trees, the occasional hoot of the owls in the churchyard, you name it, it kept waking her. Our Avril could never get used to the silence.*

We never had any kids, either, he added, pulling at an ear lobe and grimacing. Y*eah, well, that was down to me, Avril wanted a nip, but somehow, I couldn't see me as a father, so, we never had any. It's no wonder she was plagued with eczema and the like.*

He shrugged angrily. *Who are you bloody kidding, you old bastard, there was only one reason for Avril leaving you, that was your bloody womanising, gambling and boozing, no more, no less.*

Now, standing there, mulling it all over, some forty or so years later, it all seemed so totally unreal. It could have been another husband and wife that he and himself were debating.

Man and wife! he thought. *Christ! More like boy and wife, jeez! What was I, twenty-three?* He shook his head. *Twenty-three in the trousers, maybe, but more like fifteen in the head, marriage was the last thing, that I needed at that age. What I needed was a good kick up the arse, that's for sure.*

He seemed to remember that his grandfather had echoed similar sorts of sentiments at the time.

"You need your head seeing to, you bloody Berk," his grandfather barked over a pint of black and tan. "There's you still crapping yellow and you go and propose marriage to some little bloody girl who's making your shirt stir, dear God." He took another swig from his pint pot.

Cedric nodded in agreement, his medals clinking. "That's the trouble with you bloody young 'uns, you think you bloody well know it all, but you don't know your arse from your bloody elbow."

As it turned out, and, as was usually the case in those days, granddad and Cedric's warnings proved to be the case. Arthur hadn't known his arse from his elbow, and it was only a matter of time before things began to go downhill. Arthur found himself becoming increasingly disenchanted with his lot, and the allure of the marital bed became less and less attractive as Avril became more and more prone to minor ailments.

The old man remembered how he, as a young man, had sat on the edge of the bed, half-awake, absent-mindedly rubbing at the stubble on his chin, half trying to get himself motivated enough to begin preparations for another morning shift. Yawning, he got slowly to his feet and padded across the room towards his shirt and trousers, which were draped across the basket chair, which stood in the corner of the small bedroom. He pulled at the cord of his striped, pyjama bottoms, with one hand, and, at the same time, began lifting the jacket over his head with the other.

Avril lay there, oblivious, pink plastic hair curlers poking out from under the satin-edged bed sheet that half covered her face.

He looked down at her, through the gap between the top two buttons of his pyjama jacket, wondering how the snoring heap in front of him had once been the pert-nosed, dark-eyed girl, who had single-handedly managed to take his mind off soccer and beer during those pre-marital days of hot, steamy passion in Bellevue Park, or the back row of the Coliseum. In fact, any of the local hideaways that was suitably placed for teenage fumblings of a sexual nature, would be the order-of-the-day.

Is it only six years, he thought. *Jeez, it already feels more like a bloody life sentence?*

Fate then intervened, banishing his bitter, unforgiving thoughts as his pyjama trousers curled down around his ankles, sending him sprawling onto the bedroom floor. He got up cursing, and flung the striped trousers across the room, then, he picked up the heavy pair of serge, British Railway trousers from the basket chair and, balancing on one leg, began the battle of putting them on in the semi-light of the bedroom. The contest was short-lived, the trousers won.

He fell over twice more, banged his shins on the dressing table and stubbed his toe on the wardrobe before limping off to the bathroom, mouthing obscenities.

Avril hadn't stirred, but a half smile crinkled the cheeks of her hidden face.

The old man shook his head, baffled by the unreasonableness and the selfishness that had motivated his youth.

"Little wonder, that the marriage began to founder," he muttered, just as his grandfather had inferred that it would. He nodded imperceptibly, admitting to himself, that in those days, his grandfather never seemed to be too far off the mark with his observations. *He was spot on as far as my marriage to Avril was concerned,* he conceded.

A small grin replaced the fixed look to his face, as his memory banks began reprising the many other occasions when his grandfather would have been wiser to keep his outspoken comments to himself. Occasions, when trouble was not only likely, but also inevitable.

Arthur removed the unlit pipe from his mouth and pictured his grandfather, whose chin would be pugnaciously thrust out as he waylaid a total stranger, saying, in his best Presbyterian voice.

"There's only one um, Butt."

As sure as eggs are eggs, the luckless stranger would promptly fall into granddad's trap and would innocently respond.

"What's that then?"

"Friggin' stuff um!" granddad would bellow at the unfortunate, and then burst into fits of drunken laughter, as another scalp was added to his belt.

On the whole he was a lucky old sod. Arthur acknowledged, for, most of granddad's victims, would simply humour him with a nod and a smile, before quickly moving away. There were always one or two oddballs, who would see the funny side of his grandfather's macabre humour and would share in his laughter.

More often than not, a few of his more sensible victims, however, would find his humour about as funny as a wet November Thursday in Porthcawl, and then trouble was never too far away.

My stag night proved no different. Arthur recalled.

Chapter Nineteen
Conflict

In every pub that the stag party had visited that night, granddad had caught a victim, and had also come very close, in the process, to getting a fist in the dentures on more than one occasion.

Their final pub visit was to the Cobbler's Awl in High Street. It was their sixth pub call of the evening, and Arthur's grandfather was in full flow.

Downing his tenth pint of IPA, he wiped his mouth on the sleeve of his jacket and belched loudly

Turning to Arthur, he then said, "You'll soon find," he tapped the side of his nose knowingly, "that on a cold night, in marriage, the best thing in all the world is a handful of breast, and a lapful of bum."

He took another swig at his pint and nodded across the room to a thin, weasel-faced man who had snuff-stained nostrils and a Jack Russell bitch lying across the polished toe caps of his brown boots.

"Ain't that right, Teddy?" granddad shouted across to him. "What I just said?"

Teddy blew his nose in a khaki handkerchief and nodded. "Aye you're right there, lad, although our Eunice here," he pointed to the sleeping Jack Russell bitch, "she's a damn sight warmer than any soddin' woman when it gets a bit parky, and less bloody trouble, come to think of it. That's right isn't it my lovely?" He bent and patted the dog on the ribs.

The dog immediately rolled over onto its back and broke wind.

Granddad screwed up his face in mock disgust. "I'm almost on your side there, Teddy, women do make life in bed unbearable. What with their curlers and sharp elbows and thick socks, but I'd settle for that every time than have to put up with a Jack Russell that farts in her sleep."

The assembled drinkers burst into drunken laughter.

"Not a patch on Bronwyn Pugh, though," said Cedric, who had been sitting, quietly listening near the dartboard. He gazed down at the contents of his pint pot, as though it were a crystal ball. "She was a cracker and no mistake; barmaid in the Duck and Fiddle in Risca," he reminisced, a fond look on his face. "D'yer know, the size of her knockers would turn a man's legs to jelly," he licked his lips at the thought. "You talk about parky nights, she'd keep you warm, all right. She was a big girl, had nipples like walnuts." He sniggered into his muffler and his medals jingled.

The ginger-haired barmaid, with the wart on her chin, cackled with delight as she wiped at the bar top, her pendant earrings swinging like miniature trapezes.

"We don't want any of that filth here, Cedric," said Arthur's grandfather, remonstrating, not too happy with having had his thunder stolen.

He swayed as he attempted to rise to his full height of five feet five. "This young 'un is about to sample the delights of the bridal path and I don't want any ex-corporal from the bloody, South Wales bloody borderers coming in here spreading barrack-room filth."

Cedric lurched indignantly to his feet. His face puce with rage. His medals jingling. "I'll give you filth, you old sod," he shouted, shaking his fist in granddad's direction. "Who was it that brought up the question of bums and tits in the first place?"

Arthur's grandfather advanced menacingly towards Cedric, his fists clenching and unclenching.

"You ignorant old Git," he fumed. "Anyone with a bit of common knows that breast and bum can be found in any dictionary, see. They're a well-known phrase or saying, they are."

"Who are you calling ignorant? You short-arsed little Bastard," shouted Cedric. His eyes bulging with fury. "The only books you've ever read are your ration book and your bloody pension book."

Arthur's grandfather took a step towards Cedric, his fists clenched ready to do battle.

Incandescent with fury, Cedric launched himself across the snug at the advancing granddad, fists clenched, arms swinging.

Arthur's grandfather went into a defensive crouch, one hand up, protecting his chin, the other forming a fist, poised ready to counterattack. He led with a tentative probe then followed on quickly with a wild swing of the arm towards the advancing old man.

The charging Cedric's foot caught the leg of a cast-iron table and he went sprawling headlong into the side of the bar.

Granddad's wild swing missed the diving Cedric and its momentum hurled him into the fruit machine, sending glasses toppling and pints spilling.

Confusion reigned.

Eunice, the Jack Russell bitch, peed on the carpet and yapped excitedly at the ensuing melee.

Arthur and Dai went to the rescue of the two crumpled old men, while the barmaid shook the handset of the telephone at them and threatened to call the Police, if they didn't leave that very minute.

Discretion being the better part of valour, they decided that vacating the Cobbler's Awl was the wisest thing, given the circumstances.

Arthur, Dai and the two Cox boys manhandled the two old men out of the pub, literally, half-dragging them out through the front door and on up the road until they had reached a nearby bus stop, where it took all of their combined efforts to keep the two drunken old men apart until a bus arrived.

Arthur and Dai bundled granddad inside the bus and sat him down. The Cox brothers followed on behind along the lurching aisle and manhandled Cedric into another seat, well out of the reach of the cursing granddad, where he sat down with a thump, a faraway look in his eyes, and a large, livid lump on the side of his head.

Arthur's grandfather too, was not without the signs of battle, on his journey to his seat, he walked with a pronounced limp, carried his arm stiffly across his chest, Napoleon style, and repeatedly sang, in between obscenities, the first line of 'smoke gets in your eyes.'

By the time they had reached their stop both old men appeared to have forgotten their differences and had become strangely docile, so much so, that removing them from the bus proved relatively easy for Arthur and Dai and the Cox brothers, who, having got them off the bus at Chapel Terrace, guided them down the street towards their respective houses.

Cedric's house was their first call, and as they approached it, the old man with the clinking medals stopped and saluted a gnarled, old mongrel that was cocking its leg against a dustbin.

Ronnie Cox supported Cedric whilst his brother Danny, unlocked the front door with a key that was linked to Cedric's waistcoat by a long chain.

Between them they carried the old man upstairs, took off his topcoat and jacket and lifted him onto the bed. His snores followed them across the room as they tiptoed out.

Meanwhile, oblivious to all around him, Arthur's grandfather muttered.

"Where're are my chips?" and promptly buckled at the knees.

Arthur and Dai came to his rescue and propped him up against the wall, with Dai, holding him steady, while Arthur unlocked the front door of the terraced house. They manhandled the old man inside, along the passageway and into the front room, where they laid him down on the sofa. He was asleep before they had quietly closed the front door behind them.

"What now?" asked Arthur.

"I dunno," shrugged Dai. "What time is it, anyway?"

Arthur looked at his watch. "Quarter past ten, if we shift our arses, we can get a pint in the Boilermakers." He looked back up the long-terraced street. "What's keeping Ronnie and Danny?"

"Here they are, now," said Dai, pointing to the two brothers, who were making their way along the street towards them.

Arthur crossed the road and headed towards the railway. "C'mon, then, let's go," he called. "We're off to the Boilermakers. Are you two coming?"

"Not for me," Danny Cox called back. "I'm on early shift tomorrow. I can't afford another late clock this week, the gaffer will have my balls for breakfast if I'm late again."

His brother Ronnie nodded in agreement. "Yeah, me too," he shouted. "I'm off home, me."

"See you at the wedding on Saturday, then?" Arthur called back over his shoulder as he caught up with Dai, who was mounting the bridge steps two at a time.

The Cox brothers waved back, turned a corner and disappeared into Canal Terrace.

Chapter Twenty
Skittled

Dai and Arthur quickly crossed the bridge and were soon hurrying along the towpath of the canal, which ran parallel with the railway line.

In double quick time they had reached the place where a gap in the railings provided them with a short cut into Evan's Lane and the nearby club. They squeezed through the gap and trotted down the cobbled lane, reaching the main entrance of the Boilermakers Club in double quick time.

Arthur and Dai sauntered down the main passage towards the old man guarding the door, Eric Watkins, who acknowledged them with a wave of his hand as he slurped the remaining beer from a pint pot, before placing the empty glass on the table, in front of him, belching and then wiping his lips on his sleeve.

"You two have cut it a bit fine, ain't you?" He grinned, revealing several missing teeth. "You're a bit late, Lads, but I'll turn a blind eye this time, seeing as you've been on the piss, by the look of it."

"Yeah, that's right," said Dai. "It's Arthur's stag night so we thought we'd finish it off with a last pint in the Boilermakers, ain't that right Arth'?" He winked and moved his fist back and forth like a piston. "There may be some hokey-pokey about."

"You won't find much in there," said Eric indicating towards the bar with his thumb. "There's a dart match going on."

"Never know your luck," Arthur called back, pushing open the door to the smoke room, and walking towards the bar. "What're having Dai?"

Black and tan," said Dai, heading for the Gents'. "I've got to have a slash, first, though."

Arthur ordered two black and tans and took a cigarette out of a packet and lit up. He blew a stream of smoke at the ceiling and turned to survey the crowded room. A group of drinkers were gathered in the far corner, intently watching a large player with heavily tattooed arms taking aim at the dartboard.

Arthur's gaze left the dartboard and his eyes lighted on a tall, leggy blonde, who was at the back of the room playing table skittles alone. As she bent over the skittle board, the outline of her pants clearly showed through the tight, white dress that clung to her hips.

Arthur took a long swig from the stout mix and studied the blonde's legs from over the rim of his glass, watching her teeter precariously on pink high-heeled shoes.

Dai arrived back and picked up his pint. Arthur tossed him a cigarette.

"Cheers Arth'," Dai said, lighting up and taking a drag on his cigarette. He then had a huge swig from his glass, belched loudly and looked around the room, before turning back to the bar and taking another long pull at his pint.

"C'mon get it down your neck Butt, we've got a lot of catching up to do on account of those two mad old bastards and their bloody argument, slowing us up."

Dai emptied his glass with a final long gulp and put it on the bar. "Two black and tans, Taff," he called to the barman, who was absorbed in the process of rolling himself a cigarette.

Satisfied with its shape and thickness, the barman nipped off some straggling tobacco from the finished cigarette, snapped shut his tobacco tin and stuck the misshapen cigarette into the corner of his mouth and lit up.

"Coming up lads," he said from within a cloud of blue smoke.

Dai paid for the drinks and turned back to the room.

"There's Rosie Williams and Beryl Barton over in the corner," he said indicating with a nod of his head. "Why don't we go and pay our respects Arth'?" he said lasciviously, smoothing a hand over the oily hair at the back of his head.

"Yeah, go on over," said Arthur over his shoulder. "I'll be with you in a sec'. I just want to take a quick look at the darts."

Dai nodded and made his way across the room towards the two girls while Arthur nonchalantly threaded his way through the crowd of drinkers towards the skittle table and the leggy Blonde.

He stood silently besides her, watching the ball, on its string, as it swung around the central pole, in ever decreasing circles, before scattering most of the miniature skittles.

"Is this a match, or can anyone play?" Arthur asked casually, looking at the fallen skittles.

She half turned. "No, just messing about really, having a bit of a laugh, see?" She gave a nasal whinny and began replacing the fallen skittles into their upright positions on the board. As she leaned forward to steady the swinging ball, Arthur studied her profile, sizing up the tall, big-boned girl, and the long, blonde hair that framed her pale face and neck, before cascading down over her shoulders.

"Is this your regular?" she asked, not looking up as she sent the ball-on-the-string back on its travels, circling the miniature skittles.

"Yeah, that's right," replied Arthur, looking across the room towards Dai, trying to feign disinterest. He flicked cigarette ash at the floor and took a gulp from his glass.

She straightened up and turned to face him. "We're down from the Cwmbran Pioneer Club for the darts match, see."

"Who's we, then, you and the girls?" he indicated with a thumb.

"Yeah, that's right, and the boys," she said pointing across to the darts players. Arthur looked back, across, at the darts match that was in progress, taking another gulp from his glass before turning back to her.

"What's the score, then? Christ almigh...!" he spluttered, his words turning into a choking cough and his face puce, his shoulders heaving as he gasped for air.

The leggy blonde tried to help him with his predicament by slapping his back, concern showing on her face.

Arthur slumped onto the nearest seat and mopped at the stout-mix that had spread across his jacket and trousers in a dark stain, his eyes watering profusely and his throat, feeling as though it was on fire.

Gradually his coughing began to ease and he bent forward in his chair dabbing at his streaming eyes and his running nose.

"Oy! Why don't you piss off and go and cough somewhere else, Butt?" came an angry voice from the direction of the dartboard.

Arthur looked, through misty eyes, in the direction of the noisy complainant, the tattooed darts player, who was glaring at him from across the room.

"Sorry Taff," croaked Arthur, holding his hands up, indicating an apology. "My beer went down the wrong way."

"Yeah well, my sodding arrow just bloody well went the wrong, bloody way, thanks to you, so do yourself a favour, Butt, go cough somewhere else, is it?"

Arthur held up his hands, again, nodding an affirmative in the dart-player's direction, who, then turned his attention back to the match, muttering obscenities.

Arthur's breathing began to normalise, and he took a swig at the remains of the stout in his glass and sat back panting.

"Bloody hells bells, I'd thought I'd had it, then," he croaked. "I couldn't bloody breathe, for a minute there, I thought I was going to pass out." He blew his nose again and dabbed at his eyes. "I need another pint," he said, surveying his empty glass. "How about you?" He tried not to stare at the false eye, and at the gold, false front tooth that had been the cause of his choking fit. "Can I get you a drink?"

"A Babycham would be great, ta," she smiled, again revealing the gold front tooth, while the glass eye fixed him with a blank stare.

Arthur went to the bar and ordered drinks for the blonde and himself, the fumes from the night's drinking filling his head, as he leaned unsteadily against the bar.

"Jeez," he muttered. "Just my bloody luck, from the back she looks like a film star, from the front she's a bloody horror story." He rubbed at his sore throat. *Seeing that glass eye, nearly did it for me, a bit of warning might have helped, especially with me with a mouth full of black and tan.*

He veered unsteadily back towards the skittle table. "Cheers," he half croaked, his voice still not fully recovered, as he put down the glasses, trying desperately not to look at her false eye. "Thanks for helping me back there," he said gratefully.

"That's orright," she whinnied. "Any time, man, can't stand by and see a man choking, can you?" She sipped demurely at her Babycham; her eyelashes fluttering like a silent-movie vamp.

Arthur took a sip from his glass and swayed. He looked at his watch and glanced across the room, remembering his supposed assignation with Dai and the girls, but there was no sign of him. *Probably gone for a slash*, Arthur figured, dismissing Dai's absence.

He turned back to the blonde. "I'm Arthur," he said, extending his hand.

She held his hand and shook it. "Hya, I'm Pauline." She let go his hand and took a sip from her glass. "Thanks for the drink, it's very nice of you."

"Any time," slurred Arthur, fumbling in his jacket pocket for a cigarette. He found one and stuck it in the corner of his mouth, struck a match and lit up. "What happened to your eye, then?" he slurred, undiplomatically, oblivious of the social gaffe, that he had just made.

She coloured up but managed to keep her composure. "Oh, that, that happened years ago, when I was a kid," she said, dismissing it as trivial.

Arthur still hadn't realised the embarrassment that he was causing her. "What happened, then?" he asked, insensitively.

"Just an accident, that's all." She looked at her glass and took a sip, then she said, quietly, "I was climbing a conker tree, slipped and fell off and caught my face on a branch, which hit my eye as I fell down onto the ground."

This revelation was shocking enough to penetrate most drink-dulled brains, Arthur's was no exception.

"Jeez." He felt as though he'd been hit in the stomach. "I'm sorry, luv." He touched her sympathetically on the shoulder. "What a prick, I am," he slurred; a look of self-disgust on his face. "I didn't mean to upset you, honest, I just wasn't thinking straight, sorry, honest." He took a drag on his cigarette and focused on her face. "Sorry luv," he said again, touching her arm, showing her how he now regretted asking her such a thing. "I'm getting pissed so don't take any notice of me, is it?"

"Oh, that's orright man," she smiled and tapped him playfully on his arm. "Forget it, OK?"

Arthur picked up his glass and raised it. "Here's to you Pauline, you're a good 'un."

"Oy! Buggerlugs." Arthur felt a hand grip his shoulder.

He spun around in an effort to wrench himself away from the grip, which then, quickly and expertly, transferred itself from his shoulder to his throat. He grabbed at the hand and tried to prise it from his Adam's apple, which felt as though it was in the process of being reshaped.

On the other end of the hand with the death-grip, was the tattooed arm of the large darts player, and judging by the expression on his face, he was not too pleased with Arthur.

"First you ruin my friggin' darts match, Butt," he said, shaking Arthur like a ferret that had caught a rat. "Now you're chatting up my bloody girlfriend. Are you looking for a hiding or are you just plain bloody stupid, eh?"

"No, you've got me all wrong, Taff," Arthur croaked. "I was only chatting about the skittles, honest."

The grip on his neck slackened slightly, which was lucky for Arthur, as he was close to blacking out.

"For Christ's sake," he croaked. "I'm not interested in your girl, I'm getting bloody well married on Saturday." He swallowed painfully. "D'you think I'd be daft enough to go chatting somebody up two days before I was going to get hitched? Jeez, my missus would have my guts for bloody garters."

The owner of the tattoos relaxed his grip and let the arm fall to his side. "Married, you?" He let out a guffaw. "Who would want to marry a friggin' specimen like you?" He let out another snort of amusement and turned to his mates. "This clown's getting himself married on Saturday and here he is chatting up my Pauline."

"Leave him go, Gareth," one of the players suggested. "I think he's got the message, anyway, the little prick is harmless. He's three parts pissed for a start."

Big Gareth turned back to Arthur and patted him on the cheek. "You're a lucky lad, you are. It's a good thing that I'm in a good mood, Butt, now sling your bloody hook while the going's good, is it?" He turned to Pauline. "And you, get back to your bleedin' skittles, before I get mad."

Arthur held up his hands apologetically and backed away from the big man. "Don't worry I'm off, you'll get no bother from me, honest, Butt," he rasped, quickly heading for the door, rubbing at his painful neck. Arthur reached the door to the passageway and looked back towards the room for signs of Dai. "Where's that bum got to," he croaked. "He's never bloody around when he's wanted."

The blonde with the glass eye, who had returned to the table skittles, looked up and waved in his direction. Arthur managed half a grin in acknowledgement, then quickly turned and beat a hasty retreat, staggering into the passageway and slamming the bar door behind him, in a futile act of defiance, causing Eric, the doorman to look up from his football pools, a puzzled look on his face as he sucked on the end of a pencil.

"Has Dai Marshall come by this way, lately, Eric?" Arthur rasped.

"Yeah," said the old man, replacing the pencil with a pint pot, from which he took a slurp. "He left here about quarter'n hour ago with a bird in a red coat." He wiped away the froth from his upper lip with the sleeve of his jacket. "He said to tell you that he'll see you tomorrow." The old man then picked up the pencil, licked its point and marked an X on the football pool's grid.

Grim faced, Arthur staggered out into the empty street.

"Bollocks," he shouted angrily. "Wait 'til I see that bastard tomorrow, I'll give him bloody red coat."

Swaying, he thrust his hands into his pockets, broke wind and staggered off down Canal Street, the fumes of the night's drinking rising up inside him and filling his head, his eyes trying desperately to focus on the gap in the railings that he was heading for.

Arthur struggled through the gap, tearing a button from his jacket in the process, before cannoning back into the railings.

"Bloody railings," he cursed, pushing himself back into a semi-upright position and attempting a first erratic step along the canal's towpath where he proceeded to weave his way towards the railway bridge, which was slowly swaying towards him from the distance.

A high-pitched giggle followed by a manic cackle echoed across the stagnant water from the other side of the canal. Arthur stopped and spun around, listening intently; his hands thrust deep into his pockets, his upper body swaying.

The giggle came again.

"Who's that?" shouted Arthur across the fetid water. "Come on out, you git, I know you're over there."

There came a rustling from the tangled undergrowth on the other side of the canal, and through the gloom, Arthur could just make out two pairs of pale faces staring out at him from the bushes.

"Orright you twat," he snarled. "I can see you." He bent and picked up a stone from the towpath, swung back his arm and hurled the pebble across the filthy water towards the faces, then, spinning around, from the momentum of the throw, he promptly sat down on the ash path with a bump.

His aim was off and the stone, failing to reach its target, pierced the canal's weedy surface with a loud plop.

A disembodied voice came from the bushes.

"I'd give up skittles' if I were you, Butt. It's bad for the neck." There followed the sound of a raspberry being blown, and the cackle of manic laughter.

"Marshall, you git," yelled Arthur as he struggled to his feet. "I know it's you. I'll bloody have you, Butt, just you wait."

The sound of running feet and hysterical laughter came from the other side of the canal, as Dai and his female companion crashed through the undergrowth, away from the furious Arthur.

Arthur picked up another stone and hurled it in the direction of the fading laughter. His aim was better with the second effort, for it landed with a thump and clattered off into the nettles and brambles, but had no apparent effect on the raspberry-blower from across the water, whose running footsteps had, by now, rapidly faded out of earshot, leaving behind an eerie silence that cloaked the swaying Arthur, until the bark of a distant dog, eventually broke the eerie silence.

The prolonged drinking and the other misadventures of the evening had now suddenly caught up with Arthur. Lurching forward, he gripped the railings with both hands, and promptly threw up into the brambles.

He leaned, panting, his head pressed against the railings for several minutes until, eventually, his breathing normalised. Then, weakly, he pushed his body into, what approximated an upright position, away from the rusting iron. With eyes watering and nose and throat stinging, he finally staggered off, heading for the railway bridge and home.

Chapter Twenty-one
Reception

Eight days later, Arthur and Avril stood hand-in-hand outside the grey, ivy-clad walls of St Barnabas Church, Commercial Road, their faces set with forced smiles as the photographer, Gregory Luckett of Happy Pics, ducked back under his camera hood for the umpteenth time, and lisped, "Smile for the camera, please."

They had been husband and wife for forty minutes, twenty-five of which, had been taken up with the most important part of any marriage ceremony, the posing for, and the taking of, the official photographs.

Arthur's mouth was dry as dust and he licked at his lips. *God, I could murder a brown top,* he thought.

Gregory reappeared, interrupting Arthur's deliberations.

"That's it for now," he said, folding the tripod and hoisted it, and its accompanying camera, onto his shoulders. "Half a dozen more at the reception and we're all done, see you there."

He gave a sickly smile, and, with his free hand, brushed away an imaginary lock of hair from the forehead of his bewigged head.

Jeez, I hope his wig doesn't come off, he'll probably burst into tears, Arthur thought.

Gregory, the photographer, sped ahead of them, mopping at his face with a floral handkerchief as he made for the lych gate, his patent winkle-picker shoes, crunching on the gravelled path.

Arthur dismissed the thoughts of Gregory's wig and released Avril's hand in order to extract a packet of cigarettes from his trouser pocket. The audience of immediate family, bridesmaids and assorted friends, who had become part of Gregory's living tapestry, broke ranks and approached the happy couple, everyone talking at the same time and nobody listening.

Arthur lit up and brushed at the multicoloured bits of confetti that adorned the shoulders and lapels of his suit.

Turning to face Avril, he said, "What time is it, Love?"

She handed him her bouquet and peeled back the lacy hem of the mauve glove that covered her left wrist.

"Coming up to twelve."

Arthur returned the bouquet.

"Right, we'd better get a move on to the Legion, by the time we've finished the buffet and had a few pints, it'll be time for the off."

"Our train doesn't leave until six o'clock, Arth'. There's bags of time. Anyway, I want to go over and talk to the girls, for a mo."

"Aye well, don't take too long about it," he said. "In the meantime, I'll go and have a quick word with Dai and the boys."

He crunched down the path towards them.

"Orright lads," he called, blowing smoke at a weathered tombstone. "Went off ok, didn't it?"

Dai nodded. "Great, apart from the vicar, he was bloody long-winded, wasn't he? And slow, bloody hell man, if I'd known that I'd have to stand up there for that long, I'd have thought twice about being best man."

Arthur shrugged. "Yeah, well old vicar John is knocking on a bit. He's a good old boy really. He did my christening."

"You must have a good memory, Arth'," said Ronnie Cox, in admiration.

"You dull bugger, you," said Danny Cox, cuffing his brother around the head. "Arthur was only a babe in arms, then, how the bloody hell would he know what was going on at that age, for Chrissakes."

"Yeah, well he might have been a bit forward for his age," Ronnie retorted.

"Forward for his..."

"Mother told me," Arthur intervened, testily, putting a stop to the inane exchange. He turned to Dai. "Have you seen granddad or Ced?"

Dai nodded. "Yeah, Jack's gone on to the Legion with your Mam and your sister, Beryl. He said something about wanting to practice his speech before everyone else gets there."

"Oh God! He's not making a soddin' speech, is he?" Arthur dropped the remains of his cigarette onto the path and ground it into the gravel with a heel and shook his head at the prospect of his grandfather pontificating during the buffet. "So, what about he and Ced? Are they speaking to each other yet?"

"Dai grinned. "Yeah, they're good as gold, the pair of them. I've got a feeling that neither can remember too much about Friday week. I'll bet they're both afraid to raise the subject, if the truth be told."

"How come no Cedric, then," asked Arthur. "I didn't see him at the church."

"His daughter said that he had a doctor's appointment, mid-morning, but he would be coming on to the Legion straight afterwards," said Dai.

Arthur nodded. "That's good, just as long as we don't have a repeat of that bloody nonsense at the Cobblers Awl." He patted Dai on the shoulder. "Right, I'm off. I'm going to drag Avril away from those bloody bridesmaids, and get down to the Legion, so I'll see you down there, ok?"

Dai nodded.

Arthur extricated Avril from the gaggle of girls and they walked arm in arm down the gravel path towards the churchyard gate, the entourage following in their wake.

Once through the lych gate, and on the pavement side of the church, another flurry of confetti rained down over the patient couple.

Dai and the Cox brothers stood patiently at the rear of the throng, waiting until the newly-weds had been driven away in the shiny, black, beribboned Humber Super Snipe limousine, before worming their way through the taffeta-clad knot of cologne-drenched aunts and cousins, in order to reach the cluster of waving, giggling bridesmaids; making no attempt at concealing their lustful ulterior motives.

Arthur peered out of the car's back window at the passing shops and passed a hand over his face. *What the bloody hell possessed us to have the reception in the Legion,* he thought. *God-awful, wooden-slatted, fold-up chairs, splinter-laden trestle tables, overlaid with ghastly, floral-printed paper tablecloths, which ripped with the placing down of a pint glass.*

An hour and a half later, he looked down at the torn paper tablecloth and thought. *That buffet was nothing to write home about, even the Cox brothers turned up their noses at second helpings.*

Much of the proceedings, during the wedding reception, had passed him by, the old man now recalled, and memories of the forgettable buffet and the humourless speeches that followed, were now only snatches, like a dream, half an hour after waking. There were still some parts of it that he could just about bring to mind, if he were obliged to. Granddad's speech, for instance, he recalled, was surprisingly virtuous, by his grandfather's standards and had been generally well received by most of the wedding guests.

There were exceptions, of course, he remembered. *The chapel-side of Avril's family didn't seem too keen on grandad's reference to the episode of Aunty Audrey's elasticised-stocking and the coalman.*

The memory of it caused the old man to let out a huge guffaw and he looked around self-consciously, hoping that no one had heard him, but the road remained empty and silent, save for the snipping of shears, somewhere nearby.

He gave a Gallic shrug and metaphorically settled back down to savouring the memory of that particular episode of the wedding, once again seeing the looks of disapproval on the non-conformist faces at granddad's attempts at humour. Arthur's mother and sister's slightly tipsy attempts at socialising with the new Presbyterian in-laws also got a frosty, tight-lipped reaction from them, which caused the old man to give another loud guffaw.

Over the intervening years, Arthur hadn't given much thought to that day's proceedings, much of it, being either forgotten, or becoming just an assortment of jumbled images, blurred by the passage of time. So now, try as he might, the old man could not remember anything of Dai's speech, or, for that matter, his own response to it. He guessed that both were probably totally predictable and equally forgettable.

There was one small episode, however, that had stayed with him over the years, and that was the dreaded reunion of granddad and Cedric, following the previous week's fracas at the Cobbler's Awl.

Dai, Arthur and granddad stood at the bar, the buffet thankfully behind them, when the bony frame of Cedric appeared, pushing its way through the throng. Before Arthur or Dai could intervene, granddad was up and shouting.

"Over here Ced'! What'll you have?"

He beckoned to the white-haired figure with the jingling medals, who was having great difficulty in squeezing his way passed the ample buttocks of a female cousin, on Arthur's mother's side of the family who was sporting a custard-coloured fedora with matching handbag and sling-backs.

"SA will be great, I could murder a bloody pint," Cedric called, staring back at the heavy buttocks that he had just done battle with. He sat down heavily and let out a sigh.

"You look pissed off, Ced'. Has your knee been playing up again?" asked Dai, through a pall of smoke.

"Aye but there's not much that they can do about it, though," replied the old man. "He's increased my pills, to three a day, but I don't suppose they'll make much difference." He rubbed the side of his head. "He also gave me a tube of stuff to rub on me head, as well, but the bruise is nearly gone now, so I'll put the tube in the drawer, it might come in handy, one day." He rubbed at his head again. "Anyway, that's enough of me. How are you boys then, orright are you?"

Arthur's grandfather arrived back at the table and handed Cedric his glass of beer.

"It's great to see you Boyo," said granddad grinning, patting Cedric on the arm.

Cedric smiled and took the pint glass from him and drained a quarter of the contents in one gulp.

"Cheers Taff," he said and then belched.

Arthur and Dai exchanged looks of amazement at the, apparent lack of enmity between the two old men.

"That's a nasty bruise on the side of your head, Ced. How'd that happen?" Arthur's grandfather asked, pointing with his glass.

Dai looked across at Arthur, his eyebrows raised. Arthur looked up at the ceiling, waiting for the expected explosion. Cedric pulled at the lobe of his ear and screwed up his face in concentration.

"Buggered if I know, to be honest," he said. "All I know is, that it's been on the side of my head for about a week, and now it's nearly gone. You can barely see it."

He swigged at his beer and gently touched the side of his head as if to remind him that the bruise was still there.

"Funny you should say that." Granddad leaned forward in his chair. "I've had this bruise on the top of my arm for about as long as you've had the one on your head, size of a saucer, it was." He bent over and squeezed the sides of his boot. "And then there's my big toe, that's been a funny purple colour all week." He flexed his foot in the boot. "As a matter of fact, I didn't think I'd be able to get me best boots on for our Arthur's wedding, this morning."

Cedric studied the contents of his glass, shrugged and drank the last of his pint and got to his feet.

"It's my shout. Who's having what?"

"No fear," said granddad taking his empty glass from him. "Sit down, it's my round. I'm the groom's grandfather, so no arguments, besides, you've only just come in, for Christ's sake." He got up. "SA is it?" he asked, turning towards the bar, before anybody could object.

Cedric shrugged. "He's a stubborn old bugger, when it comes to buying beer, still, I'm not going to argue with him, I'll get the next round." He looked around at the assembled wedding guests. "I'm sorry, I couldn't make the service, this morning," he said, turning back to Arthur, concern in his voice. "I had this doctor's appointment, see. I couldn't afford to miss it, what with the way surgery hours are, these days." He sniffed and rubbed his nose with a cuff.

"No problem, Ced. Glad you could make it, anyhow," smiled Arthur.

"Everything go off as expected, then?" said Cedric, sniffing again.

"Oh! Yeah, it was great, thanks, wasn't it?" Arthur turned to Dai for confirmation.

Dai nodded through a cloud of smoke. "Yeah, apart from when Avril's Uncle Bernard put his elbow in your Aunty Ethel's veal and ham pie. That brought out a few pleasantries from all parties concerned, otherwise it was fine."

Cedric cackled delightedly and his medals jingled.

Arthur's grandfather arrived with the drinks and set the tray down upon the table-top. Cedric retrieved a pint glass and took a pull at it.

"Jack, your Arthur, here, was telling me about the service, everything went as planned, then?"

Arthur's grandfather sat down and lit up a Capstan full-strength and blew smoke at his waistcoat.

"Yeah, the Vicar was a bit slow, but otherwise, it went as expected, all that standing around didn't help my toe, though."

Cedric wiped his lips with the back of his hand.

"When do you reckon you injured it then?"

"Must have been about a week ago, I reckon," granddad said, smoke trickling out of the side of his mouth. "All I know is that it was there when I woke up, last Sunday morning, and it was throbbing like buggery."

"Must have happened sometime during Arthur's stag night, then," mused Cedric. "Not that you would have remembered much of that, I bet, you drunken old bugger?" He gave granddad a friendly punch on the arm.

Arthur stood up.

"I'm off for a slash, it's my shout next, so I'll get them in on my way back, OK?" He picked up the empties. "I'm having a beer, what about you boys?"

Cedric and granddad both nodded. Dai opted for a black and tan.

"How many pubs do you suppose we went in then, Ced?" asked Dai, lighting a cigarette and casually flicking the spent match across the room.

"I'd say seven or eight. What do reckon, Jack?" he looked at Arthur's grandfather for confirmation.

None was forthcoming, so the three of them sat in silence, pondering the big question. Granddad studying a beer mat, tracing around the red triangle trademark with a forefinger. Cedric screwing up his eyes and concentrating on the dusty light fitting that hung above the door that led to the Gents toilets, while Dai absentmindedly watched the barmaid's ample breasts wobble with every pull of the beer pump handle.

Several minutes later the silence was broken when Arthur arrived back at the table with the round of drinks, bringing the three silent wedding guests out of their trance-like state.

"How many pubs did we go in, on your stag night, Taff?" Dai asked Arthur, as he brought both his gaze and his mind back from the barmaid's animated bosom. He winked at Arthur, who quickly caught on.

"Dunno," he replied, shaking his head. "I lost count after the King Billy in Market Street. What do you reckon Granddad?"

After a lengthy pause, and much staring into the golden depths of his pint, granddad said, "Six, I think." He looked across at Cedric. "Wasn't one of them the Cobbler's Awl in High Street, Ced'?" He scratched his head. "You know the one what's got the barmaid with the ginger hair and the wart on her chin."

"The Cobbler's Awl," mused Cedric, touching his bruised temple as he stared at the ceiling, his eyes narrowing as fragments of memory of the lost night began to return. He touched the bruise again and stared hard at granddad, then after a short while, he quietly said, "How long have we known each other, now, Jack?"

Arthur's grandfather took a slurp from his pint.

"Bloody hell, now you're asking." He tapped the ash from the end of his cigarette. "Didn't we first meet up in Caerau Infants?" He rubbed his hand across his face and stared up at the blue haze that hung below the ceiling like Christmas decorations. He nodded in confirmation. "Yes, it was Caerau Infants, nineteen o two; Miss Protheroe's class." He took a drag on the cigarette. "Yeah, that was it, I remember first clapping eyes on you in the playground. You were boasting to all and sundry about the number twelve conker that you had, and I said that my conker would beat yours anytime."

"What's a number twelve conker?" asked Dai over the top of his pint glass.

Granddad gave Dai an old-fashioned look.

"It's a conker that's been victorious in twelve matches. Don't you bloody youngsters know nothing?" He shook his head in disbelief and took a slurp from his glass, wiping a sleeve across his mouth. "When I was a kid, I had a cheese-cutter that was a conker twenty-two, I remember when…"

"Forget the bloody conkers, for Christ's sake, will you!" Cedric hissed, interjecting. "I'm trying to establish something here."

"Orright, Ced', keep your shirt on. I was only trying to remember when we met, that's all, you did ask, remember?" replied granddad, somewhat miffed.

Cedric composed himself. "The reason that I asked, when we met, was because I was trying to establish just how bloody long, we have known each other, OK?"

"Orright, orright, I've got the sodding message," growled granddad taking a slurp from his pint. "If it's so bloody important to you about how long we've known each other, then bloody well work it out." He took another swig. "Nineteen o two from nineteen-sixty-three, that gives you... He looked at the ceiling, mentally counting, his face screwed up in concentration.

"Sixty-one years, for Christ's sake," Cedric said quietly, exasperation clearly showing on his face.

"OK, OK," acknowledged Arthur's grandfather. "I was getting there, you know I was never any bloody good at sums." He shrugged and grinned. "Now that you've established just how long we've known each other, so bloody what?"

Cedric shook his head. "Nothing, really," he replied, looking down at his gnarled hands. "I was just thinking about the past, that's all." He shrugged, resigned to granddad's lack of understanding of the situation, shook his head and smiled, dismissing the Cobbler's Awl and the futility of pursuing a pointless conversation. He changed the subject. "Miss Protheroe, Christ, do you remember that old ratbag?" He tapped the non-bruised side of his head. "What the bloody hell was her first name, now?" He bit his lower lip as he tried to recall the first name of the dragon-of-Caerau Infants. "No. It's no good, it's gone." He shrugged. "Anyway, what a witch she was, had a face like a ripped-sandal."

Granddad belched and scratched at the back of his head. "Sixty-one years, you wouldn't bloody credit it, would you? It seems like it was only yesterday." He drained the remains from his glass and reached for the fresh one that Arthur had brought.

"What were we then, five or six?"

Cedric took a swallow from his glass. "You were five, and I was six, you're a year younger than me."

"Yeah, that's right, boyo." Arthur's Grandfather held his pint glass up to the light and studied the contents. "By God we've sunk a few of these since then, eh?"

"For sure," replied Cedric over the rim of his glass, "and got into some scrapes too, didn't we?" He turned to Dai and Arthur. "We were a pair of wild, young bastards in our time, always fighting, us, see, isn't that right Jack?"

"Yeah," nodded granddad. "That's for sure, but we had more brawn than brains, in those days, didn't we?" He sighed. "I'm getting too old for all that bloody nonsense, a few jugs with my Butties, is all I require, these days, that'll do for me." He surveyed his audience, a wide grin on his face.

Cedric shook his head in wonderment, realising that his old pal Jack, had, either lost all knowledge of last week's escapade in the Cobbler's Awl, or that he had conveniently chosen to forget it, hoping, that any recriminations would fade with the fullness of time.

Whatever thought Cedric. *That's all water under the bridge now, there's no point in rehashing all of that daftness again.* He made to get up from the table, pushing himself halfway out of his seat.

"I'm going for a slash. I'll get the beer on my way back." He pushed himself fully to his feet. He leaned forward, nose-to-nose with Arthur's grandfather, and said quietly, "Listen Taff, if you can't remember your last good piss-up, then it was either a bloody Brahma of a night, or you're going senile, that's what I say." He headed for the Gents, stopped and turned. "So the next time you get arseholed and start throwing your weight around, just remember Caerau Infants nineteen-oh-two." He turned and continued on to the Gents.

"What the bloody hell is the silly old sod babbling about?" granddad asked, a bewildered look on his face. "He's the one that's going bloody senile, if you ask me."

"He was talking about Arthur's stag night. You must remember some of it, for Christ's sake," said Dai with mock exasperation in his voice.

Granddad raised his hands in surrender. "Orright, orright, so I don't remember, so frigging what? All I know is we had a bloody good night and we wet the boy's head in proper style."

"Yeah, you're right," said Dai, deciding not to push his luck. Turning to Arthur Dai said, "Anyway, talking of stag nights, I've been meaning to ask you this, all week, what the bloody hell happened to you after I went over to talk to Rosie Williams in the Boilermakers. I was expecting you to come over and help me out with the girls."

"What do you mean happened?" Arthur snapped. "Nothing bloody happened, that's what. You buggered off for a bloody knee-trembler, on the other side of the canal, and left your mate in the bloody lurch, that's what happened," he replied finishing his pint and putting the glass down with a bang.

"What are you going on about, buggered off, you git," retorted Dai. "When I looked across the room you were fully occupied, chatting up some tall, blonde piece who, was looking at you as though you were Tony bloody Curtis, so I figured you didn't need me, so I buggered off home, with Rosie."

"Yeah, well, I'm sorry about that," conceded Arthur. "She seemed too good an opportunity to miss, that's all, besides I was three parts pissed by then, so I wasn't in total control of the situation." He shrugged. "Anyway, things didn't turn out as planned, so let's forget it, orright?"

Cedric arrived, putting down the tray of drinks. "What have I missed, then?"

"Nothing," replied Arthur. "We were just talking about the Boilermakers and what happened after we left you and granddad, Friday week."

"What did happen, then?" asked Cedric, looking over the rim of his glass, a glint in his eye.

"He was telling us how things didn't quite turn out as planned," smirked Dai, turning to Arthur, his grin widening. "So, tell us, how come things didn't turn out as planned then, eh?"

"If you must bloody well know," responded Arthur, disdainfully. "I didn't like the way she looked at me."

Dai leaned forward in his seat, determined on unsettling the groom. "W

hat yer mean, didn't like the way she looked at you?"

"It was her eyes," said Arthur, defensively. "They gave me the creeps."

"How come?" persisted Dai. "Like a vampire or something?"

"No, you plonker," said Arthur, starting to get irritated at the cross examination. "If you must bloody well know, they were different colours."

Cedric wiped his lips on his sleeve. "Eyes shouldn't be allowed to put you off your stroke. I remember going out with a cross-eyed nurse from Wrexham, once, it was about six months after I was invalided home from Passchendaele. She was as ugly as sin, but I didn't let that put me off getting me leg over. What do you reckon, Jack?" he cackled.

"You're quite right there, Ced'," said granddad, trying hard to keep a straight face.

"They wouldn't normally put me off, either," said Arthur, defensively, ignoring the two old men's gibes. "Only this time it was different, see! The right one was brown, and the left one was green, and made of glass," he added quietly, hoping nobody would pick up on it.

A roar of laughter sounded around the table. "You must have been well pissed, since when has a glass eye, or anything else in that department, ever put you off your stroke before, Butty?" challenged Dai. "I've seen you on more than one occasion, chatting up birds with tattoos, hearing-aids, you name it. I remember that Peggy from Blewitt Street, when she had her leg in plaster, but that didn't stop you getting your evil way."

"Yeah well, there were one or two things besides that," admitted Arthur ruefully.

"Such as?" asked Cedric enthusiastically.

"Well she also had a gold front tooth, which didn't help, and, on top of that, she had a boyfriend built like a brick kharzi, which put the tin hat on it as far as I was concerned." He grabbed for his glass and took a huge gulp.

"No wonder you were smashed out of your brains on the canal bank," observed Dai. "What a way to end a stag night. Legless, on your arse in the brambles and not got your end away, jeez." He looked at the ceiling in disgust.

"Yeah, well you ain't heard the best part yet," said Arthur, shaking his head in disbelief. "The next day, when I went around to see Avril, she almost hit the bloody ceiling, didn't she? Said she was going to call off the bloody wedding, it took all my powers of persuasion to get her to change her mind."

"That's not like Avril," said Cedric. "She's seen you hung over before, she's always saying what a mess you are after a night on the pop. So what's new?"

"It was that bird's boyfriend in the Boilermakers," explained Arthur. "The frigging Cwmbran gorilla, when he saw me chatting up his girl, he grabbed me by the neck and damned near bloody choked me." He took out a cigarette, lit up and blew smoke at the ceiling, and continued his confession. "Well, anyway, the next day, Avril saw the marks on my neck, and accused me of having been with another bloody woman." He took another long pull at his pint. "Silly sod thought they were bloody love bites, didn't she? Well, as I say, it took of all my powers of persuasion to convince her that I got them in a scrap. I said to her, look Avril, I said, even if I was stupid enough to go out with another woman, I sure as hell wouldn't be daft enough to go and get myself bitten on the bloody neck, now would I? And of course, she had to agree, didn't she?"

"You're a jammy bastard, Tanner, that's for sure," said Dai finishing off the last of his pint. "And, I bet that it's a pound to a pinch of snuff, that somewhere along the line, you have probably, just happened to have bumped into, little Miss Thunder thighs, again, since, by accident, like?"

"Funny you should say that," said Arthur with a grin. "I did happen to bump into her two days later, as it so happens."

"Oh yeah!" said Dai disbelieving. "No love bites, this time, then?"

Arthur gazed at the ceiling thoughtfully for several moments; a smile played on his lips. "None that could be seen, anyway," he lied.

Granddad sipped at his pint in silence, his blue eyes sparkling with pride.

Cedric's medals jingled with delight.

Chapter Twenty-two
Memorials

The old man stared ahead at nothing in particular, the grin fast fading as the memory of that unsavoury episode soured his thoughts, threatening to spoil his afternoon. Unexpectedly, a bright light intervened, and brought him back to the present and back to reality. He peered intently across the motorway down towards the surrounding array of semi-detached houses, trying to locate the source of the flickering light that had so distracted him from his memories of Granddad, Cedric and Dai.

Then, he spotted it; something, somewhere on the boundary of the housing estate, was reflecting the sun's rays, flickering, as though someone was using the light to send a message.

A cloud passed across the sun, causing the reflections to cease, which gave him the opportunity to pinpoint the culprit's whereabouts.

Almost hidden by the surrounding houses was a tall, thin structure that had been the source of the glinting. His first thought was, that it might be one of those, new-fangled mobile phone masts, which have been appearing, on every available high-rise rooftop, over the last couple of years.

He narrowed his eyes, wishing that he had a pair of binoculars to hand, for, now, as the reflections had ceased, he was able to study the object, even though it was some distance away.

He scowled as he surveyed the structure, it was a church steeple and it protruded from the surrounding semis like a giant darning needle.

"Bloody rotate!" he muttered under his breath as he gazed nonplussed at the slender, aluminium structure, his eyes travelling down the length of the tower to where it married up with a squat, white, one-story, concrete building, which was adorned with narrow horizontal windows of multi-coloured glass that ran along the flanks of the building like gaudy ribbons.

He could not believe his eyes. "What the sodding hell is that, when it's home," he muttered, tossing his head in disdain. *My God is nothing bloody sacred any more, for Christ's sake!*

He was starting to get het up again, his eyes narrowing as he gritted his teeth in consternation. Having already been confronted with a three-lane highway, which was occupying the land, where his once beloved railway had been located, he was now, having to come to terms with the culture shock of seeing a modernistic church, which was now occupying what was once the hallowed turf of the Lord Ruperra Memorial Recreational Ground.

The old man may have possibly forgiven the planners, had the church been of a more traditional design, and more in keeping with his idea of how a religious building should look, but the concrete object, he was now intent upon, however, was something that he just couldn't come to terms with.

Why the bloody hell couldn't they have built something more in keeping with the old village, he reflected. *Something more along the lines of the old chapels that you can still see in the small towns in and around the valleys. You know,* he explained to himself, *grey and sombre, yet, at the same time, revered by the community, respected by all, fitting in.*

Briefly, he felt quite pleased with himself and at his silent, noble stance, until a tiny voice in his head reminded him that he had never been that enamoured with churches or chapels, anyway, and it was years since he had last set foot inside one.

He silently answered back. *It's nothing to do with bloody religion, I just get this feeling of unease whenever I have to go into one, that's all.*

He did have to admit, however, that by and large, he did find much of church architecture quite attractive, and that the history that surrounded many of the Norman and Tudor edifices, in and around the Welsh Marches, proved to be quite interesting. Yet there was still something forbidding about the ambience that was generated inside them. The seemingly, all pervasive, musty, woody, leathery atmosphere, of their interiors, always got to him, making him a bit edgy. And the way every little sound carried and echoed around the lofty interiors, smacked of the furtive, adding only to the mystique. The stained glass and the glinting gold artefacts, too, all seemed, to him, to be designed to command reverence and unquestioning faith.

It is all a bit too stage-managed for my liking, he mused, summing up the debate. *Similar to marriage, in a way,* he thought, *quite attractive when viewed from a distance, but a different kettle of fish once you step over the threshold.*

"What the hell, why am I arguing the point with myself?" he muttered angrily. *I'm getting old and bloody stupid, that's why,* came the answer.

Shielding his eyes from the glare of the sun, he resumed his study of the aluminium spire. *Never mind about any other churches, that bloody eyesore, has no saving grace about it, whatsoever,* he concluded.

He could feel his hackles rising again. To him, the aluminium spire and its attendant building, was just another example of the twenty-first century gone mad.

Those bloody, greedy bloody sods of planners and land speculators have gone and cocked it up, big time; not content with spoiling the whole bloody landscape with a sodding motorway, supermarket and housing estate, the sods have now gone and built on the bloody memo' for Christ's sake!

Which was really what his wrath was all about, it wasn't the modernistic design of the church that was irking him, any type of building, on that particular site, would have raised his dander. The fact of the matter, was, that they had built upon the sacred land of the Memo', and he was furious. It was the last straw.

He unconsciously clenched and unclenched his fists, staring hard at the church and its immediate surrounding area.

"Goddamned bloody sacrilege, that's what it is," he hissed, savagely kicking at a dandelion that was growing through a badly cracked paving stone.

They've gone and built on the Memo', he repeated to himself, still unable to come to terms with what was laid out below him. *What sort of bloody world have I come back to, then?*

He replaced the old briar back into his top pocket, stem first, and stared angrily at the expanse of rosemary-tiled roofs and their rash of satellite dishes.

"Bastards!" he hissed.

It was several minutes before he was able to compose himself, and a semblance of calmness returned.

He turned his attention back to the panorama, that could now be classified as greater Rogerstown, and surveyed the landscape, in the hope that, maybe he'd been mistaken, and had been looking at the wrong part of the village.

It had been a long time, he reasoned. *Maybe the old memory's starting to fail.*

The old man rescanned the area, but the longer he stared at the expanse of houses, the more he became filled with self-doubt.

That is where the Memo' used to be, isn't it? he questioned. *I'm not losing my bloody marbles, am I?* With his patience beginning to ebb away, his eyes, once again, traversed the landscape. *Yes, that's definitely where the Memo' used to be, I bloody well know it is, right there,* he pointed. *There, right where that sodding concrete warehouse of a church is, that's where the Memo' used to be, I know it is.*

The old man looked around despairingly; everything had changed, hardly a thing remained as he used to know it. The railway lines, the signal-box, the power station, even the Memorial Ground had been built on.

All bloody well gone, he inwardly boiled. *Built on, replaced by those modern, bloody Mock-Tudor egg boxes that nowadays, pass for houses.*

As he stared sightlessly at the concrete church, he saw only the Memorial Ground as it was in its heyday, when the summer sounds of bowling-woods colliding, and the frenzied calls of 'owzat', echoed across its green expanse.

Chapter Twenty-three
Funfair

The scent of the young, sweet-smelling grass of the Memorial Ground was revisiting his nostrils. He was back to those balmy days of summer, when the Lord Ruperra Memorial Recreational Ground would become the centre for most of the community's outdoor activities, playing host to a variety of entertainments.

One, that he fondly remembered, was the annual July visit to the town of the circus and the funfair.

It was always the same circus, Bertram Mills, he recalled.

Crowds would line the main street to watch the parade of the animals, which would come roaring, bellowing and trumpeting, Indian-file from the marshalling-yard sidings, where the circus train had been shunted, the whole cavalcade making its way down the Western-Valley road and on into the Memorial Ground.

Following on, behind the parade, would be a dozen or so members from the Railway Club's Gardening Section, shovels and buckets to hand; ready to scrape up any of the animal dung that may have dropped onto the road.

Stan Powers, who would usually be at the forefront of the dung-gathers, swore by it.

"That elephant shit is the best thing for your roses, that's known to man." He could be heard, on more than one occasion, pontificating in the Lamp and Flag.

New Members, or those, who were silly enough to listen to him for a second time, would nod sagely and make a mental note to get around to the menagerie as soon as possible, in order to get the jump on their competitors, for the precious manure.

Most of the members, who had heard it all before, would nod sagely and not take a scrap of notice, knowing that Stan was only talking his usual load of claptrap, and that he had about as much chance of winning the Miss World contest as he had of winning the Best-Rose-in-Show at the town's summer fete.

That never deterred Stan, however, for he would qualify his so-called expertise, by adding. "Mind you, it does have its drawbacks, being a bit on the strong side, like," he would say, holding his nose. "It might set your tender plants back a few weeks, but it'll soon put a stop to the missus spread-eagling herself all over the garden on her sodding sunbed."

Arthur put the empty briar back into his mouth and smiled to himself. *Yeah, the week that the circus came to the village was a time to savour all right. You were almost guaranteed a good time, anyone who didn't enjoy circus week must have had something wrong with them.*

Yes, it's true that circus-week always proved a great attraction to one and all. All, that is, except Arthur, who never went to any of the performances. For him the attraction was the attendant funfair, where all of the fun was to be had.

That's where all the crumpet was to be found. He fondly remembered. *A few pints in the Black Cat then it was off into the blue-black, balmy summer night to the funfair, where, if your luck was in, and Avril stayed at home with one of her summer-colds, you would soon be exploring the back of the big top with one of the village girls.*

It was on one such summer evening that he met up with Molly Prosser by the dodgems. After plying her with ice cream and candyfloss, he finally managed to persuade her to go onto the ghost train, with him.

As he had hoped, during the jolting, hair-raising journey through the haunted house's dark, eerie tunnel, she had screamed in all of the right places and had clung to him for protection as the car barged through skeleton-covered doors, and careered around corners where bats and cobwebs brushed past their faces.

With his arm tightly around her and his hand lightly covering a firm, young breast, and her sweet-smelling face buried in his jacket-front, he felt that his luck was well and truly in.

At the end of the ride, as they alighted from the car, a blast of air came out of the floor and blew straight up Molly's skirt, blowing it up over her head. She screamed and wrestled with the skirt, desperately trying to bring it under control while Arthur stood grinning, hands on hips, admiring the three inches of white thigh, the suspenders and the frilly, black knickers, that were on display. Now he knew his luck was in.

Big top, here we come.

Unfortunately, that was about as near to those knickers that he was ever likely to get, for as they came down the steps from the haunted-house, Arthur spotted the large, square head, with its familiar crew cut, that belonged to Molly's elder brother, Gary, who was purposely threading his way through the crowds, and, judging by the look on his face, he wasn't very happy.

Arthur studied the broad, muscular shoulders of the Rogerstown Rugby Club's number eight, and suddenly felt pretty unhappy too. Molly spotted Gary and waved to him.

Turning to Arthur, she said, "There's my brother Gary, by there." She pointed, unaware of the pending catastrophe that was heading in Arthur's direction.

She looked left and then right for Arthur, but with no success, he had melted away into the night.

Once he had put some distance between himself and the Memorial ground, he relaxed, lit a cigarette and headed for the Rogerstown Inn.

Chapter Twenty-four
Contrition

The old man shook his head in amazement. *Christ! My balls and my eyes must have been on the same string; no bloody wonder Avril buggered off with that Insurance Agent with the stamp collection.* He sucked on the empty, unlit briar, his face set as he formed a mental picture of Avril and Archie Chandler spending the intervening years together.

Archie, he guessed, would almost certainly have spent most of his waking life, when he wasn't collecting weekly insurance premiums, inspecting his collection of Balkan memorials. Arthur pictured Archie as he poured over his favourite stamps, inspecting each with a pearl-handled magnifying glass.

I bet one of his little treasures would have probably been something like, a turn-of-the-century Latvian triangular, which would have portrayed a mauve-coloured tramcar, in commemoration of the twenty-fifth anniversary of the Riga Transport system. Wow! I bet he nearly wet himself with the excitement of it all.

Avril, he thought, *was sure to be into Bovril, big time, she would be sitting in front of the telly, stirring her beef extract while applying cold-sore cream to her upper lip, while her feet would be housed in those God-awful, tartan slippers with the red pompoms, and, almost certainly, the Forsythe Saga would be on the telly.*

She's probably into all the soaps now. He grinned nastily, *and I bet she's still following the exploits of the bloody Archers.*

He pursed his lips, as he tried to remember the last time that he had seen the couple together, he scratched at his head and gazed at the motorway, nonplussed.

Then it came to him. It was the summer of nineteen seventy, not long after the divorce had become absolute. Arthur had been sitting upstairs on a number nine bus, as it waited at the traffic lights, at the Old Green crossing. Avril and Archie sat side by side in a yellow Ford Cortina, Mark-One, which was waiting alongside the bus. They were oblivious that Arthur was looking down on them, with a nasty expression on his face, as he thought, how Archie's red, jug-handle-like ears went perfectly with his thin, sandy hair and the horned-rimmed glasses, that were perched on his thin freckled nose.

The traffic lights changed to green and the yellow car, turned left, and crossed the town bridge, heading towards Corporation Road, while the number nine bus, and Arthur, continued straight on, into Upper Dock Street.

Arthur looked back at the disappearing car, thinking, *How the pair of them would make a good, sodding match, Avril, with her usual crop of chilblains, and her morbid dislike of anything of a sexual nature, and Archie, with his grumbling ulcer and a consuming passion for used postage stamps and fretwork.*

He shook his head, amazed at the amount of bile that was still in him after all those years and he let out a deep sigh. *Avril had every right to sling her hook, especially after the way that I'd performed over the years, boozing and chasing after everything in a skirt. Yeah, she had every right to give me the elbow, and to go and find a bit of happiness. Good luck to her, and if she'd found the right one in Archie, then, fine. At least, he wouldn't have strayed, that's for sure.*

He passed a hand across his face, trying to eradicate the old memories of Avril and Archie. *They've probably been very happy together all these years,* he conceded, taking the briar from his mouth and tapping it on the palm of his hand, to see that it presented no threat of combustion. Satisfied that it was safe, he pushed it, stem first, back into the top pocket of his jacket, happy to let the thoughts of Avril, and their doomed marriage, slip away.

Chapter Twenty-five
Emissions

He thrust his hands into his trouser pockets and turned his attention to the endless stream of vehicles that droned past on the motorway below him, he could feel the ire in him beginning to resurface. *If the planners had any bloody savvy at all, they would have electrified the bloody railway line, instead of digging it up and replacing it with a sodding motorway.* He ground his teeth in disgust.

"They call this bleeding progress," he muttered, nodding in the direction of the highway. *Where's the bloody poetry in any of these sodding dodgem-cars, that they're building, these days. Christ, even today's God-awful electric trains have something about them, compared to these bloody boxes on tires. The fact that they run upon rails probably has something to do with it.* He conceded, grinning to himself. *What the hell, you either like railways or you don't.*

He did, and had done so, for, as far back as he could remember. As a child, he would lie in the darkness of his bedroom, propped up on one elbow, straining to see the shadowy forms of the trucks as they trundled along the railway that ran behind the railings of the narrow lane, which separated the back-garden wall of their house, in Canal Street, from the branch line and its attendant sprawl of sidings. The squeals of the wagon wheels of the heavy coal trains and the rattle of their couplings would spellbind him, as he lay there in the gloom of his bedroom, listening to the whistles and the deep-throated grunts of the powerful freight locomotives that were hauling the coal to the nearby docks.

He folded his arms and shook his head. *Who'd have thought, that, that innocent little lad, who, used to watch the trains, face pressed against the lane's railings, would one day be in charge of a signal box, especially the one that used to be just there.* He nodded in the direction of the motorway, then let out a long sigh.

"And who'd have thought that he would have turned into a bad-tempered old sod, now standing in a place, that he doesn't recognise, while, trying to remember things that happened fifty odd years ago," he muttered grimly.

He dismissed the self-criticism and stared at the motorway and the stream of cars that raced below him.

When I started work on the line, it was nearly all steam, practically, everywhere you looked, all you could see were those great, gleaming, powerful main-line locos', not like today, all you see are tinny, pointy-nosed, bloody diesel and those electric tubes on wheels, which we are obliged to put up with.

The combination of wistfulness and prejudice had conveniently brought on a bout of forgetfulness, which rejected any acceptance, by him, that modern-day trains, which he frequently and happily used, were comfortable, fast, and clean, and, more often than not, more frequent and punctual than their fifties counterparts. But, now that he was wearing his nostalgia-hat and rose-coloured spectacles, fact and fiction had become inevitably intertwined. Logic had gone out of the window, as had his memory of the many sightings of main-line express locomotives during his preteens.

In fact, when pressed, he would have had to concede, that the sighting of a main-line express engine, on any of the valley or dockland lines, was a rarity, and the novelty of any such appearance, generally had the train spotters out in their droves.

Arthur's introduction to, and memories of, such gleaming, main line monsters, were not from the other side of the lane's railings but had taken place on the South Wales main line, in Newport's High Street Railway Station, which he would visit after school had finished for the day.

A subsequent journey to Weymouth, on the family's first holiday, in the early fifties, also provided him with the sights and sounds of railways that lay beyond the long, dark journey through the Severn Tunnel.

The memory was so vivid that he could almost hear the hiss of the steam and smell the smoke.

They had barely arrived at Newport's platform three, when their train to Bristol steamed in, with Arthur transfixed as he watched the polished, black express locomotive hiss to halt in a cloud of steam, and, while still in total awe, both he and his sister would be hurried up the steps of the carriage, and into the veneered corridor, from where, granddad would guide them into an empty compartment, where the brother and sister would bounce down with glee on the spring-laden moquette cushions.

During the journey, Arthur would remain transfixed, nosed pressed to the window of the speeding carriage, watching with fascination as the train sped through the Monmouthshire countryside, before diving into the black maw of the Severn Tunnel that would take them under the River Severn to the West country and Bristol.

As their train steamed slowly into Bristol Temple Meads, Arthur had his first taste of a busy main line; West Country railway station, with its constant arrival and departures of main line GWR express engines, each with a long rake of carriages.

Arthur stared in wonder, rooted to the spot, until chivvied along by his mother, towards an empty brown and cream bench.

The Tanner family had half an hour to wait before their connection to Weymouth was due in, so his granddad, restless as usual, decided that he needed a walk.

"Me and the lad are going to stretch our legs for ten minutes. Why don't you and Beryl go and have a cup of tea. The cases will be all right by there."

Arthur's Mother got up. "Good idea Jack," she said. "Come on Beryl, let's go and have a cuppa and a bun."

They all stood up in unison. Arthur and granddad walking away, towards the end of the platform. His mother and sister heading in the opposite direction towards the buffet.

Beneath the echoing, cavernous roof that arched over them, Arthur and his grandfather stopped and gazed at a great, glossy, green monster that stood, before them, simmering like a kettle on a stove.

That was Arthur's first experience of seeing a Great Western Castle-class engine, up close, in the flesh, so to speak.

The old man stared beyond the supermarket and the semi-detached houses, relishing every memorable moment, his eyes sparkling with delight, almost feeling the heat that radiated from the great engine's boiler and still visualizing the charcoal-coloured haze of smoke that wafted from its copper-banded chimney and the thin wisps of steam that fluttered around its cylinders, as it stood there, waiting to take the chocolate and cream carriages of the Cornish Riviera, south to Penzance.

He continued to stare at nothing in particular, letting the memories wash over him. After all those years, he could still remember the engine. "Number 5080, Defiant," he murmured. His eyes beaming as he scratched at his silvery hair. *I've got an idea that it's still around, somewhere, on one of those preserved railways, I think.*

He made a mental note to check up on it, and maybe go and have another look at it, sometime. *Yeah, it'll be nice to see the old girl again.*

Twelve years on, from Arthur's first encounter with the ex GWR, locomotive in Bristol's Temple Meads Railway Station, saw the steam era drawing rapidly to a close, and the introduction of main line diesel locomotives, throughout the country, was in full swing. This, then, was the time when main line express engines were to be seen in all manner of unusual haunts, especially during the summer months, when they could occasionally be seen travelling over the valley lines, in charge of the seaside excursions, which British Railways ran down from the heads of the South Wales valleys, to the various South and West coast holiday resorts. Only the most powerful of express locomotives would be allocated to these trains, anything less powerful would be hard-pressed to haul the long, heavy trains up the steep valley gradients, on their return.

By the late winter and early spring of nineteen sixty-four, steam-hauled trains were few and far between, diesel and electric traction having taken over, from them, for the most part.

The vigilant train spotter, however, was still able to make one or two rare sightings of these few remaining steam locomotives, as they would be seeing out their days on rugby specials.

The old man transferred his gaze to the motorway; now picturing it as the four-line track of yesteryear, on which the specials, from the Western valley, would race along, transporting the hundreds of fervent Welshmen to the away fixtures of Five-Nations Rugby tournaments.

Chapter Twenty-six
Sports

The old man was now in his beloved signal-box again.

The six-ten from Brynmawr to Newport, rattled past the Gwent Junction signal box, its bleary-eyed passengers staring disinterestedly through the moist patches, on the carriage windows, where sleeves had wiped at the condensation.

The guard waved happily from the end window of the three-car diesel train and Arthur acknowledged him with a wave as he watched the train disappear around the bend, leaving in its wake, a trail of acrid, black fumes from its exhaust, which slowly settled onto the track.

In the distance two, newly commissioned, diesel electric locomotives, double-heading an iron ore train, powerfully roared towards him on up the relief line, with a full load, bound for the blast furnaces at Ebbw Vale. Curls of grey exhaust, which issued from the vents in their roofs, dissipated in the pale, watery, wintry sky, while the united growl of their engines filled the morning air, blanketing the power station sidings with sound. Arthur watched their approach with interest, wondering if this new technology would be as good as the Standard, British Rail, class ninety-two locomotives that usually hauled the ore trains up the valley.

His thoughts were interrupted by the sight of a, down-at-heel, soon-to-be-scrapped, steam locomotive, coming in the opposite direction, heading for the down relief line with a train of empty banana vans, bound for Barry Docks. It clattered passed the signal box and its driver raised the enamel-lid of his tea can with ceremonial solemnity, toasting Arthur, before taking a gulp from it.

"Cheers," Arthur mouthed, and raised an imaginary glass aloft in acknowledgment, before closing the window behind him.

The freight train rattled through the points, taking it from the down main line onto the adjoining down relief line, its whistle greeting the growling diesels, which they acknowledged, in turn with long blasts on their horns.

The tail end of the banana vans disappeared around the bend, and Arthur restored the signals to their stop positions and signalled the train out of section. Almost immediately the main line telegraph bell announced the imminent despatch of the Nantyglo to Edinburgh rugby special. Arthur accepted it onto his section and signalled it on to the next box down the main line, which returned the permission-granted bell code. He set the signals to the off position before returning to the window and watched the tail end of the iron ore train disappear into the distance.

Arthur opened the window and leaned on the windowsill, waiting for the Rugby Special's arrival.

Two minutes later it came into view, pulled by a powerful, ex GWR Castle-class engine, which came thundering down the straight, its twelve chocolate and cream coaches swaying and clattering behind it.

As it cruised effortlessly by, Arthur was treated to the spectacle of hundreds of grinning, bottle-waving, half-cut Welshmen, all off to Scotland to wage war in the name of rugby football.

They'll all be pissed before they reach Abergavenny, he thought. *There'll be bloody mayhem inside that train before it reaches Waverly Station.*

He grinned and waved. "Good luck, you lucky bastards," he cried.

An array of red and white scarves, Welsh-dragons and a blur of white faces, rushed past and away into the distance, leaving behind a vacuum of silence.

"Lucky sods," he muttered grimly, gazing at the now empty tracks, wishing that he too, were aboard that Edinburgh bound train. He shook his head disconsolately.

No bloody chance of that, getting time off, from work, these days, is like asking for the sodding moon.

Arthur acknowledged that there was very little that anybody could do about the leave situation. It was that time of the year when the annual crop of colds and 'flu was widespread and were taking their usual toll of the general population.

Rogerstown marshalling yard had been particularly hard hit, the old man recalled. Absenteeism had been at an all-time high that winter, with every available able-bodied man covering for the sick and the disabled. Overtime working was at its peak; even rest days were being worked on a regular basis, so there was little or no chance of Arthur getting any time off, and a trip to Edinburgh was just a pipe dream.

Even if I had managed to wangle some time out of the yard master, I still couldn't have gone, anyway, he thought, shrugging his shoulders. *Tickets were like gold, in those days, and unless you had friends in high places, like those on the Committee, at Rodney Parade, or at the Arms Park, then you had no bloody chance of getting one.*

He stared off into the distance, as he struggled to retrieve fragments of memory of the times when he had been able to get a ticket for one of the big matches at the Cardiff Arms Park.

It was two weeks after the Scottish match, and much to his surprise, the chance of a ticket for the Wales match against England at Cardiff's Arms Park, had come Arthur's way, when Dai Marshall made one of his rare telephone calls to Arthur.

"It's Dai," the voice on the end of the line informed him. "How're you doing, you old sod?"

Arthur feigned ignorance. "Dai? Dai who?"

"Listen Tanner, you twat, if you don't recognise which Dai this is, then you'll miss the chance of getting a ticket for the bloody England match, orright?"

"Marshall, you git," Arthur growled. "It's weeks since you last decided to get in touch, and now, here you are, out of the bloody blue, up to your old soddin' tricks again, trying to kid me about seeing the match at the Arms Park, you plonker? You know they're like gold. Where would you get tickets?"

"Listen Butt," Dai threatened. "Do you want a bloody ticket or what? I'm wasting bloody good drinking time ringing you, you disbelieving idiot."

"Dai, you better not be having me on, because if you are, you'd better go into hiding, 'cause I'll bloody find you, make no mistake." There was just a trace of menace behind Arthur's banter.

"Certainly, I've got tickets," replied Dai. "Do you think that I would kid a mate on such an important matter? Even I wouldn't stoop so low."

Dai chuckled, adding. "Besides, this call is costing me money, and I'm low on coppers, for change."

"Ok," Arthur said warily. "So how come you've got tickets, then?" He chose to ignore the reference to Dai's financial situation.

"Remember Godfrey, the brother-in-law?" said Dai.

Arthur nodded at the 'phone. "Yeah, isn't he a Bookies Runner, or something?"

Dai ignored the taunt. "He's a cost clerk in Barwells Motors, and his boss, who is on the committee of the Maesglas Athletic Club, gave him two tickets as part of his annual bonus. So, out of the kindness of his heart, and with a little bit of persuasion from our Alice, he asked me to go to the match with him. But, here's the thing, now, he's gone and broken his ankle, so his ticket is going spare, so it's yours if you want it, Taff?"

Arthur punched the air with delight. "Dai, you're a bloody cracker, of course I want it. I'd give my eye teeth to get the chance to see Wales against the old enemy. How much do I owe you?"

"Don't worry about that, pay me on the day," Dai replied.

"Great!" yelled Arthur excitedly, hardly able to contain his elation. "How about us getting there? What about transport?"

"Train, probably," replied Dai. "I'll 'phone you in a couple of days' time and let you know the times etcetera, ok?"

"Yeah, that's terrific, Dai, don't you bloody forget, now, if I'm not at home, leave a message with Avril, failing that, get in touch with Dinky Phillips at the yard, he'll let me know."

"You know I won't forget, for Christ's sake," Dai said with exasperation. "I didn't bloody forget to ring you, did I?" Then he added, sarcastically. "I take it that you are on the right sodding shift, then?"

Arthur ignored the taunt. "Yeah, I'm on mornings. I'll ask Charlie Thomas if he can relieve me an hour earlier than usual. Charlie's as good as gold, so he'll help me out, no problem. I'll come straight down from work and meet you outside Newport Station. I should be there by about one thirty and we can be down in Cardiff by about two to quarter past. What do you reckon?"

"Brilliant," replied Dai. "I'll ring you in a day or two to confirm it all, ok?"

"Great, Dai, speak to you soon." Arthur put down the receiver and rubbed his hands in anticipation. "Great, that's bloody great," he beamed.

Five days later, the situation had changed and by then, it was all doom and gloom for Arthur. With a heavy heart and full of self-pity, Arthur rang Dai to say that he could not go to the match.

"You're joking, Arth'?"

"No, it's no joke, old son. I've got to cry off, Avril has gone down with a virus, she's rough as a skunk. The doc's given her antibiotics and has ordered her to stay in bed and not venture out for at least a week."

"Bloody hell, that's bad luck, Arth'. What a sodding shame." Disappointment sounded in Dai's voice.

Arthur nodded at the receiver. "Yeah, well there you go," he said, trying to put a brave face on it. "Some other time, maybe?" Then, as an afterthought, he added. "What about the ticket, I still owe you the money for it."

"No fear, you daft bugger," Dai replied. "I'll have no problem flogging it at the ground, on the day. I'll probably make a few bob on the deal, anyway."

"Yeah, I guess so," Arthur replied disconsolately. "I'm sorry, mate, but I got to stay home with her, haven't I?"

"Of course, you bloody well have," said Dai. "Duty calls, besides, the game is on the telly, so get a few bottles in, is it?"

"Aye, there is that, I suppose," replied Arthur. "Anyway, you have a good time, and stay away from those Cardiff girls, or they will have your keks off before you can say knife." Arthur tried to inject a little humour into the situation but failed miserably.

Dai feigned a laugh. "No problem. I'm coming straight back home, after the match."

"Orright then, Butt, I'll speak to you soon, OK?" said Arthur and he slammed the telephone receiver back on to its cradle.

If it's not one thing, it's some other bastard thing, he inwardly cursed. *If it's not a bloody virus, it's the sodding croup or some other bloody ailment. One day, perhaps a bloody miracle will happen, and she'll be well enough for me to go to see a bleeding match.*

Arthur stared out of the front window of the little stone cottage his hands clenched as he beat them in anger on the wooden windowsill.

I'm getting bloody well pissed off with her and her sodding illnesses. One day, just one bloody day, it would be nice, just to be able, to go to a match, have a few beers and then come home to healthy woman, for a change.

The old man stared down at his hands and shrugged. *No, that's not true, that's not at all true, that's only, bloody sour grapes, on my part, that's all. Our Avril was no more prone to illness than anyone else.*

In fact, the few minor illnesses that Avril had contacted had rarely stopped him from going out for a pint, he recalled. Avril was never a hindrance to his social life, and she rarely complained about his heavy drinking sessions at the Railway Club, and, it was not until late into their doomed marriage, that she actually protested, to any degree.

The old man shuffled his feet in embarrassment, nodding to himself, acknowledging that, when he was married to Avril, he had had plenty of opportunities to see lots of sport during his time at Rogerstown, particularly, in nineteen sixty four, which was their first year, in the little, stone cottage in Ebenezer Lane. That year he rarely missed a home game at Somerton Park or Rodney Parade, and the opportunities available to him during the following years, were hardly any different, the main stumbling block, that curbed his sporting activities, both as a player, and as a spectator, was, one, Arthur Tanner.

In those days many of his Saturday afternoons would be spent in betting shops, donating his hard-earned cash to the Tudor Pritchard holiday fund.

Now, some forty years later, he wished that he had taken the opportunity to go and see more of the other big games, when he had had the chance.

It would have saved me a lot of money, and maybe rescued my doomed marriage, as well. The old man shrugged. *Yeah, well, what's done is done, there's now't much I can do now, to change any of those idiotic episodes that cocked up my marriage.*

He ran his hand through his silvery hair and sighed.

Despite all of my wanderings, much of my marriage to Avril wasn't all doom and gloom, for Christ's sake. Most of the time, we were very happy together. By and large, it was pretty good.

"No, not too bad, all things considered," he murmured, mentally closing, and turning the key in the lock of the door, to the room that stored the archives, marked, *Marriage to Avril.*

He screwed up his eyes and concentrated on the stream of cars that were hurrying towards Newport and the coast, finally shutting out thoughts of Avril and that misbegotten era.

Soon, the old man was back in his nostalgic mode as he recalled some of the great sporting moments that he had not missed, his face lighting up with each new memory.

There was that time, in nineteen sixty-six, at the Arms Park, when Newport Rugby Club had won the Snelling Sevens; Dai Watkins had a Brahma of a game. He pursed his lips and gazed off into the distance. *Dai Marshall and me, we were standing in the North stand, bloody brilliant it was. Jeez, we must have had eight pints that day.*

The old man pulled at an ear lobe. "Good old Dai," he said softly, staring down at his hands.

For several minutes he stared at his leathery fingers, before finally raising his head, and pulling himself out of the gloom that the memory of Dai had heaped upon him.

With a shake of his head, he said to himself. *Hey! Come on, get your act together; this is no time to go soft on me. Dai wouldn't have wanted that, would he?* He straightened up. *Yeah, that's right; he'd kick my arse, if he were here.*

He scratched at his head and returned to searching the memory banks for other memorable sporting occasions that he had witnessed.

So, where else did we go? Let's see, now. His eyes lit up as he began to recall the golden sporting moments of his youth.

That's right, there was that trip to the Dell, in the FA Cup, when the County managed a draw with Southampton. Gerald king scored from the penalty spot.

Now he was getting into his stride. *What about that game at Sophia Gardens, when Glamorgan clinched the County Championship title by beating Surrey, that was a cracking game, for sure.*

He gave a rueful smile. *Although, I have to admit, that much of the Surrey innings had been missed, due to a session in the beer tent, with granddad.*

Three bloody cracking trips and make no mistake, there could have been a lot more if it hadn't been for me, practically living in that bloody betting shop, blowing my wages, every Saturday.

Chapter Twenty-seven
Tensions

He looked down, towards the houses and the concrete church that now occupied the area that once was the Memorial Field. *Yes, there were some cracking games on that muddy, bloody patch, that's for sure, especially during that first year, after our move into the cottage.*

The smile broadened and spread across his face, and he gave a huge guffaw and slapped at his thigh. *God, some of those matches were bloody hard. The games against Newport YMCA, they were a bugger, you could count on there being lots of blood and snot and sodding bruise. Jeez, we were lucky to come off the field in one sodding piece. Some of the other fixtures were not for the faint-hearted, either and were not much better.*

Pontllanfraith Albion, they were a tough lot of sods, and Cross Keys Nomads, Christ you could expect a good kicking at any match with them, that's for sure. He chortled, grinning hugely as he savoured the memories of those wonderful sporting moments.

His eyes lit up. "Christ, yes! And let's not forget that famous of all sporting encounters, the match against the All Stars. How could I bloody well forget that?" He laughed out loud, and looked around sheepishly see if anybody was listening, but the cul-de-sac remained deserted, and the lawn mower had long since cease to compete with the motorway.

That must have been one of the most famous matches to have been played on the old Memo', he grinned. *So famous that it made the late edition of the Argus,* he recalled.

I wonder how many of those, who were involved in that bloody fiasco, are still alive and kicking? He shook his head. *Not many, I bet, and, if there were, would any of them still remember it?* He pursed his lips. *Hardly anyone, I'd guess; I don't suppose any of the organisers are still alive. Dinky and Denzil both died years ago, and, Iorwerth Evans and Tudor Pritchard, almost certainly are. As for the rest of them,* he shrugged. *It's anyone's guess.*

He folded his arms and looked across the acres of rosemary-tiled roofs, towards the area, that once was Memorial ground, memories of the match between the Lamp and Flag and the Tudor Pritchard All-Stars, flooding back.

What a friggin' balls-up that turned out to be, that just had to be the greatest sporting disaster of all time.

That week, he remembered, there had been much consternation and gnashing of teeth among the Rogerstown Railway Club's Committee members. For they had not been consulted, regarding the proposed soccer match, between the club and a team from the T.P. betting-shop empire. Iorwerth Evans, inveterate gambler and yardmaster at Rogerstown Junction, had had the effrontery to bypass the Committee of the Lamp and Flag, and had unofficially arranged the fixture with Tudor Pritchard, betting-shop owner and well-known womaniser.

Just why the committee had been excluded from the arrangements, remains a mystery, to this day, although, it was rumoured, that Iorwerth had only agreed to the match in exchange for an extension to his credit at the betting shop. Tudor, for his part, was more than happy with the arrangements, having already pre-empted the yardmaster's decision, by, not only, booking a half page advert' in the local evening paper, but also having several dozen posters printed, and making arrangements for the engraving of a Tudor Pritchard Perpetual Cup, which, of course, he planned to present, to the winners on the day, personally.

As an extra inducement, he had also offered to fund the cost of a buffet at the Railway Club after the match.

There was also a rumour, going around, at the time, that the deal was struck, with a proviso that Iowerth also kept quiet about seeing Tudor coming from behind the circus big top, over on the Memo' ground, that July, with his arm around the waist of, Edna, Charlie Tomkin's wife.

Reginald (Dinky) Phillips, head shunter and secretary of the Rogerstown Railway Sports and Social Club, was duly called into Iorwerth Evan's office and given the news of the pending match.

"It's all arranged, Dink, all you'll have to do is get a team together, nothing much, mind, any of the lads that are spare, will do, those betting shop Nancy boys will be a sodding push over.

Dinky was speechless, he couldn't believe that someone had had the temerity to go over his head and arrange a sporting fixture, involving the Lamp and Flag, without due consultation. He was tamping mad, and he stormed out of the office muttering obscenities, which was totally out of character, for Dinky was a good and true chapel man.

He stopped Arthur by the shunters' cabin.

"Saturday night, Lamp and Flag, seven thirty sharp!" he barked. Arthur opened his mouth to reply but was cut off before he could start protesting. "Seven thirty, now don't forget, it's an emergency meeting, orright?" said Dinky through gritted teeth.

Arthur shook his head in disbelief as he watched the human-tornado sweep along the ash path, his dander, well and truly up.

Dinky disappeared into the bowels of the lamp-room, from where, the sounds of metal containers, being kicked, could be heard.

"Avril will have my guts for garters, Dink!" Arthur shouted after him, as the head shunter disappeared from view. "This'll be my third Saturday evening out this month. She'll do her nut."

It was a waste of time. There was no stopping Dinky by then, not once he had the bit between his teeth. Arthur shrugged resignedly, hitched his haversack higher up his shoulder and headed on up the loop line towards the Gwent junction signal box, leaving behind, the sound of Dinky's furious words, as they echoed around the inside of the corrugated, metal-sided lamp room.

That Saturday, Arthur had stood in the small hallway of the terraced cottage and studied his hair, in the mirror for the umpteenth time, before giving it one more going over with the comb.

"It's no good you having another sulk," he said loudly, over his shoulder. "I've told you, it's an emergency meeting. I've got to go, I can't get out of it. So, give me a break, luv, orright?"

Avril's answer came in the form of the living-room door slamming and the television being turned up full blast.

He looked at his reflection in the hall mirror and shrugged. *Well, I tried, didn't I?* He reached for his jacket, and, with it only half on, went out into the lane, and closed the front door with a slam.

The old man turned is thoughts to the little stone cottage that he and Avril had shared during the ensuing three years. Initially, living there, had taken some getting used to, he remembered, for, compared to his dockland home, Rogerstown was unbelievably quiet. Some nights, he would lie awake in bed listening to the hoots and shrieks of the owls in the nearby churchyard, and the barking of foxes echoing across the river, all a far cry from the all-pervading sounds of locomotives shunting, and the hooters and whistles of the tugs, cargo boats and steam cranes, that emanated from the railway sidings and nearby docks of Newport.

The air, of the small valley town was also noticeable for its freshness. *A good deal different from the industrial atmosphere that was ever present in and around his native dockland home.*

Arthur's rose-coloured memories of the small, country town, failed to address the fact, that, in those days, most of the houses there had coal fires. And, this, together, with the smoke and steam from the marshalling yard and power station, didn't exactly conform to the Clean Air Act of later years.

But, nevertheless, Arthur had soon grown accustomed to its ambience and had quickly adjusted to the slower pace of life of his new rural surroundings. The old man fondly remembered the lane and its rough, dry-stone wall, and the view it afforded, of the surrounding hills, the outlying farms and the dark green swathes of forestry.

He hadn't thought about that small cottage for many years, and now, that he was revisiting it, the old man was back in the cosiness of the small rooms and feeling, underfoot, the uneven flagstone-floor of the kitchen. That had always appealed to him, he recalled. The steep, well-worn stairs that led up to their bedroom, with its Georgian window and blackened, main beam that supported the ceiling, also gave him a warm, comforting feeling.

Gardening, which, over the years, had become a passion, for him, and had, in those early days of marriage, taken on a new meaning for him. He remembered, affectionately, that first day, when he had initially set foot onto the secluded little patch of lawn that lay to the rear of the cottage. There, he had been overwhelmed by the scent from the roses, the sweet-Williams and the Nicotiana, that filled the air.

The cottage garden and its plants had so captivated him, that it became, almost immediately, an all-consuming interest, so much so, that he began buying the Daily Express, for the Adam the Gardener feature. Arthur also, broke another habit of a lifetime by joining the local library, from where, over the following months, he had borrowed all of its stock of books on gardening.

Gradually, the little garden shed began to be filled with an assortment of gardening implements for the maintenance of his hallowed little plot, which he tended lovingly throughout the passing seasons. Arthur even, took the unprecedented step of joining the Lamp and Flag's Gardening Section. This alliance, however, was short-lived, for Arthur had had the misfortune to heed Stan Power's advice, regarding the spreading of elephant manure on his beloved back garden, which nearly put paid to his Dianthus and Nigella. Luckily for Arthur, and the plants, Avril's constant complaints about the smell keeping her from using the sunbed, eventually forced him to rake up the droppings and dispose of them over the lane's stone wall, lower down the hill; thus, saving his annuals from the powerful, acrid elephant manure, but, also his eardrums, from an irate Avril.

The old man thrust his hands into his pockets and looked across the motorway, towards the sparkling river. *It wasn't long before I had to say goodbye to it all,* he remembered, gloomily, picturing a young Arthur Tanner, striding down the lane, past the Black Cat Inn and on towards the main Western Valley road where the Railway Club building stuck out like an oversize military pillbox.

Chapter Twenty-eight
Committee

Although Arthur had arrived at the meeting on time, the other members of the committee, had already arrived and were restlessly waiting to get started. Arthur disregarded their haste and made for the bar and ordered a pint of bitter.

"Now that we're all here, we'll make a start, orright?" said Dinky pointedly, heading towards the committee room.

One by one they shuffled into the committee room and took their seats, Arthur sat down, next to Colin Powell, the station's booking clerk, who was busily extracting an HB pencil from the array of writing instruments that festooned his top-pocket. He set about sharpening the point with a pearl-handled penknife.

Dinky banged an empty stout bottle on the table. "Ok, let's get the show on the road and bring this meeting to order, is it?"

Arthur took a slurp from his pint pot and undid the front of his suit jacket.

Denzil Evans, the depot's store man, took a huge, black tobacco-pipe from his trouser pocket and proceeded to probe the interior of its bowl with the spike of a Swiss-Army pocketknife.

Eric Fletcher, the lamp man, cleaned the nails of his right hand with a folded-up bus ticket.

"Right, before we get down to business, are there any apologies for absence?" asked Dinky without looking up from his agenda.

Arthur lit up a cigarette and blew smoke at his lap.

Denzil shook his head and closed the spike on his knife with a loud snap, causing Dinky to look up from his agenda.

"No? Well, I have," he said. "Len Croker and Les Thomas will not be joining us tonight. Len is on a twelve-hour night shift, up at Tynycwm halt, and, according to his missus, Les' goitre is playing him up again, at least, that's what she told our Edna, in the butcher's, this afternoon."

"Does that mean we do not have a quorum, Mister Phillips?" asked Colin, looking up from his pencil sharpening.

Dinky gave him an old-fashioned looked from over the top of his half-glasses. "No, it does not! Five is a quorum and that's what we've got, so let's get on, shall we?"

Colin coloured and put his pencil back in his top pocket.

Dinky continued, testily. "As this is a special meeting, you don't have to read out the minutes of the last meeting, Colin, but you'll need to take minutes of this meeting, OK?"

"All ready to go, Mister Phillips," Colin replied meekly, opening the minute book and clicking his poised ball-pen.

"Right then, before I start, are there any questions?" said Dinky Phillips.

"Yeah," said Arthur looking up from inspecting his winkle-picker shoes. "When are we going to have a beer break, I'm nearly empty, me."

"Once I have explained to you, why you've all been called here, this evening," said Dinky. "I reckon ten minutes, quarter of an hour at most, orright? I take it you can contain yourselves for that long, can you?" Dinky was now at his sarcastic best.

Silence greeted his question, so he continued. "Now, I'm sure that you all know that I was called into the office of our great leader, Mister Iowerth Evans, yardmaster and expert on all matters concerning the sport of kings, that is, apart from knowing how to pick a winner, of course."

A ripple of laughter, lightened the atmosphere of the back room, Arthur lit another cigarette.

Denzil Evans extracted his Swiss-Army knife from his trouser pocket again and began probing the bowl of his pipe.

Eric picked at his teeth with a matchstick.

Colin undid the top button of his jacket and clicked the mechanism on his ballpoint pen.

Dinky continued. "Yes, well our noble yardmaster, then proceeded to inform me that he and Tudor Pritchard had arranged for the Tudor Pritchard All-Stars soccer team to play the Lamp and Flag, a week Saturday." He looked around the table expecting cries of disbelief and much wringing of hands.

Nothing happened.

"Well, I went for him bald-headed, I can tell you," he continued, undeterred by the general apathy within the room,

"I mean to say, as far as I was concerned it was just not on, there had been no consultation with this committee. Nobody had given the fixtures a second bloody glance, and the yard's shift roster was the last thing that the two of them had even considered. I was bloody well livid, I can tell you, and I let him know in no uncertain terms."

He passed his hand across the surface of the sparse growth of sandy hair that adorned the crown of his head. "I told him, I said, it's just not on, Iorwerth, I said, what about the Lamp and Flag's fixture list? There's bound to be a clash with your proposed dates, bound to be. Then there's Tony Croxley the union rep, I said, he'll have bloody kittens when he finds out about the shift roster being altered. Iowerth, I said, it's just not on and that's final." He leaned back in his seat and extracted a chain from his waistcoat pocket, and consulted the watch that was attached to it.

"So, when's the match, then, Dink?" asked Arthur blowing a stream of blue smoke across the table.

Denzil looked up from his pipe-bowl excavations. "Haven't you been listening, Arth'? Dinky, here, has just said that it's definitely not on, and that's final." He gave a wink.

Dinky cleared his throat. "Ah, now, when I said it's definitely not on, I didn't mean that we wouldn't be playing the match. Oh no, I was simply making sure that the Lamp and Flag didn't come out of it with egg on its face, like. It was just my way of telling him that we need to be consulted on all aspects of the clubs' administration and that we would get back to him at our convenience. There was no way that we were going to be ridden over roughshod by the likes of Mister Bloody Tudor Pritchard and the like."

"Shall I minute this verbatim, Mister Phillips or shall I precis it?" asked Colin Powell brightly.

Dinky looked heavenwards and sighed. "Whatever you've written, so far Colin, scrap it, simply write: the chairman opened the meeting and gave a brief summation of his meeting with Mister Iowerth Evans, and heads its, proposed soccer match between the Rogerstown Railway Club and the Tudor Pritchard all-stars, right?"

Colin looked crestfallen, nodded, and commenced to rule through the lines of neat writing that he had laboured over.

"Right," Dinky continued. "As I said, I did not intend to accept the yardmaster's fait accompli without getting some concessions from him, which I did." He pushed back his chair with a scrape. "Which is the next thing on the agenda. In the meantime, I shall take Arthur's premature suggestion and call a ten-minute break for those here who wish to replenish their glasses or to make themselves comfortable for the next session, meeting adjourned."

He hit the table with the empty stout bottle.

Arthur was halfway to the bar before the others had exited the committee room. Denzil joined him at the bar.

"What a frigging carve-up. It's all cut and dried, if you ask me."

Arthur called for a pint of Best and turned to Denzil.

"I could have told you that, ten minutes ago, old Evans probably promised Dinky some Sunday work, just to keep him sweet, bet you a pound to a pinch that he did."

Denzil scowled. "Aye and a new stove for the shunters' cabin, too, I bet," he turned to the barmaid. "A pint of whoosh, please Luv, oh, and a pickled egg as well, ta very much."

Arthur took a slurp from his glass. "Everything in this life's a bloody carve-up, Denz' you know that, and this club is no different, we're only here to make up the numbers." He took another gulp. "Still, it gets us out of the bloody house and away from the misery and the griping, don't it?"

Denzil looked at him over the rim of his glass. "What, are you and your Avril having a problem, then, Arth'?"

Arthur grimaced and shrugged. "Oh, you know how they are." He grinned, falsely. "Never bloody happy unless they're bloody well moaning about something or the other, we're on a hiding to nothing, us men. If we don't pay them enough attention, we don't love them any more, and we're almost certainly knocking-off somebody else. If we go and pay them a bit of attention, then we're sex mad and ought to be doctored, you can't bloody well win." He shrugged resignedly and turned back towards the committee room.

Denzil followed, shaking his head as though he had just seen a racehorse being mistreated.

Chapter Twenty-nine
Players

Once back in the committee room, Dinky Phillips closed the door and they all sat down, ready for the next session.

Arthur lit another cigarette.

Denzil chewed noisily on his pickled egg, while Colin clicked the mechanism on his ballpoint pen, as he studied Eric, who was cleaning the teeth on his comb with an old tiepin.

Dinky tidied the papers before him, squaring their sides before clipping them together with a paper clip. He cleared his throat.

"Right then, if we're all ready, we'll make a start."

Colin nervously raised a hand.

"Yes Colin, from now on you can take down this part of the meeting, verbatim," said Dinky pre-empting the booking clerk.

Colin coloured and clicked the mechanism on his ballpoint pen.

"Ok," said Dinky, leaning forward, hands splayed upon the table top. "Now, as I said earlier, I was not about to give in to Messrs Evans and Pritchard without getting something from them in return." He took a sip of his light ale. "Well, this is what they offered." He cleared his throat. "Providing that we play the match, as requested, a week next Saturday."

Denzil raised his pipe. "Hang on, a minute, Dink."

Dinky cut him off. "Wait until you hear the proposal, before you start objecting, orright?"

Denzil shrugged and commenced writing furiously on the pad in front of him.

"Right," said Dinky testily. "They said, that, if we played the match a week on Saturday, Tudor Pritchard would provide a trophy, which would be played for, thereon, on an annual basis."

"Don't tell us," said Arthur resignedly. "It's going to be called the Tudor Pritchard Annual Cup."

"You're quite wrong," snapped Dinky, stung by Arthur's obvious inference. "It's going to be called the Tudor Pritchard Perpetual Soccer Trophy."

They all groaned.

"Anyway," continued Dinky. "As I said, he's going to donate a trophy. He is also going to pay the council for the hire of the ground, and, he's going to provide miniature trophies for each of the players." He looked around the table triumphantly, "and, to cap it all, he's donating fifty pounds to the Lamp and Flag so that refreshments may be provided at the club, after the match. What about that then?" he said triumphantly, puffing out his chest and sticking his thumbs into his vest pockets.

Eric stopped the cleaning operation on his comb. "Fifty quid, jeez, we could have a right piss-up on that, that's for sure."

Dinky chose to ignore Eric. "Now," he said. "What we have to decide now, is, are we going to accept their proposition, or what?"

He looked around the table, eyebrows raised, inviting comments.

"Two things," said Arthur. "You say, he's already booked the pitch with the council?"

Dinky nodded.

"Ok, then," said Arthur, counting off on his fingers. "One, what if we say no, and two, where are our A and B sides going to be playing on that day?"

"Well to answer your first question, if, we say no to the proposition, then, he'll have to cancel the booking, unless there is another format that is acceptable to all concerned. As to your second question, the A side is away to Chepstow and the B side, who should have been playing at home, have had their match postponed, as their opponents can't field a side, due to overtime commitments at Penar colliery. So, they have now arranged to play a friendly against Blackwood, up there, so there's no problem as far as the club's other sides are concerned." He took another pull at his light ale.

"If both our sides are playing that day, who the bloody hell is going to be playing Tudor Pritchard's bunch of bloody fairies, then?" Denzil broke his self-imposed silence.

"No problem," replied Dinky\. "We'll put out a scratch side from within the yard and the club."

They all looked at him aghast.

"You must be bloody joking, Dink," said Arthur. "There's nobody in the club or up the yard who would have a clue. For Chrissakes, nobody there has kicked a ball for years."

"Don't worry," said Dinky. "As Denzil so eloquently put it, 'bloody fairies'. So, if, we can't get a scratch side to beat them, then there's something wrong, somewhere. Besides the last thing we want is a bloody walkover. We've got to make it look like it was a hard-fought game, haven't we? And what better way to do it than by putting out a scratch side?"

The members of the Lamp and Flag's Committee looked inquiringly at each other.

Arthur took a gulp of his pint.

Denzil drummed on the table top with his fingers.

Eric extracted a liquorish allsorts from his jacket pocket, picked off the coating of fluff and other extraneous matter, and popped it into his mouth, watched by Colin, who clicked the mechanism on his ballpoint pen.

Denzil stopped his drumming and looked up. "Well as far as I can see, as long as the pitch is available and we can get up a team, then I'm all for it, especially as the club is going to make some cash out of it. I reckon that it could be a good night all round."

"Yeah," agreed Arthur. "I go along with Denzil. What can we lose?"

Eric nodded. "Sounds good to me."

Colin stopped clicking his pen, rubbed his hands together excitedly and beamed his approval to all around the table.

"I'm all for it," he enthused.

"Good!" said Dinky, looking like a man who had known all along what the outcome of the meeting would be. "Now that's settled, let's get down to the nuts and bolts of the thing. What about the team? Who's going to play in what position?" He looked directly at Arthur.

Arthur shook his head. "\Now hang on a minute, Dink'. You're not expecting me to play, are you?"

"Certainly," replied Dinky. "We on the committee must set an example for others to follow. So, yes, I am expecting you to volunteer, and Denzil and Eric, I've got you all down to play."

Eric's protests were cut short by Denzil, who, to every body's surprise, said, "You can count me in, Dink'. I'm happy to play my part for the club."

Eric nodded and mumbled something unintelligible.

Arthur took a swig of his beer and relented. "Aye orright, go on then, put me down."

Colin raised his hand. "In the light of the response from around this table, I'm quite willing to..."

He was cut short. "You're running one of the lines, Colin," said Dinky, interjecting.

Colin coloured. "I'll be happy to accept, Mister Phillips, as long as somebody shows me what to do."

"Don't worry about that, Colin, we'll sort you out on the day," said Dinky, smiling for the first time since the meeting began.

"Right then, let's see, there's Arthur, Denzil and Eric. Len Crocker and Les Thomas should be OK by then, that's five. We need another six," he tapped his teeth with his pen and looked at the ceiling for inspiration. "Ah, that's right," he said, reminding himself. "There's Dennis and Albert Johnsey, who are both on the right shift. Then, there's young Terry McCarthy, Ray Deveraux and Billy Thomas, Les' cousin, oh, and there's that big Nigerian shunter. What's his name, Adey something or other?"

"Mjobo Adekunley," said Arthur, over the rim of his glass.

"Aye, that's the fella," said Dinky writing furiously.

He finished writing, capped his pen and looked up. "That's the lot, that's eleven. We're now all sorted on the playing front." He rubbed his hands together. "Now we'll take another break before sorting out the catering arrangements, OK?"

They all nodded as seats were hurriedly scraped back, prior to the dash to the bar.

Arthur moved up to the bar alongside Colin.

"what're you having, then Col? It's my shout."

Colin seemed taken aback by this sudden burst of unaccustomed bonhomie and generosity being directed at him.

He coloured. "That's very kind of you Arthur. I shall have a ginger beer shandy, if I may?"

"A pint of bitter and a ginger beer shandy, please luv," Arthur called to the barmaid.

Colin excitedly rubbed his hands together. "I can't wait to get back in there, so that we can sort out the rest of the arrangements, can you?"

Arthur handed him his ginger beer shandy and took a slurp from his own glass.

"I'm with you, there Col'," he said sarcastically. "This match is going to be one of the big events in the club's history, that's for sure." He suppressed the urge to laugh and he winked at the barmaid.

Colin took a tentative sip from his ginger beer shandy and then dabbed at the froth on his lips with a mauve handkerchief.

"I may just be able to persuade my girlfriend to come along, that's if she can swap her weaving class for another day," he said happily.

Arthur lit up a cigarette and studied the outline of the barmaid's skirt, mentally trying to guess what colour her suspenders were.

Chapter Thirty
Groundwork

"Orright, then?" called Dinky, looking around the bar. "Let's get back to it." He picked up his glass of light ale from the bar and headed for the committee room. "You too, Eric, leave the bloody fruit machine alone, there'll be plenty of time to lose your money after the meeting."

Eric dropped a dog-end onto the lino' and squashed it beneath the crepe soles of his black, suede shoes.

"I should have held those two pineapples," he muttered to himself, as he followed, Indian-file fashion into the committee room.

"Right then, are we all settled?" Dinky looked around the table over his half-glasses. "Now that we've sorted the team out, let's get down to arranging the evening's entertainment, is it?"

They all nodded.

Colin recommenced clicking the mechanism on his ballpoint pen.

Denzil brought out the huge, black tobacco pipe, gave it a whack against the open palm of his hand before gripping the stem between his teeth and giving it a trial suck. Apparently satisfied, he removed the pipe from his mouth and began to stuff the bowl with very dark, homegrown, rum-cured tobacco, tamping down the brown flakes with his thumb. He applied a lighted match to the contents of the bowl and clouds of blue smoke billowed towards the ceiling. A look of deep contentment spread across his face.

"I reckon we could have us a match and half if we play our cards right," he said taking an almighty slurp from his tankard before putting the pipe back between his teeth.

Colin looked up from the minute book, and before Dinky could interrupt him, said, "Following the match, why don't we put on a cold collation." He leaned forward in his seat excitedly.

"Better still," said Dinky, giving him an old-fashioned look. "Why don't we have a darts and skittles contest in the evening, followed by a faggots and peas supper?"

"We could get Malcolm Edwards on the organ and have a bit of a knees-up as well," offered Eric.

"I'll second that," said Denzil, through a cloud of smoke.

"I like it, I like it," enthused Colin quite beside himself with glee.

"What about a stripper, then?" asked Arthur, his face set in mock seriousness.

"Yeah," said Eric, looking up from the paper dart, that he had fashioned from a folded beer mat. "A stripper, great!"

Denzil remained tight lipped, but a great plume of smoke issued from his pipe, and his eyes sparkled.

Colin's grip tightened on his pen, his knuckles white and his eyes wide with apprehension.

Dinky, used to Arthur's little interjections, said, without raising his eyes from the agenda in front of him.

"Come on now, Arth' you know it's going to be mixed company that night. This is not the bloody Railway Club in Mill Street, For Christ's sake, the last thing we'd want is for our loved ones, and, or partners, to be confronted with a pair of bare knockers, and a G-string with sparkly bits on it, especially, while they'd be partaking of their faggots and peas. We wouldn't want that, would we?"

They all nodded their agreement.

"So, G-strings have sparkly bits on them, do they, Dink?" asked Arthur innocently.

Dinky didn't rise to Arthur's bait.

"That's what I've heard. I have no first-hand knowledge of such appendages, I can assure you, Arthur." He took a sip from his light ale and moved hurriedly on. "Let's summarise the position, is it?" He looked up, from his agenda, for any sign of dissent. "You can minute this Colin, OK?"

Colin coloured and nodded. "Can somebody loan me a pen the mechanism on mine seems to have jammed."

Arthur tossed him a Biro. "Try not thinking about G-strings, Col', you'll find your pens will last longer that way."

Colin coloured and studied the pen that he had been passed.

"So, let's see, what have we got?" Dinky scratched at his thinning hair. "We've sorted the ground arrangements out and we've picked the team, right?"

They all nodded, except for Arthur who asked, "What about the kit on the day, like?"

Dinky held up his hands. "It'll all be taken care of, Arth', shirts, shorts, socks and boots. They'll all be there in the changing rooms for you all, don't worry."

"What about sizes?" Arthur asked.

"No problem," replied dinky. "You'll be able to take your pick."

"Fair enough," said Arthur, and the rest nodded their acceptance.

"Right, having got that sorted, where are we?" Dinky studied his notes. "Oh yeah, that's right." He adjusted his half-spectacles, pushing them back up the bridge of his nose. "I'll sort out the darts and skittles side of it, but what about the catering, are we agreed on faggots and peas, then?"

"I'm all for it, me," said Denzil through a cloud of blue smoke. "But it don't half give my missus the wind."

"Well, we wouldn't want that, would we?" said Dinky, wearily. "Are there any alternative suggestions, then?" He looked around the table.

"What about an Indian take-away from the Bombay Palace?" Arthur offered.

Dinky looked at the ceiling, exasperation clearly beginning to show on his face.

"I think we'll steer clear of the exotic fare on that night, Arthur," he said po-faced. "There are too many imponderables with your foreign curry type dishes." He counted off on his fingers. "The choice of side dishes would take us all night to sort out. Do we have it with rice or chips, or both? What sort of spiciness do we opt for? If it's too hot, we'll never hear the end of it. If it's too mild they'll complain that it's not hot enough. Oh no, I think we'll give that one a miss, that's for sure."

"I go along with that," said Denzil. "I'd rather have to put up with my missus in bed, after faggots and peas than a bleeding curry, it don't bear thinking about."

"How about fish and chips, then?" suggested Colin, colouring up.

"Now that's a bloody good idea, our Col," said Dinky magnanimously. "Well done lad."

Colin's face turned a deep shade of puce. "Well, it's only a thought," he murmured staring at the table-top in embarrassment.

"I like it," said Dinky, rubbing the palms of his hands together. "Denzil can you sort that one out for us? You're pretty thick with Harry Carter the Chippy, ain't you?"

"Yeah, no problem, Dink'," replied Denzil puffing on his massive pipe. "I'll sort that first thing tomorrow, OK?"

Dinky nodded. "Well, sound him out, first, anyway, and I'll give you the total number of portions to order by next Friday, OK?"

Denzil nodded, puffing away contentedly on his pipe.

"Finally, we turn to you, Colin." Dinky looked over the top of his half-spectacles. "I want you to go and see Malcolm Edwards and see if he's available with his organ on the night. If so, book him from eight thirty to half ten. If he's not, come back to me before you do anything else, got that?"

Colin beamed and nodded to Dinky.

"Right that just about wraps things up," said Dinky, finishing up the last of his light ale. "Is there any other business, then?"

They all shook their heads.

"Right, in that case, meeting closed." Dinky used the empty bottle like a gavel.

Arthur looked at his watch; it was quarter to nine.

"What're you having then, Arth'?" asked Denzil, through a blue cloud of tobacco smoke.

"Not for me, ta," said Arthur heading for the door. "I'm knackered, me. I'm going to have an early night for a change. Besides, it's only fair on our Avril, this is the third time in four days that I've been out, this week."

Denzil nodded glumly. "Orright Taff, I'll see you, then?"

"Yeah, cheers." Arthur waved his goodbyes to all and sundry and left the bar.

He thrust his hands into his pockets and made his way home, heading up the steep, little lane, gloomily anticipating another evening of the silent treatment from Avril.

Chapter Thirty-one
Parting

As he crested the steep lane, something about the cottage seemed to be not quite right. He opened the front garden gate with a puzzled look on his face; the building was in darkness. He unlocked the front door and entered the small hall, nothing stirred; the silence seemed unnatural, almost ominous.

Arthur dismissed the feeling with a shrug. *Avril's eczema must be bothering her again*, he thought, glancing up the stairs, expecting to see a strip of light showing under the bedroom door, there was not a glimmer.

Puzzled, he hung up his jacket on a coat peg in the hall, and climbed the stairs and opened the door to the bedroom, the bed was undisturbed; there was no sign of Avril.

Arthur hurried back down the stairs and checked out the living room, it too was empty. The coal fire was barely alight, with just a glimmer of glowing embers showing through the thick, white ash that clogged the lower bars.

It's not like our Avril to go out at this time of night, he mused, frowning at the fire grate. "Perhaps she's with one of the neighbours," he murmured, with a shrug of the shoulders.

Arthur went into the kitchen. "I hope there's some cold meat in the fridge," he muttered to himself. "I'm beginning to feel a bit peckish."

He switched on the light and crossed the room to the fridge, taped to its door was an envelope. He opened it, extracted a single sheet of paper and read its contents.

"Jesus Christ!" he exclaimed, sitting down heavily onto a kitchen chair, and passing his hand over his face.

He reread the letter and then slowly folded it into four before dropping it onto the table and slumping down in the chair.

"Jesus frigging Christ!" he hissed, through gritted teeth.

He picked up the note, unfolded it and read it again, anger welling up in him.

"That's all I bastard well need!" he yelled, screwing up the note into a small ball and hurling it across the kitchen.

He got quickly to his feet and slammed out of the kitchen, into the hall, where he savagely tore his jacket from the coat peg, snapping the cotton tag from the collar in the process. Cursing at the top of his voice, he marched out of the cottage in a rage, slamming the front door savagely behind him.

Avril had left him.

He strode back down the hill, inwardly boiling, silently cursing Avril for her act of treachery; his mind working overtime.

He reached the Black Cat Inn and barged open the front door, still fuming as he pushed his way to the bar, through the throng of drinkers.

"Hello Arthur luv, pint of bitter, is it?" Arthur's pent up aggression eased slightly at the sight of two cornflower-blue eyes twinkling at him, their lashes, heavy with mascara; a tip of a pink tongue explored a glistening, scarlet bottom lip.

"Yeah, thanks Lorna," he said, his anger rapidly diminishing, as he studied the well-rounded figure of the barmaid, who, in turn, was fixing him with a seductive smile. "And, give me a large scotch on the side, as well, and get one for yourself, is it?"

"That's very kind of you, Arth'," she said, demurely lowering her eyelashes that briefly fanned her cheeks.

"My pleasure, Lorna," he said straightening his tie, his anger now totally dissipated.

The cornflower-blue eyes briefly left his face and looked down at the pint that she was pulling for him.

"Have we come into money, then, or what?" she asked placing his pint in front of him.

He lifted the glass to his lips and took a tentative sip.

"No, I just felt like pushing the boat out, seeing that it's Saturday." He brought out a packet and offered her a cigarette.

She shook her head. "Not for me luv, thanks, all the same."

Arthur took out one for himself and lit it.

"Besides," he said, automatically switching into his chatting-up mode. "We don't normally get the pleasure of seeing our gorgeous

Landlady serving in the bar on a Saturday, do we?" He took a swig from his pint pot and winked at her. "The very least that I could do, was to buy her a drink, before she goes back to looking after the moneyed-set in the lounge." He blew smoke at the ceiling. "Can't usually be bothered with us bar boys, can she?" He looked at the other drinkers standing at the bar and winked. "Am I right then, Bob?"

A heavy-set, red-faced individual, who was leaning on one elbow, at the end of the bar, grinned and adjusted his cap. "Yeah, you're spot on there, Arth'," he winked knowingly back.

The cornflower-blue eyes sparkled back at Arthur, and the moist red lips parted into a knowing little smile.

"Ah well, tonight's different," she said, deliberately including the other drinkers in the immediate vicinity. "It's the Golf Society's Annual Men-only bash, over in the West Country this weekend, so you've got me to put up with tonight, so just behave yourselves, all right?" Lorna's cornflower-blue eyes briefly turned their gaze back upon Arthur as she went to the spirit optics and poured a Scotch for Arthur and a gin for herself.

The laughter that followed soon subsided and was replaced by the usual general hubbub, as the other nearby drinkers recommenced their conversations.

"Cheers." She took a sip of the gin and placed the glass on the bar top, a half-moon of lipstick now adorned the rim of the glass. "No lady wife, then?"

Arthur shook his head. "Gone to the pictures with her sister in Newport," he lied. "Staying over, be back tomorrow, sometime, much the same as your Arnold," he observed. "I take it, that he's gone on this weekend do, as well, then?" he casually asked, looking at her over the rim of his pint glass.

Lorna took another sip from her glass. "Mmm," she nodded. "I'm going to be all on my own, unprotected." The cornflower-blues eyes asked the question.

Arthur raised his whisky glass and touched it to hers.
"I can't really see that happening, can you?" He smiled, lasciviously, answering the question.

All thoughts of Avril had been well and truly consigned to his mental dustbin, and he was now completely focused on the opportunity that had been presented to him by the absence of golf-playing husband Arnold. The conquest of Lorna had now become priority number one.

Two hours later, with the last customer long gone and the darkened 'pub now locked and secured for the night, Lorna's moist scarlet lips pressed against Arthur's mouth while he explored her well preserved forty-year old body as she lay beside him in the master bedroom of the Black Cat Inn.

Chapter Thirty-two
Recriminations

The old man shielded his eyes from the bright sunlight and scanned the nearby landscape in the hope that he might spot the Black Cat Inn or the little stone cottage that he had once rented, but the once-open landscape, with its scattering of houses, had now been built on, and, as far as the eye could see, every inch of land seemed to be occupied; shingled roofs of every hue dominating the skyline. Whichever direction the old man looked, hardly any building appeared recognisable. Many, if not all, seemed to him, to be less than thirty years old.

He fixed his eyes on a row of three-storied flats that stood, on his side of the motorway, where he would have expected to see the Black Cat's car park and beer garden.

Have I got it wrong? He asked himself, rubbing at his chin. *As far as I can remember the old Cat was somewhere near those apartments.* He stared, his hand shielding his eyes as he sought confirmation. *Yeah, that's definitely where the Black Cat used to be.* He argued to himself. *You can see part of the old wall of the lane, just behind the apartment's garages, there.*

The old man pointed the stem of his pipe towards the flats, his eyes following the line of the garages and on up, to where the section of the old lane's wall was showing.

He focused on the houses, which had been built further on up the hill, beyond the stretch of wall, hoping for more glimpses of the old lane, but he was unlucky, for none were forthcoming.

"Naw, it's no good." The old man shook his head in disgust. "The whole bloody landscapes changed. It's barely recognisable from the old days."

He studied the small stretch of old wall, slowly scratching his head.

I suppose the old Cat must have been demolished, when they erected those flats, and the cottage? That's almost certainly long gone, too, or, even worse, has been converted into one of those little rural hideaways, essential for the wellbeing of the chattering classes. Probably owned by some fat, tosser of a solicitor, or the like. He growled inwardly.

He could feel his bile returning, as he visualised the cottage with a, now, modern, mock Cotswold stone extension, loft conversion, double garage, double-glazing and PVC conservatory. He shook his head and dismissed thoughts of the little cottage's supposed desecration, being, determined to remember it as it was, and not as it might have become.

Now, as the old man stared ahead, seeing nothing, remembering that fateful night when Avril had left him. The sight of the note, taped to the door of the refrigerator, was still imprinted on his brain, some forty odd years later. He was loath to admit it, but he was still plagued with the occasional dream, which would see him, still striding angrily down the lane to the Black Cat Inn.

Even though Avril's leaving, and what was to follow, was still vividly imprinted on his memory, strangely, he had completely forgotten, until now, his escapade with the lovely Lorna, Landlady of the Black Cat.

I bloody slipped up there, didn't I? He grinned to himself. *If I hadn't buggered off back to Newport, there might have been an opportunity of nooky, on a regular basis, that dopey twat of a husband, Arnold, was more interested in the sodding golf club and his bloody Masonic friends, than keeping tabs on his missus.* He sighed. *She was good fun, was Lorna, God love her, pity that we only managed to have it off that once, because she was like a thing possessed. I was bloody knackered when I finally got back home, in the early hours.*

So bloody knackered, in fact, that he had slept right through the morning, and had not woken up until the Sunday lunchtime.

Crawling from his bed, his head thumping, Arthur wondered why there was no aroma of Sunday roast pervading the air. As he stared at the reflection of the red-eyed wreck, in the bathroom mirror, he remembered that Avril had left him, and that he would have to rely on the cold cuts, for his lunch, that were in the refrigerator.

His stomach rebelled at the thought.

It wasn't until the week following the Lorna episode that Avril finally made contact with Arthur. He had just finished working a week of nights, and had been putting off the tracking-down of Avril until after the match against the Tudor Pritchard All-Stars, but Avril pre-empted that by ringing him on the Friday, the evening before the match.

She 'phoned to tell him that she would be coming to the cottage that Saturday to pick up the rest of her clothes and various bits and pieces that were hers.

"Well, make it in the afternoon, then," he barked. "That's when I'll be otherwise engaged, elsewhere."

"Don't worry, I'll not bother you," she replied. "I'll be long gone before you get back from that stupid football match."

Before he could get in an answer, she continued. "And don't think that the fact that you haven't bothered to get in touch, has gone unnoticed, there's a solicitor's letter on its way to you."

He was about to give her a devastating riposte when she sneezed, and the dial tone followed.

"Balls to you and your frigging solicitor!" he shouted into the handset, before slamming it back onto its cradle.

Arthur had intended staying in with a couple of bottles of Worthington and an evening of television, but Avril's telephone call had so incensed him that he shelved his plans for an early night. The bottles of Worthington went back into the 'fridge, and the Avengers got kicked into touch, and he telephoned Dai, instead.

"Christ almighty! Arth'. You're still alive, then," said Dai sarcastically. "Is that really you? We, here, in the big city, had heard stories, that the night life up in Rogerstown was really wild, and seeing as how we haven't heard from you since the old king died, we thought that it had all become too much, and had finally done for you."

"Piss off Marshall, you Twat!" Arthur shouted down the 'phone with mock severity. "You know I bloody well 'phoned you three weeks ago, so don't come the-old-soldier with me, orright?" He could hear Dai sniggering on the other end of the line. "So you can stop bloody well laughing and cut the bullshit for a minute, and listen, will you?"

Dai suppressed his laughter. "Go on, then Buggerlugs, what's up?"

Arthur looked into the hall mirror and combed his hair; with the telephone-handset tucked between chin and an upraised shoulder.

"I'm getting pissed off with it up here, so I thought that I'd come down to town for a drink, for a change. What do you reckon? We can have few pints and a take away, and I can get the last bus up at half past ten, eh?"

There was a momentary pause.

"Now don't go blowing your bloody top," said Dai softly. "But I gotta say no, Taff."

"What d'yer mean no? Don't tell me that you're on nights, for Christ's sake?" Arthur said, feeling very aggrieved.

"No, there's no night shifts at Mill Street any more," replied Dai. "I only do mornings and afternoons now, but that's not the reason."

"What's the sodding reason, then?" bellowed Arthur, his dander, well and truly up.

"I've got a date," said Dai cheerfully.

"Oh, for crying out bloody loud," shouted Arthur. "Of all the sodding days to pick to go and have a bloody date, you have to go and pick tonight, that takes the bloody cake, that does."

"How the bloody hell d'yer expect me to know that you were going to ring, I haven't got a bleeding crystal ball, for Christ's sake." Dai shouted back down the 'phone.

"Orright," said Arthur, his annoyance, lessening. "Hold your sodding hair on, I didn't realise that you were courting, did I?"

"I'm not bloody well courting," retorted Dai. "This is just a one-off date, OK?"

"OK, OK, it's my fault. I should have 'phoned last week, I know," Arthur conceded.

"What about tomorrow, then?" Dai, offered, trying to be helpful.

"I can't tomorrow," replied Arthur. "We've got a do on, up at the Lamp and Flag, after the match."

"What match is that then, Butt?" asked Dai.

"Oh, just a friendly against a betting-shop side, that's all," replied Arthur, trying not to make it sound too important.

"Since when have you been going to watch the Lamp and Flag play?" queried Dai, sounding somewhat confused. "You're normally stuck in the house watching the horses on TV, on a Saturday?"

"I'm not going to watch. I'm down to play," Arthur answered, defensively.

Dai gave a hoot of laughter. "Play, what, you playing soccer? Christ you haven't kicked a bloody football for years. What in God's name possessed you to stick your hand up for that one?"

"As I said it's only a bloody friendly. Besides they're only kids, for Christ's sake," answered Arthur defensively. "Anyway, it's only right that I should give it a go, as I'm on the committee, like."

"Well good bloody luck," laughed Dai. "You'll need it, especially if there's music at the do. You'll be too bloody knackered to dance, especially with your Avril expecting a modern waltz or two."

"Avril won't be going," Arthur said quietly.

"How come?" asked Dai. "She having trouble with her swollen ankles again?"

"No," replied Arthur sharply. "We've split up."

He heard the hiss of surprise from Dai. "Jeez, how come?"

"Oh, it's a long story," said Arthur, not wanting to pursue the subject. "I'll tell you next time I see you."

"Orright," said Dai taking the hint and not pushing his luck.

Arthur changed the subject. "I tell you what," he said. "What if I go along to the do, show my face for an hour, then make some sort of excuse and leave. I'll hop on a bus and be down with you around nine, then we can hit the town. What do you reckon?"

"Yeah, orright, sounds good to me," replied Dai.

"Right then, son, all being well, I'll see you tomorrow," said Arthur. "If there's a problem I'll try to give you a ring before seven, ok?"

"Great," said Dai. "See you tomorrow, then, Butt."

"Cheers, Dai," said Arthur replacing the telephone receiver grabbing for his jacket.

He combed his hair again, straightened his tie and stepped out of the front door and headed down the lane towards the Lamp and flag, for another boozy session.

Chapter Thirty-three
Survival

When Arthur eventually surfaced, mid-morning the following day, he sat on the edge of the bed, holding his throbbing head.

Any minute now it's going to fall off and smash into a thousand pieces on the linoleum, he thought, as he gingerly explored the inside of his mouth with a tongue, which felt as though it belonged to someone else, or had, overnight, become coated with a strange substance from another galaxy.

He groaned and his stomach churned, reminding him of the seven pints of stunner and four rum and blacks that he'd consumed the previous evening.

He looked around the bedroom, at the trail of clothes that were strewn across the floor, from door to ottoman. *At least they don't have any puke on them,* he noted, as he rose unsteadily to his feet and staggered to the bathroom.

A puffy-eyed stranger stared back at him from the mirror, so he ran some cold water, and, summoning up all of his courage, doused his face. The shock of the cold water did the trick, it felt like a slap across the face and it quickly brought him out of his torpor. He splashed more of the cold water onto his face and then put his mouth under the cold-tap and sucked greedily at the stream, swallowing and belching loudly. Now, he felt that he was beginning to improve, being a hundred percent better than he was, ten minutes ago, now he only felt awful.

He ran his wet hands through his hair, and walked back into the bedroom, where he wiped them on the eiderdown, before reaching for his trousers and shirt.

He thought briefly about breakfast but couldn't face it. The memory of last night's pie and chips, that he'd eaten on the way up the steep lane, putting him right off the idea.

He poured hot water onto the coffee-powder in his cup and reached for the sugar-bowl, against which, leaned the envelope from Avril's letter, on it a message, written in pencil. *DON'T FORGET TO RING DAI AFTER THE GAME.*

"Oh shit!" he hissed, "the sodding match." He looked at his watch, it was eleven fifty-five. "Christ Almighty, I've gotta be at the bloody Memo' ground by half past one."

He took a slug of the hot, strong, black coffee and reached for a cigarette from a packet that lay open on the table, lit up and blew a stream of smoke at the ceiling, then took another huge gulp of coffee.

He rubbed a hand across his face.

I ought to have a shave by rights, he thought, but then dismissed the thought. "No, cobblers to it, I'll shave later on," he muttered.

Logic finally won the day, knowing that it would be fatal to play the match on an empty stomach Arthur was forced to open the fridge and look for food. His stomach rebelled at the sight of a half-eaten veal and ham pie, and the thought of a fried egg made him quickly shut the fridge door and to sit back down again. Finally, he made himself get up and go to the pantry.

Ten minutes later he gingerly ate at a forkful of beans on toast, which, much to his wonder, tasted surprisingly good, and, he managed to keep it down, which was a major triumph, considering the state he'd been in, half an hour earlier.

He poured another cup of strong, black coffee and washed down the last of the toast with a long gulp and settled back in his chair, lit a cigarette, and, for the first time that morning, felt almost human.

Finishing the cigarette, Arthur flicked the stub into the cold ashes that lay in the fireplace. He stretched and looked at his watch, it was twelve fifteen. He took the dirty dishes to the sink and left them there for later.

Improving by the minute, he changed his mind and decided that he still had enough time to have a bath and a shave before the one thirty deadline at the Memorial ground.

Forty minutes later, feeling more like his old self again, Arthur strode down the lane whistling, almost looking forward to the coming experience of running around after a leather ball for an hour and a half.

He arrived at the ground ten minutes earlier than he had expected, and thought about having a quick pint in the Rogerstown Inn, but dismissed the thought just as quickly, and walked through the main gate and on towards the dressing room.

Most of the team was already there, milling about, flicking ash from their cigarettes onto the tops of the footlockers, or into any handy, available football boot.

"Orright 'Arth'," said Denzil, looking up from his boot tying.

"Yeah, cheers Denz'. How yer diddling, then?"

Denzil gave him the thumbs up. "Great, Butt, ready to give those bloody Betting-shop Nancy boys a bollocking, for sure."

"How about you then, Adey?" asked Arthur. "All ready to go?"

The large Nigerian gave a wide grin. "That's for sure, my man."

Just then the door opened and in strode Dinky Phillips.

"Shit and bloody corruption!" he shouted, kicking at a footlocker in disgust.

"What's, up, then Dink'?" asked Arthur. "Forgot to post your pools or what?"

Dinky gave him an old-fashioned look. "I can't be bothered with your pathetic bloody jokes right now, Arthur. We've got a major problem on our hands." He sat down and stared at the row of coat pegs on the opposite wall, his fingers drumming on the wooden seat.

"So, what's to do, then?" asked Denzil, still bent over his boots.

"We've lost two of our stars," Dinky replied.

"Who, Dink'?" Arthur asked.

"Terry McCarthy and Billy Thomas, our main attacking force up the right flank." Dinky punched the palm of his hand.

"You make it sound like bloody El Alamein." Arthur lit up a cigarette.

"It's no joking matter, I can tell you, the whole team will have to be reorganised." Dinky searched feverishly in his inside pocket and fished out a crumpled note pad.

"Our first priority is to replace the missing players." He scratched his head. "But who's available at such short notice? That's the bloody problem."

"You'll not get anybody else at such short notice," offered Eric, who, until then, had been reading the Dandy.

"You're right, Eric, it's a bloody impossible situation."

"You'll have to play, then, Dink'," said Arthur in a matter of fact voice.

"Play, me play, don't be bloody stupid Arthur." Dinky was on his feet and shouting. "Bloody play, Christ Almighty! I haven't kicked a ball for twenty sodding years. What're you trying to bloody well do to me?"

Arthur shrugged, dismissing the tirade. "Well if you don't then we'll end up fielding half a side, and we'll be a bloody laughing stock. The Lamp and Flag will never live it down."

Dinky slumped back onto the bench, his face ashen. "Jeez, I can't allow that to happen, can I?" He looked around for support. "What choice do I have?"

They all shook their heads.

"Oh, balls to it all, that's what I say." He got up and started to remove his jacket. "If it's for the good of the Lamp, then so be it."

A spontaneous burst of applause rang around the changing room.

Denzil patted Dinky on the shoulder.

The room had more stiff upper lips than a dozen British war movies.

"You're still one short," said Arthur, bringing them all down to earth again.

"Oh, knackers," muttered Eric.

"Come on, for Christ's sake," said a muffled Les Thomas, his face inside his football shirt. "We don't need eleven to beat the arse off those poofters, do we?"

"Absolutely," agreed Denzil, his back stiffening with pride.

"You're quite right, of course, Les," responded Dinky, having now regained his composure. "Nevertheless, we do need a full team, and a full team we shall have."

He got up and stomped from the room.

Five minutes later he returned, leading a protesting Colin by the arm.

"It'll be orright, Colin, trust me," he cajoled. "We'll play you out on the wing, where, you won't get any bother, honest."

"But you said that I'd be running the line, Mister Phillips. I'm not sure that I can do the wing thing."

"I know that, lad," Dinky purred. "But we're in a bit of a jam, like, and you're the only man available that we can trust." He put his arm around Colin's shoulder and gave it a squeeze. "Don't let the Lamp and Flag down will you? We're relying on you."

Colin coloured. "Gosh Mister Phillips, when you put it like that how can I possibly refuse."

"Good lad," said Dinky slapping him heartily on the back.

That's when Mjobo split his shorts.

"Oh, Christ man, look what's bloody happened here." He pointed to his crotch, where the shorts had entirely disintegrated, leaving only the waistband intact. Mjobo was now wearing two legs instead of shorts.

Dinky was horrified. "Buggeration!" He stamped his foot in rage. "That's all we bloody well need; they were the largest size that we had."

"Well I can't play like this, can I?" shrugged the big Nigerian.

"I know that, I know that," snapped Dinky. "Let me think a minute, will you."

He paced the floor of the dressing room for several minutes then suddenly stopped.

"Right, got it," he said and strode from the room.

Five minutes later he slammed back into the dressing room.

"Our Edna is on her way over with a spare pair, she'll be about ten minutes, OK?" He wiped at the perspiration on his brow with his sleeve. "In the meantime, for Christ's sake cover yourself up, will you?" He pointed at Mjobo's exposed parts.

"What with?" said Arthur, grinning. "We don't have a bucket big enough."

The dressing room echoed with laughter, even Dinky managed a half smile.

Still grinning Arthur started to get changed. He picked up a shirt, shorts and socks and put them to one side and went to the row of boots, on the corner shelf, and began to sort through them.

"Hang on!" he muttered. "All these are too big." He went through them again. "Hey Dinky these are too bloody big."

"Do me a favour, Arth' give it a rest," said Dinky wearily. "I can't take any more of your merry quips."

"I'm not joking," Arthur said, holding up a boot. "Eight is the smallest that I can find."

"What do you mean the smallest? Eight is your average, for Christ's sake." Dinky was starting to lose control. "How bloody small do you want them? You didn't tell me that you had deformed feet."

"They are not bloody deformed," said Arthur angrily. "They're just small, that's all."

Dinky sat back down with his head in his hands.

"Well that's the best you're going to get. Roll up a couple of pairs of socks and shove them into the toes. You probably won't know the difference."

He looked thoroughly demoralised.

A car horn sounded, breaking the silence.

"That'll be Edna with the spare pair of shorts," Dinky said getting slowly to his feet. "I'll just be a sec'."

Arthur sat down on the hard-wooden bench and lit a cigarette.

"This is bloody brilliant, this is," he complained, rolling up a pair of socks and stuffing them into the toe of one of the boots, then going through the same procedure with the second boot, before carefully, easing his foot into it, the second boot quickly followed and he got to his feet.

"Bloody rotate!" He stamped down onto the changing room floor. "Now I know how Coco the bleeding clown felt like." He tested the boots again with a couple of quick stamps on the floor. "I'll never be able to bloody run in these."

Denzil gave him an encouraging slap on the back.

"You'll do great, Arth'. Don't worry about that, orright?"

Arthur shrugged. "I'll give it a go, anyway."

The door of the dressing room burst open and Dinky stomped in, his face like thunder.

"These are all that our Edna could find, that were big enough. You'll have to make do with them, orright?" He tossed them across the room to Adey.

The big Nigerian caught them and held them up at arm's length, for inspection.

"They're bloody Khaki! I thought you were going to get football nicks?"

"I told you," Dinky hissed in exasperation, "they're the only ones that Edna could lay her hands on."

Adey held them close to his face, giving them a close inspection.

"What the frigging hell, are they?"

Dinky coloured and got angrily to his feet.

"They happen to be my sister-in-law's rambler's shorts, if you don't mind, Christ! She'd have kittens if she knew what they were being used for, she'd be turning in her bloody grave."

He sat back down muttering and busied himself with the tying of the laces on his boots.

"Sorry, Dink'," apologised Adey. "I didn't realise."

"Ah well, you weren't to know," conceded Dinky.

"What did she die of, Dink'?" asked Arthur brightly.

"She had a heart attack whilst climbing Twmbarlwm," replied Dinky solemnly.

"Jeez! She wasn't wearing these, was she?" Adey hurriedly dropped them onto the bench.

"No, of course she bloody well wasn't," Dinky barked. "It's her spare pair."

Adey didn't seem entirely convinced, but he shrugged and reluctantly began climbing into the large expanse of khaki.

Denzil coughed and looked at the ceiling.

Arthur bit his lip as he pulled the number-seven shirt over his head.

Colin sat immobile, his white legs sticking out of his shorts like pipe cleaners.

Dinky broke the silence with a clap of his hands.

"Right then lads, let's get our act together. We kick off in ten minutes. So, let's get out there and limber up, is it?"

"Any team tactics, then, Dink'?" asked Denzil attempting a straight-legged bend.

Dinky nodded. "Yes, play your own game."

Eric looked totally mystified.

Denzil quickly straightened up after his knee gave an ominous click.

"Aye, right, then," he said, doubtfully.

Chapter Thirty-four
Combat

Play your own game, jeez what a bloody scream. The old man grinned. *Poor old Dinky didn't have a bloody clue.* He stared at the motorway. *Play your own game, what a bloody laugh that turned out to be.* He folded his arms and slowly shook his head. *I don't know who the bloody hell we thought we were kidding; we must have looked a right bunch of bums when we ran out onto the Memo' field that day...*

Compared to the immaculately turned out Betting shop team, 'a bunch of bums' was probably an apt description for the Lamp and Flag select eleven, ten of whom ran on to the pitch sporting faded red shirts, white shorts and red socks, while the eleventh member lumbered onto the pitch, bringing up the rear, sporting a nifty pair of khaki shorts, complete with two, button-down back pockets and a reinforced gusset, encasing his muscular, black behind.

Following Mjobo onto the pitch was the Tudor Pritchard Eleven, resplendent in purple and white striped shirts with purple collars and cuffs, white shorts and purple and white-hooped socks. They ran onto the pitch, looking lean and fit, and, to Arthur's dismay, very athletic. The sparse strands of onlookers clapped and cheered them.

The referee was the local police constable, Gethin Thomas, with Iowerth Evans and Tudor Pritchard running the touchlines.

Gethin tossed the coin and the Betting-shop team won. They decided to play towards the power station end and following a loud blast from the constable's Acme Thunderer, they kicked off at three o'clock sharp.

By twenty past, the Lamp and Flag were three down.

"Some frigging walk-over," wheezed Les Thomas as he chased back towards the Railway Club's goalmouth. "Nobody told me that we'd be playing a bunch of bloody, super-fit nineteen-year- olds, roll on bloody half time, I'm bleeding knackered."

Arthur nodded in agreement but was too exhausted to speak.

A long ball down the wing found the Tudor-Pritchard right-winger, who cut inside Stan Evans, danced around Mjobo Adekunley and then cut back outside, towards the touchline. Len Crocker advanced from his goal line, in an effort to narrow the angle, hands splayed ready for action.

The winger cut back inside, widening the angle and let fly with his left boot. The ball scorched past Len, into the back of the net.

"Shit and corruption," panted Dinky. "We're getting frigging stuffed."

The Lamp and Flag kicked off for the fourth time. The ball sailed up the pitch into the opposition's penalty area, where their tall, rangy centre half met it, and headed it back up the pitch, his headed pass finding the Betting-shop number nine, who chested it down and poked it forward, as he ran towards the waiting Arthur, who, ran, manfully towards the ball, optimistically swinging a boot at it, in the hope that he could clear it up field, before the centre forward could get to it.

Amazingly, his foot connected with it, and the ball bulleted back towards the onrushing centre forward, catching him squarely in the groin. With an agonised howl, the Betting-shop player went over backwards and lay curled up on the grass clutching at his testicles, mouthing obscenities.

At the same time as the ball hit the number nine, Arthur's right boot flew off his foot, at a tangent and hurtled forward, hitting Constable Thomas squarely on the back of his head.

Following the impact, the constable, immediately joined the prone centre forward on the ground, senseless.

"You dirty bugger!" cried an incensed old lady from the front of the small crowd that stood on the touchline. "You ought to be locked up for fouling like that."

She angrily hurled her umbrella at Arthur, who ducked, and watched it sail over his head, catching Mjobo Adekunley squarely on the nose.

"Oy, Oy, Oy! That'll be enough of that," shouted Tudor Pritchard, waving his flag furiously, running on to the pitch towards the crouching Mjobo, whose nose, which was, now, streaming with blood.

Through tear-filled eyes the big Nigerian, could just about make out a blurred figure, with arm raised, running towards him. Thinking that he was about to get another smack in the face, Mjobo raised up an arm in defence of his face, and with the other arm let go a haymaker of a punch, which caught Tudor Pritchard on the point of the chin, instantly felling him to the ground, where he joined the other two casualties.

The All-Star's tall centre half threw himself at Mjobo, fists flailing at the black man's large gut. Stan Evans and Les Thomas rushed in to separate the two mauling men and one of the Nigerian's flailing arms caught Les and sent him spinning to the ground, where he joined the All-Star's centre forward, Constable Thomas and Tudor Pritchard.

Mjobo, still having vision problems, stumbled backwards over the crumpled figure of Les, pulling down the centre half and Stan in the process.

That's when all hell broke loose.

The rest of the players joined in the melee, followed by girlfriends, wives and mothers. In fact, the whole female population of the crowd seemed to descend upon both sets of players, attacking some, defending others, soon it was "perm' any eight from ten".

Players were fighting players, spectators were fighting spectators, and players were fighting spectators.

A St John's ambulance man, who was tending to the fallen referee, was suddenly upended and dragged screaming into the milling throng.

Colin, the clerk, could be seen fleeing along the riverbank, minus his shorts, followed by two stout females in hot pursuit.

Denzil, who had had enough, was making his way back to the dressing room dragging his right leg, and shaking his head in disgust.

Arthur, who had immediately vacated the playing area, following the umbrella incident, had beaten Denzil to it by five minutes and had changed and was heading away from the fracas just as the two police vans arrived.

Ten minutes later, it was all over, with the police arresting all the remaining players, plus, two-dozen spectators.

The game was abandoned and the presentation cancelled.

The do was scrapped.

Arthur climbed wearily back up the hill and returned to the cottage, where he telephoned Dai and then went to bed for a couple of hours. That evening he caught the bus to Newport, where he and Dai proceeded to try and drink the King Billy dry.

An account of the ill-fated match made the front page of the local newspaper, the following Monday, its banner headlines proclaiming: *Soccer riot at valley town — 32 arrested.*

Several weeks later, following the court case, twelve of the players were fined for disorderly conduct, with the remainder of those arrested, being bound over to keep the peace.

Most of the spectators, who were arrested, ended up spending much of that fateful Saturday in the cells of Maindee Police Station, in Newport, before eventually being let off with cautions.

The All-Star's centre forward's severely bruised testicles became the talk of his squash club, who subsequently lost the league title due to his incapacity.

Police Constable Thomas was off work for six weeks, during which time he could be seen in the reference library wearing a neck brace.

Iowerth Evans was banned from all of Tudor Pritchard's betting shops and, as a reprisal, Tudor Pritchard was banned *sine die* from the lamp and Flag.

Dinky Phillips suffered a sprained wrist and a broken pair of half-glasses, and a week of the silent treatment from his wife, on account of her late sister's khaki Rambler's-shorts, which were in dire need of restoration in the gusset area.

Mjobo Adekunley, the big Nigerian shunter, could be seen, walking the sidings, sporting an injured nose that was twice its normal size and resembled a boxing glove.

On hearing of the station booking clerk's escapade, Colin Powell's girlfriend, disowned him, returning his Christmas present, *The Chipmunks Greatest Hits,* LP, together with a withering letter, condemning him for his shameless exhibition of sexual excess with local Girl Guide Mistress, Olive Blakewell and her sister Josie.

The boot that caused all of the damage was never recovered, and two weeks later, Arthur received a bill, from the club's committee, charging him ten shillings and sixpence for replacement costs. Furious, Arthur sent in his resignation and told them to go and stuff themselves. Six weeks later, he said goodbye to the little cottage and to Rogerstown Junction, when he moved back in with his mother, sister and grandfather at Newport.

Chapter Thirty-five
Puddings

Slowly, the old man rubbed the palms of his hands together, and then, absentmindedly, tested every finger on both hands, with finger and thumb, searching out every wrinkle and ridge, each a reminder of the passing years. Finally, he finished his inspection, thrust his hands into his trouser pockets and turned his attention back to the motorway, watching, the seemingly endless traffic, snaking its way into the distance towards Newport.

Some of the cars were angling off, away from the mainstream, and were scuttling along the motorway's slip road, towards the junction with the road leading to the housing estate and the adjacent supermarket. He watched, as, one by one, the vehicles peeled off, some taking the road to the housing estate and the safe haven of the brightly painted carports, others going into the supermarket's car park.

From his vantage point, the old man studied the toy-sized cars, as they homed in on their respective carports, then he switched his attention to the supermarket and the shoppers, who were scurrying about the forecourt like ants, their trolleys glinting in the sunlight.

From his standpoint, the roofs of the hundreds of cars that were parked at the front and sides of the supermarket looked like a patchwork quilt of steel.

"Lowry meets Legoland," he muttered. Arthur scratched at his head. *How the bloody hell did we ever manage to do without supermarkets, all those years ago, beats the hell out of me,* he thought.

His Mother, like most housewives in the Docklands area, was still shopping at the neighbourhood shops in the early nineteen sixties, very often visiting the local fishmongers, the butcher's shop, or the fruit and vegetable market, several times a week.

Fresh food was the order of the day, and very often, all that graced the interior of the new refrigerators of those lucky enough to afford such luxuries, was the Sunday joint and Friday's fish.

The concept of frozen food still proved an anathema to most, and it wasn't until the Supasaver, had been built on the old bombsite at the end of Commercial Road, that most of Dockland's womanhood, finally succumbed to the temptation of the pristine and tempting world of self-service, and frozen packet meals.

The years of wartime austerity had finally been put behind them. The brave new world of television sets, vacuum cleaners and twin-tub washing machines was beckoning.

The marketing age had arrived.

Arthur's Mother was no exception, and, once smitten, she availed herself of its cut-priced, vacuum-packed offerings. Although, it would take her many months before she was persuaded to actually buy anything frozen. From then on, it was the only place to shop.

Granddad, on the other hand, would have none of it, and, as usual, proved to be his normal stubborn self when it came to airing his opinions on the subject of shopping…

"I don't want anything to do with those bloody new-fangled places and their sodding wire trolleys." He bellowed cantankerously, from behind the evening paper. "What do we want with one of those sodding delicatessen things, anyway? If, I was ever bothered about getting any of that bloody foreign muck, I would go around to old Aswar's in Lewis Street, wouldn't I? Besides, what's wrong with the Home and Colonial, it's got all that a man could want, in the way of edibles, and it's fresh, none of that bloody frozen rubbish." His face appeared from behind the evening paper. "What do you reckon then, Arth'?"

Arthur looked up from the jigsaw puzzle that he and his young niece, Nicola were getting wrong together.

"Personally, I'm all for frozen food, me, especially the curries."

Granddad scowled. "Yeah, well you would, wouldn't you? You youngsters, you're all the same, you want to forget all that foreign muck and get some decent grub inside you, like egg and chips and the like." He flicked cigarette ash in the general direction of the fire grate. "As a matter of fact, I could go a plate of egg and chips right now, our Edith," he said blowing cigarette smoke at the T.V. screen.

"Go, is the right word there, Jack," answered his daughter from the back kitchen. "You can go and find someone to get it then, orright?" Arthur's grandfather scowled and said nothing. "There'll be no more food in this house tonight, not until the Christmas puddings are potted and labelled, anyway," said his daughter's voice as it competed with the sound of pots and pans being moved around.

Granddad showed his displeasure by rustling the newspaper each time he turned a page, muttering, each time, under his breath until he had finished reading the final page. He folded the paper and tossed it onto the table, with disdain.

"I see the County lost again on Saturday. It's no wonder the crowds are dropping. They only had six thousand there for their last home game."

"Yeah, well there would have been six thousand and one if you'd gone over to support them instead of spending all afternoon in the betting shop," said Arthur, not looking up from the puzzle.

"You won't catch me paying two bob to go and see that shower, that's for sure." Granddad slapped the newspaper twice with the open palm of his hand to emphasise his point.

Arthur's niece, with tongue protruding from the corner of her mouth in concentration, had managed to make two unmatched pieces fit together, transforming, what should have been Noddy's face, into, part headlamp and part sunflower.

"No, they don't go there, Nicky." Arthur prised out the mismatched pieces. "See, they're the wrong shape, and they're upside down." He held up the offending pieces, to show her. "Carry on like that and you'll have Noddy and Bigears looking like something out of Dan Dare."

"Her name is Nicola. How many times do I have to tell you?" said Arthur's sister, Beryl as she staggered into the kitchen with an enormous earthenware bowl three-quarters full of Christmas pudding-mix. She heaved the bowl up onto the table-top. "Don't anybody bother to offer to help," she said through gritted teeth.

Granddad looked up from examining the cuff on his shirt.

"Can you manage then, our Beryl?"

She gave him a dirty look and took Nicola from Arthur's lap.

"Come on, it's time to stir the pudding mix and make a wish, before we start filling the basins."

Arthur's mother came into the parlour, bearing a tower of pudding basins and holding a wooden spoon.

"Right then, Dad, you have the first stir." She handed the spoon to granddad. "And don't forget to make a wish."

Granddad scowled. "Fat lot of good wishing will do, if last year's stirring is anything to go by. County had to apply for re-election and my horse fell at the first in the National." Grudgingly, he took the spoon from his daughter and stirred the pudding-mix, using both hands on the spoon, before passing it to Arthur. "And, it's no good you wishing for Avril to come back, either, she's moved to Southport," he lied, giving a malevolent grin.

Arthur ignored the taunt and stirred the pudding in silence. He handed the spoon on to Beryl.

"There you go, Sis', give it a good 'un."

She stood Nicola on a chair and guided the child's hands around the handle of the spoon and together they stirred the mix. Finally, Arthur's mother took her turn, slowly wiping her hands on her apron, before taking the spoon in both hands and slowly moving it through the sticky, yellow mass.

"There," she said putting down the wooden spoon. "Now we can start filling the basins, Beryl, orright?"

Beryl nodded and picked up her young daughter.

"Give me five minutes, Mam, while I get Nicola off to bed, then I'll give you a hand, OK?"

Her mother nodded.

"Right then, I'll go and get the muslin, string and labels." She disappeared into the back kitchen.

Beryl carried her daughter to the door.

"Come on then, young lady, time to go up the wooden hill to Bedfordshire, isn't it?" The child protested and wriggled in her mother's arms.

Arthur stepped forward; arms outstretched.

"Here, let me take her up, our Beryl. I'll read her a story."

"Thanks, Arth'," she said, passing over the child. "There you go, let Uncle Arthur take you up, is it?"

"Come on sausage, when we get up those stairs, I'll tell you all about Noddy, you know, the one with the funny cap on the front of your jigsaw-puzzle box," said Arthur, hoisting her onto a shoulder. The little girl nodded and sucked at her thumb.

"How long do you intend to be up there, then?" asked granddad. "I'm thinking of going to the Legion for a bevy, soon." He wiped a layer of pudding-mix from the wooden spoon, with a finger and suck it off the gnarled digit.

Arthur shook his head.

"Not tonight, I'm going to have an early one. I'm on mornings tomorrow."

Granddad grimaced. "I thought that you were on afternoons, the rest of the week?"

"Only after tomorrow, I've swapped shifts with Tommy Banks."

"How come?" scowled the old man. "Must be bloody important to give up a shift of mornings for afternoons. I couldn't stand afternoons, me, all that rushing to make the pub before shut tap. I found that to be very unsettling."

"He's got an appointment at the dentist's, having the first fitting of his new front teeth," explained Arthur.

"He's a bit young to be having false teeth, ain't he?" said granddad. What's he got pyorrhoea?"

"No, there's nowt wrong with his gums. It's his teeth they were knocked out in a collapsed scrum when the Railway Club, in Station Street, played up at Fleur de Lis in the first round of the East Mon Cup, the hooker's knee caught him in the gob."

"Poor sod!" granddad said with some feeling, buttoning up his waistcoat. "He'll never live that one down, for sure." He threaded his watch-chain through a buttonhole in the waistcoat. "Up at Fleur, was it? And lost, I expect?"

Arthur nodded and hoisted his niece higher up his forearm as her weight seemed to have become increasingly heavy.

Granddad wound his scarf around his neck.

"Bad enough having to play up there, in the middle of bloody nowhere, and getting beat, and then to have to come back home without your front teeth as well. Christ he'll never live that down."

He plucked his jacket from the back of his chair.

"Are you coming for a pint, then? I'm only going for a couple. I don't intend to say out half the night."

Arthur peered around the half-asleep child and looked at the clock that sat on the mantelpiece. Temptation tugged at his arm. *Go on,* it said. *A couple of pints won't hurt.*

"Give me a quarter of an hour, OK?"

His Grandfather scowled and sat back down.

"Yeah, well, don't be long. I can't wait around here all night surrounded by puddings and women being busy."

Arthur grinned and took the youngster off to bed.

Thirty minutes later granddad and Arthur threaded their way through the press of bodies in the smoke-filled back room of the Legion and headed towards the bar.

Two-and-a-half hours later, they staggered homewards, very much the worse for wear.

Pissed as farts, the old man gleefully recalled.

Chapter Thirty-six
Plastered

The incessant ringing of the fire engine's bell was beginning to annoy Arthur, as he watched the fire tender racing across the Fleur de Lis rugby pitch, which appeared to be the size of Dartmoor, and just as bleak, and yet, seemed to him, to be perfectly normal. As in most dreams, the implausible was accepted without question.

As the fire engine got nearer, its bell became correspondingly louder. A manic Tommy Banks was at the wheel. His brass Fireman's helmet at a crazy angle. His huge toothless mouth gaping.

The bell's sound had become agonisingly loud.

He sat bolt upright in his bed, groaned, and looked at the luminous face of the alarm clock, which told him it was a quarter to five. He reached out and silenced it. A mallet pounded at the inside of his skull. His tongue, now replaced by an old slipper.

"Dear God," he groaned, letting his head fall back onto the pillow.

His brain felt as though it was bouncing from side to side inside his skull, like the clapper of a bell.

He lay there for a moment, trying to focus his thoughts as he peered at the faint glow of dawn that distinguished the curtains from the rest of the darkened room.

As his brain gradually returned to normality, he realised that it was a quarter to five, and that a morning shift was beckoning. He groaned again and slowly swung his legs out of bed.

Arthur's first attempt at standing failed miserably and he fell back onto the bed with a thump. His second try met with more success and with the aid of the headboard he managed to stay upright, swaying in the gloom, knees trembling.

Edging his way gingerly around the bed, he groped for the light switch, which he pressed. The world around him exploded in a great starburst of jagged light, as the sixty-watt bulb said good morning.

He shielded his eyes and felt around for his shirt and trousers, discarding his pyjamas in the process. Finding them, he struggled into the coarse British Railway trousers, pulling them up over his legs and hips as he teetered precariously, one buttock on the edge of the bed.

He pushed his feet into his slippers and staggered out of the bedroom onto the landing, feeling his way along the banister, his legs like jelly. Slowly Arthur started down the stairs. His head pounding, and his eyes watering profusely.

Equally slowly, the trousers, which he had forgotten to button, descended down off his hips, gathering momentum, with every step, and in a trice, slid down over his thighs, passed his trembling knees, and curled around his ankles. So, when Arthur took the next step, the inevitable happened, the trousers playing their part in his downfall. With a cry of despair, Arthur plunged headlong down the staircase, coming to the bottom step, where he lay, pain searing through his foot and on up into his right leg, the offending trousers, still wrapped around his ankles.

The ambulance brought him back from the hospital at quarter past four that afternoon. Granddad and Arthur's mother helped support him as he did a Long John Silver impersonation along the passage and into the kitchen, where he slumped down onto a chair, with a moan. His mother gently eased a cushion under the plaster-encased leg.

"You're not to put any weight on the leg for at least twenty-four hours, the plaster has to be totally dried out, that's what the Staff nurse in casualty said, anyhow."

"The way I feel I won't be putting any weight on it ever again," said Arthur, through gritted teeth.

"Well at least, it's not broken, anyway," said granddad cheerfully as he unbuttoned his waistcoat.

"It's as bad as a break, Dad," his daughter interjected indignantly. "The man in the plaster-room said that it was a bad dislocation, and they can be worse than breaks." She took the kettle from the hob and went into the back kitchen to fill it from the cold-water tap. "A very rare dislocation, too, that's what he said!" she yelled, over the drumming of the water that filled the kettle.

"What's rare about a dislocation?" asked granddad, looking over the top of the Radio Times. "I had a dislocation once, when we played Saint Mike's in the semis of the Lord Tredegar Shield. The trainer, Danny Singleton, ran on to the field, and, before you could say knife, he'd put it back, no trouble."

Arthur's mother reappeared with the full kettle and put it back on the hob.

"That was only your finger Dad. Arthur's is a bit more serious than that, for God's sake." She wiped her hands on her pinafore and tossed her head in disgust.

"Serious!" Granddad exploded with indignation. "It might have only been a finger, but it was bloody serious, I can tell you. Jeez, we were twelve six down, and me a key member of the attack, being outside-centre and all."

"Yes, well that was fifty years ago, and this is now, so shift your elbows so that I can lay the table." She flapped the cloth in mid-air and let it gently settle onto the table-top. Grandfather scowled and scraped back his chair to get out of range of his irate daughter.

Arthur eased his leg on the cushion.

"What's for tea, then Mam? I've only had a Kitkat and a cup of tea all day."

She turned to him sympathetically and smiled.

"What do you fancy then, luv? You must be famished."

"I could murder a plate of beans on toast," he said, trying to look hard done by.

"Coming up luv, anything for the wounded soldier," she said over her shoulder.

Arthur cringed, he'd been waiting for this moment to arrive and had been dreading it. He knew that as soon as he had moved back in with his mother and sister, he'd be the target of their combined maternal urges. Now his worst fears were coming true.

And me stuck here with this bloody leg in plaster; I've got no chance. He groaned at the thought.

His mother looked up from laying the table, concern on her face.

"What's up luv, your leg playing you up, then?"

The fact that he was twenty-eight years old, separated from his wife, and twelve and a half stone in his knickers, didn't make a scrap of difference, he was his mother's little boy again, and nothing was going to deter her now.

"No, it's all right," he explained. "Just a bit of pins and needles, is all."

"Brilliant, our Edith," exclaimed Granddad, coming out of his reverie, suddenly rejuvenated. "A plate of beans on toast will go down a treat," he rubbed his hands together in anticipation.

"You'll have fry-up like the rest of us and like it," said his daughter, banging down the empty teapot. "Besides, there's only one tin of beans left, and they're for Arthur."

"One tin?" responded granddad, incredulously. "The amount of time that you spend in that fancy supermarket, I'd have thought we'd have a bloody kitchenful of beans by now?"

His daughter stood hands on hips and gave him a hard look.

"It took me and our Beryl three trips down to Wondasdave, just getting all the ingredients for the puddings, the Christmas cake and the minced pies. The tinned stuff has had to wait, that comes Friday with the rest of the normal shop." She smoothed down the front of her pinafore, testily. "I've spent a fortune getting all the Christmas goods in, and all you can do is sit there and moan, you, ungrateful hound."

She bent over the solitary tin of beans and attacked it with a tin-opener. "So, until Friday you'll have to make do, like the rest of us, so tonight, it's either fry-up or meat-paste sandwiches, take your pick." She clattered the cups and saucers onto the tablecloth. "And don't sit there scowling, make yourself useful, go and get the milk and sugar, and put the tea in the pot."

"Bloody fry-up." Granddad thrust his hands into his trouser pockets and slouched off to the pantry, scowling.

Arthur grinned; knowing that granddad would be silently mouthing obscenities as he reluctantly carried out his orders.

Arthur dispatched the last forkful of beans and took a slurp of tea.

"That was great, our Mam," he said wiping at his lips.

His Mother looked up from her eating.

"I'll be getting some more tins in soon; do you fancy some spaghetti hoops for a change?"

"Terrific," replied Arthur. "And I tell you what, I wouldn't say no to a tin or two of those sausage and beans as well, if you can manage it?"

"Manage it? Certainly, we can manage it, anything for our little invalid." She beamed. "Another cuppa, then?"

"Not for me, Ma, I'll wait till supper, now," he said, suppressing a belch.

"I'll not say no to another cup, our Doris," Granddad said, forking up the last of his bubble and squeak.

"Well you know where the pot is." Arthur's mother said gesturing with a fork, not looking up.

Granddad wiped at his mouth with the back of his hand and got to his feet, scowling and reached for his cap.

"On second thoughts I'll not bother," he said, standing on his dignity. "I'll go and give Cedric a visit. He may be plagued with intermittent wind, but at least you get a friendlier reception there." He pulled on his jacket and belched into his hand. "Bloody fry up!" he grumbled.

"Don't forget your scarf. There's a cold wind forecast." Arthur's Mother said as she gathered up the used plates.

Granddad scowled at his daughter and took down his scarf and wrapped it around his neck.

"Four years up to my armpits in freezing cold mud in the bloody trenches and I managed to survive. Now, I'm only going two hundred yards down the bloody road and I've got to wrap up like a sodding Eskimo." He reached for the door handle, pain in his eyes.

"Oh, Dad." Arthur's mother called.

"What now, for Christ's sake." He turned, defeat etched on his face.

"Pick up an Argus on your way back from Ced's, will you? Ta."

He nodded dumbly, the last of his defences breached. "And don't forget that, Tommy Cooper's on at half past seven, will you? You like Tommy, you wouldn't want to miss him, would you?"

If he had had a sword, he would have snapped the blade over his knee and surrendered, but as he hadn't, he simply acknowledged defeat with a limp wave of the hand and closed the door behind him.

Arthur picked up the Radio Times and scanned it.

"Oh good, the Avengers are on at eight, with a bit of luck we might see Emma Peel!" He grinned at his double entendre, but it fell on stony ground, being lost on his mother and sister.

He sighed and adjusted the cushion that was supporting his leg, lit up a cigarette and settled back to watch Alan Whicker interviewing Tessie O'Shea.

Thirty-five minutes later the sound of the front door banging shut caused Arthur to look away from the TV. Granddad came in, unwinding the scarf from his neck.

"You weren't long, then," Arthur said, turning his attention back to the screen.

Granddad took off his cap and placed it on a coat-peg.

"As much as I like old Ced', a quarter of an hour, twenty minutes, is about as much as I can take these days. I'll be glad when he's finished with those sulphur tablets."

He struggled out of his overcoat and the sound of bottles clinking came from within its depths.

"Bad, was it?" Arthur asked, wrinkling up his nose.

"Bad!" Granddad tossed the evening paper onto the table. "Bad is not the word for it, bloody appalling would be closer to the mark. Takes your sodding breath away. The sooner he's off those goddamned tablets the better." He hung up his overcoat and delved into the huge patch pockets and extracted four-pint bottles of Bass. "These might come in handy, eh?"

"What oh." Arthur rubbed his hands together in delight. "A plate of Cheddar and pickled onions, as well, would round the evening off very nicely, thank you."

"Too bloody true, our Arthur," agreed granddad, unbuttoning his waistcoat and opening the Evening Argus at the sports page.

"Let's leave it until we've watched the Avengers, is it? You never know, we might see Emma Peel." Arthur grinned.

Granddad looked up from the evening paper. "Don't be tupp, we're bound to, she's always in it."

Arthur gave a sigh of exasperation. "Yeah, that's right, I forgot that." He turned his attention back to Cy Grant and his guitar, but Cy and his calypso soon took second fiddle when the pins and needles struck. "Bloody pins and needles," cursed Arthur wriggling his toes and easing his leg into a more comfortable position.

He looked grimly down at the plaster cast and silently cursed.

The sooner I'm back on my feet, the better. All this lying around is going to drive me bloody bonkers. He punched at the plaster-encased leg. *All that crumpet out there and me stuck in the bloody house for the duration. I'll be lucky to be back in action by Christmas.*

The old man pulled at an earlobe and continued to stare at the crawling lines of distant cars and the scurrying shoppers, no longer seeing them. *Busted marriage, busted leg, busted life.* He shook his head. *Jeez, what a pathetic sod I must have been, sitting there, feeling sorry for myself, poor bugger. Poor Bugger? I don't think. I'd never had it so bloody good, that's for sure, waited on hand, foot and bloody finger, not having to go to work for a couple of months and still getting paid to sit at home all day. No wonder I was bored and frustrated and depressed by that prolonged period of inactivity — what was it, a whole week?*

He shook his head again and looked down at his lower torso.

"What wouldn't I give to be twenty bloody eight again; never mind having a leg in plaster," he muttered. *You wouldn't hear me complaining, that's for sure.*

In fact, as he now recalled, apart from that first week of enforced inactivity, his spell of sick leave had been very pleasurable, and the plastered-leg proved a Godsend...

Just eight days after Arthur and granddad had staggered home from the Boilermaker's, Arthur hobbled back down its tiled passage, leaning heavily on one of granddad's walking sticks and being supported under the arm by Dai's hand.

As Arthur and Dai entered the bar, a cheer went up from the regulars.

Granddad and Cedric fussed about him like a pair of old hens and Mavis, the barmaid, made a point of leaving the bar and coming over to him, and, bending over, planting a big, wet kiss on his lips, much to the pleasure of the regulars, who cheered, as they surveyed the upper halves of her two large freckled breasts, which, somehow, defied gravity by remaining inside her low-cut blouse.

Granddad found a low, padded barstool for Arthur's plastered-leg and gently lowered it down onto it. Cedric bought him a brown-top and Dai offered him a cigarette, while granddad lit it for him.

It was the life of Riley.

"When's the plaster due off, then, Arth'?" asked Cedric, wiping away froth from his lips.

"Four to six weeks, according to the staff-nurse in the Fracture and Orthopaedic unit," said Arthur with a feigned expression of pain on his face.

"Still, it's kept nice and clean, considering," remarked Dai, a malevolent grin on his face.

Arthur's eyes narrowed.

"what are you grinning at, Marshall, you git? You're up to something, I bloody know you of old."

Dai laughed out loud.

"Nowt, honest, it's just that, I hate to see a clean plaster, it's unnatural, ain't that right lads?" He looked around for their support.

Then, before Arthur could stop him, Dai was down on all fours, pen in hand, writing on the plaster cast.

"You twat, Marshall. I knew you had something planned, you sod, you," hissed Arthur, screwing his head around, in an effort to read what was written on the plastered leg.

Dai had drawn an arrow, from ankle to thigh, pointing up, with the message. *This way to heaven, girls.*

This proved such a hit with the rest of the regulars, that Arthur could only sit there helplessly, unable to prevent the further attacks on the plaster cast, as one by one, most of the regulars added their messages to the once white surface.

At first, he feebly tried to fend them off, but soon gave in and, with resignation on his face, he looked towards the heavens in exasperation.

Ronnie Cox was the last to get a go at the well-scrawled-on plaster. Wielding a permanent marker pen, he wrote. *By hook or by crook I'll be the last on this leg.*

"You dull bugger, it don't even rhyme," said his brother, Danny, admonishing him.

Arthur read the message and burst into laughter, and, one by one, the rest of the regulars crowded around, to read the leg. Laughter ringing around the room as the contents of Ronnie's message was relayed from drinker to drinker.

Ronnie looked around the room, perplexed. "Well, I can't see what's so bloody funny."

Amid all the guffawing and hoots of derision, what had been missed by all and sundry, and Arthur in particular, was the fact that, not only had Ronnie used a permanent marker-pen, when writing his message, but, in doing so, he had also gone beyond the top edge of the plaster. The bare bit of Arthur's leg, above the plaster, now sported the cryptic message, *is leg.*

Chapter Thirty-seven
Saturnalia

The plaster cast was eventually removed, three weeks before Christmas, and, in order to strengthen the emaciated leg, during the ensuing weeks, Arthur took to going to the local swimming baths, each day, where he would spend an hour trying to complete as many lengths of the baths as possible

After just three sessions, not only was the leg responding well to the exercise, he had also managed to get himself involved with Doreen, the local swimming club's breaststroke Champion, a title that he could have claimed for himself, except that the breast stroking, that he employed, was entirely out of the water.

A week after their first meeting, they sat side by side on the tiled edge of the shallow end of the swimming pool. Doreen seemed strangely attracted by Ronnie's handiwork, which had, by now, become a dark-grey smear on Arthur's thigh.

"That's a nasty bruise on your thigh, Arthur," she said, pointing at the remnants of Ronnie's message that was still defying all efforts of removal with soap and water.

She raised a leg and adjusted the wet swimming costume that clung to her classically formed bottom, her eyelashes working overtime in the allure department.

"Oh that." Arthur looked down at the offended mark and shrugged. "Yeah, got it when I fell over, trying to rescue a bloody tabby from going under the wheels of a coal-lorry, last week," he lied.

"Did it survive?" she asked, concern showing in her emerald eyes. Her bright, red lips forming a pout.

"No danger," he said, warming to his task. "Went straight under the lorry, full pelt and on up the lane towards the canal. While, Muggings, here," he pointed to himself, "went arse over tip in the road. What a plonker, eh?"

She shook her head in disagreement. Her dark-red hair dancing on her shoulders.

"Of course you're not. I think that you were very brave to try and save a poor defenceless cat like that." She lightly touched at the would-be bruise. "Is it still tender?"

He shook his head as he looked at the reflections dancing on the surface of the water, trying to appear unaware of the cool hand on his thigh.

With a bit of luck, my lovely, it'll be me who'll be doing the thigh touching and you'll be on the receiving end. He turned to her grinning malevolently. "No, it doesn't hurt at all."

The swimming paid off, the old man recalled, grinning.

The exercise did the old leg a world of good, not to mention other important areas, and Doreen seemed reasonably happy with the situation.

By the time that Christmas week was upon them, the calf of his leg had regained much of its former meatiness. His limping was barely perceptible, except, that is, during the follow-up visit to the doctor's surgery, then inexplicably, it became much more pronounced.

The doctor examined the injured heel and ankle.

"Ok, you can put your sock and shoe back on, Mister Tanner." He turned back to his desktop and hurriedly scrawled his findings on Arthur's notes. "Yes, the foot seems have made a very good recovery. I think it is now safe for you to return to work. How does it feel to you?"

Arthur shrugged. "Well it's not too bad at the moment, doc, but every so often it seems to lose its strength and I end up limping again." He gave the doctor a pained look.

"Really." The Doctor gave Arthur an old-fashioned look, over the top of his half glasses. "Yes," he mused. "The injury may just have left you with a little weakness in the calf muscle." He gave Arthur another searching look before opening a desk drawer and extracting a pad of forms. "Very well, I'll give you another sick note for a fortnight, that will take you into the New Year, after which, I would expect the leg to have fully recovered, and you can go back to work."

"Thanks doc," said Arthur gratefully retrieving the sick note from the doctor, and, with a wan smile, limped from the room.

He closed the door behind him and strode down the passage and out through the front door, rubbing his hands together.

Two more weeks off, bloody brilliant. Christmas, here we come. He grinned widely.

Arthur and Dai sat in the crowded, men-only bar of the Engineers Arms, drinking black and tans. It was Christmas Eve and they had been out on the town for two hours, and had now reached that stage of drinking when melancholia was setting in and they were beginning to feel sorry for themselves, with each reminiscence drifting somewhere between the maudlin and the absurd.

"Do you realise that today is the tenth anniversary of the Western Movie Club, Arth'." Dai took a long swallow and wiped at his lips. "Ten years." He let out a huge sigh. "Jeez, it seems like bloody ten minutes." He nudged Arthur. "The good old days, eh?"

He leaned back in his chair and studied the ceiling.

"Aye, that's when the old Western Movie Club was at the height of its powers, when; there would have been at least a dozen of us, here, on Christmas Eve, at least a dozen. Let's see." He held up his splayed fingers and counted off on them. "There was, you and me, the Cox boys, Squint Carter, Bloggs Barton, Andy Taylor and his cousin Derrick, oh, and, there was, Spud, Alec, Gary, and Dezzie." He lifted his glass to the heavens in mock salute.

Arthur shook his head and stared into his pint glass.

"Do you know I'd forgotten most of them?" He shook his head again. "Living in Rogerstown has probably had a lot to do with it. I expect, you know how it is, once you lose track of people…" he ended lamely.

Dai nodded.

Arthur took a long pull of the dark brown liquid and smacked his lips.

"Where the bloody hell have they all got to; I wonder?" he scratched at his chin.

"They're all over the bloody place," Dai replied.

"Like where?" asked Arthur.

Dai started counting off on his fingers again.

"Take Squint, for instance. He's married and living in Leicester. Bloggs, he emigrated to Canada. Spud and Gary both went to Saudi, working on some distillation plant or something." He drained his glass and rose from his seat. "Same again, Arth'?"

Arthur nodded, looking over the rim of his glass.

"Yeah, ta," he said, finishing off the last of his beer, handing his empty glass to Dai. "It's just the two of us now, Taff," he sighed. "Just the two of us."

He watched Dai make his way to the bar, feeling the effects of the alcohol's fumes, which were filtering to his brain.

Dai came back from the bar with two fresh pints, his eyes slightly glazed. He passed a glass to Arthur and sat back down heavily.

"What about Andy and Derrick, then? I haven't seen them for years," slurred Arthur.

Dai took a tentative sip from his glass.

"Derrick's living in Maindee, married to that Gloria, who was an usherette in the Regal?" He nudged Arthur's arm. "You remember, Gloria, big-blonde job? Father was Tommy Morris the window cleaner."

Arthur sat up in astonishment.

"What, Gloria bloody Morris? Spud married Gloria bloody Morris?"

Dai nodded "Got a couple of kids, as well."

Arthur shook his head in amazement.

"Jeez, Poor Bugger. Can you imagine that? It must be like being married to Harpo bloody Marx in a skirt."

Dai snorted and coughed as his pint went down the wrong way.

"For Christ's sake, not while I'm drinking, you plonker."

Arthur grinned. "What would you rather be, Dai Marshall coughing on a pint or Spud having to face the sight of big Gloria ever morning?"

Dai wiped at his lips.

"No bloody contest. I'll settle for a good cough every time."

Arthur gave a guffaw. "And what about good old Andy, then? I suppose he's settled down too, eh? Got him a nice little number in a drawing office, somewhere? Council house in Somerton, I bet, and a four-year-old Austin Mini, am I right?"

Dai took a swig from his glass.

"You're way off, Taff. Our Andy boy's gone the other way."

"What d'yer mean, the other way? Moved to the West Country, d'yer mean?"

Dai took a longer swig and looked around furtively.

"Bloody West Country, my arse. No, he's, you know? S-hook job," he said demonstrating a limp wrist.

Arthur looked flabbergasted.

"You're pulling my plonker, you git, ain't you? What? Andy, a sausage-jockey? Get out of it, no way."

Dai shook his head.

"No bull Arth'. I saw him myself, only last week, walking in Belle Vue Park, holding hands with that Robby Pinkly."

Arthur shook his head in disbelief.

"You know," said Dai, "the hairdresser, who's got that shop in Corn Street."

Arthur looked visibly shaken.

"I can't bloody well believe it. Andy a bloody poofter." He shook his head in despair. "What's the bloody world coming to, for Christ's sake. It's all beyond me, that's for sure."

Dai sipped at his beer in silence, waiting for Arthur to get a grip on himself.

Arthur finally broke the silence, his face set.

"When the Western Movie Club first started, you had your Jerry Lee and Elvis and the rest of the rock and roll boys, from the States. Later on, from the mid-sixties till now, you've had all the Liverpool groups and the like, which is great, 'cause they've taken rock and roll further along the road." He took a huge gulp of brown-top from his glass. "You with me so far?"

Dai grinned drunkenly.

"Not a frigging clue, but, carry on."

"Before I do, it's my shout." Arthur struggled to his feet. "What is it, then?"

"I'll try another," Dai said, finishing off the tail end of his drink.

"We'll have a couple of rum and blacks, as well, is it?"

Dai puffed up his cheeks.

"Aye, go on then."

When Arthur staggered back with the drinks, he placed them on the table and flopped back down into his chair.

"Now, as I was explaining." He took out a packet and extracted two cigarettes, tossing one across to Dai. "Where it all went wrong," he continued, "was in the early sixties when you had all those bloody Bobbies hogging the charts."

"I don't remember any coppers in the charts, Arth'. Besides, what's that got to do with Andy going queer, then?"

"Not coppers you plonker, Bobbies." Arthur leaned forward in his seat. "Bobbies for Christ's sake!" He waved a hand in the air dismissively. "And never mind, bloody Andy, listen to what I'm saying."

Dai looked nonplussed.

Arthur blew smoke at the ceiling and hiccupped. "Now look." He tapped the table-top with a finger. "There was Bobby Bland, Bobby Rydell, Bobby bloody Darin, Bobby Vee, Bobby Vinton, Christ, there was even a bloody song called, Bobby's girl."

Recognition dawned upon Dai's face.

"Right, got you. So, it was all the Bobbies that cocked it all up, then?"

"Certainly, it was," slurred Arthur. "If it wasn't for the Beatles and the Stones, the rock and roll heritage would have been lost forever, no thanks to the Bobbies of this world." He sniffed with disdain and took a sip from his glass of rum and blackcurrant.

They lapsed into silence, both contemplating the effect of the Andys and the Bobbies of this world, and what life would have been like, without rock and roll.

"Bobby Crowther," said Dai emphatically, breaking the silence.

"Who the bloody hell is Bobby Crowther, when he's at home?" slurred Arthur. "I've never heard of him, what's he sing, then?"

"He wasn't a Singer. He was a dog," hiccupped Dai.

"What are you bloody well going on about, dog. What do you mean a dog? Are you talking about a mutt?" said Arthur, trying to focus his eyes.

Dai stubbed out his cigarette butt.

"Yeah, a dog. He was a greyhound that my cousin Proctor won in a card game, in the Old Comrades' Club, Cardiff."

Arthur stared at Dai in amazement.

"Your something else, you are. One minute we're discussing bloody Bobbies, the next, were onto sodding greyhounds and some plonker called Proctor." He took another sip of the rum mix. "Proctor, what sort of bloody name is that for a man, then?" He broke into a cackle. "Bloody Proctor, you've kept that one quiet, all these years, ain't you? It's no wonder no bugger's ever heard of him."

"Well, he's not my cousin really," confessed Dai, on the defensive. "A few times removed, to be honest. He was my Aunty Annie's second husband's nephew."

"Bloody rotate! If he was any further removed; it'll take three bleeding weeks to find him, which is just as well, with a name like bloody Proctor," Arthur roared with laughter.

"Oh, bollocks to bleeding Proctor," retorted Dai irritably. "We were talking about Bobby Crowther, right?"

"Yeah, yeah, all right, all right, calm down, for Christ's sake, so what about him, then?" said Arthur trying to ease the tension.

Dai relaxed and leaned forward.

"Like I said, Proctor won Bobby in a card game, but he never made it beyond the autumn, though."

"How, come?" Arthur hiccupped again.

Dai gave a reverential sniff.

"Got hit by a tram the following Sunday morning. Got killed stone dead." He leaned back in his seat and belched. Rum fumes filled the air.

"Hit by a bloody tram," Arthur grimaced. "Now that's what I call bloody hard luck. Poor old Bobby, he could have been a champion."

"Not, Bobby, you plonker." Dai looked to the heavens in despair. "Proctor, it was Proctor who got hit by the tram, not Bobby Crowther, for God's sake."

"What happened to good old Bobby, then?" Arthur slurred his concern.

"Dunno. I'm only going by what our Audrey told me when I was a kid." Dai flicked ash from his cigarette and reached for his pint glass.

Arthur gave him a scathing look.

"How the bloody hell did we get onto this stupid bloody subject, anyway?"

His ears had started buzzing, and he blew his nose, hoping it might sort out the ear noise.

It didn't.

Dai shrugged. "Don't look at me Taff. You were the one who started all that crap about Bobbies and the like."

Arthur slumped in his chair.

"Yeah, that's right, bloody pop stars." He waggled his finger in the offending ear, to no avail. So, he took out a packet of cigarettes and offered it to Dai. "Ciggy?"

"No, it's my shout," said Dai, pulling out a packet offering it across the table.

"Cheers." Arthur took one and they both lit up.

"D'yer know, Dai, I can't bloody get over how all of our mates have all just faded away into obscurity, just like that." Arthur snapped thumb and finger together. "Know what I'm saying?"

Dai nodded gravely.

"Yeah, well that's how it goes. Everything changes, nothing stays the same."

Arthur took a drag from his cigarette and shook his head.

"I've got a funny feeling that Christmas, this year, is going to be a real bummer." He shrugged. "It's nothing that I can put my finger on, just a feeling, that's all."

"Yeah, I know what you mean, there's not a party on the horizon, nothing." Dai's shoulders drooped despondently. "Anyway," he said. "At least there's that Doreen. I expect you'll be sorting out her Christmas stocking, eh?" Dai gave a knowing look.

Arthur scowled. "No chance. She's buggered off to her sister's in Ipswich, until after the New Year."

Dai feigned a pained expression on his face.

"No nooky this Christmas, then?"

Arthur leaned forward towards Dai.

"I tell you what. Next bloody year we ought to book up for Christmas at Butlins, up at Peeliweeli."

"Where the sodding hell is Peeliweeli, for crying out loud?" asked Dai frowning.

"Up, North Wales, somewhere," Arthur slurred. He dipped his finger in his beer and proceeded to draw a map of Wales on the table-top. "By there, on the coast, up Wrexham way."

Dai nodded, but looked mystified.

"Bit cold for a holiday camp, this time of year, ain't it?"

Arthur gave a snort of scorn.

"No, you daft Git. It's all indoors this time of year. There's snooker, table tennis, cinemas, dance halls, stacks of bars, they've got the lot." He grinned lasciviously, "and dollies coming out of the woodwork, looking for a Christmas present. That's what we should have done this bloody year and bugger the sodding Western Movie Club."

"Yeah, well we'll know better next time, eh?" said Dai, starting to feel depressed again.

"I hate bloody Christmas," snapped Arthur. "And all of the paraphernalia that goes with it. All those sodding coloured glass balls and bloody crackers, I hate them."

"I hate tripe and onions and Mario Lanza," Dai responded, leaning back in his chair, a silly grin on his face.

"I hate gas capes and Stenhousemuir," Arthur chortled back at him, a manic look on his face.

"And Gorgonzola, and cane furniture," Dai cackled, wiping at his eyes.

"Scoutmasters, ginger moustaches, and chest expanders." Arthur held his aching sides, barely able to get the words out.

"You're drunk, you twat." Dai accused him, his eyes streaming.

"So I am." Arthur screamed hysterically.

The room suddenly went quiet and heads turned in the direction of the two drunken pals. Sally the barmaid told them to keep the noise down.

Arthur did his best, trying to restore a bit of composure to proceedings, but it was proving difficult.

Dai wiped at his eyes and blew his nose, loudly. The resulting trumpeting, setting them both off towards hysteria, again.

Arthur struggled to his feet, his eyes, wet from the laughter

"C'mon Butt, it's almost shut tap, let's bugger off and get a take-away curry, is it?" He burbled.

"Good idea, Arth'," said Dai, wobbling to his feet. "Let's go Cinders, the curry house awaits." He staggered towards the door, turned, and blew a resounding raspberry back at the smoke-filled room.

Arthur pushed him through the door.

"Move your arse, you daft sod, before somebody takes exception to your Christmas message."

They left the fug and the heat of the bar and reeled out into the December night, the cold night air hitting them like a slap in the face.

Dai pulled his coat collar up around his ears and pressed his chin into its neck.

"Buggeration, it's cold enough for a bloody walking stick, General," he said, blowing on his hands.

Arthur struggled to maintain a straight face.

"Yes, Corporal, it is indeed, in fact, it's cold enough for ten men. But fear not, help is at hand, a good, hot curry awaits us, at yonder mess tent."

Dai clicked his heels and broke wind in mid salute.

Arthur tucked an imaginary swagger stick under his arm and returned the salute.

"We'll have no laughter in the ranks, Corporal, lead the men to the Simla Palace at the double."

A cyclist careered down the hill towards them, ringing his bell frantically.

"Get out of the way you pair of drunken bastards!" he yelled, as he sailed by, just missing Dai.

"Bollocks!" Dai yelled after him, flashing a vee sign for all that he was worth.

"And a merry Christmas to you too, you Git," Arthur shouted. "May you and your saddle soon part company."

They both saluted ceremoniously and headed for the Indian take-away restaurant.

"Forward the vindaloo light infantry!" cried Arthur, pushing open the blue glass-panelled door.

Arm in arm, they staggered through the doorway and into a world of aromatic spices, red and gold flock wallpaper, chicken-off-the-bone with fried rice and poppadums.

Ten minutes later they wove their way down Dock Street towards their homes.

Christmas day, just ten minutes way.

Chapter Thirty-eight
Christmas

The shriek of a toy tin trumpet blasted Arthur out of his dreams, forcing him to open one eye and look at his watch. It was nine thirty, it was Christmas morning, and his head felt as though a form of medieval torture was being applied to the top of it. He explored his lips with the dead ferret that had swapped places with his tongue.

On the other side of his bedroom door, a three-year-old niece thought she was Louis Armstrong as she blew on the toy trumpet that she had recently discovered in her Christmas stocking.

Arthur groaned, knowing that soon the parcel containing the toy drum would be unwrapped and then the one-man-band, and his misery, would be complete.

He decided to cut his losses and get up.

Having washed and dressed, he made his way gingerly down the flight of stairs, with the strangled notes from the toy trumpet following him.

He opened the kitchen door and the aroma of Christmas food, in preparation, wrapped itself around his nostrils. Herbs, spices, assorted fruit and vegetables vied with the chicken and pork, the whole heady mixture filled the air.

Remarkably, his hangover left him and he suddenly felt hungry.

He wished his mother and sister a merry Christmas and received a kiss on the cheek from each for his trouble, before being shooed out from under their feet.

He returned to the kitchen, made himself some toast and tea and made his way down the passage, heading for the front room and relative peace.

His young niece had, by then, as expected, unwrapped another parcel and had found the drum, and was now accompanying herself. Arthur slipped into the front room and quietly closed the door behind him, and the efforts of the one-man-band becoming muted.

He stood and looked about the room. Coloured paper chains hung from the ceiling and sprigs of holly peeped out from behind picture frames. In the bay window a Christmas tree stood draped in sparkling tinsel, and shiny red and blue stars hung from the tips of its branches, slowly revolving from the heat of the room.

The combination of the pungency of the pine needles, and traces of lavender-scented furniture polish, gave the room an unreal, almost forbidding sort of atmosphere. He placed the tea and the toast on the dining table and rubbed his hands together in appreciation.

"That's what I like to see, a real fire," he murmured.

"Just as well that some of us can bloody well get up in the mornings, then, ain't it. Otherwise it would bloody well stay unlit, wouldn't it?"

Arthur's heart leapt in his chest.

A cloud of blue smoke drifted upwards, closely followed by granddad's head, as it appeared above the settee's back.

"Christ all bloody mighty!" Arthur gasped, retrieving the cup and saucer from the table and slopping tea over his thumb, in the process. "You scared the bloody shit out of me. It's a good job it's Christmas otherwise you'd have to be confined to barracks for the duration."

Arthur's grandfather, unmoved, licked at a thumb and turned a page of the Radio Times.

"Where did you get to, last night, then?" he asked, without looking up, and not waiting for an answer, continued. "Me and Cedric were in the Boilermaker's until gone half eleven. We had a cracking night. Della, the steward's missus, was in her pots, went arse over tip during the conga and landed up against the piano, and caught Albert Stanbury a whack across the head with her elbow as she went down, bloody brilliant!" Granddad's eyes gleamed at the thought. "Old Albert went staggering across the room, fell on his arse and emptied the contents of his pint pot down the front of Irene Titheridge's trouser suit. She was bloody furious. She was so sodding mad that she fetched the steward a smack around the ear with her handbag, for laughing." Arthur's Grandfather gave a huge guffaw and poked the fire; a shower of sparks danced up the chimney.

Arthur grinned and bit into the crisp, buttery toast, washing it down with a swig of hot, sweet tea.

"Dai and me went to the Engineers." He took another sip of tea. "We hoped we might see one or two of the lads from the old Western Movie Club days, but we were the only two to turn up."

"I didn't know you were into Cowboys and Indians?" Granddad looked up from the Radio Times, quizzically.

"What the bloody hell are you going on about, cowboys?"

Western movies, you said, that's cowboys if ever I heard it," granddad said, flicking over another page.

"Don't be bloody daft. It has nothing to do with sodding cowboys. It's just a name we had for our Thursday night piss-ups at the King Billy, back in the late fifties, that's all. Nothing to do with bloody cowboys." He finished off the rest of the toast.

Granddad dismissed Arthur's explanation with a shrug, turning another page.

"I see that plonker, Cliff Richard is on the box tonight. Two bloody hour special and not a bloody pub open, to escape to."

"Great!" Arthur beamed. "Who else has he got on with him, then?"

Granddad turned back a page and scanned the lines of print.

"Sandy Shore, Val Doonican and Mike Yarwood."

Arthur rubbed his hands.

"That'll do for me, especially if he sings *move it*."

Granddad scowled. "Yeah, well, I'll be bloody well moving it, that's for sure. I'll be moving it into here, with a few brown ales and sod bloody Cliff bloody Richard. I'll leave him to you and the women, in the kitchen."

"What about the women in the kitchen, then?" Arthur's mother pushed open the door and marched in, carrying an assortment of packages.

"Granddad doesn't want to watch Cliff tonight, so he's coming in here and leaving the telly to us in the kitchen."

Beryl, also laden down with brightly coloured packages, followed in behind Arthur's mother, accompanied by Nicola on trumpet.

"Right, Jack, Arthur, shift your backsides," said his mother, as she and his sister unloaded the packages onto the settee, much to Granddad's chagrin.

The ceremony of exchanging Christmas presents then commenced, and for the next hour the sound of tearing paper, and oohs and ahs of surprise and delight filled the air.

Arthur ended up with the usual two shirts, three pairs of socks, and a tie, plus, the more acceptable, Dennis Wheatley novel, two Boot's record tokens, and a gas-powered cigarette lighter from his Mother.

Granddad unpacked a succession of packages containing things that were, apparently, to assist in his leading a well-ordered life.

A scarf, socks, handkerchiefs, fleece-lined gloves and slippers, each, in turn, grudgingly acknowledged with a forced smile. A broad grin soon appeared on his craggy face when the bottle of dark rum, the drum of fifty Capstan full-strength, followed by the 1969 *News Chronicle Book of National Hunt Racing,* emerged from their holly-printed wrappers.

"Cheers Arth'." He raised the bottle, acknowledging his grandson's presents.

Arthur shrugged his shoulders with embarrassment.

"That's orright, get it down your neck, enjoy it."

"Oh, no you don't. You leave the top on that bottle until tonight," granddad's daughter admonished him, a smile playing on her lips.

Granddad scowled and placed the bottle on the floor between his feet.

Arthur's mother got to her feet and went across to the sideboard.

"Shall we all have a small sherry, yes?"

Granddad visibly brightened at the suggestion.

"That's a good idea, our Edith." He grinned and turned to Arthur. "Then, Arth' and me will pop down to the Legion for a couple of quick halves while you girls rustle up the grub, is it?"

"Now, you're talking, Granddad." Arthur held out his hand and took the proffered Oloroso Fino from his mother.

"And it better be a couple of quick halves, mind," she said, raising her glass to her lips. "You two, make sure you're back here for half one, without fail, or heaven help you." She sipped at her drink, her little finger cocked.

Granddad drained his drink in one go.

"Don't you fret none. We'll be back by then, no problem." He turned to Arthur. "Are you fit then?"

Arthur emptied his glass and rose.

"Right, then, let's do it."

They all rose together and filed out of the room, the women heading for the kitchen, and the men, for their coats and scarves and the front door.

As Arthur and granddad stepped out into the street, the trumpet and drum recommenced their cacophony.

Ten minutes later they were at the entrance to the British Legion Club.

Arthur's grandfather pulled open the frosted glass door and they walked down the green-tiled passage towards the main bar. He opened the door and they entered a smoke-filled, room, crowded with Christmas morning drinkers.

Arthur stood on tiptoe, craning his neck as he looked over the sea of heads across to the other side of the room.

"There's Dai and Cedric, over by the door to the Gents." He indicated with a thumb, yelling across to his grandfather above the din. "You go on over, I'll get them. What are having, SA?"

Arthur's grandfather nodded, turned and headed across the room.

"See what Ced' and Dai are having, ok?"

Granddad gave a thumbs-up sign and shoulder-charged his way through the crowd of bodies.

"Come on, let the dog see the bloody rabbit, then!" he yelled.

Arthur pushed his way through the throng in the opposite direction, towards the bar, and ordered two pints of SA, from Stan, the barman, who was sporting a false red nose and a purple and green paper hat on the back of his freckled, balding head.

Acknowledging the order, displaying a mouthful of discoloured teeth, he yelled above the din. "Coming up Arth'."

Arthur turned away from the nauseating sight of Stan's teeth and caught sight of a pale-faced Dai, who was threading his way through the throng, towards him.

"You look like a man who could do with a pint of electric lemonade?" said Arthur, grinning. "Are you OK? You look a bit dodgy, to me."

Dai blanched visibly.

"Strong lager? You are joking, that'll probably do for me, the bloody state I'm in." He winced and rubbed at his stomach.

Arthur took a slurp from his pint glass.

"What's up? You're never hung over, for God's sake."

Dai shook his head.

"No fear. It'll take more than the amount of beer that I had last night for me to have a hang-over," he lied. "Anyway, I didn't have all that much, did I?"

Arthur shook his head.

"Close on a gallon, I s'pose."

"Right," Dai confirmed. "No, it was that sodding vindaloo, that's what did it for me. I must have been to the lav' half a dozen times since about six this morning."

"Anyway," said Arthur, dismissing Dai's misery, out of hand. "Here's granddad's pint. What are you and Cedric having?"

Dai took the glass from Arthur.

"Well, I've already had one port and brandy, so I'll try another, with a bit of luck that ought to settle the old guts, eh?"

Arthur shrugged. "I don't suppose it'll hurt, any. What about Ced'?"

"He wants a pint of SA."

Arthur nodded and turned back to the bar.

"Add a pint of SA and a port and brandy to that order, orright Stan?"

The barman nodded, adjusted his paper hat to a more rakish angle, then turned to the optics, humming; *All I want for Christmas is a Beatle*.

Arthur collected the drinks and passed the port and brandy to Dai.

"Here, get this down your neck, that'll sort you out."

Dai led the way, single file, through the crowd of drinkers.

"If I fart now, I'll clear the bloody room," he called over his shoulder to Arthur.

A carroty-haired woman in a two-piece vermilion suit and cream stiletto-heeled shoes, overheard Dai and gave him a withering look, turning to her husband, and complaining, nodding in the direction of the departing Dai. Her husband bent his head to hear her, then, straightened up, grinning widely.

Miffed by her husband's obvious lack of concern, she dug him in the ribs causing him to slop beer onto the toe of one of his suede shoes.

"Aw, bloody hell, Grace, watch where you're putting your elbow, for God's sake, will you."

Indignantly, she thrust an empty glass at him.

"Here, laughing boy, I'll have another brandy and Babycham."

He scowled and took the glass from her.

Dai and Arthur reached Cedric and Granddad's table and handed out the drinks.

Dai pulled up a chair, sat down and raised his glass.

"Merry Christmas everybody."

They all responded by raising their glasses.

"Who's had a new cap for Chrissy, then?" Dai winked at Arthur and granddad.

Cedric's eyes flashed.

"What's wrong with me cap, then?" He glared at Dai. "Our Alice bought this in British Home Stores. They don't sell any rubbish in there, I can tell you." He thrust out his chest. "This is quality headwear, this is, and no mistake."

"Don't get your arse in your hand, you daft old bugger." Arthur's grandfather gave Cedric a friendly nudge. "He's only having a bit of fun. It's Christmas, for God's Sake."

The incongruity of his statement was lost on them all.

"Yeah, that's right Ced'," Arthur agreed, sipping at his pint. "Dai didn't mean nothing by it. Did you, Butt?"

Dai shook his head.

"As a matter of fact, I wouldn't mind a cap like that myself," Arthur said, taking another gulp from his beer, trying to placate the old man.

The colour was slowly returning to Dai's face and he was swiftly becoming his old self again.

"Yeah," he said. "I could do with a check cap like that, that's for sure." He fought to keep a straight face.

Cedric rose to the bait again.

"That's not bloody check, you ignorant young sod, this is your genuine tartan, this is."

Before Dai could pacify the old man, a voice sounded above the babble of the Christmas morning drinkers and pierced through the tobacco smoke.

"Tanner, you old git."

They all turned towards the sound.

"Well, I'll be buggered," said Arthur getting to his feet and pushing back his chair. "Ernie bloody Parry, for Christ's sake." He moved from his seat and punched the approaching figure playfully on the shoulder. "How long have you been home, then, you sod?"

Ernie Parry countered Arthur's punch with a friendly slap.

"Got home last night." He dragged a chair up to the table and joined them.

"Brilliant!" exclaimed Arthur sitting back down. "You all know Ernie, don't you?"

The assembled drinkers nodded.

"Ernie, you remember this lot, don't you? Dai Marshall, Jack, my granddad, and Cedric Mathias." He pointed them out in turn, using his glass.

Ernie nodded. "'Course I do." He held his glass on high. "Merry Christmas all," he said taking a huge gulp from the glass, then he ran his hand over the short, ginger tufts that made up his army haircut. "Where d'yer get that hat, Ced, pinch it off some Jock at the Arms Park, then?" He let out a huge guffaw and looked around the table for a response.

Cedric went puce with anger and struggled to get to his feet. Dai and granddad held him down.

"He's only bloody joking, Ced'." Arthur's Grandfather patted him on the shoulder. "Calm down, for God's sake, it's bloody Christmas," he repeated.

"Yeah, only joking, honest." Ernie grinned, over the rim of his glass. "Here, have a whiff." He offered an opened tin of cigars around the table.

Somewhat mollified, Cedric took a cigar and accepted a light from Ernie and sat back in his chair, took a swig from his pint glass then surreptitiously removed his cap and stuffed it into his jacket pocket.

"So, when are you back to Germany, then, Taff?" Arthur asked.

"I'm not," replied Ernie, blowing smoke at the table. "I'm off to Ripon in January for three months, then it's on to Brecon 'til July, then it's demob and balls to the poxy army." He emptied his glass with a huge gulp. "It's my shout. What are you all drinking, then?" he belched.

"Those brandies and port have done the trick," said Dai rubbing at his stomach. "I'll try a brown-top, Ern', ta."

"No problem," said Ernie, collecting the empties. "What about the rest of you lads?"

"Make it brown-tops all round, is it?" Arthur looked around for confirmation.

They all nodded.

"Right oh," said Ernie, rising.

"Hang on, Ern'. I'll come and give you a hand," said Arthur getting to his feet.

"That's all right, Taff. I'll get a tray, no bother."

Ernie left his seat and threaded his way through the blue haze towards the bar.

"I wonder where he's staying?" mused Dai. "His mam and dad are both dead, as far as I recall?"

Granddad nodded. "Yeah, died within days of each other, must be at least seven years ago."

"He'll be staying at his brother Ronnie's house, I expect." Arthur offered, as he watched Ernie's progress to the bar.

"Another piss-artist," Cedric murmured.

"Who is? Ernie or his Brother?" laughed Dai.

"Both of them, all of them," Cedric replied. "All the Parry's, were well known for their drinking, especially old Granny Parry. She lived on pickled eggs and glucose stout." He took a slurp from his glass. "It's a good job that they decided to bury her when she passed on. If they'd had her cremated, the bloody roof of the crem' would have blown off." Cedric cackled manically.

"Brown-tops coming up!" Ernie yelled as he approached the table.

Arthur noticed that he had a bottle of scotch in his jacket pocket.

He must have bought that from the bar while he was up there. I didn't notice him with it before, he thought.

"You won't be missing it, then, Ern'?" said Dai with a wink.

"What, the Army?" said Ernie, sitting down. "You must be bloody joking, Butt." He took a swig from his pint glass and grinned. "I'll miss the crumpet, of course." He looked into space wistfully. "Especially Maria, from Dortmund, God, she was a big, strong girl, nutcracker thighs, you know what I mean?" He gave a coarse laugh and looked around the table for approval.

The rest joined in the laughter.

Arthur's Grandfather playfully dug Cedric in the ribs.

"Nutcracker thighs, eh? Ced'. What does that remind you of, then?"

Cedric shrugged his shoulders.

"Go on, then, tell us." He lifted his glass and took a slurp.

"Mother Ramona Treadgold," granddad said with a gleam in his eye. "Usherette in the Plaza, lived in Coomassie Street with her old mother, Florrie. They had a lodger with a carbuncle on his neck."

Cedric visibly brightened; a smile of recognition lit up his face.

"Freddie the bump!" he said. "Freddie the bloody bump, I'd forgotten all about him." He took another pull at his drink. "Freddie the bump," he murmured to himself.

Granddad nodded. "That's him, worked in the glue factory over on Corporation Road. Jeez, what a pong from those rotten bones, remember, Ced'?"

Cedric wrinkled his nose in mock disgust.

"Remember, jeez, when the wind changed you could smell them bones right across the river, and, bloody Freddie, you could smell Freddie from a hundred yards away, too, no trouble." He grimaced and shook his head. "It beats me what Florrie saw in him, especially with that lump on his neck and him smelling like a bloody, pole cat's armpit."

Arthur's grandfather tapped the side of his nose knowingly.

"He was keeping the widow happy, wasn't he?" He lifted his pint and surveyed his audience over the rim of his glass.

"Keeping her happy!" Cedric gave a scornful laugh and showed his multicoloured teeth to the world. "Keeping her bloody happy, you must be bloody joking, Jack."

"Ah, but don't forget," grandad said. "He was a single man. He was bringing in charge-hand's wages. He had no dependants, neither." He tapped the table top with a forefinger and took a slurp from his glass, and, with a wicked smile upon his face, said, "And don't forget the special bonus that Freddie always made available to the widow!" He looked around the table. "Who's round is it, any way?"

"Never mind whose bloody round it is. What about this special bonus, then?" Cedric leaned forward in his seat, his eyes sparkling with expectation.

The rest of them had all stopped drinking and were listening intently.

Granddad looked about him furtively, making sure there were no eavesdroppers, and, with an expressionless face, he leaned forward towards Cedric and whispered.

"She never wanted for glue!" He let out a huge guffaw and sat back in his seat roaring with laughter. He slapped his thigh. "Never wanted for glue!" He turned and yelled across the room to a white-bearded old man, who had nodded off under the moth-eaten moose head that stuck out of the wall, by the honours-board. "Ramona Treadgold's Mam. I said, she never wanted for glue, did she Charlie?"

The old man woke with a start and held his glass of stout aloft.

"Yeah, same to you Jack, and many of them." He took a slurp from his glass and then subsided back into his own private world under the moose-head.

Arthur's grandfather wiped away the tears of laughter from his cheeks and looked around at the assembly of grinning faces.

"Never wanted for glue. What a cracker, eh?"

Dai blew his nose and sighed.

"No more, for Christ's sake, please, I'll bust a gut if I hear any more."

Arthur slapped the table with delight and the glasses jumped.

Ernie was doubled up, clutching at his sides. An inch of ash broke away from the end of his whiff and disintegrated on contact with the knee of his trousers.

Cedric face was as dark as thunder.

"Bollocks, you daft old sod," he hissed and took a gulp from his glass.

Arthur wiped at his eyes and snorted.

"That was a bloody cracker, eh, Ced'?" He poked Cedric playfully in the ribs. "Never wanted for glue! I like it." He rocked back in his chair, gripping his sides.

"That's it!" Cedric said, struggling to his feet. "I've had just about a bloody gutful of having the piss taken out of me."

Arthur's grandfather put a hand on Cedric's arm.

"Hang on, you daft old bugger. Don't go getting your arse in your hand. It's only a joke. There's no need for you to get all hot and bothered, Butt." He patted Cedric's arm. "Sit down and have another pint, is it? We'll all be going soon, so one more pint, then off, ok?"

Cedric's expression gradually softened, and he grudgingly sat back down.

"All right, one more pint, then I'm away, and if you tell me its bloody Christmas, one more time, I'll bloody well swing for you all." He drained his glass. "And no more bloody stupid jokes, eh?"

"No more jokes, promise." Arthur's grandfather held up his hands in defence. "Right, who's having what, then?" He looked around the table.

"Sit where you are Jack, it's my round." Dai got to his feet. "Scotch all round, yeah?"

They all nodded and Ernie passed around the box of whiffs again.

"Hang on Dai. I'll come and give you a hand." Arthur got up and followed Dai to the bar.

"Six double Bell's, and no daft bloody comments," Dai said to Stan the barman, who was now wearing a pink plastic Groucho Marx nose and a black moustache with spectacles attached. Below his stubbly chin, and hiding his greasy collar was a green bow tie that lit up in a series of irregular flashes.

"Six double Bell's coming up!" he yelled to the room. The light from his flashing bow tie, reflecting off the optics on the row of bottles of spirits that stood on guard above the till.

"That'll be twelve and a tanner, ding bloody dong!" He held out his grubby hand for the money, a crooked grin on his face.

Dai and Arthur collected the drinks and headed back towards their table.

The woman with the white stiletto heels and the carrot coloured hair, now looked decidedly worse for wear. Her lipstick was smudged and the second button on her vermilion jacket was undone, revealing the top half of two pallid hemispheres.

Dai belched loudly as he squeezed passed her.

"Pardon me, I'm sure!" she said in a nasal twang, staring after Dai with flashing eyes and tossing her head in disdain.

Dai looked back at her.

"Pardon you?" he said with a half laugh. "Pardon you, with tits like that you ought to be bloody locked up, never mind bloody pardoned."

She gasped, turning to her Husband.

"Did you hear what that young sod just said to me, our Merv'?"

"Aye, and quite bloody right an' all," said her husband draining his glass. "Do yourself up and drink your drink, woman. By the time that we get home that sodding chicken will be burnt as black as a darkie's arse!" He turned and staggered off towards the door, not waiting for her to respond.

Arthur looked back at the bickering couple and grinned.

"Talking about grub. Where are you eating today, then, Dai?"

"I'm having grub around at our Sandra's," said Dai sighing. "The whole bloody family will be there, as usual."

"You don't sound as if you're looking forward to it, Butt?"

Dai shook his head.

"You can say that again, there'll be our Sandra's in-laws, and their god-awful kids. Sandra's husband, Nick, who will have on that stupid, bloody, striped apron, which he insists on wearing when he carves the bloody bird." He sighed again. "And, it's a pound to a penny that Auntie Marge's paper hat will fall off onto her plate, at least four times before somebody takes it off her head, without her noticing. It's guaranteed, happens every bloody year without fail." He looked at his watch. "It's all due to begin in about half an hour. I can't bloody well wait!"

Arthur laughed. "Aye, ours will be the same, I expect. We'll be ten minutes late because of granddad, and I'll get the bollocking for keeping him at the pub."

They reached the table and handed out the whiskies. "Where are you eating, this year, then, Ced'?" Arthur took a sip at the whisky.

"I'm round at our Iris's," the old man replied through a cloud of cigar smoke.

"That's in Baldwin Street, ain't it?" asked Ernie.

Cedric nodded and took another sip from his whisky glass.

"What time are you eating, then, Ced'?" Granddad leaned back in his chair and surveyed the room.

"I said that I'd be back for half one." Cedric pulled out a battered pocket watch and flipped open the case. "Quarter of an hour, time for another, is it? It's my shout."

"Not for me, old son. We gotta be going," said Granddad, putting a hand on Cedric's arm. He turned to Arthur. "Drink up Arth'. I'll only get a bollocking off your Mother if we're late."

Arthur grinned at Dai and winked.

"Bollockin, that's a bloody laugh, that is." He drained the rest of his whisky. "Are you coming around the house tonight, then, Dai?"

Dai put his empty glass on the table.

"Yeah, do you want me to bring a few bottles?"

"Brilliant!" said Arthur.

"Yeah, and bring some money as well, we'll be having a few hands of pontoon. Cliff bloody Richard is on the box," interjected granddad.

"Great!" Dai rubbed his hands in anticipation. "A few brews and a game of cards, sounds good to me." He turned to Cedric. "How about you Ced', are you going around, then?"

"Yeah, of course, I've been going to Jack's every Christmas night since the old King died. That's right, ain't it, Jack?" said Cedric.

"That's right. He's never missed a Christmas night, at our place has Ced', about half seven, OK, Ced'?"

Cedric nodded as he drained his glass.

Arthur, granddad and Dai got up to leave.

"See you later, then, Ced'. Cheers Ernie," said granddad.

"Cheers all." Ernie waved his glass at them and turned to Cedric. "Have you got time for another, Mr Matthias?"

"Aye, why not," Cedric replied. "I could sink another, at a pinch."

"Don't you keep your Iris waiting, now," admonished Arthur's grandfather.

"Don't worry," Ernie cut in. "I've got the car outside. I'll give Mr Matthias a lift, home, is it?"

Cedric nodded his approval and waved goodbye as Arthur, Dai and granddad, weaved their way through the throng.

Granddad pushed open the door and they entered the tiled passageway that led to the outside door.

The powerful aroma of floral disinfectant, urine and stale beer assailed their nostrils.

"I think I'll chance it and wait until I get home," Arthur said, wrinkling up his nose in disgust as he passed the doorway to the lavatory. "I can't face going in there."

"Too bloody true!" said Dai holding his nose.

Granddad said nothing as he buried his nose into his scarf.

The cold, street air hit them and they let out joint sighs of relief as the front door closed, separating them from the stench of the passage.

Arthur's grandfather extracted his nose from the depths of his scarf, breathed in deeply and let out a long, satisfying sigh.

"Ah, that's better." He blew his nose and took another breath. "Jeez, that bloody passage smelled like a Cherokee's loincloth, and I'm dying for a slash. As soon as I get into Mill Lane, I'll be topping up the canal."

"I won't be able to hold on till I get home, either," said Dai, looking back over his shoulder as he turned to cross the road. "Ouch," he shouted, as he walked into the bumper of a parked car, that he hadn't seen. "Who the frigging hell put that there!" He rubbed at a shin and stepped back from the kerb to survey the offending vehicle, his full bladder temporarily forgotten.

The car was a pink, nineteen fifties, Vauxhall Cresta with white-walled tyres and enough chromium trim to outdo the new bar in the Tredegar Arms, in George Street.

Arthur peered into the car's interior.

"I wonder who owns this little lot, then," he said looking suitably impressed.

"Ernie Parry," said Dai without hesitation.

"What makes you say that, then?" asked granddad.

"I just know it, that's all," said Dai kicking at one of the tyres. "It's got Ernie bloody Parry written all over it. It's just the sort of thing that he'd have, isn't it? I bet he's borrowed it from Honest Stan's car show-room, that's where his brother, Tommy works."

"Right now, I don't give a tuppenny toss who it bloody belongs to." Granddad crossed his legs in anguish. "I just want to get home and bloody relieve myself, that's all."

"Yeah, you're right there, see you later tonight," said Dai dashing across the road and disappearing into Mill Lane.

Arthur and granddad waved after him as they hurried on up James Street towards their house and blessed relief.

Chapter Thirty-nine
Missing

Arthur and his grandfather sat contentedly in the lavender-scented front room, legs stretched out towards the fire grate, their stomachs full of the Christmas fare that they had tucked away.

The young niece had been taken to bed, exhausted and Arthur's mother and sister were ensconced in the kitchen, sherry and Turkish Delight to hand, watching, the White Horse Inn on-ice.

Arthur puffed on a whiff and blew smoke at the glowing coals before taking a slurp from a glass of milk stout.

"I'm as full as ten men, me," he said rubbing his bloated stomach. "If I don't see another mince pie this year, I'll be more than happy."

Arthur's grandfather, probed at a back tooth with a matchstick, his face contorted.

"Got you, you little bugger," he said, triumphantly holding aloft the matchstick and inspecting the impaled prey. "That's been plaguing me ever since dinnertime." Tossing the matchstick, and the offending microscopic piece of matter, that once was part of a cockerel's breast, into the fire.

He leaned forward and extracted a bottle of India pale ale from the crate at their feet, prised off the metal cap with his pocket bottle-opener and poured the hissing mixture into a glass. He then held the glass and its contents up to the light for inspection, like a would-be TV wine buff, before taking a long slow swallow of the liquid. He belched loudly and held the glass in placed on the arm of the settee beside him.

"Ah, that's better," he said, his eyes half closed as he settled back against the cushions.

Then belching again, granddad wiped at his lips with his sleeve and undid the top button on his trousers.

"You're right there, Arth', that third bowl of trifle nearly did it for me." He took his pocket watch from his waistcoat and looked at it. "What time did Dai and Ced' say they were coming around?"

Arthur checked his wristwatch.

"Half seven, Dai said, in about ten minutes time."

He got slowly to his feet. "If we push the settee to one side, and pull the table over towards the fire, it'll make more room and give us all a bit of heat. I'm not playing bloody cards over by the door, the draught's enough to cut your sodding legs off."

He lifted one end of the heavy mahogany dining table an inch off the carpet before quickly dropping it back. "Jeez!" He straightened up, gingerly feeling the small of his back. "That bloody thing weighs a ton, you'll have to give us a hand with it."

Arthur's Grandfather finished the repositioning of the settee and went to the other end of the table, ready to lift.

"Bloody youngsters, today." He shook his head. "Weak as buggery, no bloody staying power that's their trouble. They ought to stop bloody playing with themselves and get out in the fresh air and do a bit of walking, get some exercise."

"Oh yeah, and when's the last time that you were out getting some exercise in the fresh air, then?" said Arthur through gritted teeth.

"I go around to the betting shop and the off licence most days, that's far enough for a man of my advanced years," puffed granddad.

Arthur grunted and moved forward gingerly. Granddad followed suit, and, between them, they struggled across the room with the heavy table.

"This'll do, here," said Arthur, dropping his end and sitting down on the arm of the settee, blowing hard.

Granddad went back to his newly positioned seat, and his glass of pale ale, and stretched out his legs towards the glowing coals, wriggling his toes.

"I tell you what, there's not much to beat a good fire and a couple of decent brews, to hand. What do you reckon, then?"

Arthur nodded contentedly and reached for another bottle of glucose stout.

Granddad lit up a Capstan full-strength and blew smoke at the coloured Christmas decorations that were slowly waving above his head from the heat of the fire, and with half-closed eyes he murmured.

"Yes, this'll do for me."

For the next twenty minutes the pair sat in silence, contentedly soaking up the luxury of the warmth from the coal fire.

Eventually, Arthur stirred himself and looked at his watch.

"Dai's late, it's nearly five to. It's not like him to be late for a game of cards and a beer." He looked at his watch again and shook his head.

Granddad, not trusting, the accuracy of Arthur's modern wristwatch, consulted his own, prized, half-hunter, and having studied it to his satisfaction, acknowledged that Arthur's pronouncement was more or less right.

Sitting upright, he wedged his feet back into his slippers.

"Yeah, you're right, Arth'. Old Ced's generally on the ball, too, especially when it comes to a hand of Find-The-Bitch." Granddad got to his feet and stretched. "How are we doing for snacks and the like?"

"It's all here, don't bloody panic," said Arthur, pointing to the sideboard. "It's all there, on the sideboard, there's nuts, tangerines, dates and figs, but not the box of Milk Tray, mind, that's for sis' and mum."

Granddad scowled. "I'm not bothered with those tarty, soft-centred thingys, a handful of walnuts will beat your chocolates every time, they were made to go with your Worthington IPA, are walnuts." He threw his dog-end into the fire. "As a matter of fact, I think I'll crack a few now, pass the bowl over, Arth'."

"Hang on, Jack, let's wait until Ced' and Dai get here, then we can all get stuck in, is it?"

Granddad scowled again and sank back into his seat.

"Yeah, all right, then."

As he reached for his glass, there came a knock on the front door.

"That'll be them, now, I expect," said Arthur getting to his feet and making for the front room door.

A minute later he and Dai entered the room, both looking distinctly troubled.

"You're late," said granddad picking up a pack of cards and ruffling through them. "I could have been a few shillings up by now. What're you drinking, then, Dai? The beer is over here on the floor." He gestured towards the fireplace. "Where's Ced', then? Is he not with you?"

Dai slowly undid the buttons on his overcoat.

"No, you won't be seeing Ced' tonight."

He hung the coat on the hook on the back of the door.

"How come?" granddad asked, puzzlement showing on his face.

"There's been an accident," Dai said, softly. "Ced' and Ernie Parry have been in a car crash."

"Whereabouts?" asked granddad quietly, the colour draining from his face.

Dai sat down gingerly and leaned forward in his seat.

"Over in Baldwin Street, not long after we left them at lunchtime." He passed a hand over his face. "A copper, at the hospital, told me that eyewitnesses said that the car took the corner too fast, hit the kerb, and turned over on its side, before crashing into a lamppost."

"Who was driving? Not that bastard, Ernie bloody Parry, was it?" hissed Arthur, making a fist. "In that sodding Cresta that we saw parked outside the club, lunchtime, I bet?"

"Yeah, that's the one," Dai replied, grim faced. "The one that was dripping in chromium."

"You wait till I get my hands on that prick, Parry, he'll wish he'd never come home on leave, the twat!" Arthur clenched and unclenched his hands in anger.

"You can forget that, Arth'," Dai said quietly. "Ernie Parry won't be doing anything from now on, he's dead."

Granddad and Arthur stared in silence, shocked by Dai's news.

"Jeez!" Granddad shrank back against the cushions, his hands trembling, the glass of beer that they held, dancing on the padded arm of the settee. "Was he crushed, then?" he asked quietly.

"No, bled to death," said Dai, puffing out his cheeks and shaking his head in bewilderment. "Do you remember, that when he went up to buy a round, in the club, this morning?"

Arthur and his grandfather nodded silently.

"Well, he came back with a bottle of scotch, sticking out of his jacket pocket," said Dai. "He must have bought it at the bar, remember?"

Arthur and Granddad nodded again.

"Yeah, well," said Dai, continuing with his account of the accident. "According to the cops, the bottle must have broke apart when the car turned onto its side, but it didn't smash into pieces, not like you'd expect it to. The neck just snapped off and the rest of it just sort of split into a couple of jagged pieces, one of which went into the side of Ernie's neck."

"Dear God!" Arthur's face was drawn and ashen.

Granddad stared at the carpet.

"Yeah, they said that there was blood everywhere," said Dai grimly.

"What about Ced'?" Granddad asked quietly.

"They found him underneath Ernie, also covered in blood. He had a length of jagged glass sticking out of his side."

"Oh, balls! Not old Ced'." Granddad's eyes were moist. "Old Ced', my mate, dead, I can't bloody believe it."

Dai shook his head. "No, Ced's not dead, for Christ's sake."

"Not dead? You said he had a frigging slice of glass sticking in him, and that he was covered in blood," Arthur said, in disbelief, his face thrust forward, challenging Dai.

"That was Ernie's blood," replied Dai. "And, yes, you're right, there was a long piece of jagged glass sticking in Ced's side, which had gone right through his overcoat, but that's as far as it got. When they undid his overcoat, they found the point of the glass was buried in the peak of his cap, which was folded up in his jacket pocket. You know, the tartan one that he'd had for Christmas, the one that we were all taking the piss, about?"

The colour was returning to granddad's face, he leaned forward towards Dai.

"So. it didn't go into his body, then?"

Dai shook his head.

"No, that sodding cap saved the old bugger."

"So, how bad his he, then?" asked Arthur.

"He'll survive," replied Dai. "The poor old sod, has got a lump on the side of his head the size of a bloody duck egg and two of his ribs are broken, and, he's got a mild concussion. I went round to see his daughter, just before coming here, and she said, that, as she was leaving his bedside, in ward eight, he sat up and asked if she would bring him in a couple of bottles of Guinness. So, no change, there, then," Dai grinned. "His daughter, said that he should be out of hospital by next Wednesday."

"Aha!" Granddad slapped his knee with glee. "I knew the old Bugger wouldn't let me down." He wiped at an eye. "The old Bugger," he said fondly, then coughed into his hand to hide his embarrassment. Then, getting to his feet, he said, "Right, first things first." He was now back in his, I'm-in-charge mode. "Arthur, go and get my bottle of rum, will you? We're going to celebrate the old sod's good fortune, and drink to his recovery." He grinned widely, rubbing his hands in anticipation. "Then we can play some cards."

Chapter Forty
Reflections

The old man absentmindedly inspected the permanently bent-up, arthritic, little finger, on his left hand, as he fondly recalled granddad, Dai and Cedric. He explored the little ridge of hard skin that had been formed by his mother's wedding ring that he had worn on the little digit for many years after she had died.

He explored the callous, feeling the imaginary little gold ring as if it were still there.

Everyday wear and tear had eventually caused the ring to break in two, it becoming so thin, that, finally, one day, the gold just gave way and it fell from his finger.

Arthur still had the two little crescents of gold, which he kept wrapped in tissue paper, in a small ivory snuffbox that sat on a downstairs windowsill in the living room of his old fisherman's cottage that overlooked the golf links, and the Atlantic Ocean.

The box had pride of place, sitting between the yellowing, fish-bone Buddha, from Bangkok, and the hand-painted ashtray that he'd bought in Kusadassi.

He released the finger and thrust his hands into his trouser pockets and turned back to the motorway.

It's been a while since I've unwrapped that tissue paper and had look at mam's wedding ring, he thought. He made a mental note, that he would inspect the pieces of gold upon his return to Cornwall. *Maybe I'll go into Penzance and find a jeweller who can repair it, you never know, it may be possible.*

He stared across the valley, while memories of the family, which had been locked away for such a long time, resurfaced.

The old man pictured his mother, as she was, when he was a young boy. Then, a tall, proud, handsome woman, whose shiny, nut-brown hair, would be gathered at the nape of her fine neck, tied with the familiar mauve bow. Her blue eyes would twinkle, whenever she laughed, but could become ice-cold chips when she was provoked. *Just like granddad.* He smiled at the thought.

She wore that ring for forty-eight years, four as a wife, and the remainder as a widow, jeez, that must have been bloody tough on her.

Arthur's father, also Arthur, had died, eight months and seventeen days into the start of the Second World War, going down with his torpedoed ship, somewhere in the North Atlantic.

Arthur senior was just twenty-three years old, and, it was his first voyage.

Arthur's mother, who was fourteen months younger than her husband, was just six weeks away from giving birth to Arthur Sydney Tanner, when the letter from the Admiralty came.

Over the ensuing years Arthur's dead father was rarely mentioned, and, when the subject came up, it was never discussed for any great length.

It was as if his mother had locked away all the hurt and grief, so that it never got to see the light of day again. There were no pictures of him on display and contact with his side of the family had become less and less frequent with the passage of time.

Even previous to Arthur senior's death, there had been scant correspondence with his family, who lived in rural Somerset, and, by the end of the war, this had virtually become non-existent, except for the exchange of Christmas cards.

By the time Arthur had left Tredegar Wharf Infants and joined Powell's Place Junior School, all contact had ceased, and any thoughts of relatives across the Bristol channel had faded into the dim and distant past.

All that Arthur knew of his father and the in-laws was what little information he was able to glean from his grandfather, who would grudgingly give out very limited amounts of information, after a few pints. Arthur's sister, who still had some childhood memories of the long, lost father, who had kissed her goodbye for that last time, when she was three years old, would provide a few snippets, but these were few and far between. So, apart from the sparse information that Arthur had managed to glean over the years, the only evidence of his father's existence was the thin gold band on the finger of his mother, now pieces in a box on a windowsill in Cornwall.

She had never remarried, and over those same ensuing years, her father, Jack, Arthur's grandfather, gradually took over the role as head of the household, so that, by the time Arthur was in his early teens he had come to look upon his grandfather as a father-figure, even though he still referred to him as granddad.

Arthur left school at fifteen and immediately applied to British Railways for a job as a booking boy in a signal box. He was successful, and after passing an interview at the Regional Headquarters at Newport High Street Railway Station, he started at Maesglas goods yard the following Monday.

That evening, granddad put down the Evening Argus, cleared his throat and said, "I see that there's a house in Rutland Street for rent, number eighteen. Two-bedroom, and in good nick, so they say."

Arthur's mother looked up from her sewing.

"Yes, I heard. "Mrs Watts's old place, wasn't it?"

Granddad nodded. "Yeah, that's right."

"Know anybody who might be interested, then?" she turned her attention back to her sewing.

"I might be," granddad said, clearing his throat again.

His daughter looked up sharply.

"What do you mean, you might be?"

Granddad picked up the newspaper again and, casually started to turn the pages, feigning disinterest.

"I said, I might be, that's all." The sporting section rustled.

She put down her sewing.

"Stop hiding behind that paper Jack and put it down."

Arthur's Grandfather complied.

"Now, what are you on about, you might be, might be? Since when has this house not been good enough for you, then, Jack?"

He thrust his hands into his pockets.

"I knew you'd start, as soon as I mentioned the idea, I knew you'd start."

"Start, I'm not starting," her voice had taken on a hard note. "I'm not starting. I'd just like to know what's put this daft idea into your head? You going potty in your old age, then?"

Granddad held up his hands in surrender.

"Listen our Edith, will you? Just let me tell what I've been thinking, ok?"

She folded her arms in front of her and with a straight face, said, "Go on then, I'm all ears."

"Well, I've been thinking, Arthur has left school now, and is working for a living, bringing in a wage. Before you know it, he's going to be the man of the house."

She interrupted him.

"Dad, I know Arthur's growing fast, but he's still only fifteen, for God's sake. You've been like a father to him and Beryl. I don't know what any of us would have done without you being here. This is your home." She looked at him, her face softening. "You don't have to go, you daft old softie." She got up and went over to him and squeezed his arm tenderly. "You daft old softie."

"I know that, lovely," he said. "You're not listening, though, are you? It's the sensible thing to do. Arthur is going to be grown up before you can say knife."

She tried to speak but he held up his hand.

"No, let me finish, before you know it, you're going to have two young adults in this house, wanting more space. Our Beryl's been working nearly three years, already. She's buying clothes and the like, going dancing, seeing boys, no doubt? Arthur will soon be the same, you'll see, before you know it, he'll want to start bringing young ladies home, like any normal growing lad." He waded on, not letting her get a word in edgeways. "So you see, it makes sense for me to move out, there'll be more space all round, and we won't all be falling over each other. Don't get me wrong, It's not that I feel that I no longer belong or anything." He folded his arms and looked her in the eye. "It's just the most sensible thing to do, and I'll only be around the corner, in the next street. It's not as though I'll be going to the other side of the world, is it?"

She gave a small smile.

"You're a crafty old sod, Jack. I'll bet you've been planning this for months, haven't you?"

He grinned and picked up the evening paper again.

"I've not agreed nothing yet."

"This has got to take some thinking about," she said smoothing her apron. "There's probably a million things about it that haven't been thought of, I bet."

"Well you better think fast then, the landlord wants my answer by Saturday," he said quietly.

Two days later granddad's daughter, Edith, relented.

"Oh, all right, you stubborn old man, go to Rutland Street, if you must."

Granddad grinned and rubbed his hands in delight.

"I knew you'd see sense, our Edith." He got up and headed for the door, his arm already threading its way into the sleeve of his jacket.

"Where are you off to, now?" she asked.

"Just over to see Cedric Mathias, his daughter has got a three-piece suite for sale."

She laughed out loud.

"Fair play, Jack, you take some beating, that's for sure."

And so, granddad moved into Rutland Street and Arthur moved out of the box room and into the back bedroom that had been vacated by his grandfather.

Nine years later, soon after Arthur and Avril had married and moved to Rogerstown, granddad left his little house in Rutland Street and moved back in with his daughter.

By that time, Arthur's sister Beryl, who had been married for three years, to Terry, was living on the other side of town.

Not many years would pass before they would all be reunited under the one roof again.

Granddad. He smiled, fondly remembering the old man again. *He was like a father to me and Beryl.* He shrugged disconcertedly. *How bloody strange life is, when you come to think about it.*

He shook his head at the irony of it all.

There's mother, widowed, before I was born, following in the footsteps of grandfather, who too, was widowed when his wife, Gwynneth died in childbirth, leaving him with the job of bringing up his daughter single-handed. He shook his head. *And, just like mam, he never remarried either. Then, to top it all, there was poor old Sis', married to Terry for eight years and trying for a family all that time, and after all the false alarms and the miscarriages, when she finally does become pregnant, she is also widowed, and just before she had Nicola.*

He clenched his fists; his arms straight down his sides.

"The bloody Tanner curse!" he said out loud, squinting into the sun-filled middle distance and shaking his head, filled with rage.

He stood there, for some time, rigid until his newfound bout of anger slowly ebbed away. Finally, having regained his composure, his thoughts returned to his lost family and friends.

Mind you, our Beryl did remarry, when she was in her forties, he recalled. *Nice chap too, it turned out, name was Alec, treated her well, and took to Nicola straight away.*

The smile faded. *Now, she and Alec have both passed on.*

He sighed and thrust his hands back into his trouser pockets.

It's funny, when people you knew and loved are no longer around, how the old memory can play tricks, you think you remember them accurately, until when you come across pictures of them, then there's a difference from the memory, there's always something that's never quite right. The old memory gets altered by time and before you know where you are, none of it's real any longer.

Arthur wiped at an eye as he stared at the sprawling housing estate and its attendant supermarket.

"All gone," he murmured to himself. "All gone, Mother, Granddad, Sis, Alec, Terry, Dai, Cedric, all dead."

Others had simply disappeared, like the Cox brothers, who, he hadn't seen or heard of, for over thirty years.

Or Avril, he conceded as an afterthought. *God knows where she is?* He shrugged. *Could be anywhere, who bloody knows?*

He chose not to remember that his niece, Nicola, had recently mentioned that she had seen Avril in Boots the Chemist, in Cardiff, not three months ago.

What about you, then, you sad old sod? he asked himself. *What happened to Jack-the-Lad?*

He kicked at a stone.

He's turned into a grumpy old sod, that's what, a grumpy old git, who has spent the last hour, standing here, trying to recapture the past.

He inspected the bent-up little finger again. *Forget the bloody past, you daft old sod, concentrate on the present, there won't be that much more, so make the bloody most of it.*

Although he had to admit that making the most of the present was not all plain sailing, for today's technological challenges were proving easier-said-than-done.

When faced with the truth, he grudgingly conceded, that he was sadly lacking in both the knowledge and the will, to handle many of the new-fangled gizmos of modern life. He grinned. *About the only bloody aspect of cutting-edge of technology, that I can handle, is using a sodding bread knife.*

As far as he was concerned, the door to the state-of-the-art department of the new Millennium was still very firmly shut. His lack of the essential modern amenities in life was painfully obvious.

You've never driven a car, you only have the mobile, because texts are cheaper than telephone calls, and you've only just about mastered that. He studied the horizon, lips pursed in concentration. *You wouldn't know the bloody Internet, if it hit you in the face, and you're still playing vinyl LPs on a thirty-year-old record player, you still smoke, you're not politically correct, in any sense, and you don't give a shit whether your food is genetically modified or not. You're still eating beef, regardless of the constant warnings from the Popular Press, and best of all, you must be the only person in Britain, who still hasn't bloody well seen the film, Zulu.*

He grinned widely. "Yeah great, isn't it," he said out loud.

Chapter Forty-one
Perrenials

"Hey, are you, all right?" a voice asked.

Arthur spun around on his heel. "You what?" He looked around trying to locate the voice.

"Up here," said the voice. "I said, are you all right, I was a bit concerned as you've been standing there for over an hour, now."

Arthur stepped back with a start, searching for the whereabouts of the voice. He looked up to the top of the manicured hedge of the nearest bungalow, there, the upper half of a balding head, with horn-rimmed spectacles attached, showed above the hedge that surrounded the corner bungalow's garden.

"I just wondered if you weren't feeling too well, that's all," said baldhead.

"Oh, yeah, I'm OK, thanks." Arthur pulled out a handkerchief and blew loudly into it. "How long have you been there, then?"

"About an hour, or so," answered baldhead. "Haven't you heard the mower going?"

Arthur shook his head, and lied. "Sorry, can't say that I have, I must have been miles away."

Baldhead looked somewhat miffed but nodded nevertheless.

"I've been giving my hardy annuals a bit of a sort out; you know how it is this time of year?"

Arthur studied the Chad-like figure and reasoned that baldhead must either have very long legs or be on the last rung of a very short ladder, for the head remained, unmoving, at cheek height, above the privet, spectacles glinting in the late afternoon sun.

A gloved hand, holding a trowel, appeared, joining the head, and rested on top of the manicured hedge, while another hand, complete with handkerchief, joined it and proceeded to mop at baldhead's baldhead.

Arthur shook his head.

"Sorry, I'm not into gardening." He lied again, hoping that the owner of the glinting spectacles would bugger off and leave him alone.

The disembodied voice carried on regardless.

"One has to keep a careful watch on one's hardy annuals, you know, what with all the pests and diseases about, they can be a proper worry, this time of the year." Without warning, the head disappeared, and the scraping of metal on concrete, could be heard.

A gate opened and baldhead, complete with the rest of his body, appeared, consternation showing on his middle-aged face.

It was just as Arthur had expected, baldhead was obviously a son-of-the-soil, for, as well as the obligatory gardening gloves, he also sported green Wellington boots and an apron with a large single pocket in the front, kangaroo style, protruding from it, rubber-handled seccateurs.

"I hope that you don't think that I was spying on you, or anything, because I most certainly was not."

"No, not at all." Arthur retrieved the empty pipe from his top pocket and blew through it, just to be certain that it was unlit, regardless of the fact that it hadn't been smoked since early morning. "No, I was just surprised to see you, that's all," he explained.

"Well, that's all right then, isn't it," said baldhead, relief showing on his face. "Now, are you sure that you are all right, you wouldn't like a glass of water, would you?"

"No, honestly, I'm OK." Arthur began to feel a bit irritable. "I was just on my way, anyhow."

"Just admiring the view, then, was it?"

Arthur gave him a scathing look. "You must be bloody joking," he hissed. "You call that a view." He pointed towards the housing estate. "That, my friend, is a bloody eyesore, who ever is responsible for defiling this valley, ought to be bloody well shot!"

"How do you mean, defiling?" A look of apprehension showed through the lenses of baldhead's spectacles, and he took a step backwards and put a gloved hand on the gate's latch, ready to make a rapid retreat to the sanctuary behind the privet.

Arthur gestured angrily.

"All those bloody houses, and that grotesque, concrete bloody monstrosity that passes for a church, it was never like this forty years ago." His arm swept around in an arc. "All that land, over by the supermarket, that was all fields, then. Over there," he pointed, "that's where the Memorial Ground used to be. Ran all the way down from the main road to the river and right across to the power station."

Baldhead ventured a step forward, curiosity getting the better of him.

"Yes, I've heard mention of a power station that used to be somewhere over on the other side of the motorway. Mind you, that was long before Claire and I moved here, of course."

Arthur shrugged. "Sorry, I didn't mean to shout. It's just that it's all so different from when I lived and worked here. It's come, as a bit of a shock to the old system, you know? I shouldn't have expected you to know about any of this." His arm swept in an arc again. "You're too young to remember, that's for sure."

Baldhead took another step forward, reassured, that, for the immediate future, his safety was no longer in jeopardy.

"Yes, I can understand how you must feel, coming back to a place after so many years, and seeing so many changes, must be a bit of a bitter pill to swallow."

"Yeah, well," Arthur shrugged resignedly. "I suppose we're all a bit wary of change, especially when you've felt comfortable without it, over the years. It's me, I'm just getting old and cranky, that's all." He managed a thin smile.

Baldhead nodded and cast an eye back to the valley.

"So, whereabouts did you live, then?"

Arthur pointed towards the tower block in the distance.

"Behind those flats, there." He nodded. "Just behind them there used to be lane that ran from the Black Cat, right up to the top road. I lived in a small cottage about three quarters up from the bottom."

"What's the Black Cat?" asked baldhead.

"Used to be my local," smiled Arthur. "It was at the bottom of the lane. Getting there was easy, coming back up with a bellyful of beer, was not so easy, though, I can tell you."

Baldhead's face had disapproval written all over it.

"I wouldn't know about that; Claire and I are teetotal."

"Me too, now." Arthur lied, feeling a thirst coming on.

"Quite right, too, drinking only leads one down a slippery slope, that's lined with problems."

Arthur nodded sagely. "Especially if you've got a weak bladder."

Baldhead chose to ignore Arthur's last remark.

"So, where did you work, then? In the power station?"

"No bloody fear, I was on the railway, signalman, just down there." He pointed towards the nearside lane of the motorway.

Baldhead removed his spectacles and gave the lenses a wipe.

"What, where the motorway is? There used to be a railway along there?"

"Certainly," said Arthur, who then spent the next ten minutes telling baldhead all about Rogerstown and the railway that ran through it, pointing out the route that the lines used to take and where the marshalling yard used to be, and how it played host to the hundreds of coal trucks, from the Western Valley collieries, that kept the power station's boilers supplied. He went on to describe, in great detail, how there were countless trains assembled at the marshalling yard each day; each one, leaving at half hour intervals, bound for destinations all over Britain.

Baldhead's eyes were beginning to glaze over; he shuffled his feet, wiped his spectacles again, beads of sweat were decorating his brow.

"Oh well, time to do a bit more, I suppose, hardy annuals wait for no man," he said desperately.

Arthur glared after the departing figure, annoyed that his own passion for railways and the days of steam hadn't been able to compete with baldhead's hardy annuals.

"Yes, its time I was heading back to our Nicola's place, I guess," he said.

Baldhead opened the gate and turned.

"Is that your daughter, then?"

Arthur shook his head.

"No, never had any children of my own. No, Nicola is my niece. It's her daughter, Petra, who's getting married on Saturday, that's why I've come down, for the wedding."

"Come down? You live away, then?" baldhead asked.

Arthur nodded. "Lelant in Cornwall, I've lived there ten years, now, ever since I took early retirement in the mid nineties."

"Sounds very nice," said baldhead.

"Yes, it is," replied Arthur.

"Well it's been nice to have met you. Have a good wedding," said baldhead, retrieving his pruning gloves from the front pocket of his apron.

"I will, especially if the beer is free," Arthur said, grinning.

"I thought you didn't drink any more?" baldhead asked sternly.

"I lied," said Arthur gleefully.

The gate slammed shut.

Chapter Forty-two
Reunion

Arthur studied the closed garden gate before turning for one more look at the valley, then, slowly, he set off, making his way back out of the cul-de-sac and across the road towards the lane, the canal and his niece's home.

He looked at his watch. It was four-o-clock. *Just a nice stroll back along the canal for an hour or so, and we should just make it to the Old Ridgeway Tavern, where a couple of pints of Best and an evening Argus, will do me a treat.*

He rubbed his hands together in anticipation, the disappointment of seeing the desecration of the old haunts of his youth, soon deposited into the recycle — bin of his memory banks, banishing any remnants of nostalgia that may have remained.

He rounded the anti-sheep gate and crunched his way along the ash path until he came to the canal basin with its armada of houseboats and gleaming launches. *A bit different to when I was a lad,* he thought, retrieving his pipe from his pocket. *Jeez the only boat along this stretch in those days was that rotten old, sunken, coal barge that we used to dive off.*

He stopped and looked across the now clear, crystal water, which mirrored the hulls of the crafts that gently swayed upon its surface. He looked beyond the boats, following the water's progress to the first lock that was a half a mile away.

Not a bloody soul! He tossed his head in disgust and gave a trial suck on the pipe and spat into the canal. The spittle broke the mirrored surface and sent a series of tiny, circular waves on a journey across to the fern-strewn bank on the opposite side of the canal.

Arthur took out a golden brown leather pouch from his inside pocket, unzipped it, and, with gnarled fingers, proceeded to work strands of dark brown tobacco from it, into the bowl of his old briar.

Not a bloody soul! Fifty years ago, this towpath would have been jam packed solid with kids, filling their jam-jars with frogspawn, or, later on, nearer Midsummer, netting the newly hatched tadpoles and newts.

He watched the rings in the water as they reached the other side of the canal. *When we were kids that water would have been all covered with pondweed. We would have had to make a hole in it before diving in, or we would end up with a mouthful of the stuff.*

He grinned to himself, letting the childhood memories wash over him.

He delved into a jacket pocket and fished out a box of matches, picked out a match and scraped it alight along the sandpapered edge. He held the flame to the contents of the pipe's bowl and puffed rapidly, before shaking out the match and flicking the dead stick into the canal, where it floated along, competing with the midges and long-legged water-boatmen, thronging the surface.

For several minutes he ambled along, puffing away contentedly, sending huge plumes of blue smoke into the air, which sailed languidly above the water; rising and dissipating, as it crossed the hawthorns and crack willows that lined the other side of the canal.

He stopped and removed the pipe from between his teeth, and studied the surrounding countryside. Through the gaps in the greenery, on the opposite bank, he could see patches of meadowland rising in undulating steps towards the hog's-back that was Ridgeway Hill, the other side of which, just a half a mile away, as the crow flies, was his latest watering hole, the Old Ridgeway Tavern. He sighed and looked enviously at the hill.

Twenty years ago, I would have climbed that hill, no problem, that would have saved me at least a half hour, always assuming that I could cross the bloody water, without getting wet. He dismissed the pointless debate and shrugged resignedly. *I get out of breath climbing out of my trousers, these days. Trying to make it to the top of Ridgeway Hill would probably do for me, anyway.*

He continued walking again, knowing, that he would have to go the long way around, which would mean, following the canal as far as the next lock and then crossing the water via the attendant humped-back stone bridge, before beginning the climb up the less-steep, Black-Ash path.

His teeth clamped shut on his pipe again and he resumed puffing contentedly on it. His eyes fixed on the Black Ash Path lock, which drew ever nearer with each step.

When he finally reached it, he sat down on the huge, square timbered spar that was bolted to the lock gate and protruded out towards the towpath. He looked down into the now empty lock; a trickle of water ran down its slime-covered brickwork sides to the foot or so of water some thirty feet below the rim.

His mind jumped back fifty or so years as he remembered how, on one hot summer's day in the early Nineteen-Fifties, Ronnie Cox had showed off, by mimicking a tightrope artist, arms extended out, as he made his way along the top of the lock gates, slowly inching one foot in front of the other.

The members of the gang all held their breath.

Suddenly, a moorhen burst out of the reeds, sounding her alarm to the rest of the canal's wildlife.

Ronnie, momentarily distracted by the commotion, teetered precariously on one leg before he plunged into the canal, on the other side of the lock, with a howl of despair.

Luckily, for Ronnie, his fall was not into the empty lock, for he almost certainly would have been killed. Being a strong swimmer, he easily made it back to the canal bank side. Unluckily for him, he was then forced to sit out the next hour, on the wooden arm of the lock gates, clad only in his brother's short-sleeve, Fair-Isle pullover, while his sodden clothes dried in the sun.

Arthur snorted at the memory and removed the pipe from between his teeth, before he choked on the smoke. *What a bloody sight,* he grinned, seeing Ronnie again, pulling on his dried-out clothes, which, he had, like Alice, mysteriously, grown too big for.

"Our mam will kill us," he kept repeating forlornly, looking like a replica of a Norman Wisdom character.

Arthur shook his head, got to his feet and slowly made his way across the bridge, feeling the moss-covered, surface of the age-old stone.

He reached the other side and stopped and tapped out the contents of his pipe against a rusty Great Western Railway boundary marker, then blew down the stem of the briar, and, satisfied, that it was empty, put in back into the top pocket of his jacket and began the climb up the Black-Ash path.

A quarter of an hour later he wheezed to a halt at the summit, and plumped down onto one of the public benches that adorned the local beauty spot. He turned and looked back, his eyes following the route that he had taken, along the ribbon of canal, back to its basin, where, the now, miniature houseboats, were tied up.

I don't suppose that I'll be doing that walk, again, in a hurry, he mused, turning and looking down the hill, to the 'pub, which lay about a quarter of a mile away, along with the little group of adjoining shops.

Beyond their roofs, in the far distance, was a sprawl of newly erected apartment buildings, which, along with the marina, had replaced the acres of redundant railway lines and wharves that had once swathed the river's banks and most of the surrounding dockland.

He shielded his eyes in an effort to pick out some familiar landmarks that might lead him to locate the site where his mother's house had once been, but, disappointedly, just like Rogerstown, of an hour or so earlier, there were very few points of reference, that allowed him to locate any part of the area that would have been familiar to him.

"Enough of bloody memories," he muttered, abandoning the search and getting to his feet. He studied his watch it was five forty-five

My God! The paper shop shuts in ten minutes. I'd better shift my arse. He got up from the bench and walked briskly down the hill, making it to the newspaper shop with three minutes to spare.

He pulled an evening paper from the outside rack and went in and paid for it.

As he walked back out, from the shop, he glanced at the back page, just to give himself a taster, prior to downing his first pint.

The headlines screamed at him.

NEWPORT RUGBY TO GROUND SHARE WITH PONTYPOOL IN NEW £90k. STADIUM AT CWMBRAN!

"Bloody rotate!" he exclaimed. "I can't bloody believe it, ground sharing with the bloody enemy. What's the sodding world coming to?"

That's when he went headlong over the taut dog's lead that extended from the female arm, on the one side of the shop doorway to the collar of the West Highland terrier, on the other side.

Arthur ended up on all fours, on the pavement, staring at a pair of very expensive, suede, high heel shoes; which led onto a pair of very shapely calves.

"God Almighty!" he said angrily, as he struggled to his feet, dusting down his trousers. He looked down at the pavement.

"Oh bollocks!" he cursed, seeing the bits of broken pipe that were scattered in the gutter.

"My Donegal Rocky!" he cried. "That was my favourite bloody pipe, that was. It must have fallen out of my top pocket, when I went arse over tip, over your bloody dog's lead."

He was red-faced and furious.

"Still swearing, then, I see, Arthur?" The female said in a matter of fact voice.

Arthur retrieved the broken pieces of pipe, stuffed them into a jacket pocket and looked up, his gaze travelling up the pale-green, knee-length dress that clothed the slim figure, then on, up, past the string of pearls around the slim neck, to the handsome face of the unsmiling female stranger.

He stared at her grimly, his mouth set.

"What the bloody hell do you expect, for Christ's sake. There're acres of bloody land, to be found, around here, for dog-walking. But no, you have to go and choose this bloody patch of pavement, right outside the shop doorway, I bloody ask you." He looked down at his trouser legs, checking for stains from his fall, there was none, but he brushed at the non-existent dirt regardless, before straightening back up and bringing his attention back to the female, still fuming.

He scowled at her.

"How the bloody hell do you know my name, anyway?"

Suddenly, recognition showed in his eyes, and in an astonished voice, he half whispered.

"My God, Avril!"